ROBIN GIDEON

ROYAL RAPTURE

ZEBRA BOOKS
KENSINGTON PUBLISHING CORP.

For JVD tai-pan
rg

ZEBRA BOOKS are published by

Kensington Publishing Corp.
475 Park Avenue South
New York, NY 10016

First Printing: August, 1993

Printed in the United States of America

One

"Give it your all, Ivor," Anton Talakovich said to the young man in fencing garb.

"But Prince Anton, you've just finished a complete match against —"

"Let me worry about that," Anton said a bit too sharply, sliding the protective mask over his head. Anton reminded himself that he was angry with himself and not with Ivor.

He slashed an "X" through the air, breathing in deeply in preparation, then assumed the opening stance.

"At your command," Ivor said, touching his fencing foil to the prince's.

Ivor was fresh, and the prince had already finished an arduous lesson, followed immediately by a complete match with his instructor. Under other conditions, Anton would have been reasonably satisfied with the morning's fencing instruction and exercise, but not this morning. Anton was angry with himself, and true to his nature, he needed to cleanse his soul with the honest sweat of strenuous exercise.

The clang of fine dueling foils filled the large, airy, renovated room on the third floor of Castle Talakovich. Anton parried Ivor's thrusts, pleased with the young man's fencing skills, though they fell short of his own. The duel began tentatively at first, as Ivor

5

tested Anton, assessing how much or little the fatigue had slowed him down.

Advancing and retreating, Anton felt perspiration breaking out on his body, and the deep, slow ache of muscles that were beginning to burn with fatigue.

Anton responded instinctively to Ivor's attack, his body finely honed from countless hours of fencing practice and instruction since the age of six. He allowed his mind to wander, to think about the *real* reason he felt the need to punish himself with a second fencing match immediately after his weekly instruction.

The answer to the anger was Catherine, and Anton knew it. No, that wasn't entirely true. Only about one third of his anger was directed at her. Twice that measure of anger was directed at himself for ever becoming involved with her. Catherine had been the one to initiate the affair with Anton, and consequently, she felt it was her right to determine when the affair should end. Anton, easily bored, particularly with wealthy young women not nearly as entertaining in or out of bed as they'd like to think, was not the type of man to let someone else—not even a lover—make such decisions in his life. He'd been nice enough, and even presented Catherine with a gold bracelet as a separation gift.

Catherine had made quite a scene of it, complete with theatrics, hysterics, and plenty of those crystal tears she could shed at a moment's notice—tears that were not born in her heart. The scene took an ugly public turn, and though Anton was hardly a villain in the matter of the affair's end, she had made sure that his name was muddied up a bit, just for good measure.

Anton was most furious with himself for not having seen it coming. He shouldn't have let himself taste Catherine's charms in the first place, and once he had, he should have spotted the sadistic twinkle in her

6

eye the first time they disagreed on even the most trivial matter.

Anton promised himself that he wouldn't make the same mistake again with another woman like Catherine, but he knew himself, and women were his one real weakness. He was surely tiring of the game he'd been playing for too long now with the facile, frivolous debutantes who were becoming less enjoyable to seduce all the time. The pursuit, once an end in itself, was now a pale breath of once vibrant air, the capture a hollow triumph.

The thing of it was, the women in his social circle who cast an eye in his direction were too much alike. Sometimes, it was impossible for Anton to distinguish memories of one from those of another once the affair had ended. Their smiles were uniformly coy; their fathers were uniformly wealthy and titled; the way they murmured, "no, no" just before pulling him into their bedrooms all had a strikingly similar, lilting, false quality to it.

The prospect of rushing out to plunge himself into exactly the same vexing state as the one he was in now didn't at all appeal to Anton, though for the life of him he couldn't see any alternative. Going without women in his life was an *not* an option — not for a man whose blood ran as hot as the prince's.

His mind switched gears with characteristic abruptness to a second source of frustration: Napoleon of France. Sooner or later, that damned little lunatic would need to be dealt with. Not for a second did Anton believe the peace treaty between Napoleon and Czar Alexander of Russia was worth anything at all. Reports from Anton's agents in France, as well as what he'd been hearing from the czar, suggested that Napoleon had been rattling his saber more and more all the time.

For an instant, Anton looked into Ivor's eyes. He saw angry determination there, and it pleased him.

One of the reasons Ivor was such a good opponent was that there was plenty of anger in his soul. To whom exactly that anger was directed, Anton wasn't quite certain. It could well be directed at him, though he didn't think so. For bouts such as this, Anton fought fair and paid well.

The clang of dueling foils grew louder as the battle intensified, until at last Anton slashed the winning stroke and touched the tip of his weapon to Ivor's protective vest, directly over the small red circle over the heart. It would accomplish nothing and would be unjust to take his anger out on Ivor by needlessly prolonging the match, and he knew it.

"You nearly got me that time," Anton said, removing his face shield and ruffling his sweat-dampened blond hair. "Your skills are improving all the time."

"It wouldn't have been so close if you hadn't had a match right before mine," Ivor commented. He was pleased with his own performance and skill, though he realized he'd lasted as long with the prince only because he was fresh going into the match and Anton wasn't.

"Go to the kitchen and have a bite to eat. Tell the cook I sent you, and that meat and wine should be served liberally."

Ivor grinned broadly. "That's more than kind."

"No less than you deserve," the prince replied as the young man hastily exited the fencing room.

Anton pulled a towel from the rack and began drying his forehead. What he needed to do was roust the anger from his soul through solid work, and with Napoleon's constant and escalating political machinations, there was plenty for Prince Anton to do.

Perhaps Anastasia's companionship would put him in a better frame of mind. As Anton's sister, she was the only person in the world whom he trusted completely, and her presence almost invariably cheered him out of the doldrums.

8

Natasha sat in the finely upholstered, overstuffed chair in the castle library and tried to calm the rapid beating of her heart. For the third time in the ten minutes that she had been alone in the enormous room, she pulled the small, wrinkled handkerchief from her fist and tried again to remember not to wring the damp patch of lace and cotton. After all, it wouldn't do at all to let Princess Anastasia Talakovich, Natasha's intended employer, know exactly how desperately she needed employment.

She didn't want to be there. She needed a job, to be sure, and the rubles to be made as Princess Talakovich's personal seamstress would go a long way toward quieting Aunt Aggie and Uncle Ivan's continual complaints of the "enormous" expense they had been forced to bear since Natasha had come to live with them. Maybe, in time, she might be able to squirrel away enough money to get a small room in a boarding house in Moscow, far from the influences and insults of her aunt and uncle.

"Stop it," Natasha said aloud, whispering to herself. This was *not* the time to start wondering about what problems she faced in the future. Her interview with Princess Talakovich in just a few minutes presented problems enough. "Concentrate on the reasons you're here now!"

She heard the enormous door to the library open, but she did not turn in her chair to greet the intruder. She studied the handkerchief, which was damp and wrinkled in her palm. Then, afraid the cloth would miraculously reveal to the princess how desperately she needed employment, she tucked it into the cuff of her sleeve.

"And who might *you* be?"

Natasha spun in the chair, then leapt to her feet at the sound of the rich, cultured male voice. She had anticipated seeing Princess Anastasia, not Prince Anton.

She had seen him before, of course. Between Prince Anton and his sister, Anastasia, they owned enough land in and around St. Petersburg to form their own country, though that would never be necessary, since the Talakoviches were close associates professionally and privately with Czar Alexander.

He was dressed for fencing, and his shirt was opened almost to the waist, showing a generous expanse of chest that glistened with fresh perspiration. A towel was tossed negligently over his shoulders. Her gaze lingered upon his naked chest a few seconds longer than necessary, until Natasha almost forcibly made herself look away.

The prince was a familiar figure, speeding through the countryside in his private carriage, rushing to this business meeting or that romantic tryst. The prince's flair for business was exceeded only by his panache for seduction, according to some. Others maintained that his seductive skills far exceeded his business acumen, though this latter opinion was held chiefly — or at least most adamantly — by women who had an intimate knowledge of Anton's abilities.

"Pardon me," Anton said, moving forward with a grin pulling at his lips, causing the dimple to appear in his cheek. "I didn't mean to startle you. I am Prince Anton Talakovich, and you are . . . ?"

Seeing him now so close, in the flesh, was oddly disorienting to Natasha. She had been told a hundred times by her aunt and uncle that the Talakovich blood was stained, tainted, and that the prince was a devil — perhaps even the anti-Christ.

He didn't look evil at all, with his dazzling smile and his immaculate white shirt of priceless silk now damp with perspiration. His shirt was open nearly to his waist, affording Natasha an almost completely unhindered view of his chest. His pectorals were clearly

10

defined, and as the prince moved his arms to toss the towel he'd used into a chair, Natasha watched the muscles in his chest ripple beneath the skin.

She wondered why a lazy, rich prince would have such an exquisitely developed physique. His waist was narrow, which perhaps made his thighs appear a bit more powerfully developed than they really were, though Natasha's trained eye made her wonder if the closeness of the cut of his trousers could add to the impression in a decidedly flattering manner. Everything about the prince exuded energy, sensuality, and power, as though at any moment he could spring into action in another fencing match, or indulge himself in physical activity of a sensual variety that would be no less taxing upon his magnificent body.

"And you are?" Anton repeated, standing at ease, accustomed to having a numbing initial effect upon some women. His smile was indulgent and only faintly sardonic.

"Natasha . . . Natasha Stantikoff."

In the blink of an eye a thousand crazy ideas burst through Natasha's consciousness. Should she curtsey to the prince? Aunt Aggie had said that the prince had a weakness for women. She even told the story of the fishing fleet heiress from Minsk who had almost literally thrown herself at the prince at a party last year in Moscow.

"Stantikoff? Should I recognize the name?"

The question rankled on Natasha's nerves. She didn't really expect a man like Prince Anton to know all the people who lived on his land, but the way he'd voiced the question reinforced the polarity in their social positions, and let Natasha know just how cavalier Anton was of his elite status.

"No, I should think not," Natasha replied, her disorientation now vanished, replaced by annoyance, which was swiftly transforming to anger. "I've never been known for committing a crime against the czar,

11

if that's what you're implying."

Anton flashed a jaunty half-smile. He was not accustomed to being rebuked by young women, especially not in his own library, and not by a woman who hadn't been his lover. There were several women whose contempt for Anton was almost legendary, though that had more to do with lovers overlapping in Anton's life than anything else. To his credit, Anton had never made any promises of permanence with any of his previous lovers, so he had therefore not broken his word, though this technical distinction did absolutely nothing to salve the wounded egos of the women who had hoped to become Anton's wife, and in doing so to enjoy some of the enormous wealth that went along with being a Talakovich.

"That isn't what I meant at all," Anton replied smoothly, annoying Natasha because he wasn't in the least bit ruffled by her open lack of respect.

He took Natasha's hand in his, smiling, his gray eyes locking with her brown ones. She tried to remove her hand, but Anton, with little effort, held her firm.

"I beg your forgiveness," Anton said, that humorous timbre back in his voice now as though the world was an infinitely amusing place to be. He seemed anything but repentant.

He dipped his head to kiss the back of Natasha's hand. His lips were warm, soft, slightly moist, conjuring up a fluttering sensation of what those lips would feel like pressing against her mouth. The very instant the disturbing thought entered Natasha's head she forcibly jerked her hand free, and took a stumbling step backward.

He had kissed her hand, nothing more than that, and certainly nothing that could be construed as untoward. But when Anton kissed her hand—or maybe it was the way his cool gray eyes seemed to assess her like a connoisseur—Natasha felt as though she was being caressed in a most intimate manner.

"I'm here to see Princess Talakovich. She said she would see me. She's looking for a good seamstress."

"Ah, yes! My dear sister! It would seem that she has all the luck in the family, at least as far as visitors go."

"I've heard Lady Good Fortune has visited you often enough," Natasha replied, then bit her lip because such naughty double entendres were hardly appropriate at a time like this.

"Touché!"

Anton went to the wheeled cart holding a tray of heavy crystal decanters, and though it was only two o'clock, poured himself a finger's worth of the Norwegian vodka that he had shipped to St. Petersburg from Oslo especially for himself and some of his closest friends. He offered Natasha a drink, and was neither displeased or surprised when she declined. She didn't seem the type of woman to use hard liquor.

But what kind of woman *was* she? Anton had always prided himself on his ability to see through a woman's outward appearances quickly to tell the type of person they truly were in just a matter of seconds, but so far, Natasha had remained a mystery to him . . . and nothing intrigued Anton more than a curvaceous mystery with eyes that could make a man forget all about his business responsibilities.

She was beautiful, Anton noted, making a point of looking at her while pretending to be rearranging the liquor bottles and glasses on the tray. Her hair was dark brown, or perhaps auburn, was fashionably swept up and piled atop her head, with loose, curling tendrils falling down along her cheeks. She had a high, wide forehead, which Anton believed indicated intelligence, though he knew intelligent people without such a forehead. Though he did not know the young woman now standing in his library that well, he suspected she was quite intelligent. Her eyebrows were full, and very dark, almost black, suitably framing

13

eyes that were inquisitive, darted quickly, and held in them the mysterious quality of someone who is hiding something . . . perhaps even from herself. Her nose was by no means dainty, though this certainly did not displease Anton, and neither did her wide, sensual mouth—the lower lip being slightly fuller than the top—that silently promised unimaginable pleasures.

"Do you find something amusing?" Natasha asked. With fifteen feet now separating her from the prince, her bearings and self-confidence—the hallmarks of her personality for nineteen years now—had returned almost to normal levels.

"No."

"Then why are you laughing at me?"

The smile instantly vanished from Anton's face. He recognized in her voice the insecurity that she tried hard to keep hidden, and her pain touched him deeply.

"I was not laughing at you. I was only smiling, and even that was because I was thinking how very beautiful you look."

Natasha made a sound of disgust and turned away from Anton. She could not imagine being beautiful in the old, faded dress she wore. Not even Princess Anastasia—and everyone knew that she was the most beautiful woman in St. Petersburg, and probably in all of Russia—could look beautiful in the faded blue dress that was much too worn and old-fashioned.

"Do you really think I'm that gullible?" Natasha asked.

Anton shook his head, swirling the vodka around in the crystal goblet. It didn't surprise him at all that Natasha didn't believe his words. Half the time even he didn't believe the words he spoke to women. Just the same, it was surprising, mildly annoying, and entirely beguiling that such a beautiful woman—a woman clearly out of her social class in Castle Talakovich—should have the nerve to be so challenging, especially since it was apparent that she was at the castle in hopes of employment.

Anton looked at Natasha carefully then, assessing her as he would a business associate that he had yet to determine the trustworthiness of. What qualities and characteristics did she have? he mused. She was intelligent, and beautiful enough to be very distracting. She was also stubborn, and quite willing to do battle—at least verbal battle—with anyone, if her pride or her stubbornness was piqued. She was poor, as witnessed by the dress she wore, which was not only old, but had also never been of the finest quality. She was also skilled, since Anastasia was even more particular about her clothes than Anton was, and that was saying something. If Anastasia had called Natasha to the castle to discuss being her new seamstress, then Natasha's skill had to be considerable.

"No," Anton said at last, breaking the silence that had developed between them. "I don't think you're that gullible. I don't know yet exactly what I *do* think of you, but I *don't* think that you're gullible."

Natasha felt as though she had won a small victory over Anton, and she had to fight to keep from smiling. She turned partially away from the much-too-handsome man and went to the high windows that overlooked the castle courtyard. It was a beautiful day, and suddenly Natasha wanted to be anywhere but where she was, doing anything other than jousting verbally with Prince Anton. She had enough problems in her life without his contributions, and she was certain that behind the ready, handsome smile and the vitality in his gray eyes, the prince was nothing but trouble.

"I'll go see what's keeping my sister," Anton said then. "It's rude of her to keep you waiting."

Natasha turned away from the windows, and for the first time smiled genuinely at the young prince. "You don't need to go," she said, her voice softer than

15

she wanted it to be. "I'm in no hurry, and the truth is that I've arrived here a little early. I didn't want to be late, you see."

"Yes, I understand completely," Anton replied. "Then perhaps you'd allow me to give you a tour of this drafty old castle?"

Natasha paused, thinking about the offer. What on earth had prompted her to ask the prince to stay? The words had escaped her lips before she'd really thought about them, and now she regretted her impulsive action.

"No, thank you," Natasha heard herself say.

She saw the disappointment show on Anton's face briefly before he masked his feelings once again. She guessed that he was a man who often masked his true emotions, and because of this, she felt a strange comradeship with him.

"I'd like to," she added then, speaking the words without really thinking about them first, which wasn't usual for her. "I just don't want to miss Princess Anastasia."

Anton smiled as he approached, and the expression had a devilish impact on Natasha's senses. His smile was cool and confident, causing the dimple in his cheek to form. Natasha noticed for the first time that his chin was faintly clefted and that when he smiled at her, she felt a tingling in the pit of her stomach.

She took a step backward, not wanting to be too close to the prince. He was a man who could touch her without actually putting his hand on her, and that made him far more dangerous than any man Natasha had ever known.

"Please, allow me to show off my home. I seldom get the opportunity," Anton continued, his fingertips lightly touching the sleeve of Natasha's dress. "I am really quite proud of it. Over the past two years, Anastasia and I have put a lot of work into it to make it more comfortable."

Natasha wanted to correct the prince, but to do so would surely have angered him, and been unseemly. "Done the work" indeed! He and Anastasia had *not* done the work, they'd hired laborers to do the work, and they'd probably underpaid those laborers, too! Natasha held tightly to this thought, not wanting to think too highly of any of the Talakoviches, and certainly not of this one whose reputation with women was both considerable and despicable.

"If you insist," Natasha at last replied.

She was, in fact, curious to see the castle. Natasha promised herself that she would not be impressed in the least little bit by his broad shoulders, his narrow hips, his beautiful clothes and dashing smile, or the intensity in his eyes that made her wonder if he always attacked life as though it was an unrelenting challenge.

Anton offered his elbow, and Natasha hesitated only a moment before slipping her hand around it. It would be absurdly prissy of her to not take his arm while getting a tour of his castle, she told herself. And besides, it wasn't as if anything of a romantic nature necessarily had to transpire between them. He was simply showing off his castle to her, bragging as the rich so often do, showing off the fine and beautiful baubles in his life that were beyond the purse of craftsmen and artisans like Natasha Stantikoff.

So why, since she really had nothing but contempt in her heart for seducers like Prince Anton, and since she had been told for years that he and his kind were, in essence, the devil incarnate, did she have this fluttering feeling in the pit of her stomach, and in places . . . lower? And why was she suddenly so aware of her body, of the swishing of skirts against her legs as she walked, and the gentle rise and fall of her breasts inside the tight-fitting bodice of her dress as she ascended the stairs leading to the second floor of the castle? Why was her heart thudding, even now that

17

she had recovered from the shock of being confronted with the prince?

It took a moment for Natasha to realize that Anton was talking to her again, explaining whose portrait was displayed on the stairway wall they had just passed.

"He was your uncle?" she asked, silently damning herself for not listening to Anton as carefully as she should have, letting her fears and her emotions get in the way of what she had been told she must do.

"My great uncle," Anton said, and there was just the slightest flutter in his voice that indicated his feelings for the man were deep and sincere. This surprised Natasha, since everything she had heard about Anton indicated that such emotions were beyond him. "He died a long time ago, but when I close my eyes, I can still hear him talking. That man could tell the most fantastic stories. Even when I knew the stories were all just the stuff of his imagination, it didn't matter because he told them so well."

Natasha studied him out of the corner of her eyes as they went down the hallway of the second floor. She wished that she hadn't witnessed his love for his deceased great-uncle. Prior to that, she had been able to see him completely as an exploiter of the peasants of Russia, and seducer of women, rich and poor alike, who lacked the good judgment to avoid scoundrels like Prince Anton Talakovich.

"Anyway . . . the family just isn't as large as it used to be," Anton said, his voice soft and reminiscent. "It's just myself, my sister, and Auntie Nina left." He patted the hand that Natasha had resting on his forearm and smiled softly at her. "But I'm sure I'm boring you with my family background. Everyone knows what's happened to my family."

"Yes," Natasha replied, and quite suddenly she realized her answer could be misinterpreted. "I mean, no."

18

Anton smiled, realizing Natasha's difficulty.

Everyone *had* heard about the misfortunes of the Talakovich family. A family reunion at a lush hotel in Moscow ended in tragedy when fire consumed the hotel, and most of the Talakovich family along with it. Then there was the carriage accident that caused the death of Anton's mother, and the battlefield death of Anton's father and brother.

Yes, everyone knew of the tragedy that seemed to surround the Talakoviches, but what Natasha's aunt and uncle seemed most concerned about was the Talakovich fortune, which they were convinced was ill-gotten, stolen from Natasha's family by foul means, in a conspiracy to keep Ivan and Aggie downtrodden and helpless against circumstances beyond their control.

The castle was not nearly as lavishly appointed as Natasha had anticipated. Though many of the rooms were magnificently filled with the finest furniture, plushest pillows, porcelain, and artworks of glittering value, other rooms were barren, empty of everything save cast-off furniture that was worn out and some broken tools and household items that someone with good intentions intended to fix, but never had. In one room Natasha paused long enough to ask Anton if he had been the one to break the ornately carved bentwood chair, and his smile and casual shrug of shoulders told her he had, but it had been so long ago that he couldn't remember the event.

"I think , I was playing tag with Anastasia," he said, already stepping out of the dusty room. "We were children."

From all the stories that Ivan and Aggie had told her over the years, she half expected a corpse to fall out of a closet, or to find some poor soul chained hand and foot to a wall

"What were you like as a child?" Natasha asked, looking up at the prince as they moved down the hallway.

"Just a child, no different than any other. I had a lot of money, I suppose, but I wasn't really aware of it. When you're a child, rubles mean very little. People, not things, matter to children."

"You sound like you were lonely as a child."

Anton stopped walking so quickly that Natasha, who still held lightly onto his arm, was spun around so that she faced him. His mouth, which had previously been so animated as he talked lovingly of his house and family, was now pressed into a grim, tight line, and in his gray eyes was a frozen hardness that chilled Natasha's blood.

"You ask too many questions," he said.

"I'm sorry," Natasha replied, abashed.

She dragged her gaze away from Anton's with some difficulty. She was aware that she had crossed a barrier between them that she should not have, and though little physically had changed between them, she felt the walls of his self-protection come up to surround him, isolating her, freezing her with its glacial iciness and resolve.

"I'd better return you to the library. My sister hates to be kept waiting."

They walked in silence back to the library. Natasha wondered if her statement concerning Anton's loneliness had destroyed her chance at becoming his sister's seamstress. She *needed* the employment desperately. Natasha was certain she would lose her sanity if she had to remain in the same house with her aunt and uncle much longer.

At the library door, Natasha turned to Anton, and for no more than a second, their gazes met and held.

"I didn't mean to pry into your past," she said softly. "Or make you angry."

"I never get angry," Anton said, and Natasha knew he was lying, hiding his anger even now. "Good luck with Anastasia," he said, then turned on his heel and walked away.

Alone again, Natasha suddenly felt like there was no air in the room. There was a forcefulness to Anton's personality and strength of will that was almost overwhelming when he was near, and for a few seconds after his departure, it was as though he'd taken all the air in the room with him when he left. Natasha wondered whether she could work in Castle Talakovich for the princess without being inexorably drawn in by his enigmatic force of will and the alluring, seductive aura that hovered about him like a second physical presence.

The door to the library opened and Natasha gasped in surprise. She suddenly found herself facing Anastasia Talakovich, and the look on the princess's face said she was not happy.

Two

"Would you please step in?" Anastasia asked, stepping aside so that Natasha could enter.

"I truly am sorry, ma'am," Natasha said, feeling her ears burning with embarrassment. "I didn't mean to be late. It's just that — "

"There's no need to apologize," Anastasia cut in, silencing Natasha as much with the sternness in her eyes as in the way she held up her hand. "You were with my brother. I am only too familiar with how he is when beautiful young women like yourself are nearby."

Natasha found it difficult to look directly at the princess. Anastasia did not really resemble her brother, though she was definitely an extremely attractive woman. The similarities for the most part began and ended with the brilliant gleam in the eyes that seemed to bespeak a superior intellect that was extremely intimidating to a woman like Natasha Stantikoff.

Like her brother, Anastasia was fair-skinned, and her blond hair — the color of gold that Natasha rather envied — had a healthy sheen to it. Her nose was small, straight and pert, unlike Anton's, which had a slight bump on it high at the bridge, making Natasha wonder whether the prince had broken his at some time. But though Anton was robustly physical, his

22

shoulders broad and powerful, his chest expansive, his thighs strengthened by countless hours in the saddle, Anastasia was very slender, her hands so dainty and pale white they seemed almost childlike.

It was in the eyes that the family bond between Anton and Anastasia made its presence irrefutable. The keen intellect that each possessed seemed to shine through in the brilliance of her eyes, and looking into Anastasia's gaze was a bit unsettling for Natasha.

Although Natasha herself possessed both a fine intellect and an abundance of talent in many areas, she lacked a sophisticated formal education that seemed *de rigueur* among the fine-bred elite in Moscow, and especially in the gaudy decadence of St. Petersburg.

"Please, be seated."

Anastasia waved absently to a nearby wingbacked chair. The princess then went to the elaborately braided pull cord hidden behind a curtain near the fireplace wall. Even before Anastasia had taken her seat in the chair that faced Natasha's, the library door opened and the butler — stony-faced and awesomely efficient — stepped into the room.

"Yes, ma'am?" he asked in a grave, formal tone.

"Some tea would be nice," Anastasia said, *noblesse oblige* placing a smile on her mouth now.

The moment the door closed, the scowl returned to Anastasia's face, framing her mouth with lines that faintly marred her beauty.

"My brother has a way of sidetracking certain people," Anastasia said, leaning toward Natasha. She patted the younger woman's knee in an almost maternalistic fashion, even though only two birthdays separated them.

"And I'd be willing to bet that the certain people he sidetracks are all women."

"You know Anton well already," Anastasia said, then smiled brightly. "I hope he didn't inconvenience you too badly."

23

"Actually, he was quite charming," Natasha said.

She looked away for a moment and thought, *And devilishly handsome, and witty, and able to make a woman forget all about her past and her future unless she's very careful.*

Forcing herself back to the present, a little surprised that Anastasia was worried about her feelings and apparently not angry that she was late for their meeting, Natasha said, "I understand that you have already seen a number of the gowns that I made for Alexa Chowicz. If you would like, I can make a gown or two for you as well, provided you supply me with the material, and then you will be able to judge for yourself the work I can do for you."

"That won't be necessary," Anastasia said, her smile now indulgent. "I don't work for free, and I don't expect Pou to, either. I've seen your work, and it's excellent. I wanted to meet the person possessing those skills."

The tea arrived, and Natasha was shocked once again at the princess, and at how attentive she was, concerned that her visitor's tea was brewed to perfection, going so far as to say that honey, fresh sliced lemons, and cream were all available, and should Natasha desire anything else, that, too, would be made available with just a snap of the fingers.

"This is wonderful," Natasha said, sipping her tea. It *was* truly wonderful. Tea of fine quality was a luxury beyond her financial limitations, and fresh lemons and sweet honey were treats that she rarely enjoyed. "You've been more than kind."

In the short time that she had been in the Talakovich Castle, many of the things that she had heard and believed to be true about Anton and Anastasia had proven — at least at first glance — to be false. Anton was something more than just a ruthless, coldhearted satyr, and Anastasia bore little resemblance to the loud, shrewish woman who ruled her castle with a

24

whip, as Natasha's aunt and uncle had long insisted.

"There is something that you must know," Anastasia said, breaking the silence. "If you work for me, you work for no one else." She smiled to soften the blunt impact of her words. "I am a selfish woman when it comes to my clothes, a vain woman when it comes to the way I look and how I appear in public. You are a very talented woman and I demand that your skills be devoted exclusively to me." She smiled very brightly then, displaying a dimple that was reminiscent of Anton's, and gleaming white teeth. "Of course, I pay handsomely for such exclusivity."

Natasha returned the smile, but there wasn't much joy in her heart. If Anastasia had talked with Alexa about the dresses she had made, then it was also likely that they had discussed Natasha's fee, which hadn't been much. To make matters even worse, Alexa had been a peevish tyrant during all the fittings, continually complaining that she was over-paying for services rendered.

"Yes, ma'am," Anastasia said, and though she tried to swallow it, disappointment rose in her voice.

"Alexa and I sometimes move in the same social circle," Anastasia said quietly. "That is where all similarity ends. She found you quite amusing."

Natasha's jaw clenched in anger as she pictured the wealthy debutantes laughing over how hard she had worked for the few meager rubles that had grudgingly been placed in her palm. The fire of defiance showed in her eyes, and in that instant she realized that Princess Anastasia Talakovich's previous concern had all been nothing but a ruse, just one more role that she played like an actress on stage. When the princess was kind, it was nothing more than *noblesse oblige* for the "lower classes."

"You surprise me," Anastasia said, her green eyes twinkling like jewels. "You show your anger. Most people don't dare do so with me."

Natasha set her tea cup and saucer down with a rattle of fine china. She stood quickly. She'd heard quite enough. Natasha knew that Ivan and Aggie would be furious with her if she didn't get a job soon, but she couldn't remain silent another second. Her aunt and uncle would just have to find some other method of getting their grasping little hands on the rubles necessary to finance their indolence.

"If you'll excuse me, I'll be leaving now. It's rather obvious that a working agreement between us is unlikely."

"Please don't leave," Anastasia said, rising to her feet and moving so that she blocked Natasha's path to the door. "I'm afraid you and I don't know each other very well yet, and that's caused some misunderstanding." She shrugged her slender shoulders, and Natasha noticed enviously how perfectly petite the princess was. "I find your anger charming because it proves to me that you have spine and spirit and pride."

Natasha tried to move past Anastasia, but the princess moved to once again block her escape.

"Alexa is a smug, condescending witch," Anastasia continued, the green fire still flashing in her eyes as she moved right then left to block Natasha's escape, determined to have her say before the seamstress left Castle Talakovich. "She thought it was enormously entertaining to pay you so little for your wonderful work."

Natasha had been a physically robust, active person all her life, enjoying horseback riding and the rough and tumble games she'd played with the neighbors as a child. She was taller and more curvaceous than Anastasia, and certainly much stronger. She *could,* if it really got to that, simply throw the princess out of her way.

What was the penalty in St. Petersburg for knocking a princess to the floor? she wondered.

26

"Don't even think that!" Anastasia said, backing up quickly and more than just a bit theatrically until her shoulders were against the library door. Her grin beamed even brighter, which in no way cooled Natasha's anger.

"Think *what?*" Natasha bit the words out angrily, wanting desperately to give her rage vent, knowing full well that if she did she'd make the biggest mistake of her life.

"Don't think about hitting me, or whatever it was you thought about just a moment ago." Anastasia reached behind her back and without looking twisted the locking bolt on the library door. "Please don't. I hate violence, and the truth is that bruises look truly horrid on my skin because it's so pale. When we were children I received a hundred bruises from Anton."

She did not want to smile. Natasha was as angry as she could ever remember being, and despite this — or maybe because of it, and because one of St. Petersburg's most beautiful and wealthy women was blocking the doorway with an expression that would not be out of place if she had been tied to railroad tracks — she almost started to laugh.

"It's a strange ability I have," Anastasia continued, her words coming out rapid-fire. "I can guess what people are thinking. That's why I knew you were thinking of hitting me." She shrugged her slender shoulders again in an almost nervous gesture. "You're thinking that's a really strange ability, and you're right, it is."

Natasha's anger had faded into confusion. She wasn't entirely certain what she had expected Princess Talakovich to be like, but it certainly wasn't like this. And Anastasia's seeming ability to read her mind made her feel very uncomfortable.

"So Alexa thought it laughable — paying me such a paltry fee. What did you think of it?" Natasha asked. She'd never dreamed she'd hear herself using such a tone with a princess, or asking such a question.

"I think it typical of Alexa, and I think it was hideous." Anastasia's smile faded then, and her body posture relaxing from the theatrical to the natural. "She likes stepping on people when they're down, and she really loves paying less than she should. That's part of the reason why I demand you work only for me. Like I said, I'm selfish that way. I'll pay you enough so you'll never have to listen to Alexa complain again. Besides, when Alexa finds out you're working exclusively for me, she'll raise the roof with her self-righteous screams of indignation."

Warily, Natasha asked, "So what will you pay?"

Anastasia gave her the figure, and the blood drained from Natasha's face. "That's three times — no, more than three times — what Alexa paid me for each gown."

"It's four point three times more, to be precise. I'm paying you what you're worth, not what you'll accept."

For a second Natasha turned away from the princess. She needed a moment to clear her head. The Princess Anastasia was proving as confusing and enigmatic as the prince, and Natasha's emotions had been bouncing up and down too long that day for her to put too much faith in her own perceptions.

"My brother and I can be a trifle . . . much, I know," Anastasia murmured, moving away from the door to place her hand lightly on Natasha's shoulder. "But in spite of everything you've heard about us, we really are not that much different from anyone else."

Natasha looked into Anastasia's eyes, searching for the truth that she was certain was hidden. But looking into those jade green eyes, all Natasha saw was ingenuousness. The princess, it seemed, was telling the truth.

"Nothing beyond a vast fortune, keen intelligence, enviable beauty . . . trivialities like that," Natasha said sarcastically, finding it difficult to believe that Princess Anastasia thought she was nothing more than common folk, with common naivete.

"Let's not split hairs, shall we?"

The last of Natasha's anger faded then. She felt the tension between them fade, too, and with a weary sigh she started to laugh softly, and the princess joined her.

"Please, can't we sit down and start this all over again?" Anastasia asked, her tone and expression so sincere that Natasha thought she was either being very honest or was a very skilled, dangerous liar. "I'm afraid you will find that many people harbor opinions about me, and most of them haven't bothered to learn if there is any cause for their opinions. Rumors have as much destructive power as the truth." She took Natasha gently by the arm and led her back to the overstuffed leather chairs they had so recently vacated. "Come, let's finish our tea, and discuss all the latest fashions, shall we? I must warn you though, my tastes run toward the flamboyant."

"Scandalous is more the word for you, from what I've heard."

Anastasia tossed her blond head back and laughed aloud. "You've got spirit, Natasha! I think we're going to be great friends!"

The time passed easily, and it wasn't until the maid came to ask Anastasia what she'd like for her evening meal that Natasha realized she had better leave if she wanted to make it home before dark.

"Won't you stay and dine with us? It really has been wonderful becoming acquainted."

Natasha was tempted, not so much because she looked forward to the scrumptious meal that would be served, or because she wanted to prolong her time with the princess. Natasha just did not want to return to the small house that she shared with her aunt and uncle. Once there, she would have her chores to do, and the evening meal to prepare. The housework and cooking were considered just a fraction of the work that Natasha was expected to perform in payment for her aunt and uncle having taken her in after the death of her parents.

"I must leave," Natasha said through a smile that never quite reached her eyes, nor warmed her voice. "Thank you for your kind offer. Perhaps another time?"

"Are you certain? I promise, I'll protect you from Anton."

They laughed then, freely, easily. Surprised, Natasha felt as though she had made a friend that she would have all her life, though she was not a person who made friends easily.

"No, thank you, but I mustn't. I'll return tomorrow, and we'll begin your new wardrobe that will turn heads and make the tongues wag."

"Maybe we can design a few items for you, too," Anastasia said, slipping her arm through Natasha's as they left the library. "Perhaps you'll allow me to teach you to be scandalous!"

Natasha didn't hesitate a second to shake her head. She was much too modest and certainly too curvaceous to wear the gowns she made for the flashy, wealthy debutantes of Moscow and St. Petersburg.

They parted company at the wide, double doors in front of the old castle. Anastasia was already thinking about the notes that Anton would want her to transcribe, and the papers that she needed to read before supper. Never for a second did it occur to her that her guest had arrived on foot, or that she had an eight-mile walk home which would take her two hours at a brisk pace.

When the solid *thunk!* of the castle's heavy oak door closed behind her, Natasha felt relief wash over

30

her. She had not only survived her time with Anastasia, she had secured well-paying employment, and made a friend besides.

It would be dark in an hour, Natasha guessed. Maybe in even less time than that. She wondered what Ivan and Aggie would say to her, and what she would say in response to their probing questions. They believed that she was not entitled to any privacy at all, which was just one of the many things that annoyed her so about living with them.

For the hundredth time in the past two weeks, Natasha thought about leaving her aunt and uncle's house, and forging out on her own. Perhaps in Moscow she would be able to find meager lodgings she could rent cheaply, or—

Ruthlessly, she stilled such pointless thoughts. She knew in her heart that such a move was not possible. Ivan and Aggie took every ruble she made from her work, leaving her nothing at all. And Natasha was sage enough to know what happened to women who arrived in Moscow without a family to protect them, or money to secure the comforts of roof and bed.

And there was Aislyn to think about. Poor, naive, trusting Aislyn who had a child growing inside her, and no place to live. Aislyn, who wept when she confessed to her parents that she was pregnant, and who had been rewarded for her honesty by being thrown out of her home. Granted, Natasha didn't have much of a home to offer Aislyn, but it was better than the cold forest floor.

With a sigh, Natasha raised her head, squared her shoulders, and started toward the gateway of the Talakovich castle grounds.

The pounding of hooves against the lush grass startled Natasha, and a moment later, when she saw Prince Anton leaning over the neck of his stallion as he urged the horse into an even more frantic gallop, her heart began racing as swiftly as the horse's.

31

Her first thought was of their angry parting several hours earlier; her second was how commanding the prince looked sitting astride the mighty stallion.

Three

Anton pulled the stallion to a neighing, prancing halt directly in front of Natasha. She backed away, rather frightened by the heavily muscled gray beast, even though she had ridden and worked with horses most of her life.

"Good evening, miss," Anton said through a beaming smile, removing his hat and bowing low with a theatrical wave of his arm, though he remained on horseback. "I have just discovered that you are travelling on foot. And that, Natasha — or must I continue to call you Miss Stantikoff? — simply will not do."

"I thought you were angry with me," Natasha said suspiciously.

"That was before," Anton replied, as though it answered everything.

Natasha had survived one encounter with Anton, and she had not wanted to see him again so quickly. She needed time to herself, away from the troubling influences of Anton and Anastasia. She needed to spend time with her thoughts so that she could once again remember — and even more than that, *believe* — that the Talakoviches, and all the wealthy gentry like the Talakoviches, were her enemy, and to think that they were anything other than that was foolishness.

"If I'd known earlier that you were walking, I would have prepared my carriage," Anton continued, dismounting so that he would be less intimidating. He was aware of what it was like having to look up to a man on horseback.

His stallion pranced a little, wanting to run. Natasha suspected that the horse and his master were both restless creatures by nature, males who needed to stretch their long legs and exhilarate in the full velocity of their lives.

"I enjoy walking," Natasha said, though in truth she had not at all been looking forward to the eight mile journey.

"And I don't mind taking you," Anton replied without hesitation. "Please, just give me a moment and I'll have the carriage readied." He reached out to take Natasha's hand. His gloves, she noted with professional interest, were made of the finest kidskin available, and were soft as butter. "Come with me to the stables. It won't take but a moment."

The pink tip of Natasha's tongue passed lightly, swiftly over her lips to moisten them. Whenever Anton was near, her throat felt constricted, her mouth and lips bone dry. She did not realize the erotic image she presented to Anton when she moistened her lips, or the way the innocent, nervous gesture sent fire racing through the prince's veins.

The stable hands were clearly rather shocked that Anton had brought a woman to the stables with him. Apparently, this was an entirely male domain.

She noticed that the stable hands smiled to themselves as they cast glances her way. Were they all thinking that she was Prince Anton's lover? Probably, she decided bitterly. It wasn't true, and if Natasha had any say in the matter — which she most certainly did — it never *would* be true. But circumstances made it impossible for her to speak her mind and declare her innocence.

The stable hands quickly and silently harnessed a matching pair of chestnut geldings to the prince's newest and most lavish open carriage. It was an impressive display of power and authority, and Natasha viewed it with mixed emotions. Though Anton had not raised his voice to them, there was command in his gray eyes, and everyone knew that unless the stable hands were impressive for the young lady at the prince's side, there would be hell to pay.

"You don't need to crack the whip," Natasha said out of the corner of her mouth, keeping her voice low, as the two hanging lamps on the carriage were lit.

Anton smiled at her, his arm sliding casually around her waist as he prepared to help her up into the carriage. "I haven't cracked the whip with them," he replied. "I pay my men well, and they know what is expected of them. More often than not, these men have nothing better to do than gamble away the money I pay them."

Natasha wondered if discretion was one of the traits that Anton looked for in stable hands. Was that why the men all looked at her as though she was Anton's latest lover—because they'd already seen so many of his lovers?

Natasha knew the idea of the prince having lovers shouldn't bother her, but it did, and in ways and for reasons that she didn't want to contemplate.

She didn't want to think about Anton's lovers, just as she did not want to feel the pressure of his gloved hand against the small of her back. But she couldn't forget about Anton's reputation, nor could she deny the way her senses reacted to his closeness, to his most innocent touch—if, in fact, any touch from the prince could be considered innocent.

Did every woman respond to him this way? If so, then it was no wonder that the rumors maintained that he had slept with every debutante within a two hundred kilometer radius of his palace in St. Petersburg, and with every beautiful woman—married and single—in all of Paris. It was said that if the walls of

35

his Paris apartment could talk, Napoleon's government would topple from the scandal.

"This is my newest treasure," Anton said with unabashed pride as he helped Natasha up into the carriage. "I had it commissioned almost two years ago."

"That long? So even a prince has to live with frustrations?" Natasha asked with a mocking eyebrow arched.

"You don't know the half of it," Anton replied, taking the reins and urging the team into motion.

The gameskeeper and the groundskeeper both were open-mouthed with shock when they saw Natasha in the carriage beside the prince. Natasha noticed this, though she did not ask why it was so strange. Could it be that the prince did not invite ladies to his castle? That would explain the shock on the faces of the servants and staff.

"Ignore the looks you're receiving," Anton said as they rolled beneath the high archway gate on the thick surrounding wall that separated the castle from the countryside beyond.

"You can read thoughts as well as your sister." It was a flat statement by Natasha. Could Anton read her thoughts so clearly that he knew how agitated his proximity made her?

"It's a myth that Anastasia and I can read people's thoughts. The myth, mind you, has served us well in our business dealings. But it is a myth nevertheless. We're wrong as often as we're right."

"Why tell me that? You were more impressive when I thought you could read minds."

Why indeed? thought Anton. Honesty had never been his strong suit when it came to women. He did not lie outright, but the omission of salient facts had long served him well in his association with the fairer sex.

"We didn't exactly part company on a friendly note. I didn't want you to have the wrong impression of

36

me."

"I shouldn't have been so prying. It's a fault of mine, I guess. I've always been curious."

"Don't apologize. Curious people tend to be interesting people, and are rarely boring or tedious. I have little patience for boring people."

Natasha looked at the sun low on the horizon and knew that it would be dark by the time they reached her house, and very late by the time Anton returned to Castle Talakovich. Wasn't he worried about being robbed at night?

"Where do you live?"

"I'm living with Ivan and Aggie Pronushka."

"Pronushka? But you're a Stantikoff."

"They're my aunt and uncle. My parents died five years ago in an accident. Since then, I've been living with Ivan and Aggie. They live near —"

"I know where they live," Anton said a bit sharply. He tapped the reins to the horses, hurrying them slightly.

There was a lot of distance to cover, though he really wasn't in any hurry to part company with the unaffected seamstress who was so different from the well-bred, insipid debutantes he usually found himself sharing a carriage with.

He was glad that she was the first woman he'd taken for a ride in his new carriage. It wasn't burdened with memories of any other woman, and for that, Anton was grateful.

"You know my aunt and uncle?" Natasha asked, surprised. She could hardly imagine a circumstance that would warrant a man as powerful and influential as Prince Anton Talakovich associating with Ivan and Aggie.

"I know *of* them," Anton replied.

Before Natasha could continue asking questions, Anton began talking of the countryside, telling one anecdote after another, hardly listening to his own words. He knew of Ivan and Aggie Pronushka, true enough, and it was a topic he did not wish to pursue with their niece.

The Pronushkas had been spreading rumors about him and his sister for years. Ivan was an alcoholic, and Aggie was not much better, from what Anton had been able to learn. They had inherited a small plot of land from either a brother or father, and thought that the little patch of rocky land and some trees would miraculously allow them to live like the czar, even if they didn't bother to farm the land.

First, the Pronushkas sold the lumber on the part of their land that was wooded, and when the trees were gone and the money spent, they began selling off the farmland in strips. Anton, through his legal council, was able to buy the land cheaply because he was willing to put up all the rubles immediately upon the sale agreement.

The Pronushkas had never bothered to educate themselves, to learn a trade, or to even use the wealth that they had inherited in a wise fashion that might benefit them for many years. Instead, they spent their money quickly, foolishly, on things that had no lasting value, and when at last they were without a coin in their purse, without skills to sell, without anything but their anger and their bitterness to keep them going from day to day, they turned their contempt upon the Talakoviches, who had bought their land and their lumber. Ivan and Aggie cried to any and all who would listen, complaining that they had been robbed by the wily and unscrupulous Anton and Anastasia Talakovich.

"You seem far away," Natasha said, studying Anton's profile. His mouth pulled up on the right side in a half-smile, forming the dimple that played with Natasha's senses as it danced on Anton's cheek. Natasha thought somewhat enviously that no man had the right to have dimples that deep.

"Not really. I'm right here with you."

"You are now, but you weren't a moment ago."

"Now who's reading minds?"

Natasha laughed softly, feeling a little more comfortable, becoming at ease with the prince. It was, after all, a beautiful evening, and she was riding in the most luxurious and comfortably appointed carriage she'd ever seen, much less ridden in. There was no reason at all that she shouldn't enjoy herself.

"Over there, near the bend in that river, is where Anastasia and I learned to swim," Anton said, nodding to an area a short distance from the road. "There's a flat section in the river bed; no drop-offs, and the bottom is sandy."

"Carefree days of youth?"

"Yes. But not so carefree when we returned home with wet hair. Maman was always livid with Anastasia and me for something or other." Anton chuckled. "And then there was the time the Crakow woman caught us swimming near the swing tree, and we had to grab our clothes and make a run for it. She saw, as she put it, our aristocratic arses, and when she told Papa, he kept us locked in our rooms for a fortnight."

Anton pulled his gaze away from the river, turning his attention back to the road, and Natasha could tell that he was forcing himself not to think of such things, even though they seemed to be rather pleasant memories.

As she surreptitiously looked at him out of the corner of her eyes, not knowing what to say and feeling the silence pushing them further apart, she wondered if he was really the heartless, greedy monster of a man that Aggie had always claimed he was.

"The road moves away from the river further up, but over there—you can't see it from the road—is where we tied a rope to a tree and used to swing out into the river. We became pretty good at doing tricks and flips through the air, though Anastasia didn't re-

39

ally have the hand strength to hold the rope very well."

While Natasha had a difficult time picturing Princess Anastasia, so fine-boned, delicate, and feminine, swinging from a rope out into a river, she could easily picture Anton, as a youth, doing exactly that. She could also picture *herself* swinging out into the river, swimming to her heart's content, feeling the water rushing along her naked body as she and the prince gloried in their youth. Yes, her and Anton, naked and unencumbered and—

"What's wrong?" Anton asked suddenly.

"Nothing!" Natasha snapped, shocked at how forcefully she had responded to the ridiculous thought of her and Anton as youths swimming *sans* clothes. "Why do you ask?" she asked, trying to compose herself.

"Your whole body jerked just a second ago."

Natasha did not want to continue talking about herself and her errant thoughts. "Where did you have this rope swing?" she asked, wanting to get the subject off herself.

"Just down the road, and to the left. This road follows the river all the way to the sea."

"Where, exactly," Natasha prodded. She thought such conversation was harmless enough, and it was pleasant chatting with Anton. What she did not need was another display of Anton's anger.

"I'll tell you what, I'll show you the secret swing tree," Anton said through a smile that beamed, even in the waning light.

He pulled the carriage to a stop and set the brake, then leaped from his seat to help Natasha down. Instead of merely taking her hand to help her down, his strong, long-fingered hands encircled her waist, and when Natasha gave a little hop to go from the carriage to the ground, Anton held her just a moment or two longer than necessary before lowering her gently to

40

the ground.

His strength surprised and delighted Natasha. She was a tall, broad-shouldered, voluptuous woman, and yet Anton held her easily, without even the slightest show of strain, and she was left to wonder how a prince, who probably hadn't done a lick of hard labor in his entire life, could have developed such a powerful body.

"I hope the tree is still there," Anton said with a jaunty, boyish smile.

"You don't know?" This surprised Natasha, since it was apparent from all that the prince had said that the area was a special place for him.

"I haven't been back here since I was a lad," Anton replied. He placed his hand on the small of Natasha's back, guiding and hurrying her down the winding path through thickening trees.

"Why not?" she asked, trying to ignore the heat of his palm, which seemed to go straight through his gloves and her dress and into her blood.

He stopped so abruptly that she took several steps forward, then had to stop and turn back toward the road to look at him. Her immediate thought was that she had infuriated him once again by asking some question that he found much too invasive, but instead all she saw in his expression was profound confusion.

"You know, I really don't know why I *haven't* been here in so long. I've thought about the swing tree often enough, but I guess I just figured it was all something from my past, a part of my youth that I left behind when I became a man."

"Giving up your past seems a terribly heavy price to pay for becoming a man," Natasha said quietly.

Anton looked at her quizzically, his eyes narrowing in concentration. Something that may or may not have been a smile pulled at his mouth, and then he started walking again toward the river, his pace now much slower.

Natasha made a point of staying far enough ahead of him as they walked down the path so that he wouldn't have his hand against her back. She'd noticed that he had removed his kidskin gloves.

The area where Anton and Anastasia had swung out into the river was thickly overgrown with trees, and quite well hidden from the road. It was much darker here, surrounded by trees and in a natural low spot of the geography. What little sunlight was left of the day was mostly shadows that did nothing to hide Anton's handsome features.

"There it is," Anton said, suddenly rushing forward.

There was no rope attached to the limb high overhead, and Anton was quite certain that much of the river bank had been eroded away during the recent spring floods, but all in all it was just as he had remembered it, and the sight of it now made him almost giddy with excitement.

"You should have seen us," Anton said, standing at Natasha's side. His hands were clasped behind his back as he watched the cool, clear river flowing slowly past. "Anastasia and I used to swing for hours out into the river. We did it so much the grass right where we're standing stopped growing. There was a long, bare patch of ground right here worn away by our feet from us pushing each other higher and higher so we could swing further out into the river."

Natasha could picture the scene clearly, but what she did not like about the scene was that she could see in her mind's eye an adolescent Prince Anton, as naked as the day he was born, frolicking on a sultry summer's day. She looked down and saw the grassy bank had recovered from the youthful footsteps of old.

"It appears as though nobody has been here in quite a while," she said absently, suddenly feeling the need to whisper, as though she were standing in an old church, as though there were kind-spirited ghosts all around her.

"I rather like that," Anton said, also whispering now, his thoughts far away. "I'd like to think that this place is private."

"You should have come here before this." Natasha took a step further away from Anton, as though to give him room to let his happy memories dance around him. "You shouldn't let memories fade. There's nothing more important than your past," she said, thinking about her own deceased parents, and the loving memories she cherished of them.

"Yes, there is."

"Oh? And what's more important than the past?"

Anton turned away from the river and took several steps until he stood directly in front of Natasha. He placed his hands lightly upon her shoulders, his face cast in light and shadow, his features starkly gaunt and surprisingly unguarded.

"The present," Anton answered after a moment.

A mystifying shiver made its way unbidden up Natasha's spine. She looked up at the prince, thinking him quite easily the most handsome man she'd ever seen, and easily the most enigmatic.

He has a beautiful mouth, she thought as he placed his hands lightly on her shoulders. *Very sensual lips. And, dear God, he's going to kiss me with them!*

43

Four

His lips brushed against hers, light as a feather. It was a tender kiss, strangely tentative, particularly in light of the nature of the man giving the kiss. So when Natasha leaned toward Anton to deepen the kiss, to press the plush softness of her lips more firmly against his mouth, she was surprised at her own behavior. Then she realized that she was reacting precisely as Anton had wanted her to.

One second it was Anton initiating the kiss, and the next it was she, and though a soft warning bell tinkled in the back of her mind, Natasha ignored it as Anton's long, strong arms wound slowly around her waist.

This is madness, she thought as Anton's right hand came upward to cradle her head, his fingers pushing into her oft-admired luxurious mass of auburn hair. *Divine, beautiful, exquisite madness!*

He angled her head slightly to the side to more completely seal her mouth with his own. And when Natasha felt the tip of his tongue run the circumference of her mouth, she heard a low, throaty sigh, and realized with astonishment that the sigh had come from herself.

Natasha had been kissed before, but what had happened in her past had not prepared her for her own reaction to the prince's kisses. On the other two occasions that she had been kissed, one boy had left her feeling nothing at all. The other boy had tried to wedge his thick, slimy tongue between her lips, and the sensation was so shocking and horrifying to Natasha that she had nearly gagged.

So why, with such unpleasant experiences of past kisses, was she tingling — most pleasantly — from head to foot now? And why, as Prince Anton Talakovich's tongue lightly traced the outline of her mouth, was she willingly opening her lips, trembling slightly with a mixture of anticipation and trepidation?

Her heart pounded against her ribs. Natasha's hands still hung limply at her sides, and in the back of her mind she wondered if there was something she should be doing with them that she was not. She could feel the strength of his chest pushing against the fullness of her bosom, making her breasts flatten within the demure bodice of her hand-me-down gown. Her nipples felt achingly tight and erect. Her scalp tingled as Anton's hand moved very subtly, his long fingers entwined with her hair.

When Natasha felt the tip of Anton's tongue probe experimentally between her lips, she shocked herself again by meeting his tongue with her own. Instincts and passion guided her. The kiss became deeper, more satisfying, more exhilarating in a hundred different ways.

She moaned loudly this time, the sound of unexpected pleasure soaring upward from deep within her soul. She opened her mouth wider, swirling her tongue against Anton's, leaning into him to further heighten the pressure against her breasts.

He moved her head again, initially confusing Natasha, then delighting her when he nipped at the silken flesh of her neck with his strong white teeth. She gasped, a soft sound borne of surprise, pain, and excitement. The pinprick of pain caused by Anton's teeth was smoothed away a moment later by the wet

45

warmth of his rasping tongue sliding over the same spot, spreading the fire of desire that had ignited deep within Natasha, and was slowly working its way through her limbs to the tips of her fingers and toes and everyplace else in between.

Natasha's passionate confusion over what was happening was matched by Prince Anton's, a fact that gave him no peace of mind whatsoever. *He* was more than just a little bit experienced in such matters, and *he* was not supposed to be so carried away by emotions—certainly *not* by emotions caused by just a little kiss!

Anton darted his tongue against Natasha's and sensed that she did not have much experience in kissing men, at least not in kissing men this way. Until only a second earlier, he had always viewed inexperienced women as something of a nuisance, a bother, because they had such a tendency to become confused over what they were supposed to be letting their heart feel and what they were supposed to be letting their body feel and do. But Natasha's innocence heightened the fever in his blood, and flashing across the surface of his mind was a series of fairly vague yet thoroughly erotic images of the rapture that would be his if he was the man to free the passionate woman he sensed was imprisoned behind the bars of an old-world sense of propriety and the cheap woolen gown that had seen much better and far more fashionable days.

He felt the way her body trembled, and the resistance she had to the pleasure now coursing through her. Pulling her body closer, Anton sealed off her tiny moan of pleasure with his lips, thrusting his tongue deep into her mouth.

Her breasts, as full and round as any his own erotic imagination could conjure, were a firm cushion against his chest, and when her knees bumped against him, he was certain that she had to feel his burgeon-

46

ing manhood pressing against her, straining to be freed from the imprisoning confines of his trousers.

But if she did feel it, she pretended she did not, and she never moved her hands from her sides. She did nothing to deny Anton, and nothing to urge him on, and for a man like the prince, Natasha's ability to control herself was an aphrodisiac to his senses, a challenge that he simply could not ignore.

What a fool I am! Anton thought suddenly as his brilliant mind, which he never allowed to get involved with the cravings of his body, reminded him that Natasha was a commoner, *and* was probably soon to be an employee. No man in his right mind took advantage of that situation, not if he intended to have peace in his own home. Other damned fools might use their power and influence to seduce the hired help, but that also meant that before long everyone in the castle knew about the affair, and whatever pleasure the sex had brought was easily outweighed by the turmoil that it triggered.

Taking Natasha firmly by the arms, Anton pushed her away slowly but firmly. She continued to keep her eyes closed for several seconds, affording Anton the chance to look at her—truly study her for the very first time—and the loveliness that confronted him was even greater than he had first seen. With her lips slightly parted, glistening from his kisses, she looked as though she could have been sleeping standing up, dreaming of some supremely erotic incident, her hair tousled and disheveled by the ardency of his kisses. She finally opened her eyes, which were a rich chestnut brown, the color he had at first thought was common he now realized was infinitely rare, even unique, and stunningly beautiful.

She was breathing quickly and deeply, making an effort to regain control of her senses, and this pleased Anton, since he had been worried that his kisses had left her unaffected. As she breathed in deeply, her breasts rose and swelled inside the bodice of her gown, drawing Anton's attention. The neckline was not in keeping with fashion, and with this Anton was deeply dissatisfied, since the decolletage hardly showed any cleavage at all, unlike the much more pleasing Empire fashion, currently in vogue, which in some cases revealed almost the entire breast.

With some effort, Anton dragged his eyes from her bosom up to her face, though looking into her eyes had just as much effect upon his riotous emotions as looking at her bosom.

He watched the tip of her tongue move around her lips. Was it a nervous gesture, or was she seeking to taste his lips once again, to somehow taste again the kisses he had just given her?

"I'm sorry," Natasha said then, her voice very soft.

Those two words shocked and dismayed Anton. He was only too aware of the inequalities of the Russian social system, and never a day passed when he was not thankful and grateful that he had been born at the top of the social register. Just as Anton was aware of his position, so, too, it would seem, was Natasha Stantikoff.

In a flash of awareness, Anton realized that Natasha had seen the disapproval on his face — the expression put there by his dissatisfaction of his own actions — and she had immediately assumed that she was to blame. In Russia, it was always the workers, peasants, serfs, and servants, who received the blame, no matter who was at fault.

Her apology twisted the knife of guilt and obligation in Anton's heart, and he shook his head slowly, searching for the right words that would make her believe he was not the kind of Russian aristocrat who used his power and wealth to foist sexual capitulation upon beautiful young women of a lower social station.

"No, Natasha, I am the one who should apologize," Anton said.

He turned away so that he wouldn't have to look at her. Apologizing for kissing a beautiful woman was not something he'd done before, and it was causing him considerable confusion.

"You're not to blame," he continued. "Frankly, I don't even know why I brought you here, or why I'm here myself." He looked up at the horizontal limb high overhead, imagining that the swing rope was still tied there. "This was a mistake. One must leave one's past where it belongs—in the past."

A residual tremor shivered through Natasha, and she hugged herself. She could not say why she had felt such pleasure in his kisses, or why the contempt that her aunt and uncle had tried to imbue in her for the Talakoviches vanished the moment she was in Anton's arms. All she was certain of was that buried deep within herself there was a passionate woman, a woman she'd kept hidden—but unforgotten—for nineteen years, a woman Anton had given her just a glimpse of only a moment before.

Even though he was no longer touching her, Natasha was still able to feel where his fingers had pushed through her hair, dislodging the coiffure she had worked so hard at that morning before beginning her trek to Castle Talakovich. Her scalp continued to tingle, and so did her nipples. She could still feel the heat of his hand against the small of her back, and the extraordinary feel and taste of his tongue playing gently, erotically against her own.

"Come, I'll take you home," Anton said then.

He's as confused by this as I am, Natasha thought. *He didn't intend for this to happen any more than I did. But he apologized for kissing me . . . and yet his heart was in that kiss . . . I know it, I felt it. Who is this man?*

The remainder of the ride home was wrapped in thick silence. A few efforts were made at conversation, but neither Anton nor Natasha were able to distance themselves from their thoughts and doubts enough to make room for the witty repartee that had sparked their previous conversation.

"The house is behind that wind break," Natasha explained, nodding to a copse of trees on the north side of the road. "Perhaps it would be best if you didn't take me all the way home. My aunt and uncle . . ."

Her words died away, and Anton did not press the issue because he could well imagine why she did not want him to see the way she lived. He pulled the carriage to a stop, then leaped out, moving around to help Natasha down, but she had already stepped out.

"Good evening to you then," she said, then turned away and walked down the gravel road into the darkness, moving quickly, not wanting to taste his kisses another time before she left him.

Anton watched her disappear around the trees. Listening carefully, he heard the sound of a door slam shut as Natasha entered her house. At last sure that she was safe, he leaped back into the carriage and tapped the reins to the team, turning them around.

It was dark, and he had to hurry back to St. Petersburg to meet the American mercenary who, he hoped with all his heart, had been successful in his negotiations. The necessary finances must be acquired for his country to secure the weapons of war. Somehow, they had to prevent the destruction of his beloved Mother Russia by that little madman from France, Napoleon Bonaparte.

"You're late," Aggie said, her fleshy face twisting in a disgusted scowl as she kicked her feet up on the ottoman, pulling the footrest a little closer to her chair, which caused Ivan's feet to fall off the ottoman.

"Aislyn had to do the cooking, and you know she doesn't cook nearly as well as you. Then she started complaining about not feeling well, so she went to bed without even cleaning up the dishes."

Aggie was shaking her head with disgust as Natasha, still in her best gown, pushed her sleeves up and started pumping water to wash the evening dishes.

"I hope your day was spent doing something other than just avoiding your chores around here," Aggie continued, turning in her chair so that she could continue to berate her niece.

She glanced at Ivan, who was glassy-eyed from liquor, cradling the small glass in his hands as he stared absently into the fire. On the floor at his side, tucked between his chair and the wall, was the bottle of vodka that he purchased from the man in the Gdin valley, who made the cheap liquor himself from his own potatoes. Ivan was more interested in the volume and alcohol content of his vodka than he was in its smoothness or taste.

"Aren't you going to say anything to her?" Aggie at last prodded, keeping her voice down to give the outward appearance that she was not being overly disrespectful to her husband, yet making sure she spoke loud enough so that Natasha knew she was egging Ivan on.

"Why? You're doing a fine job of keeping her in line," Ivan shrugged. He watched Natasha pumping the water handle, smiling drunkenly and lustfully.

As soon as Natasha put the boiler on the stove to heat water, she mumbled something about needing to change out of her good dress—though it really wasn't very good at all—if she was to do her chores, then went to the small bedroom she shared with Aislyn.

She found her friend laying in the bed they shared. Aislyn was on her back, her right hand resting lightly upon her stomach. She was pale, and when she

51

looked at Natasha, her eyes brimmed with tears.

"I'm sorry to leave the dirty dishes for you to tend to," Aislyn said quickly as Natasha sat on the edge of the bed, looking down at her friend sympathetically. "I would have done them myself, but I started feeling so weak and your uncle kept leaning close to me, looking at me with that way he has, and every time I had to smell his breath I just — "

"Shhh! There's nothing to explain." Natasha put a cool hand on Aislyn's forehead. She didn't feel feverish, but she was pale. Some women handle pregnancy easily, others have a nine-month struggle to endure. Aislyn, it seemed, was going to fall into the latter category, and whether Natasha liked it or not, it was up to her to do what she could to make life easier for her pregnant friend.

"I have happy news for you," Natasha continued after a moment, smoothing a lock of Aislyn's hair away from her forehead. "I don't think we'll have to be here much longer. Princess Talakovich has hired me to be her personal seamstress, and she's promised to pay me a fortune!" Natasha leaned close, not wanting Ivan or Aggie to hear what she had to say. The walls in the old house — particularly the interior walls — were not very thick. "I should be able to save up enough money to get us both out of here. I've only got to work hard, that's all."

Aislyn smiled wanly. She had heard her friend say such things before. That was their dream — to escape Ivan and Aggie and their insults and cruelties. Freedom was always just around the next bend in the road, according to Natasha. All she had to do was work very hard, and they would have what they needed to set themselves up in Moscow, perhaps as helpers in one of the boarding houses there, or maybe in one of the many hotels that served as temporary housing for high-ranking soldiers and foreign businessmen and dignitaries who were now so much a part of the Moscow life.

"If not for me, you could leave right now," Aislyn said, her voice an exhausted whisper.

"That's not true, and you know it! What would I do in Moscow, without any letter of introduction, without any money? You know that leaves only one thing left for a woman in a big city like that." Natasha squeezed her friend's hand. "Don't you give it another thought. We're friends, and we've got to protect each other. We're all we've got, you and I." Natasha leaned low to kiss Aislyn's forehead. "Go to sleep now. I'm going to change into my work clothes, finish up the dishes, and then I'll be to bed."

She had missed supper at the Talakovich Castle, and now she would go to bed without anything, but Natasha didn't mind. The day *had* been fruitful, and if the princess was as good as her word and would really pay what she had promised, then surely it would not be long at all before Natasha could pack her meager belongings, grab Aislyn, and escape this living hell that was her home.

When she stepped out of her bedroom, she found Aggie going through her small clutch purse. Natasha kept nothing in there but a brush, a couple of extra hair pins and combs, and some extra sewing needles and thread.

"Empty, I see," Aggie snapped, throwing the purse down on the floor. "Empty again." She began wagging a fat finger Natasha's direction. "We weren't born to support you, you ingrate. You must earn your keep, just like everyone else. You'd better start bringing in some rubles — and quick! — or your uncle is going to throw you right out that door, do you hear? He'll throw you out the door right along with that lazy, pregnant friend you invited in without asking our permission."

"She had no place else to go!" Natasha snapped. Then, in a much softer tone, her heart sinking as the reality of her home life began to once again seep into her pores like a virus, she said, "I'll be bringing in coin soon. I'll give you every ruble I make."

"How much? And when is 'soon'?"

Natasha related the story of her interview with Princess Talakovich, carefully not mentioning that she had found Anastasia delightful company. She didn't even think about mentioning Prince Anton, and what she had thought about him.

"They'll probably rob you blind," Aggie said softly, but the statement was only spoken out of habit, and bore little resemblance to her true thoughts. "Thieves, those Talakoviches. You've heard how they did all they could to destroy your uncle and me, how it was the Talakoviches that stole our land. They did it because they knew that Ivan and me were competition for them. They destroyed us because they knew the only way they could build their fortune was if they destroyed your uncle and me."

Natasha knew enough to nod her head and murmur "uh-huh" at the appropriate times, but she did not listen to her aunt. She'd heard the stories and the excuses all before, and they simply did not ring true, especially not now after she'd met Anton and Anastasia, and she knew them to be something other than the heartless monsters Ivan and Aggie insisted they were.

It was very late by the time Natasha finished cleaning the house, washing and putting away the dishes, and washing and wringing Ivan and Aggie's stockings and undergarments. When she crawled beneath the blanket in bed, Aislyn whispered another apology for not helping with the work, and for needing to take up half of the bed.

"You just get to sleep and save your strength," Natasha said, pulling the blanket up around her shoulders. "And don't concern yourself about a thing. I'm going to get us out of here. That child of yours is not going to grow up here, with Ivan and Aggie to poison his mind. I promise you that."

Natasha was exhausted and hungry, but the moment she closed her eyes, she saw Anton's face. And laying quietly there in bed, she could remember—and almost feel again—all the sensations that had rippled through her when Anton's lips had kissed her with such devastating effect, awakening within her a hunger far deeper than even the heartiest meal could satisfy.

It was a long time before sleep finally claimed Natasha, and even then, she continued to dream about Prince Anton Talakovich.

"I thought you'd be in bed by now," Anton said to his sister as he entered the library at Castle Talakovich.

"There are just a few papers I wanted to go over once more before I give you my opinion on the proposals." Anastasia arched her back, stretched her arms high over her head, then rubbed the back of her neck.

"Go to bed," Anton said in his older-brother voice that was at once commanding and compassionate. "Anything in those proposals tonight will still be there in the morning."

"I suppose you're right."

Anastasia rose from her chair and glanced at the grandfather clock opposite the fireplace. It was very nearly midnight, and though she was curious as to where her brother had been for the past several hours, she kept that curiosity to herself. Anton would not lie to her about his social and sexual life, but sometimes Anastasia found that while ignorance might not be bliss, turning a blind eye to a brother's excesses did keep a loving sister from worrying overmuch.

"Sleep well," Anton said as his sister left the library.

When he was at last alone, he went to his desk and lit the candle there, angling the reflecting mirror to throw the maximum amount of light on the desk top and the stacks of papers and documents.

He hoped that Anastasia would sleep well, though he knew that such a wish for himself was absolute folly. His mind felt like it was on fire. Though such mental agitation was certainly nothing new to Prince Anton Talakovich—a businessman renown throughout Russia and Europe for his shrewd, cunning mind—what was different about his searing unease was the cause: a woman.

He couldn't focus his mind on business, and that's what was most troubling. Anton had long felt that one of his greatest assets was his ability to concentrate on a single problem for endless hours, turning the matter this way and that to look at it from every conceivable angle until, in the end, however Anton decided to attack the problem would be the absolute best way to challenge it.

After he had turned his carriage around and started back to the castle, Anton had allowed himself ten minutes to think about Natasha, and mentally relive all the sights, tastes, touches, and scents that he had enjoyed with her.

The ten minutes came and went in the blink of an eye. Ten minutes just wasn't nearly enough to let his mind do justice to the time he had spent with Natasha, so he allotted her memory an unprecedented additional twenty minutes. He did not think for thirty straight minutes about any woman, much less one he was not having an affair with.

At the end of thirty minutes, Anton decided it was time to banish Natasha from his thoughts, and concentrate for a while on all the business matters that were continually pressing in upon him.

There was that little lunatic in France to think about, and the czar himself had put Anton in charge of seeing to it that loans for weapons were secured in such a fashion that Napoleon—who was, in theory, Czar Alexander's friend and Russia's ally—never suspected their fortification efforts.

It was the czar's opinion—and Anton and Anastasia's as well—that behind Napoleon's proclamations of peace and calls for unity and sovereignty lay deceit, treachery, and a burning imperialistic drive that would one day bring well-armed and trained French soldiers to march in anger upon the soil of Mother Russia.

Caleb Carter, the American mercenary and Anton's only real friend besides his sister, was expected at the castle soon. He'd spent months in England, Switzerland, Sweden, and elsewhere, securing potential loan agreements and arranging for the finest pieces of heavy artillery made to be secretly shipped to St. Petersburg. When Caleb arrived at the castle, there would be even more for Anton to focus on.

So with all that on his mind, it should have been child's play for Anton to forget all about a seamstress in an old woolen dress. The problem was, he wasn't a child and neither was Natasha, and no matter how many times Anton turned his thoughts toward the arcane business practices of the international banking community, his focus faded and Natasha, once again, rose to the forefront of his consciousness, demanding his total awareness.

"I've got to concentrate," Anton whispered to himself, rubbing his temples lightly, staring at the cover page of a contract on his desk.

He wasn't even close to falling asleep.

Five

"You've got to tell me everything about him," Aislyn said in the morning. She looked radiant, healthy, and happy after a long night's rest, and her smile warmed Natasha's heart. "Is he as handsome as I remember? I saw him once when his carriage went through the village. Is he as wicked as all the women claim?"

Natasha rolled her eyes theatrically, as though her friend's questions were almost too trivial to even comment on. Actually, Natasha was almost embarrassed to find herself enjoying the brief, private celebrity status she was receiving from Aislyn after commenting in an off-hand manner that it had been Prince Anton who had given her a ride home in his own carriage.

"Tell me everything!" Aislyn said, her excitement making it hard to keep her voice at a whisper. She tucked the sheet under the mattress, making the bed while Natasha washed her hands and face in the cool water basin beside the chest-of-drawers.

"There's really not that much to tell you about him," Natasha replied with a smile, at last giving up the charade that Prince Anton's presence in her life was nothing extraordinary. "He's as handsome as you remember. It was the first time *I've* seen him up close, and he's beautiful. Everything but his eyes."

58

"Why not his eyes? What's wrong with his eyes?" Aislyn demanded. She pulled the nightshirt over her head and dropped it onto the bed, then sat on the small bench in front of the water basin where Natasha had been moments earlier. She worked a soapy lather into a wash cloth and began washing her arms, shoulders, chest, and neck, all the while looking at Natasha through the reflection in the mirror.

"It's not that there's anything *wrong* with his eyes, its just that they work too well."

"Too well? That doesn't make any sense."

"Of course it doesn't. I just don't know how to put it."

Natasha went to the one window in the small bedroom and looked out. It would be dawn soon, and just as soon as she finished her chores around the house, as well as cooking breakfast for her aunt and uncle, and cleaning up afterward, she would be on her way once again to Castle Talakovich. The prospect of seeing Anton again alternately horrified and excited her.

Thoughts of Prince Anton had never been far from her since their parting. His gorgeous grin, so boyish and yet so masculine, had haunted her dreams and now continued to haunt her thoughts.

"Well, try!" Aislyn said, exasperated at Natasha's delay. Being both pregnant and abandoned, reality was not a comfortable place for Aislyn to be, so she welcomed the make-believe world of Prince Anton.

"His eyes see everything," Natasha said quietly, still staring out the window. Her voice sounded as far away as her thoughts were. "They're gray and most of the time they seem very cold . . . but now and then you can see a spark in his eyes, an inner warmth, as if he's hiding a raging bonfire. He tries to hide that, of course, but if you look at him closely and if he lets his guard down, you get a chance to feel that warmth."

"His eyes—you're sure they're gray? Not blue or

59

green?"

"I'm positive of it."

"That's an unusual color."

"He's an unusual man.

The bedroom door opened then and Uncle Ivan stuck his head in, getting to see Aislyn's soapy breasts before she covered herself with her hands. It was the conversation about Anton that had made Natasha and Aislyn let their guard down. Both women knew that Ivan liked to burst in on them unannounced particularly early in the morning and late at night in hopes of seeing a little more skin than he should.

"Hurry up in here," he said, as though his only reason for looking in the bedroom was to speed the women along. He kept his voice low as a thief so that Aggie wouldn't hear him. She didn't at all approve of his voyeuristic bent. "I want breakfast on the table in thirty minutes."

"Yes, sir," Aislyn said quietly, arms crossed over her bare bosom, her head down in shame.

Natasha said nothing, knowing that if she argued with her uncle at all, he would only come deeper into the bedroom and confront them, thereby prolonging his time in their room. But though she kept her tongue silent, the contempt she felt for her uncle screamed from her dark eyes, shouting the obscenities at the man that her upbringing would not allow her to voice aloud.

When they were alone again, Natasha went to the door, leaning a shoulder against it so that it couldn't be opened while her friend rinsed the soap from herself. There were no locks anywhere in the house, and whenever Natasha questioned this, Ivan asked her what it was she needed to hide from her "generous and caring aunt and uncle."

"We must get out of here," Natasha said softly, still trembling from the anger she felt deep in her soul for the way her uncle abused the power he had over herself and Aislyn. "Sooner or later, he's going to demand more than just rent from us."

Aislyn had just pulled her old dress over her head. "Not from us, just from me," she replied, and the defeat she felt showed in the tone of her voice, and tugged at Natasha's heartstrings. "You are his niece, and he might like to look at you, but he probably won't go any further than that. I'm no relative to him at all, and he's already told me that it wouldn't make any difference if he and I—" the hideous memory choked off Aislyn's words temporarily "—if we did that thing that men and women do, since I'm already with child."

Overwhelming rage and frustration washed over Natasha. She had suspected that when she wasn't around, Uncle Ivan was making unwanted advances to Aislyn, but she hadn't asked her friend about it. Now her worse—or *almost* her worst fears were confirmed. If she didn't get herself and Aislyn out of the house soon, Ivan would get what it was he craved.

"Be strong," Natasha said, a thin thread of almost lethal anger running through her tone. "Just for a little while longer, you've got to be strong. And don't give in to my uncle. No matter what he says, don't give in to him."

"I won't." The words were spoken without an ounce of conviction in them, heightening Natasha's determination and sense of mission.

She left the bedroom, forcing her anger to remain buried deep inside. If it showed on her face, she might have to explain her anger, and she was too volatile to lie effectively.

It was while Natasha was washing the breakfast dishes and Aislyn was outside near the garden where she was weeding that Aunt Aggie came forward with a smile on her face that was decidedly out of character.

"You know, Ivan and I were thinking . . ." Aunt Aggie said.

61

Natasha dried her hands on a towel, turning to face her aunt. She said nothing, simply stared, waiting for the words that she was certain she would not like hearing.

"You know how bad the Talakovich thieves have treated your family in the past, and maybe you getting a job with the princess is divine providence?" Aggie nodded her head, as though she was just now realizing this. She didn't fool Natasha for a second. This whole speech was planned out. "Maybe this is God's way of helping us all get back on our feet again."

"How so?" Natasha asked. When she'd told Ivan and Aggie what she would be paid for her seamstress services, she cut the figure in half, guessing—and accurately so—that they would take every ruble of her income.

"Everyone knows that Princess Anastasia is a woman of loose moral character. Goodness, the stories I've heard about what that woman's done!"

"They were rumors, Aunt Aggie. Nothing but rumors. I wouldn't believe a word of it." *Especially since you're the one who probably made up the rumor in the first place,* she thought bitterly.

"A woman of loose morals is no woman at all!" Aggie snapped, as though she herself had never cheated on Ivan, which everyone knew wasn't true. "She flirts outrageously, and it doesn't just end at flirting either, I can tell you."

"So what are you saying? What does any of this have to do with me?"

"I'm saying that she's got more gems and jewels than she knows about or can even remember, and sometime if you're with her for the evening, maybe you can slip one of those gems into the pocket of your dress? Heavens, she'll never miss it, and we both know that whatever you take from her is certainly no more than what we deserve. She probably bought the gems with money she stole from your uncle and me

62

anyway!"

Natasha stared at her aunt, and for one of the few times in her life she was speechless, utterly dumbfounded by what she'd heard. There she was, on the eve of beginning the highest paying job she'd ever had (even if she only considered the amount that she'd told Aggie she was receiving), and the first thing that Aggie could think of was to get even more money—not earning but by stealing it.

If there'd ever been any doubt in Natasha's mind that Ivan and Aggie had lost their property through their own foolish, self-destructive conduct, that notion vanished. Ivan and Aggie were, at base and in the very core of their hearts, thieves—and *lazy* thieves at that! They were completely incapable of honesty.

"And what am I supposed to do with the jewelry that I steal?" she asked at last.

"You give it straight away to your uncle and me." Aggie's eyes took on a bright light. She did not hear, because she did not *want* to hear, the condescension in her niece's tone. "Ivan knows a man who will give us a good price for anything we can bring him. And don't worry, he sells everything he gets in Moscow, so nobody will ever know where the jewels and gems come from."

Not only are they thieves, they're stupid thieves, Natasha thought, utterly astonished that Aggie actually believed the people in Moscow who had the money to afford such priceless jewelry as that which Princess Anastasia wore wouldn't recognize it. The princess was famous for her jewelry, and all of it was not only of the finest quality, but flamboyant and original, as befitting her *joi de vivre*.

"I'll get caught," Natasha said quietly. There was a ringing in her ears. Did Aggie really think she would go along with such an outlandish—and illegal—scheme?

"No, you won't. You're a clever girl." Aggie's eyes

63

narrowed, and the tone of her voice dipped menacingly. "And you know who you owe for putting a roof over your head all these years, don't you? You know that Ivan and I took you and Aislyn in when nobody else would."

"Aislyn hasn't been here that long."

"That's right, she hasn't. And in the time that she's been here, she hasn't had your uncle in her bed, either, has she? Now who do you think has kept him from jumping between her thighs, eh? It's been me, that's who! And just how long do you figure he'll be satisfied with getting a look now and then at what he's not touching?" Aggie moved very close to Natasha, almost daring her niece to back down, ready to pounce at the first sign of weakness. "Ivan won't wait much longer, I can tell you! Ivan may be a drinker, but the vodka hasn't unmanned him yet. Not by a long ways! He's always been a bull, and he's got more than just eyes for that young friend of yours. So you think real long and hard about that, and whether or not you're too high and proud to do what it is I tell you." Aggie's mouth twisted into an ugly sneer, and her eyes went up and down over Natasha as though inspecting a brood mare. "And don't look at me with those big, offended eyes, missy. You don't need me angry with you, and the moment Ivan thinks I won't geld him, you'll find out he wants to do more than just look at you ladies.

"So perhaps when you're in that big castle, you can find yourself alone with the prince, and maybe when that happens, you can find yourself on your back with your thighs open wide. That'll make the prince think kindly of you, and maybe then you can find your hands inside his pockets as well as his pants, if you know what I mean."

The words bore into Natasha, each one burning holes in her psyche. Aggie was not making idle threats. She meant every word, and Natasha had not one moment's doubt that if she did not comply with the demands presented, then a blind eye would be turned toward Ivan's abuses.

Natasha finished her morning chores, and after another warning to Aislyn, telling her to stay far from Ivan during the day, Natasha began the eight-mile walk to Castle Talakovich.

It was shortly after six o'clock, and she hoped to be there by eight, eight-thirty at the latest.

He was operating on adrenaline and not much else, but that was nothing really new for Prince Anton Talakovich. The few hours' sleep he got during the night didn't prevent him from waking up before dawn to awaken and alert his personal cook and coachman of his hastily concocted morning plans.

Before the sun was up, Anton was on his way in his finest closed carriage drawn by matching black geldings. Beside him on the seat was a wicker basket laden with food. There was cold chicken, cold roast beef, hard and soft boiled eggs, a small pitcher of fresh cow's milk wrapped in a towel and packed in ice, along with a bottle of champagne being similarly chilled. There was also a steaming silver pot of coffee wrapped in a towel, with a matching pot for tea.

Having no idea what kind of foods Natasha Stantikoff enjoyed best, Anton simply had his cook pack everything possible. It was a typical move of Anton's: when in doubt, go to excess.

What was not typical was that he was taking particular pains to please a young woman not from his own background. In the past, a trinket or bauble was sufficient to let whatever woman he happened to be sleeping with at the time know that she was appreciated, and that sex with her was not entirely without tender affiliation to Prince Anton's heart.

But how did one go about entertaining a woman

who had nothing at all? Giving a diamond necklace seemed much too extravagant, and Anton highly suspected that should he make such a gesture, he'd probably be unintentionally insulting. He didn't know Natasha that well yet, but his instincts told him that she was a proud woman, and if he tried a grand gesture, she would think that he was trying to *buy* her favors, and that would simply never do.

What was he to do if he arrived before the household had awakened for the day?

Anton didn't want to dwell on that possibility now. He did not relish the opportunity to at last confront the troublesome Ivan and Aggie Pronushka, but he surely wouldn't back down from one.

There had to be some way of getting Natasha away from her aunt and uncle on a permanent basis so that these little complications wouldn't have to enter his life, Anton thought. He was long accustomed to tailoring other people's lives to suit his own interests.

The moment the thought entered his mind, his entire body flinched as though he'd been jolted by lightning. Was he really pondering a *permanent* arrangement to see Natasha?

No, only temporary permanence, he thought with a certain stubborn, cold-hearted refutation.

The carriage slowed, and Anton looked out the window. The sun was just turning the horizon pink with its first rays of the day, and Natasha's home was still a mile away. He leaned out the window, about to question the coachman, when he saw her on the road, walking with a brisk stride, a cloth bag slung over her shoulder.

Anton's heart did a crazy little leap in his chest when he saw her. She was even more beautiful in the morning than at night, he decided. Her hair was done up nicely, but the swiftness of her stride had pulled loose several strands, which now danced about her cheeks. Her face was slightly flushed from the exertion of keeping the fast pace she'd set since leaving her house.

Anton noticed instantly that she was wearing the same dress she'd worn the day before, which probably meant it was the best one she owned, and the only one she felt was presentable at Castle Talakovich. He noticed, too, with equal measures of dismay and pleasure, that the dress's decolletage was very modest, and that beneath the austere material with its old-fashioned styling her heavy round breasts rose and fell with her determined stride.

For the nth time since first meeting her, Anton tried to tell himself that the only reason he was so fascinated with Natasha Stantikoff was because she was so different from the wealthy, abominably bored and thus boring debutantes he usually found himself in bed with.

"Good morning!" Anton called out.

Natasha had been looking at the ground ahead of her, and her head snapped up at the sound of his voice. She smiled immediately, then the smile vanished just as quickly as it appeared, which caused a million conflicting explanations to speed through Anton's mind.

When the carriage stopped, Anton opened the door wide and stepped out, bowing low and pointing toward the open door as he did so. "Your carriage awaits you, my lady."

Natasha peered into the closed carriage as though looking into the cage of some dangerous animal in the Moscow zoo. The fragrant smells of fried chicken wafted through the air, making her mouth water in anticipation. Her morning had been so hectic and disquieting that she'd left without eating breakfast. Missing that meal, combined with the evening meal on the previous evening that she also had not eaten, left her ravenous now.

"Where were you going?" she asked. It just didn't

seem right to her that Anton should go through all this trouble just to bring his sister's new seamstress to the castle for her first day's work.

"I *was* going to your house," Anton said, the smile still on his face though he did not at all appreciate the suspicious way Natasha was looking into the carriage as though it was a trap that had been set and would be sprung the moment she stepped into it. "Now, once you step in, I will be going back to Castle Talakovich."

The right side of Natasha's mouth pulled upward in a smile of appreciation that she tried futilely to keep to herself. "You came all the way out here just to bring me to the castle?"

"More precisely, I came all the way out here to see if you were in the least bit hungry while I brought you to the castle. It's a minor but critical distinction."

Anton reached into the carriage and, with a flourish, removed the white towel from over an oval, ornately carved silver tray laden on one side with thick slices of roast beef, and on the other with pieces of fried chicken. The fare now, in the light of day, seemed terribly heavy, and Anton had to bite his lip to keep the apology unvoiced.

Natasha looked at Anton, then at the road that lay ahead of her. It was clear to Anton that she was not the type of woman who could easily accept gifts from men as her just due. Rather, she was suspicious of gifts, possibly *especially* gifts from men, and Anton wondered if she had been hurt in the past, lied to and disillusioned by a man.

He made a mental note to have some discreet inquiries made. It was none of his business, he told himself, but just the same, he would find out whether any man had hurt Natasha Stantikoff . . . and should that be the case, perhaps pay a visit to the offending, swinish cretin to discuss the benefits of gentlemanly conduct.

Quietly, and without the forced humor that he had used earlier when he surprised Natasha on the road, Anton said, "It would please me enormously to accompany you to Castle Talakovich. If you've already eaten, don't feel obligated to partake." He held his hand out, and when Natasha took it to enter the carriage, his smile was broad and thoroughly unaffected.

"Do you always treat your new workers this way?" Natasha asked, taking her seat opposite the food.

"Just the special ones," Anton said, sitting down beside her. It was not mere coincidence or happenstance that the food was placed on one seat cushion, making it necessary for Anton and Natasha to sit next to each other.

"I didn't realize being Princess Anastasia's seamstress made me so special," Natasha said offhandedly, looking at the food that was so very close, but not wanting to be so unladylike and bold as to uncover the trays herself.

There are a lot of good seamstresses around, and none of the others would be allowed to set foot in this carriage, Anton thought, enormously pleased that Natasha really did not realize how special she was.

"Hungry?"

Natasha nodded, inhaling deeply, savoring the smell as though she could taste the air. "A little," she said, vanity making it impossible to admit to being famished.

"Then let's get started," Anton replied, opening yet another basket to reveal fine porcelain plates and gleaming silverware.

Natasha's hunger had, at first, made her oblivious to the efforts that Anton was making to please her. Did she prefer white to dark meat, or would the roast beef be more enjoyable than the chicken? he asked. And if it hadn't been such a spur of the moment decision to meet her and have this rolling breakfast, Anton assured Natasha, he would have had cut fruits in their juices in bowls chilled for her. Perhaps next time all of that would be possible, Anton said, though the raised eyebrows over inquisitive gray eyes suggested that whatever Anton wanted had a way of becoming a reality in short order.

The seasoning on the chicken was different from anything Natasha had tasted before, and it was delicious. Chicken, though, is a messy food to eat, and part of her wished that she had opted for the roast beef. She wiped her hands repeatedly on the elegant napkins that Anton had provided, but the quality of the cloth was such that Natasha felt rather guilty for soiling the fine fabric.

Natasha ate, though perhaps not quite as much as she would have liked, and drank two cups of the fine tea, though it had become tepid during the trip from Castle Talakovich.

She looked out the window of the carriage, watching the countryside coming to life in the morning. After her initial shock at discovering that Anton had come in his carriage to take her to the castle, she had quickly become comfortable with him, though there could be no denying the tingles she felt in her stomach — and down lower — whenever their eyes met.

"More?" Anton asked, reaching for the silver tea server.

"No, thank you. I've had quite enough of everything," Natasha replied.

"It is certainly much too early for the wine," Anton said, though there was a hint in his voice that if Natasha wanted some wine, his opinion on the matter was quite changeable.

"Some things are better after the sun goes down, not just as it is coming up," Natasha said in all innocence.

"Some things, but not everything," Anton replied, arching a brow above a cool gray eye.

Natasha looked out the window, hot embarrassment turning her cheeks pink, making her throat and chest feel warm, her ears feeling on fire. She had meant for it to be just idle chatter, but Anton had turned the comment into something lascivious.

"That isn't what I meant," she said quietly, refusing to look at Anton.

Though he did not make a sound, she could hear him laughing inside, and it irked her enormously. She could picture his thoughts, the amusement he felt at embarrassing the naive country girl, and the more she thought about this, the angrier she became.

"You mustn't be angry," Anton said, looking at Natasha over the gold-edged rim of his coffee cup. "I only meant for it to be humorous."

"At my expense," Natasha shot back quickly. She turned on the carriage seat to face Anton, her chestnut eyes darkening with building anger. "You think everything about me is funny, don't you? Well, I'm not as silly as you think, and I'd appreciate it very much if you'd stop reading my mind."

Anton leaned across the seats to set his cup and saucer down on the silver tray on the facing seat. When he turned toward Natasha again, she could still see the amusement in the corners of his eyes, but he was no longer laughing inside.

"Natasha, you must believe me when I tell you that I did not mean to insult you, or belittle you in any way." He took one of her hands between his palms. "Contrary to the stories that you might have heard, I'm really not the demon legend makes me out to be."

Natasha looked at him, wanting to believe him, feeling the warmth of his hands surrounding hers. He'd used the word *legend* concerning himself, but he used the word without great boastfulness. He was virtually a living legend, and this was something that he accepted as fact, as another person would accept the color of their hair, or being tall or short, or some other feature about themselves that they couldn't change, even if they wanted to.

What would it be like to live with the burden of legend continually weighing upon your shoulders? she wondered.

For good or evil, everyone had profound opinions concerning Prince Anton Talakovich. No one, it seemed, felt neutral about him. Certainly not Aunt Aggie and Uncle Ivan, who felt Anton was the most pernicious and predatorial creature ever to walk on two legs, and not the legions of women from eighteen to forty who had sampled the sensual charms of the prince.

"You must learn to trust me," Anton said. He turned Natasha's hand so that the palm was upward. With a forefinger he began tracing the lines on her hand. "The gypsies believe that the future can be foretold by the lines on the hand."

"Do you believe that?" Natasha asked. She could hardly picture a man as brilliant as Anton accepting such superstitious beliefs.

"There are several bands of gypsies who travel through my land several times a year. I confess, I have stopped them in the past, and when I did, I got a chance to know some of them. There's an old woman — a dark-eyed gypsy from the Balkans, I believe — who read my future from the lines in my hand, and in a crystal ball."

His fingertip moved across Natasha's hand in a manner that was subtly caressing. Natasha watched his fingertip roaming around the palm of her hand, and she tried to tell herself that it really wasn't that stimulating to be touched like that — really not stimulating at all. But as Anton's fingertip followed the line of her thumb, moving upward until he touched the delicate area between the thumb and palm, she could have been touched on the breast and not have been so deeply affected.

"What . . . what did the gypsy woman tell you?"

Natasha asked softly, her mouth feeling dry as she tried to make conversation.

"She said that someone very interesting would be entering my life soon."

Natasha smiled a bit nervously. "And how long ago did she tell you this?"

"Last fall, as the caravan was moving to the south, where it is warmer during the winter." Anton's fingertip slid higher, touching the inside of Natasha's wrist. "Your heart is beating fast," he said, tilting his head back to look into Natasha's eyes.

She laughed, a bit more nervous than before, and pulled her hand away.

"The carriage seems to be moving very slowly," Natasha commented, looking out the window.

Quite suddenly, the carriage seemed to be very small, closing in around her. Anton's presence, his all-pervading, heady sensuality, dominated the air, forcing her to inhale it, to become a part of it and affected by it whether she wanted to or not.

"I told the driver to take his time. I didn't want our breakfast to be disturbed."

He looked at Natasha's profile, finding her even more lovely in the morning light than she had been in the pale evening moonlight. As she sat as close to the far wall of the carriage as possible, staring out the window, Anton was afforded the opportunity to look at her leisurely, to caress her with his eyes, and forever memorize the subtle features that made her distinctly her own person, in all her loveliness.

And why was she so fascinating? he wondered. He had been with enough women in his life for him to realize there was a difference between any companionship, and exciting companionship. In the wild days of his youth, he had thought that touching any woman was as much as he could hope for; over the years he had become more discriminating, though his amorous exploits were still, to say the least, prodigious.

"I don't want to be late for the princess," Natasha said softly, still looking out the window.

"Don't worry, I'll take care of everything."

Anton let the direction of his gaze drift downward, following the slender line of Natasha's throat, to the modest decolletage. When the carriage hit a bump in the road, her breasts bounced gently, and he felt the tightness in his stomach become greater.

Why her? he wondered again, realizing that it was really quite ridiculous that he was so aroused by her clothed breasts. It certainly wasn't like he had never felt a woman's firm breast in his hand before . . . but he had never held *Natasha's* breast, and the thought of it now took his breath away.

Natasha turned then to look at him, and when she did, Anton guiltily pulled his gaze up from where it had been lingering.

"Why me?" she asked softly, confused, her rich brown eyes narrowed in concentration and doubt. "Why so much attention to me? You can have any woman you want." Her eyes narrowed even more, and she added with disapproval in her voice, "Everyone knows that."

The bluntness of the question, the boldness of it, shocked Anton so thoroughly that for a moment he was speechless. He was supposed to be the one with the preternatural ability to read minds, and now she was the one setting him back on his heels. It was not a sensation he appreciated, though in spite of this his respect for Natasha's intellect and abilities went up considerably.

"I don't really know why you . . . fascinate me . . . so," he said slowly and carefully, studying Natasha's face as he spoke. "I'm being honest with you now. I truly don't know why you play with my mind." He looked away from her for the briefest moment, collecting his thoughts, choosing his words carefully, hellishly confused over why he was speaking the truth to this seamstress. "I'm sure I could concoct a much more romantic lie, but the truth is that I don't know *why* you . . . enthrall me . . . only that you do."

Natasha was as confused—but by no means insulted—by what she had just heard as the prince was at himself for saying the words. She hadn't been slighted at all. She looked at him, thinking it so enormously odd that such a brilliant man could know such confusion.

Was this all just part of his seductive act? If so, it was working magnificently. She had prepared for smooth, unctuous words and flattery, and if he'd spoken that way to her, she would have laughed in his face, and easily been able to cast him aside—so she wanted to believe.

His confusion and his apparent honesty now touched something deep within her, and if it hadn't been for the much-too-recent memory of Aunt Aggie suggesting that she whorishly give her body to Prince Anton in hopes of gaining his trust so that she could steal from him, she might even have invited his kiss.

"I'm different, that's all," Natasha said with quiet detachment. "You're not accustomed to talking with the hired help. If I was another wealthy young woman from an aristocratic family, you wouldn't give me a second glance."

Anton shook his head. "It's not that simple. At first, that's what I thought too, but then I realized I was only lying to myself. I haven't been able to put my finger on it yet, Natasha Stantikoff, but there is something beguiling about you, something deliciously and strangely compelling . . . addictive, even . . . like a sorceress . . . bewitching me with your spell. . . ."

Each word touched Natasha intimately. As he spoke, he moved over in the carriage, trapping Natasha against the side. He placed his left hand lightly upon her knee, touching her through her long dress, and his right arm slid around her shoulders, pausing briefly to brush aside several loose strands of auburn hair at the nape of her neck.

"Anton," she whispered, about to tell him to stay away.

She could not say more because his mouth, wide and seductive, slanted down over hers, sealing off her breath, cutting off any words of protest she might have uttered. He leaned into her, pressing her backward, turning toward her as the kiss grew more fierce, heated with the suppressed hunger that had been toying with Anton's emotions since he had first kissed her the night before.

Natasha turned her face away from him finally, needing to breathe, needing to no longer taste his kisses so that she might think clearly. She gulped in air, trembling softly as Anton's warm, moist lips caressed her throat.

She couldn't let Prince Anton kiss her because it was exactly what Aunt Aggie wanted him to do, and no matter how tremblingly erotic it was to be in Anton's arms and feel his kisses deepening, Natasha could not be the type of woman that her aunt wanted her to be, *that* type of woman who considered sex a business venture, and her body just another weapon in her arsenal to get what she wanted.

"I can't," she whispered, balling her hands into small fists, pushing them against Anton's chest. She squeezed her eyes tightly shut, afraid that frustration would allow tears of embarrassment to flow. "I can't . . . I just can't!"

Six

Anton's mouth pressed against her throat, her cheek, the corner of her mouth. She felt the tip of his tongue tracing the line of her lip, and she trembled, wanting to speak, afraid that if she did she would not say the words of denial that needed to be said. His tongue played against the corner of her mouth, seeking entrance without attempting to force its way in. He was waiting for an invitation, confident that she would give it to him, gold-plated and engraved as though to some wildly decadent party given by the elite who were far beyond the staid rules of conformity guiding the rest of the world. His confidence rather annoyed Natasha, though it did nothing to mute the delicious sensations she was feeling.

She shivered and sighed, and when she felt the smooth fabric of Anton's white shirt against her palms, she realized belatedly that her fists had opened of their own volition. Beneath the thin layer of his fine shirt she could feel the hard, lean muscles of his chest.

He had, she thought then, a working man's body, and he had no right in the world to have one since from birth he had been and would always be part of the elite, landed gentry of Russia.

"You beguiler," Anton whispered, his light, feathery kisses travelling from one corner of Natasha's

77

mouth to the other, pausing briefly along its journey to kiss the tip of her chin. His tongue caressed her lips teasingly, silently requesting entrance, seeking willing capitulation to the deeper pleasures they both desired, though only one dared openly seek. "You say you can't, but we know you can. You were made for pleasure."

He tried to kiss her mouth, but again Natasha turned her face away from him. She was breathing deeply now, her chest rising and falling as she struggled to control the torturous emotions speeding through her system. Even as she denied herself the pleasure of his sweet, sensual kisses, her hands, as though driven by a desire that was greater than her sense of propriety, explored more boldly the great expanse of his chest, sliding beneath the exquisite jacket to feel his shoulders.

"Don't," she whispered with little conviction as Anton kissed her throat, working his way to her ear. She felt his sharp teeth grasp her earlobe, and though she cried out softly, she made no effort at all to get away from him.

She turned her face toward him, determined now to put an end to this madness, this sheer, utter lunacy, and when she did, Anton leaned away from her. His eyes, gray and smouldering with fiery passion, bore into her, burning her soul and igniting her senses.

"No?" he asked, looking straight into her eyes.

Natasha hesitated. She was frankly intimidated by the intensity she saw in his gray eyes. All she had to do at that moment was repeat that single, two-letter refutation, and he would cease the erotic assault on her senses. But she did not tell him to stop. She did nothing at all but sigh softly and looked first into his eyes, then at his mouth, thinking that it was entirely unfair of him to kiss her so sweetly when he knew fully well that she could not remain unaffected.

He leaned into her again, pressing his mouth over

hers, kissing her more hungrily than before. When his tongue again touched her lips, Natasha opened her mouth just slightly, touching the tip of her tongue to his. She moaned then, trembling with rapidly building desire as his slowly deepening, erotic kiss gently and irrevocably stripped away her resistance.

She felt his left hand at her knee raising the hem of her dress, and though the sensation of movement of fabric against her legs was not in the least bit unpleasant, she felt that she simply must stop him. Allowing a kiss or two, she told herself, was not going beyond the boundaries of decency . . . but to go further than that, to let Anton caress her in the way he clearly wanted to, was beyond any standards of acceptability.

And once again, Aunt Aggie's hideous declaration that if she would just spread her legs for the prince she'd be able to control him echoed in Natasha's mind, and the agonizing power of those horrible words, and the calloused, mercenary mentality behind them, hit her with startling, flinching effect.

Her hands shot down from Anton's chest to ball the skirt of her dress in her fists, holding the material tightly on either side of Anton's hand, making it impossible for him to raise the material higher.

"There's no need to fear . . . It'll be magic, my beguiling one," Anton whispered, his lips caressing Natasha's ear as he spoke.

He kissed her again, deeply and passionately, and Natasha slanted her head slightly so that his mouth could slant down more perfectly against her own. She thrust her tongue into his mouth, reacting to his kiss with shameful abandon, behaving as she had promised herself she never would.

She clutched onto the skirt of her dress, balling the material in her fists as much as an act of frustration as to prevent the garment from being raised, entirely unaware of the conflicting signals she was sending to Anton by kissing him so passionately while at the same time clutching to her dress as though afraid he would rip it from her body at any second.

"Sweet . . . beguiling," Anton whispered, catching Natasha's lower lip between his teeth and biting softly.

She cried out then, a high-pitched sound of excitement and surprise, and the sound of it lit a bright fire in the prince's blood.

She felt Anton's left hand moving higher, from her knee to her thigh, and though he touched her through her dress, the sensation was so profound that Natasha was convinced she could feel his fingerprints upon her flesh. When his hand was at her hip, Natasha stopped breathing. His fingertips were frighteningly close to the moist, ravenous juncture of her thighs, where all her sensations seemed to rush toward and gather, pooling, becoming incessantly stronger and more demanding. Natasha's knees parted, as though possessed by some demonic urge from nature, and the moment she became aware of this, she clamped her knees together again, tightly this time, a defense against the desires that confused and delighted her.

I can't think when he kisses me.

She accepted this as an irrefutable truth, and she realized that she would do nothing to stop his kisses. They tasted too good on her lips, and the way the pleasure from them spread slowly to every part of her body was something she wouldn't even try to deny.

She was focusing on Anton's left hand to the exclusion of almost every other sensation. When the hand curled around her hip to cup her buttocks, squeezing tightly, Natasha sighed and shivered as a fresh burst of moisture and heat curled outward from her femininity like liquid gold reaching the most minute crevices in some exquisite mold.

Still she clutched her dress with both hands, concentrating on Anton's hand as it touched and caressed her, wondering with trepidation and excitement where it would travel next, not doing anything at all to either impede its progress or guide its movement. It seemed to her then that the hand was distinct and separate from Anton, an entity in itself, a passionate traveller upon the landscape of her body.

With her knees clamped together, the pressure in that mysterious place between the points of her hips, down low and in deep, became even greater. Aware of this, of the sensation of hunger in her body and soul that Natasha had never believed a woman could feel, of her pantalets being moist and clinging uncomfortably to her, Natasha sought desperately for some definable way of deciding what she would allow Anton to do, and what she would not.

"Relax . . . you're so tense . . . It takes away the pleasure when you're tense," Anton whispered, his breath warm and teasing against Natasha's ear as he spoke.

I can stop him now, Natasha thought then. *If I tell him to leave me alone, he will. I've just got to tell him to keep his hands to himself. I'll tell him this very moment.*

And she might have done exactly as her better judgment dictated if Anton's caressing left hand had not crept upward until the tantalizing fingers curled around the swell of her breast. He caught the risen tip of her nipple between his finger and thumb, squeezing lightly, and fresh honey moistened the petals of her womanhood.

Natasha opened her mouth to cry out, but the sound was silenced by Anton's fiercely possessive kiss. Her arms were knotted with tension as she squeezed the fabric of her dress frantically, and though everything that Natasha believed about herself said that she should end this insanity now, she angled her shoulders so that both her breasts would be exposed to Anton's touch.

If Natasha was confused at her own actions, it was only fitting, because she had thoroughly confused

Anton. He was well-versed in the art of seduction, and he knew all the subtle signs of passionate arousal in a woman. But what he did not understand was Natasha's *intellectual* resistance to what her *physical* self was all but screaming for. To add another ingredient to this cauldron of confusion was the fact that she was holding onto the skirt of her dress as though it were a lifeline to sanity, which made what was *beneath* that skirt, what she was protecting so feverishly, all the more alluring to Anton.

"Easy . . . easy," he purred, as though trying to gentle a frightened mare.

The tone was not one which Natasha found entirely pleasing, and she rather resented what she perceived to be the prince's casual and condescending attitude.

"I can't — " Natasha gasped, but before she could tell Anton that she could not *continue,* he kissed her words away, and she knew that he only thought she meant she couldn't *relax.*

As she danced her tongue against Anton's, Natasha felt the small, cloth-covered buttons of her bodice come unfastened beneath Anton's fingers.

This is too easy for him, Natasha thought a bit peevishly, realizing that Anton had unfastened the buttons quicker and easier with just one hand than she had been able to fasten them that morning using both hands.

As the bodice was released and the decolletage opened, the pressure against Natasha's full breasts lessened, and only then did she realize how swollen with tension and desire her breasts felt. She sighed, squirming against Anton and the side of the luxurious carriage, as his fingertips followed the upper line of her chemise. She felt his finger dip into the cleavage of her breasts, sliding beneath the pale fabric of the undergarments, and she moaned, a low, throaty sound of passion that was becoming stronger with each passing moment. What was most shocking of all was that Natasha had not thought she was even capable of such a sound.

"Yes, you can," Anton whispered, tugging loose the top bow that held the chemise closed.

The second ribbon came loose, and Natasha held her breath, squeezing her eyes tightly shut, knowing there was only one more slender ribbon of fabric that held the chemise closed, and once that was untied, she would be bared to Anton's hands.

Would he look at her? she wondered. What if he didn't like the way she looked?

She tried not to think about that, but such fears and insecurities were too close to the surface to be easily ignored. Natasha wished then, suffused by wild irrationality from sexual tension, that the sun would miraculously be blotted from the sky, that there would be a total eclipse so that Anton wouldn't have the chance to look at her, and inversely, she wouldn't have to see anything, all she had to do was feel the sensations — all so new and exquisite — that Anton was introducing her to.

When the third and final ribbon was loosened, Natasha could no longer breathe. Anticipation and nervous tension made her suck in her breath and hold it, though she was unaware of it, just as she was unaware of the fact that by holding her breath in, she was puffing her chest out, making her breasts look even larger and more inviting than they normally were.

"The scent of you is an elixir to my blood," Anton whispered, his lips warm and soft against Natasha's collarbone as he inhaled deeply, filling his lungs with the woman that so mystified him.

He pushed aside the chemise slowly, separating it enough so that the entire front of her body was exposed, while leaving her nipples as yet hidden from his hungry eyes. He wanted the unveiling to be postponed, to be savored as a starving man would savor a delicious meal, or a man dying of thirst would swirl cool, clean water in his mouth for a long time before actually swallowing it.

With the tip of his finger, he followed the line of fabric down the front of Natasha's body, touching her very lightly, following from the hill of her breast down to the flat of her stomach. He edged the cotton aside just enough to see the outermost darkened area of her areola.

The cotton, Anton noted with a strange detached logic, was very old, had been washed many, many times, and was extremely soft and pliant. He suspected that the chemise would be comfortable to wear, but he still felt it was something of a shame that Natasha — whose skill at making such garments was extraordinary — should not have the money necessary, or the time, to make fine undergarments for herself. Besides, breasts as exquisite as these should be ensconced only in the finest, softest, smoothest silks and satins, Anton decided with a connoisseur's eye for detail and nuance.

He leaned partially away, looking at Natasha, sensing her confusion, unease, and excitement. Her breasts were firm beneath his fingertip as he slowly, enticingly eased the two halves of the chemise's fabric further and further apart. The nipples that he had yet to see were blunt dents in the faded cotton, silent testimony that his kisses and caresses had not left the seamstress unaffected, though she had not explored his body with her hands nearly so intimately as he had explored hers.

"Your skin is so beautiful," he whispered, spreading the chemise further, displaying more of the dark aureolas, leaving now only the passion-peaked nipples still covered. "Not a blemish. Nothing but you . . . beautiful, mysterious you."

Natasha turned her face away from Anton, her lower lip caught between her teeth as she waited anxiously for Anton to slide his hand beneath her che-

mise to touch her breasts once again. Her body ached
with the need for Anton's touch.

So why was he taking so long? Was this some game
on his part, some sophisticated and decadent game to
see if it was really possible to drive a woman mad with
want? Or did he want to humiliate her?

None of that was true, Natasha told herself. Anton
was not the monster that Ivan said he was. He wasn't!

I've got to breathe.

The single, logical thought came to Natasha not
out of any loss of sensation from Anton's caresses—
and his damnable avoidance of certain areas of her
body that now desperately craved his touch—but out
of the deepest and most primordial part of her brain
that worked to keep her heart beating and her lungs
breathing.

And just as she breathed, she felt the warmth of
Anton's mouth, hot and wet, close over the crest of
her right breast.

She cried out sharply, unmindful of the driver who
no doubt could hear her cry of ecstasy. Anton took
much of her breast into his mouth, his cheeks hollowed with suction, feasting upon her bounty. He
scraped his tongue over the nipple, sending lightning
bolts of pleasure shooting through Natasha's body,
the pleasure so fiercely intense it was almost painful.

Her body jerked hard and she released the death
grip she'd had for so long upon the skirt of her dress,
now pushing her fingers into Anton's silky hair to hug
his face to her breast.

She felt everything Anton did to her, and each
touch, each minute sensation, heightened her pleasure, sending her soaring into a world that she had
never been to before, and though she believed that
nothing could feel as good as what she was feeling
now, Anton knew there was still a journey ahead of
them both—a pleasurable journey that he was only
too willing to guide Natasha—before she discovered

the farthest reaches of pleasure.

"Shhh! My darling, shhh!" Anton whispered.

It registered in Natasha's brain that she should not make quite so much noise. It registered there, but did nothing to change the way she responded to Anton's touch. She was incapable of stilling her response to Anton. She was too inexperienced in these matters to be calm while Anton's sharp, devilish teeth nipped at the inflamed tips of her breasts. And when his fingers and thumb rolled her nipples, now slickened from his kisses, Natasha could do nothing other than shiver.

She felt Anton moving up on her body, his lips brushing against her chin, and she pulled him to her fiercely, meeting his kiss with an open mouth, inviting and receiving immediately the slick, probing tongue that had set her breasts aflame and totally stripped away her decorum.

Anton leaned into Natasha, pressing her deeper into the plush, leather cushions of the carriage. He had taken the closed carriage, he now realized, in hopes that something like this would happen when he picked Natasha up at her home.

But what was happening now had gone beyond his expectations. Natasha's voluptuous, quivering body responded to each of his caresses, and though at first he had suspected she was feigning her excitement — he had, in the past, known a few women who tried to get their hands on the Talakovich fortune by pretending that even a casual, sideways glance from Prince Anton caused them to swoon and climax — he now realized that she was reacting so strongly because each sensation was entirely new to her.

He could not say whether or not Natasha was a virgin, but one thing that was certain was that she was a woman who had never found any pleasure in a man's arms before, and this knowledge — this awareness that he was the first man to show Natasha pleasure — heightened Anton's pleasure.

86

"Relax, my darling, and let yourself go," he whispered, cupping her breast in his hand, pressing his fingers deep into the firm, luxurious mound as his lips nibbled at Natasha's mouth.

He no longer cared if she shouted so loudly that the coachman and all the neighboring villagers they passed heard her and knew what was happening in the Talakovich carriage — and everyone would know who owned the carriage, since his family crest, known by everyone for hundreds of miles in all directions, was etched on the side doors. All that mattered to Anton was that he show Natasha the mysteries of passion; that he be the key that unlocked her ecstasy.

Her arms were around his shoulders, and Natasha was hardly aware at first that her dress was being raised until she felt Anton's hand against her knee. Irrationally, her first thought was of the hideous, torn condition of her stockings, but that fear did not last long, replaced by a greater fear — that of ending up in the same unacceptable condition that Aislyn was now in — that exploded in her brain. She felt his fingers caressing the smooth flesh of her inner thigh, sliding her dress higher and higher on her legs, and the tingles that came from his touch seemed to go straight to the small, throbbing bud of burning sensation hidden between the slick, tender folds of her womanhood.

"You can't . . . we mustn't . . . we shouldn't," Natasha managed to say.

She cleared her throat and across the surface of her mind she wondered if there had been some drug, an aphrodisiac that superstitious men professed worked with unresponsive women, that made them crave carnality. Maybe Anton had put that in the food, or in her tea?

It was a ludicrous notion. The only thing driving Natasha mad with desire was Prince Anton Talakovich, and he certainly needed no gypsy's magic to make a woman desire him.

"Yes, we can, and we should," Anton countered. He moved Natasha so that she was almost prone on the carriage seat and he was partially reclining upon her, his long legs tumbled onto the floor of the carriage. His hand crept higher on her leg, pushing her dress up, his fingertips now following the top edge of her stocking. "We mustn't stop now. We've gone too far. There's no turning back."

That's not true, Natasha thought, but did not say because Anton had leaned into her, kissing her hungrily, taking her breath, her resistance, her strength of will, all away.

The riotous emotions going through Natasha hindered some of the glorious sensations that trembled through her voluptuous body. She could feel Anton's powerful chest against her breasts, and his silk shirt rubbing against the lust-hardened tips heightened her passion. She felt, too, his hand against the inside of her thigh, and the way his fingertips brushed closer and closer to the core of her hunger. And more than anything else, she felt her own pulse, her passionate heartbeat pounding strong and true, in her womanhood.

What would it feel like for Anton to touch me there? she wondered, pushing her fingers into his slightly wavy, tawny colored hair as his tongue entwined with her own.

Natasha had spoken several times with Aislyn about men, asking what it had been like to be with a man and so forth. From what Aislyn had said, the pleasure of a man's companionship rested primarily in his ability to provide a warm and comfortable home, and in return for those creature comforts, a woman was expected to provide sexual gratification.

From all that Natasha had been able to glean, it wasn't supposed to feel so good, not like this, like her body was on fire and burning out of control from the inside out, and her head was ready to explode, and that if she could not kiss Anton and feel his tongue sliding between her lips she would undoubtedly die at that very moment.

The erratic wanderings of her mind ceased their desultory fears the next instant, and became entirely focused, when Anton's skilled hands untied the drawstring of her pantalets, and his long fingers tugged the material down and brushed lightly over the rather smallish, triangular thatch of curly auburn hair.

Her reaction was driven by the demands of her body, not the dictates of morality or propriety that her logical mind seemed so fixated on. She raised her foot, kicking it up so that it was near her backside, the sole of her slipper flat on the seat cushion. Her other foot dangled over the edge of the cushion near the floor, legs now spread wide and inviting, breath coming in quivering little gasps, heart pounding, hips twitching from side to side.

This is absurd for me to be so aroused, Anton thought as he sought, then found, Natasha's secret place.

He touched her lightly there, pleased that she was so warm and honied and passionate, yet displeased that his own response was very nearly as unbridled. He felt that he should be more aloof, more in control of his own emotions and desires instead of as wildly aroused as he really was. It was his own ego that demanded he be more cavalier about this encounter— Natasha Stantikoff wasn't his first woman, and Natasha wouldn't be his last, that little voice whispered inside his head—and simply accept the satin-skinned seamstress as just another amorous conquest.

But instead he was frantic. His manhood throbbed, straining against the tight contours of his breeches, and he thought of releasing a few buttons to free himself, but decided that he would wait, and allow Natasha to do that for him.

"Oh . . . oh . . . oh . . ." Natasha moaned breathlessly, trembling from head to foot as Anton touched her.

She shoved her hands beneath his jacket to force his chest against her own aching breasts. Her hips seemed to gyrate of their own volition, unable to remain motionless while Anton touched her, the pressure alternating between being firmly demanding, so that she had no choice but to respond to him, and so light that she raised her hips up to him in wanton offering, seeking to deepen the contact.

She received her unspoken wish a moment later, when Anton probed more deeply with his fingertip, delicately and expertly, and for the very first time in her life Natasha had the sensation of Anton not merely touching her, but being *inside* her.

Her first reaction was to clamp her thighs together, but Anton was too well versed in the art of seduction, too schooled in all the various reactions that women have to such stimulation, for her to deny him. Within a matter of seconds Natasha, as she continued to hold tightly onto Anton's chest and kiss him sweetly, opened herself to his caresses once again. She kept her eyes closed, her thoughts not even on the kiss that she shared, but on the caresses that aroused her so magically, and stoked the inferno of this wildfire.

Slowly, carefully, tenderly, Anton pushed more deeply into her, and when at last he cupped her womanhood in his hand, he rubbed the heel of his palm against her tingling bud, eliciting yet another surprised cry of ecstasy to be ripped from her passion-addled brain.

"N-Nothing . . . can feel this good," Natasha managed to gasp, shivering on the carriage seat as Anton's hand began to move back and forth, sending slick friction shooting through her so that she could hardly breathe and could not kiss. Her mouth felt desert-dry from gasping for air.

"I'm going to prove you wrong," Anton said with a

devilish smile, sliding off the seat. He curled his long legs beneath him kneeling on the floor of the carriage.

Natasha stared at Anton, wildly confused and not a little horrified at the thought that he had suddenly decided he'd done enough to her, and would do no more. She felt suspended in midair, and unless she was taken higher, she would surely plummet back to earth, and the landing would not be a gentle one.

"Let me take care of everything," Anton said in that much-too-confident tone, easing away from Natasha's grasp.

"Don't stop," Natasha whispered, a little frantic, part of her wanting to close her chemise and bodice to hide her breasts, and part of her wanting to act brazenly so that Anton would continue with all the glorious things that he had been doing.

She reached for him, wanting to pull him near again, but he caught her hands by the wrists, bringing them together to clamp them together in one hand. He trapped her hands over her head against the wall of the carriage.

"Just let me take care of everything," Anton said, and with his free hand pulled Natasha's dress up to her stomach, a devilish smile curling his mouth into a smile of seduction that no woman could resist.

Seven

Natasha heard what Anton had said, and though she really did want to follow his wishes—he seemed far more competent in these matters—*forcing* herself to be calm was impossible.

"Gently now. Gently. These are feelings best savored, not devoured."

Natasha felt utterly exposed and terribly vulnerable lying there on the carriage seat. She tried to calm her breathing, listening to Anton's soothing, seductive words. Despite the buzzing in her brain and the rippling tingles that shimmered across the surface of her skin, she forced her chaotic emotions to become if not orderly, then at least somewhat controlled.

Anton was whispering to her, telling her she must trust him, to leave "everything"—and she really had no solid notion of what all that single word was to encompass, but she sensed that it was quite a lot—to him, and Natasha believed him.

Perhaps the prince was a thief and a liar and a scoundrel, but he was capable of touching Natasha's soul, even without putting a hand on her, and that was reason enough for her to believe him, trust him completely, just this one time, and concerning just this one topic.

"Much better," Anton whispered, adjusting his position slightly so that he was more comfortable, sitting on the heels of his brightly polished boots as he knelt at right angles to Natasha. "I want you to concentrate on what you're feeling, to really think about it so that you don't miss anything, so that even the most minute sensation can be savored."

She turned her head upon the carriage seat to look into the face of the man whose low, soft, melodic voice had stripped away her fear.

"Close your eyes, and let yourself *feel*," Anton said.

Natasha closed her eyes and thought about all the separate and yet distinct and precise sensations registering in her brain. She felt the gentle rocking motion of the carriage as it moved slowly along the old road, and felt the motion of her right foot, dangling in midair over the edge of the seat. She felt Anton's powerful left hand release her wrists. Natasha kept her arms resting loosely on the seat above her head because it kept them out of the way. She didn't want to do anything that would present obstacles to Anton's continued erotic performance.

"There should be shrines and temples built to honor you," Anton said, amazing himself since he was only being half-flattering and mostly honest.

He was glad that she had settled down enough so that he could take a more leisurely perusal of her charms. When he'd told Natasha that she must concentrate if she would gain the greatest appreciation of what she was capable of feeling, he'd only been telling a partial truth. Anton wanted her prone and motionless upon the carriage seat so that *he* could let his eyes feast upon her magnificent bounty.

Anton touched her, his right hand sliding lightly along Natasha's thigh, grazing against the satiny flesh just above the top of her stocking. He brought his left hand down her forearms, brushing over her face lightly, a fingertip tracing the bridge of her nose before making an oval path around her mouth.

Natasha's tongue crept out between full lips tentatively to taste Anton's finger. He watched, fascinated, as she sipped the fingertip briefly. The sight of her lips surrounding his fingertip provided a bit more stimulation than Anton had expected, conjuring uninhibited mental pictures that made his arousal strain even more mightily against the buttons of his breeches.

"Much better," he whispered, needing to hear his own voice to be assured that he was in control of himself.

This early-morning tryst had become more wildly erotic than Anton, a fairly cynical man, had allowed himself to imagine possible. He took his hand from her mouth, bringing it down over her taut breast, which swayed gently with the rocking motion of the carriage.

No woman has ever set my blood on fire so! Anton thought, amazed that he was actually now touching the woman who had created the image in his brain that had made sleep the previous evening a near impossibility.

He touched her, trying to judge her responses to his caresses more than the pleasure he received in the contact. Her eyes were closed, her face impassive, her mouth open just slightly. When he brushed his fingers once again against the slippery petals of her femininity, Natasha gasped softly, her body arching slightly, her knees unconsciously parting just a little further.

Watching her voluptuous body tremble and writhe beneath his hands sent heat surging through Anton. As he pressed his long fingers deeply into Natasha's breast, he realized that his hands were shaking badly, and that his heart was hammering against his ribs so strongly he would not have been at all surprised if his heart leaped right out of his chest.

He sensed that she was getting closer to passion's culmination much quicker than she had anticipated, or perhaps that she had never been there before.

Either way, the fact that he was exciting this strangely vexing, stunningly beautiful seamstress was playing havoc with his own control. Anton pushed her dress higher, working his fingers and thumb with as much pressure as he dared against Natasha to draw extreme satisfaction. He caught the erect tips of her breasts with his other hand, rolling the passion-hardened buds between forefinger and thumb, watching the patina of expressions that transformed Natasha's face as sizzling desire swept over her.

For long moments, Natasha seemed on the very edge, and though Anton used all his considerable skill, he could not take her further, send her soaring into the physical oblivion of ultimate satiation. He waited, using all his skill, judging the thousand signals that Natasha's body sent out which spoke of what she was feeling, and what her response to those feelings was.

She was stubbornly holding back.

Anton had seen this happen several times before with his lovers, though never before had he taken it quite so personally. Natasha was, whether she was consciously aware of it or not, holding back, keeping herself in check, reining in her emotions — and Anton refused to believe that he could not make her give herself over to him totally.

Whether it was from fear or inexperience or maybe even because the rocking motion of the rolling carriage was disturbing her, Anton could not say. All he *could* be sure of, and with the angry confidence of a man whose goals and desires are very seldom thwarted, was that he wanted to please Natasha more than she ever had been before, that *he* would be the one to show her physical desire's highest summit, and *he* wasn't going to be thwarted in his quest — not even by Natasha herself.

"Just let yourself go," Anton whispered, bending over, kissing Natasha's upraised, bent knee, his tongue flicking briefly into the soft hollow of her knee. "Don't be afraid. Just let yourself go."

For Natasha, being at the brink for so long was no longer something that felt good. Rather, it was painful to hang there, as though suspended in midair though not floating, every muscle in her body flexed into painful knots, her teeth clenched and her eyes alternately squeezed tightly shut, then opening wide.

She felt Anton's warm lips against the inside of her thigh, his tongue trailing lightly along the flesh, touching her with moist, featherlike caresses, and at last she started to relax.

He's going to kiss me, she thought in the crazily chaotic manner, simultaneously horrified and fascinated at the possibilities, which was all her mind was capable of at that moment.

She felt his arms slide around her thighs as he bent lower, and Natasha placed her right hand lightly upon his broad shoulders as he bent lower, moving now out of view. She felt his breath, warm and tantalizing against her heated center. Very slowly, she began to relax, to become calm and almost serene, the purring, deep, sultry words of praise and desire having its inexorable effect upon her.

She had thought that nothing could feel quite so stimulating as having Anton's hands touching her, caressing her body in those intimate places that she had never allowed any man to see or touch. Only moments earlier, Natasha had thought that nothing could feel that good, or that frustrating, since the caresses had turned her body into a jangled mass of raw nerves and frustrated pressure. She'd felt like a mainspring that had been wound too tightly, so tightly that the pressure could never be released.

And then she felt Anton kiss her down low, the faint raspiness of his cheeks against the smooth, tender surface of her thighs, the strong, commanding feel of his steelish arms encircling her legs, his hands upon her thighs to hold them apart.

He touched her with his tongue, then probed deeply, and though Natasha was wildly confused, her body went limp and pliant.

"Oh, Anton . . ." she whispered, rolling her head from side to side on the leather carriage seat.

She had thought that nothing could feel better than Anton's touch, and he had proven her wrong with carnal kisses that slowly carried her away from the edge of the abyss that she had been teetering so precariously and so frustratingly upon. It was as though he'd lifted her in body and soul, carrying her now into another realm. Before, she had felt as though she were hanging in midair, now she felt weightless, able to float and soar, at one time both utterly serene and calm and yet mentally focused with an intellectual clarity that Natasha had never before known.

Natasha ran her hand lightly over Anton's shoulders, feeling the great strength of him through the fine fabric of his jacket.

She felt as though she were in a vortex, slowly moving faster and faster through an empty black space filled only with feeling, with the sensations of the mind and body.

Onward, faster and faster, accelerating so rapidly that Natasha thought she would surely crash into something, completely unable to slow the meteoric ascension until at last she felt herself convulsing, her body shivering through white-hot waves of incredible, searing heat.

She tried to sit up, to push Anton away from her because if he did not stop—and stop this very instant—then surely she would die because no mortal could withstand such feelings, could be the recipient of such ecstasy, without going mad, or bursting into flames.

She tried to push him away, to make Anton stop those exhilarating, intimate kisses that were much too private for Natasha to even think about, but he would not stop for even a heartbeat, and when she felt her head bounce against the carriage's seat cushion, she realized that spasms had suddenly made it absolutely necessary for her to make her body as straight and prone as possible.

There was no fight left in her, no resistance, not even any fear, though she was wildly confused about what had just happened. Once the spasms subsided, Natasha was much too sensitive to allow Anton to continue, though she lacked the strength to do much more than tremble through the aftershocks of her release.

"S-stop," she whispered weakly. "Please, you must stop. I c-can't take . . . anymore."

Natasha was sprawled out on the carriage seat, her bodice stretched open to reveal her breasts, her dress pushed up to her stomach, her pantalets bunched around her left ankle. She felt totally vulnerable, and at the same time more at peace than she had ever been.

She watched as Anton slowly unfurled his body, turning in the carriage so that he now faced her. When he looked at her, his cool gray eyes held triumph, and Natasha wondered whether he could be the victor without her being the victim.

"What happened?" she asked.

Anton merely smiled, brushing away a curling strand of Natasha's hair from her eye. Then he took her hand by the wrist, and though Natasha thought he was going to kiss her palm, as he had before, Anton had quite a different thought in mind. He placed her hand upon the long, prominent ridge in his breeches, forcing her fingers around the bulging fabric to squeeze tightly. His eyelids fluttered briefly, and a tremulous, rumbling groan of pleasure came from him.

"I love it when you touch me," he whispered.

Anton moved his hand, but Natasha did not move hers away. She was fascinated by what she felt beneath her fingers, against her palm. Fascinated . . . and frightened. It was too large, she was certain, to cause her anything but pain. Perhaps that was why Anton had become so skilled with his hands, and with those kisses that shredded her sense of propriety and decorum. He had learned all those skills to make up for the pain that he later inflicted upon the women he showered his charm upon.

She was frankly frightened by the size of him, but she did not move her hand away from him, nor did she believe that she would not let Prince Anton Talakovich have his way with her. In a thousand different ways, he was the most unusual man Natasha had ever met, and he was certainly the most brilliant. Everything about him touched her in one way or another, and now, as she felt his manhood throbbing against her palm through the fabric of his tight-fitting breeches, Natasha wanted to know everything there was to know about this erotic new universe that Anton was leading her through.

Anton saw the trepidation in the depths of Natasha's brown eyes, and he smiled reassuringly, bending down quickly to brush her lips with his own.

"Don't worry, my darling, I will make it magnificent for you. You mustn't be frightened."

The afterglow of her climax was wearing off, and with it, lucid thinking was returning — much too quickly for Natasha's liking. Quite suddenly, Natasha felt horrendously vulnerable, and with her dress all askew, terribly wanton.

She began pulling her bodice together when Anton took her hands in his own. He shook his head slowly, his eyes ablaze with hunger.

"Don't hide yourself, my darling. We're a long way from the castle, and a long way from finished here."

His eyes locked with Natasha's. His right hand went

down to the front of his breeches and he unfastened the first button, then stopped.

"You do it for me," he said, still holding onto Natasha's hand, guiding it downward.

I've let this go too far, and now I can't stop it, Natasha thought, intensely curious to know and see and feel exactly what it was that was trapped inside the tight breeches, straining to be freed.

She placed her hand upon him, and his arousal swelled in response. It was a living thing, she thought, just waiting to attack her. And if she had any sense at all, she would have stopped this foolishness long ago, or even now she would throw herself out the carriage door and walk home.

I shouldn't be doing this, Natasha thought as her trembling fingers fumbled with the top button of Anton's breeches.

It was at precisely that moment that the carriage came to an abrupt halt. Anton, still kneeling on the floor of the carriage, fell forward upon Natasha. She heard him utter an obscenity between clenched teeth, and the vehemence of it shocked her, since he had never spoken in such a manner in front of her before. The harshness of the single word also let Natasha know that he would not be stopped in his quest to possess her, no matter what.

From outside the carriage, a voice rang out calm and clear in the morning air, and with a slight accent, the origin of which she could not place.

"Reach for your weapon," the voice said, "and you'll be dead before you get the pistol from your jacket."

Anton cursed again, bolting to his feet, having to remain hunched over in the carriage. "Don't move, or make a sound," he said, then leaped out of the carriage, slamming the door behind him.

Natasha scrambled to a sitting position, struggling desperately to tie and button all that needed to be tied and buttoned if she was to be presentable.

If the carriage had been stopped by thieves, she didn't want them to know what she had just done, and though she told herself that it really shouldn't matter what savage outlaws thought of her, hot shame colored her cheeks . . . because *she* cared about what she thought of herself, and now that she was alone in the carriage—alone and desperately frightened—she felt that her willful abandonment to passion in Anton's arms and to his magical kisses must surely be terribly, sinfully wrong.

Eight

Anton's emotions were moving in every direction at once as he burst out of the carriage with his hands outstretched and open so that the dangerous, deadly man who'd stopped the carriage would see immediately that he was unarmed. When Anton had heard the voice, he recognized it instantly.

Anton came to a standstill, breathing a sigh of relief, making a patting-down motion with his hands to his coachman. Everyone was still alive, and he wanted it to stay that way.

"What in hell brings you here?" Anton asked Caleb Carter, who was riding the tallest and most ill-mannered looking gray stallion the prince had ever seen.

"Is that any way to greet an old friend after a long absence?"

Caleb grinned then, and though he didn't want to, Anton returned the smile. When Caleb dismounted, the two men clasped hands and slapped backs in playful camaraderie.

Anton stepped away to look at his old friend. He was not entirely pleased with what he saw. Caleb's cheeks were sunken, his eyes hollowed slightly with fatigue. His dark hair that curled over the collar of his jacket was a little longer than he usually wore it, and Anton attributed this to a frantic schedule rather than a changing sense of fashion. During his trek back to

St. Petersburg, Caleb had lost weight, and since he was even more gaunt than usual, it heightened his appearance of being a dangerous, haunted, hungry predator.

The coachman set the brake and got down from his seat, clearly disapproving of the American who first showed the temerity to stop the prince's coach, then make threats to discourage any reprisals.

In a low voice, since Caleb was standing very near, the coachman said to Anton, "You just give me the nod, and I'll see he rides away from here as quick as he rode in."

Anton's smile broadened, and he shook his head. "You've tempted Fate once and have lived to tell of it. Don't you think you've run your luck out about as far as you can take it?"

The coachman was a good man who'd been in his fair share of scrapes and fights, and his ego wouldn't let him easily accept the foreigner's threat.

"He doesn't look so much to me."

Anton's smiled vanished then. "If you believe that, then you are in a minority of one in all the world. And if that man really did mean to do you harm, there's absolutely nothing you could do to stop him. Now get back to your position and stay there until I tell you it's time we continue on our journey back to the castle." His expression and tone softened as he concluded, "You've done exactly what you should have. You've done just fine."

"Aye, sir," the coachman said gloomily, returning to his position.

Though he pretended to be greatly resentful of the fact that Prince Talakovich had prevented him from finding out just exactly how tough Caleb Carter really was, in truth he was greatly relieved to have the opportunity to back down without losing too much face. There was something in Caleb's eyes, which seemed to see everything, and all at once, that was distinctly unnerving, even to a man like the coachman. Caleb Carter had an aura that warned others that he had killed before, and would kill again if it was necessary . . . and there was nothing anyone else could do to stop him.

"Have you been to the castle?" Anton asked Caleb quietly, only now fully collecting his senses. It had been quite a shock to him to one second be waiting for the rapturous feeling of the most beautiful woman he'd ever known unbuttoning his breeches, to the next moment be easing the tensions between a proud old coachman and an American mercenary whose deadly skills were *ne plus ultra*.

"Not yet. I was headed there when I recognized your crest," Caleb said, waving a hand toward the door of Anton's carriage. "But now that we're together, perhaps your carriage will be more comfortable than my saddle. I've been on that horse so much over the last three weeks . . ." Caleb rubbed his backside to emphasize his point.

"I'd like to help you, but right now the carriage is occupied, and I'd rather not feel crowded."

Caleb just grinned, knowing instantly the gender of the person Anton was sharing his carriage with. And then, as though on cue, he saw a beautiful face move into the carriage's open window. The eyes were large, brown, and luminous, framed with what seemed to be unruly, slightly wavy auburn hair. The woman hid herself in the recesses of the carriage immediately after making eye contact with Caleb.

"I understand your need for privacy," Caleb said, already turning back to his horse. "I'll ride on ahead. Give me a chance to bathe the dust of the road from my bones, and eat something, then I'll tell you everything I've learned since we were together in London."

"You remember the way to the castle?"

"It's been five years, but I still remember."

Caleb rode away quickly. Anton, with his critical

eye for details, took note that his friend's horse was thin, his ribs showing plainly, leaving Anton to ponder how many days Caleb had been pushing full-out to get to St. Petersburg.

It didn't seem to Anton that any of this was a good omen, but he refused to let himself dwell upon it for long. After all, there was Natasha Stantikoff still in his carriage, and some unfinished desires that had yet to be attended to.

"Who was that?" Natasha asked, her tone quavering just slightly as Anton returned to the carriage. The moment he had the door closed, the carriage started moving again.

"A friend of mine. My only real friend, actually. I met him a long ago, when we were in England together."

Anton took notice that Natasha had refastened all her buttons, though this did not particularly disturb him. He'd opened her bodice once, and he could do it again. The carriage was still far from the castle, and despite the unexpected intrusion of Caleb, the coachman knew enough to keep the homeward pace slow and leisurely.

"Let's not talk about him now . . . not when there are more interesting matters to concern ourselves with," he said, his tone smoky with renewed passion.

Anton tried to kiss Natasha, but she pushed away from him. She was not in the least bit pleased with herself for what she had allowed Anton to do, and she certainly wasn't happy with him, since she was convinced that he had drugged her somehow, which had been the cause of her inappropriate behavior. That had to be the reason those wild things had happened, since if she'd been herself and thinking clearly, she wouldn't have allowed the prince anything more intimate than a kiss.

105

"How can you think about such things now? How, after that man was here?"

"He's gone now," Anton said, sliding over on the seat, pinning his voluptuous guest against the padded side wall of the carriage.

"I don't like that man," Natasha said resolutely, quite suddenly very convinced that she had gotten involved with something much more complex and dangerous than she had foreseen, and she wasn't at all certain that she could cope with the challenges now facing her.

"You don't know him." Anton was not in the mood to *talk* with Natasha, and even if he was, it wouldn't be about another man.

"I still don't like him," Natasha said sternly. She pushed his hand from her knee. "He looks dangerous. He looks like a man who has killed men."

Anton ceased his efforts to unfasten the bodice buttons of Natasha's gown, moving away from her. "He *is* a dangerous man, I assure you, and he has killed before."

Her jaw dropped open. She looked at Anton not as though he came from a different social strata than she, but an entirely different world. "You know that about him, and still you call him your friend?"

Anton's gray gaze hardened, becoming frigidly cold, and Natasha could almost see the protective walls coming up around him, sealing her out.

"Caleb is my friend. The best I've ever had . . . the only real friend I've ever had. Yes, he's a dangerous man, but he's only a threat to evil people. And as for my continued association with Caleb, I think you will find that when you reach a certain level in the world of politics and finance, naivete is not something endearing and sweet — it's just stupid, and usually fatal."

Natasha reacted to the words as though she'd been slapped, and in a way, she had been. Anton's harsh words left no room for doubt about who was the

106

wealthy landowner, and who was the poor, but talented working girl hoping to earn enough to rent an apartment of her own. It was the anger that Natasha heard in Anton's voice — anger that bordered on contempt — that shocked her more than anything else. In a single moment of epiphany, Natasha saw the brilliant, driven, ambitious young man that she had heard so much about, the young man who had outwitted and out-maneuvered much older and far more experienced businessmen throughout Europe and Russia.

Softly, Natasha said, "You see tenderness as a weakness. Is it so evil of me to distrust a man as—" she searched for a word to accurately describe the American, but only one word came to mind "—*menacing* as your friend."

Anton looked deep into Natasha's eyes for long moments. He realized that part of his anger was because his desire had been thwarted, and he was still hungry for the release that now, quite clearly, Natasha was not going to give him. And it was patently absurd for him to be protective of Caleb Carter. If ever there was a man in all the world more capable of defending himself against all enemies, it was the articulate American mercenary that Anton had learned to love like a brother.

He turned and looked out the window. It was too painful for him to look at Natasha, her face still a little flushed from their passionate encounter, and realized that she did not want him to touch her. She was so close, but the abyss between them now was a chasm not easily bridged.

"We'll be to the castle soon," Anton said, still looking out the window.

A minute later, Anton shouted for the coachman to pick up the pace. With the mood inside the carriage as icy as it was, there was no reason to dawdle.

107

Castle Talakovich was just the way he remembered it.He had been there one time before, five years earlier, for a single night, after Caleb and Anton had gotten involved in an ill-fated attempt to help some villagers on the island of Crete attain freedom from their despotic ruler.

Seeing the castle three hundred yards in the distance, with its formidable stone and iron gates and surrounding walls, Caleb was suddenly overwhelmed with fatigue. He had been fighting his own exhaustion for weeks now, and with a comfortable bed and safe surroundings soon his to relish, the tension and adrenaline that had kept him going for so long now had vanished.

He patted the big gray stallion's neck. "Soon you'll be in a corral, with plenty of oats and clean water, and you won't have to carry me around for at least a couple weeks, I promise, ol' boy," Caleb said.

He sympathized with the animal, who had lost much weight during the long, arduous, deadly trek across much of Europe and Russia. The horse Caleb had bought prior to this one had been shot out from beneath him after a less than successful attempt to purchase sabres from an Italian weapons manufacturer.

Allowing himself to slump in the saddle, Caleb thought back to how an educated American should find himself in St. Petersburg, doing the crazy things he had been doing for the past years.

It had all started out innocently enough. Caleb came from a wealthy family, an only child, and when his aging father took on a young, extremely attractive, highly sexed new bride, it became quickly apparent to everyone in the household, including the servants, that the new Mrs. Carter, who wasn't much out of the teen years herself, had more than just a maternal affection for the young Caleb Carter.

Caleb's father, a man whose power and influence matched his ego, did not take kindly to the competition his son represented, even if Caleb had done absolutely nothing to seek his stepmother's attention.

It wasn't long before Caleb was packed off to school—the farther away, the better, as far as the elder Carter was concerned, and price was no object. Caleb found himself in England, attending Eton, and sharing a room with a brilliant man of the same youthful age of sixteen. The roommate was Prince Anton Talakovich.

The boys were outcasts in a dozen different ways. Both were younger than their other classmates, and both received extremely high grades from their teachers. Both boys had an iconoclastic sense of humor, and liked to taunt the Fates in a myriad of ways. Both boys had been born into great wealth, though they really didn't see much of it now themselves. Both were a bit more handsome than they really had any right to be, Anton fair-haired and exuberant, Caleb dark-haired and broodingly alluring.

Individually and collectively, they fascinated the women with whom they came in contact. And when the older boys decided to put these bright young men in their proper place, Anton and Caleb banded together tighter than ever, and their bond of mutual trust and interdependence took form and solidified permanently.

Now nearly fifteen years later, Caleb could say without hesitation that the only man in the world he trusted completely was a Russian prince; the only man in the world Anton trusted completely was an American mercenary—that, too, hadn't been planned.

It wasn't that Caleb had set out to be a mercenary. After graduating from Eton, he returned to the United States, and soon figured out that his father wasn't at all pleased with the way his wife's eyes lighted up whenever Caleb entered the room. And when some ruffians on the street began making comments to Caleb's stepmother as she walked down the street, Caleb stepped in to defend her. Before the dust had settled, daggers were drawn and two men lay dead in the street, with a third and fourth bleeding badly. In the end, Caleb stood victorious but alone. His stepmother had abandoned him during the fracas to face the police by himself.

Caleb had long suspected that his father had something to do with the death of his mother, but he'd never really believed the man could be truly viciously murderous — not until he discovered that it was his own father who had put the local political and legal machinery in process to demand that action be taken against Caleb in the deaths of the "fine young men slain in the prime of their lives by the hot-headed Caleb Carter."

It took about three days for Caleb to figure out that he had been tried and convicted even before going to court, and that his father most definitely was not on his side. It wasn't until, pressing his ear to an upstairs heating vent, Caleb heard his father laughing with his young bride about how Caleb would soon be out of the picture, and that he wouldn't inherit a penny of the family fortune, nor drain another cent from the family savings, that Caleb realized the enormity of his father's greed and savagery.

On that night, he realized his father had probably had his mother murdered.

Caleb ran away that night with little more than the clothes on his back, and before noon the next day, the newspapers were saying that Caleb Carter was an escaped fugitive, guilty of cold-blooded murder.

He wandered aimlessly for a while, feeling rather sorry for himself, and desperately needing cash. He became acquainted with a portly, elderly gentleman in New York. The man liked to gamble, and conse-

110

quently often had large sums of money with him, so he needed a bodyguard. Caleb accepted the position, and attacked it with all the zeal that he had attacked the books during his Eton days.

The finest soldiers were hired to teach him, and Caleb learned quickly all there was to know about fighting with guns, daggers, sabres, and with his bare hands. A small man with lightning reflexes from the Orient had been hired to teach Caleb how to use his body as a weapon, and how to throw even much larger, heavier, and stronger men to the ground. Caleb also learned from this man how to sit motionless and let his mind go blank, to let all his thoughts flow freely, or to stop altogether so that serenity could fill him.

He learned all this and more, and when his services were no longer needed by the old gambler, he was on the road again, this time possessing extraordinary skills of an unusual variety.

Before long, staying in America seemed too risky for a young man like Caleb, who valued his freedom above everything else, so he booked passage back to England, using a false identity. He'd hardly been in London a week when he read in the newspapers of a brash young man from Russia who, rumor had it, had purchased half the fine diamonds in the city, and had given all those beautiful baubles to the equally beautiful young women who'd been seen accompanying him throughout fashionable London.

The newspaper didn't give the young man's name, but Caleb knew there could be only one Russian that successful both with women, and with business: Prince Anton Talakovich.

They were reunited when they were both just twenty-two, and since then, for the past eight years, Anton had needed Caleb's wisdom, intelligence, and deadly skills countless times. For the better part of the past eight months, Caleb had been travelling

111

throughout Europe, working to arrange financing so that a suitable standing army could be mobilized should Napoleon Bonaparte decide to send his troops eastward. The current army, financed by the czar, was poorly trained, poorly outfitted, and possessed firearms that missed their mark when they did shoot, and misfired as often as not.

Anton did not want to see his beloved Mother Russia overrun by the madman from France, and he couldn't allow the news to get to France that he was putting together the machinery necessary to fortify the western border against an enemy that, at least theoretically, was an ally. Consequently, a multilingual American who had a first-class mind and a taste for intrigue was the perfect choice to see foreign bankers and investors for the loans needed for the weapons of defense.

Caleb was weary of it all. He was weary of walking into this bank president's office in Zurich, or that one's office in Bonn, and having to discuss such sensitive matters, knowing that the man he was talking to really didn't care whether there was bloodshed and war or not, only whether there was a profit to be made by the war. Caleb had to work with such men, but he didn't have to like them at all, and on the three occasions when he was attacked by men determined to find out everything that Caleb *wasn't* telling them, he hadn't a moment's hesitation or doubt in killing his attackers.

He needed to rest now, to regenerate his soul and once again, at least for a little while, be reassured that the world was not inherently evil, and that he did not have to look in every shadow to see where the next assassin might be lurking.

The guard on the east gate looked at Caleb with wary eyes, but he'd been given Caleb's name, and allowed the American to enter.

The stable boys who took his horse looked at him

the way so many other people did — as though he was a very dangerous man, and they feared him. In all the time that he'd had such an influence on other people, Caleb still had not gotten accustomed to being feared. He wore his deadly skills with unconscious ease, and no matter how hard he tried to appear as just another businessman, it was his eyes and his walk and the fluid grace of all his moves that gave him away, and created fear in men, and fascination in women.

A butler escorted him to his room, and Caleb sighed with contentment. Anton, it appeared, had thought of everything, including providing an assortment of dressing robes and loose, fur-lined caribou slippers for him to wear.

"The prince will be arriving later," Caleb told the butler, keeping the smile to himself as he thought about the auburn-haired beauty who had made riding to the castle in the carriage impossible. "Please let him know that I'll need some time before I'm ready to see him. Until that time, I'd like a hot bath drawn, and some food brought to me."

The butler nodded and left the bedroom without a sound. He, like the other servants at the castle, had been forewarned that a friend and business associate of the prince's would be spending some time at the castle, and was to be shown every consideration. With nothing more than a look, Anton had let the staff know that to show the guest anything less than princely service would result in severe consequences.

A large room had been made up for him. The chest of drawers was completely empty, which made Caleb smile, because he no longer had any clothes to fill the drawers with. All his clothes except those he wore had to be left behind some time ago, when a potential banker became more than just a little bit curious as to the identity of the man that Caleb worked for. Caleb had to make the decision of whether he wanted to keep his clothes, or keep his skin, and he chose the latter.

The bedroom windows faced west, so there would be no morning sun, and Caleb was thankful for that. He had always been a night person whereas Anton was much more a day person, and they often joked about this, since it was one of the few ways in which they differed.

He stripped out of his clothes and tossed them onto the floor, then slipped his arms into one of the four robes that had been placed on the bed. The robe was purple, thick, clean, and felt positively wonderful against his skin. Next he stepped into a pair of loose slippers, and Caleb sighed loudly. He'd been without physical comforts for quite some time, so it was doubly wonderful now to have such quality garments and surroundings.

The butler returned shortly to tell Caleb that his bath was ready at the last door down the hall on the right. He thanked the butler and waited until he was alone once again in the guest bedroom. Then, from his pile of clothing, he removed the small, stiletto-bladed dagger and sheath, and slipped them into the folds of his robe along his ribs before leaving his room.

Even in Castle Talakovich, it wouldn't be entirely wise to let his guard down completely. Caleb had made too many enemies in his past eight years to believe that there weren't people in this world who would pay a fortune to have him murdered.

He entered the bathing room and smiled. Anton's touch—his brilliant mechanical flair for the little touches that made life easier for himself and others—was instantly apparent. The bath tub was oversized, which made for comfortable bathing, but it was also placed on a short trolley track so that it could be rolled easily out the opposite door. Also, the base upon which the enameled tub was fastened was hinged at one end, so that to empty the tub, rather than removing the water one bucket at a time, it could just be tilted and drained quickly and easily.

Caleb crossed the room and opened the far door. His smile broadened when he saw the sluice gate in the floor, and overhead, the spigot. Caleb remembered years earlier, when he and Anton had lain in their dorm room beds thinking of the future, and all that they'd like to change, how the prince had said it was silly and inefficient to have hot water brought to an upstairs bedroom. His idea was to have an upstairs room reinforced, with a solid brick floor put in to prevent accidental fires, and in this upstairs room, there would be a stove for boiling water. Through a series of hoses, the hot water would drain directly into a tub one floor below, letting gravity do the work that hired servants usually needed to perform with considerable effort.

"Still changing the world to suit your needs, eh, Anton?" Caleb muttered to himself as he stripped out of his robe, hung it on the back of the door, then stepped out of his slippers.

He poured fragrant soap into the steaming water, swirled it around with his hand, then eased himself into the tub. The water was almost too hot for him to withstand, but even that felt good. He had gone much too long without a proper bath, and he was determined to make up for it now. The soaps that had been placed out for him were all fresh bars that had never been used before.

He bathed himself, then bathed himself again, and by the time he went through the ritual a third time, he finally felt clean enough again to call himself human. An assortment of towels, all neatly folded and freshly laundered, awaited him, and Caleb stepped out of the tub, dripping wet but squeaky clean, and was just reaching for a towel when the door opened and all hell broke loose.

Nine

Princess Anastasia Talakovich was perhaps the only person in the entire castle who did not know that "Prince Anton's American friend" had arrived. So when she stepped into her private bathing chambers and found herself staring at a tall, handsome, and completely naked man, her first thought was that one of her stable hands had decided to use her private bathing chambers to take a bath. To make matters even worse, there was a dagger on the floor near the tub, and everyone knew that the princess absolutely forbade any weapons to be brought into the castle.

"What do you think you're doing?" she snapped, bending quickly to reach for the dagger.

She was long accustomed to men doing what she told them, either because they worked for her, or because they were hopeful beaux who either wanted to get their hands on her fortune, her body, or both. What Princess Anastasia was not in the least bit accustomed to was dealing with a man who had no fear of her at all, and moved with such startling speed that she was left speechless.

The moment her fingers closed around the handle of the dagger, Caleb's strong fingers closed tightly around her slender white wrist.

"Let it go," the man said, his fingers like steel bands

surrounding her wrist.

Anastasia was too proud, too frightened, and much to angry to even consider releasing the dagger. She struggled to pull her hand free from his grasp, but he continued to hold her tightly. When she braced her feet and pulled hard as she straightened up in an attempt to free herself, Anastasia caused the big man to lose his balance briefly, stumbling toward her, his broad, naked chest striking her.

A moment later Anastasia felt trapped between the solid, ungiving surface of the door against her back, and the heat and texture of the lightning-quick man pressing against her chest. He pulled her hand above her head, trapping her wrist against the door so that she could do no harm with the dagger. One second of struggle later and Princess Anastasia had both her hands pinned against the door above her head.

"Take your hands off me, you repellant swine!" Anastasia hissed, looking up into the man's eyes.

She knew then that she had seen him before, though she was too mentally agitated to say where or when their paths had crossed in the past. It was especially troubling to not only be suddenly confronted in her own bathing chambers, but by a naked man who exuded danger.

"Drop the blade."

She closed her eyes for only a moment to compose her senses. She knew that this man could easily break the bones in her wrist if he wanted to, and that so far he had opted not to let this violent encounter get *that* extreme. When she opened them again, there was the faintest hint of a smile on the man's lips, and at last Anastasia remembered where and when she'd seen the man before.

"Caleb Carter," she said, her fear evaporating with the recognition, though her anger diminished not one bit.

His eyes narrowed briefly, then recognition brightened them. "Anastasia? Little Anastasia?"

It had been five years since last he'd seen her, and then she was a brilliant, precocious sixteen-year-old girl who was all coltish arms and legs and held only the promise of the woman that she now had become.

"I'm not *little Anastasia!* I was *never* little Anastasia!" She squirmed, trying to pull free her hands, distinctly aware of the American's nudity, and how the full length of him was pressed against her. "It's *Princess Talakovich* to you!"

"Well, Princess Tal-a-ko-vich," Caleb replied, slowly and sarcastically drawling the syllables of her name out, "you're holding my blade, and you'd better let go of it before you get hurt."

He was naked, and Anastasia was thankful that she didn't have to look at him. And though she most certainly did not wish to prolong the contact between herself and Caleb, she also could not accept a threat—even a veiled threat like the one he'd just given her—to go unchecked. She had never bowed to any threat before—not even as a child—and she wasn't about to start doing so now.

"You'd better get your hands off me, or you're going to get hurt," she said with a haughty, imperious tone that belied the fact that a handsome and entirely naked man she hardly knew was pressed against her, holding her hands above her head. She looked challengingly into Caleb's eyes and raised her knee just enough to brush against the inside of Caleb's thigh. "Hurt in ways a man does not want to be hurt, and dressed as you are, you are particularly defenseless."

Anastasia had thought the counter-threat to knee him in the groin would be sure to put Caleb in his place and let him know who wielded the power in Castle Talakovich. The fact that she believed this was proof of how little she actually knew about the foreigner who worked with her brother in a capacity that Anton had never really explained.

Instead of backing down, Caleb kicked her left foot to the side, forcing her legs apart, and then wedged his hips in tight between her thighs, making it impossible for her to knee him in the groin.

Anastasia tried with greater force now to get away from Caleb, but he had her pinned more firmly than ever against the door. She tried to close her legs, but Caleb had protectively positioned himself between her thighs, making it impossible. His groin was pressed against her own, and they were separated only by the layers of her dress and pantalets, and the pressure against her brought a wave of sensation that Anastasia had never before felt — and one she did not appreciate.

"Never, *ever* threaten me," Caleb whispered, distinctly aware of the lushly feminine woman he held trapped against door.

Part of him realized that the safe and intelligent thing to do at this moment would be to remove his dagger from her hand, release her, and promise to explain his presence in the castle as soon as he had fully dried himself and put fresh clothes on. One simply did not manhandle a Russian princess in her own castle in St. Petersburg — not without paying a heavy penalty for the offense. This was even more true should the offending male be a foreigner.

The glitch in Caleb's logic was and always had been his love of adventure, and its corollary, danger. Anastasia was much too beautiful for him to release her before he absolutely had to.

In his mind's eye he travelled backward in time to when he'd first looked upon Anton's little sister, thinking her to be a lovely girl of sixteen, so full of energy and spirit. She had become even more beautiful than Caleb had imagined she would, her figure becoming fuller, more curvaceous, though she had maintained her natural slenderness.

The plunging bodice of her Russian-fashion gown

119

allowed Caleb, assisted by his greater height, a soul-gripping view of pale white breasts, small and perfectly shaped. Caleb leaned forward just enough to touch his naked and still slightly damp chest against her, watching with fascination as her breasts compressed within the daring decolletage, droplets of water soaking into the fabric of her gown.

A shiver worked its way up Anastasia's spine. With Caleb's gaze going from her face down to her breasts, she was suddenly made aware not only of Caleb's naked body, but of her own body, and with that awareness she suddenly felt the heat and strength of him. She no longer tried to free her arms, though they remained trapped above her head, and she stopped wriggling because it only served to allow Caleb's slender hips to move deeper between her thighs.

It was against her nature, but Anastasia closed her eyes, inhaled deeply, and whispered, "I'm sorry." But even as she spoke the apology, she was planning severe retribution for making her apologize when she felt she hadn't done anything wrong in the first place.

She waited for a response, but received none. Time seemed to creep at a snail's pace. Caleb was not the kind of man she could control with an icy look or a stern comment.

Once, several months earlier, she and Anton were talking about a greedy, corrupt foundry owner in Prussia who had threatened to welch on a contract that was half-completed, and Anton had mused aloud, "Maybe I should have Caleb visit the Prussian. Caleb has a way of making troubles disappear." There had been a chilling confidence in Anton's voice at the time, but since Anastasia had only met Caleb once before, and that had been years earlier, she hadn't thought much about it.

With Caleb now pressing his naked body against her, holding her captive, seemingly oblivious to his own nudity, Anastasia could imagine the fear a man would feel if Caleb had been sent to put an end to troubles for the business interests of the Talakovich family and the Czar's Russia.

"I said I'm sorry," Anastasia repeated, opening her eyes to stare challengingly up at Caleb.

He had leaned back enough so that his chest was no longer pressed against her bosom, and that made it easier for Anastasia to think clearly. She did not want to look at his smug expression, but when she let her gaze trail down, Anastasia caught herself appreciating the fine, defined lines of his pectorals, and she noticed the two areas on his chest where the water had been blotted away—by her own breasts. The scent of him, all masculine and freshly soaped and scrubbed, toyed with her senses.

With the fierce resolve of a woman who had the power to turn his life into a holy hell, she looked Caleb straight in the eyes and unflinchingly said, "I said I was sorry, now take your hands off me and get out of here."

Caleb smiled then, showing a set of even white teeth. His hand slipped upward from her wrist to pluck the deadly dagger from her fingers. Then he took a step backward, releasing the princess, only slightly embarrassed by his nudity.

She turned her back to him the moment she could, but even that wasn't quick enough to prevent her from seeing the powerful muscles in Caleb's biceps, shoulders, and chest, and the wash-board ripples of muscle in his abdomen.

A rush of warmth went through Anastasia, elicited both from the embarrassment of being in the same room with a naked man she hardly knew, and the unanticipated excitement she felt at seeing such a spectacular specimen of the human male.

"We'll talk about this later," Anastasia said, tiny aftershocks of the adrenaline that had rushed through her making her tremble slightly.

She opened the door but didn't even take a step out of the room because Marta, Castle Talakovich's oldest and most beloved servant, was shuffling slowly down the long hallway. In a flash, Anastasia realized that no possible explanation for her being in a room with a naked man would satisfy the kindly old woman's iron-clad sense of propriety.

"Change your mind about leaving me?" Caleb asked, sliding his long arms into the sleeves of the purple robe as Anastasia carefully closed the door.

"Be quiet," Anastasia whispered, leaning forward so that her forehead was against the door, her eyes squeezed tightly shut in frustration. She hated the amusement she heard in Caleb's tone, even tinged as it was with the accent that Anastasia did not at all find appealing. "Marta is in the hallway, and I'd rather not have to explain to her what you and I are doing in here together."

"Marta?"

For a moment, Anastasia wondered what title to give the old woman. She had been nanny to both her and Anton, but she certainly hadn't held that role in a long time, and simply calling her a servant seemed drastically inadequate to the woman who had wielded such power in Castle Talakovich over the past forty years.

"A servant," Anastasia said at last, realizing the title itself sounded somewhat demeaning.

Caleb made a huffing sound, and Anastasia gritted her teeth. She couldn't wait to get away from the man. How could any one man exude menace and at the same time find humor in her predicament? Years earlier, Caleb had spent several days at the castle, but all Anastasia remembered of him then was that he was a man who did not speak, seldom blinked, made no sound when he moved, and stayed to himself except for when he was locked away in Anton's office discussing whatever political machinations the men had to deal with.

She felt his presence behind her and she cautiously checked over her shoulder. It wasn't until she saw that Caleb had put on a purple robe that she turned completely to face him.

"I gave that robe to my brother for his birthday a couple years ago," Anastasia commented with brittle nerves, clearly not happy that a man she did not like was wearing it now.

"If you want me to, I'll take it off." Caleb reached for the knotted sash at his waist.

"No!"

Anastasia glared at the American. She had heard that Americans had no royalty, and consequently had no understanding of civility and manners, and after spending the last five minutes with Caleb Carter, she easily believed it.

Angry, she turned back to the door and opened it just an inch. Marta — ever the efficient servant and an absolute stickler for cleanliness — was busy adding a light polish of mineral oil to the woodwork railing, paying special attention to the spiraling vertical support struts. Along the railing overlooking the main floor landing below, Anastasia guessed that there had to be at least fifty of the hand-carved struts, each and every one of which would be gleaming by the time Marta finished her work. But Marta, though loyal and dedicated, was also advancing in years and declining in speed, which meant Anastasia had no choice but to stay in the humid bathing chamber with the intolerable Caleb Carter.

She closed the door, careful to do it so quietly that she didn't draw Marta's attention.

"Damn!" Anastasia whispered. She felt it was utterly absurd that a woman of her vast fortune, living in a large old castle with many rooms, should find herself imprisoned in her own bathing chambers.

"Such language from a lady! Tell me, can you be a

lady *and* a princess, or are the two exclusive of each other?"

Anastasia wheeled upon Caleb, her blue eyes spitting flames of hatred, and only Marta's presence not far away kept her from shouting out her contempt.

"No, the two are not exclusive, you boorish barbarian! Why do you have to insult me?"

Caleb ran his fingers through his thick ebony hair, which was now only slightly damp. There wasn't even a hint of a smile as he replied, "When you call me a repellant swine, don't expect me to be thunderstruck by the accuracy of your observation."

"You attacked me," Anastasia said in explanation.

"You grabbed my dagger," Caleb countered. "What did you expect me to do?"

"To act like a civilized human being."

Caleb shrugged, and with both hands this time, smoothed his damp hair back off his forehead. Anastasia wished he would stop doing that because every time he did, his robe opened up just a little more, showing off more of his chest, which had a strange way of drawing her gaze, even though she told herself that there was really nothing at all interesting, either physically or intellectually, about Caleb Carter.

"I'm not civilized," Caleb said quietly. "That's precisely why I'm so valuable to your brother, and your czar."

"*Your* czar? He's not yours as well?"

Caleb smiled slightly, tugging at his lower lip as though the question itself was a little silly. "No, he's not my czar. I'll help him, but that doesn't make me one of his subjects."

As Anastasia looked at Caleb, she realized that there was absolutely nothing about the man that she liked. He was an American away from his homeland, and apparently he felt little or no loyalty to his adopted country. He was brusque, forceful, and thoroughly unapologetic.

The only thing that he had going in his favor, she decided, was his looks. His hair was black as midnight and parted on the left side, and his eyes were dark brown. The robe had slipped open at the chest, and she saw an old knife wound on his chest where someone had apparently tried to stab him in the heart and failed. He looked, she thought, like a hungry wolf, a rogue wolf, the kind that sheepherders in the countryside feared so much because they were so difficult to hunt or trap.

He was handsome, and the dangerous quality that hovered about him was appealing in a strange, erotic way to Princess Anastasia, whose life had been pampered, and who had always been protected from men like Caleb. But even though there was a distinctly alluring quality to the American, Anastasia knew that any involvement with him would only end in disaster.

"Between the two of us we ought to be able to trick one old woman, I should think," Anastasia whispered, deciding that she would rather risk getting caught by Marta than spending any more time with Caleb.

She opened the door and peered through the crack. Marta was on her hands and knees oiling the base of the corner post of the railing. A sense of guilt came over Anastasia, and she made a promise to herself to have a younger servant doing such chores in the future.

Then she closed the door and turned back to Caleb again.

"Will you go out there and talk with her? Turn her so that her back is to me, and keep her attention until I can slip down the stairs?" It rankled Anastasia's sensibilities to have to ask Caleb for anything, but under the circumstances, she didn't see any other way around the situation.

"Just give me a minute, then make your move."

"This kind of deception ought to be second nature

125

to you," Anastasia said with insulting condescension, then opened the door to the bathing chamber so that Caleb had to leave. She felt a certain triumph in having had the last word with the abrasive American, and she could hardly wait to tell her brother that Caleb absolutely *had* to leave the castle immediately.

She waited thirty seconds, then opened the door and peered out. When she did, she saw Caleb taking Marta by the elbow, assisting her to her feet. He was smiling in a most charming manner, and it bothered Anastasia, because even though he'd smiled at her, she'd never seen quite that smile from him. To Marta, an old servant, he would be respectful and charming; to her, mistress of the castle and a princess of royal blood, he would not show her any civility whatsoever!

Anastasia slipped out of the bathing chambers and down the stairway, keeping her eyes away from Caleb, and hoping she'd never have to see him again.

Ten

"Is there anything wrong that you want to talk about? Something I can help with?" Anastasia asked Natasha as they worked in Anastasia's enormous bedchamber.

"No!" Natasha replied, a bit more quickly and defensively than she would have liked.

Though it had been over four hours since she had been in Anton's arms in his carriage, she still couldn't keep the blush from creeping into her cheeks with distressing frequency, nor had she been able to fully concentrate on her work, even though this was her very first day on the job, and Princess Anastasia had made it absolutely clear that she expected nothing less than superb craftsmanship.

"You seem flushed," Anastasia continued.

She was standing on a small stool to achieve the right height while Natasha took all her body measurements and made a mock bust so that Anastasia wouldn't have to be present for every fitting.

"My brother hasn't been troubling you, has he?"

"No!" Natasha answered, once again more quickly and defensively than she would have liked. Then, looking a bit more closely at the pale-skinned princess, she said, "I was thinking that *you* appear a bit flushed. Is there anything troubling you?"

Natasha brought a cloth ruler from Anastasia's underarm to the point of her hip, then made a notation on a slip of paper.

"Me? No, there's nothing amiss with me," Anastasia replied, and this time it was her turn to be quick.

Natasha tucked a new series of pins between her lips and gave her employer a suspicious look. "I could be wrong," Natasha mumbled, the words coming out indistinctly because of the pins. Her tone, however, said that she did not for even a second believe that she was wrong.

For a moment, the two women exchanged looks, and then it became glaringly clear to them that they were both lying, and that they probably had no need to lie. Then they started laughing, which caused the pins to fall from Natasha's mouth. Anastasia leaped down from the stool to help her new friend retrieve the pins, and in her haste, she knocked heads with Natasha, eliciting yet another peal of laughter from the two of them.

"Let's leave it alone for a while," Anastasia said when their hilarity finally began to subside. She wiped away tears of laughter from her eyes.

Anastasia rose to her feet, dressed only in undergarments and an intricately embroidered corset, and slipped on a light dressing robe. Then she sat on the settee in a corner of the room, and poured a small glass of wine for herself, and one for Natasha.

"Have a glass of wine with me," Anastasia said, knowing that it would be positively scandalous for her reputation if anyone from her debutante society should discover that she socialized with her servants. She didn't care a whit what anyone thought about it. She patted the cushion beside her. "Sit and talk with me."

Anastasia had noticed that Natasha was wearing the same old gown that she'd worn the day before, though she had yet been able to figure out some way of bringing the subject up without sounding either intrusive or condescending. She wanted to enlarge Natasha's wardrobe without making it seem like an act of charity.

Natasha sat down, leaning slightly toward Anastasia. There had always been something about Natasha that had made her approachable, something that made other people want to confide in her, trust her. Perhaps that was why Aislyn had sought out Natasha over anyone else in her time of need; perhaps the poor, pregnant girl simply had no one else to turn to. Whatever it was, people tended to trust Natasha, and though Anastasia was unaware of it, she, too, felt drawn in by the seamstress's gentle, caring heart.

"Tell me what happened that has disturbed you," Natasha said, her voice soft, concerned. "It helps to talk about what takes away our happiness."

"It's nothing, really. There's a man who works for my brother in an . . . odd capacity. I ran into him earlier today. He surprised me, and he is really quite a . . . different type of man. His eyes are . . ."

Anastasia shook her head, angry with herself because the images of Caleb's naked body had never strayed far from her thoughts. Perhaps most disturbing of all was that she had not seen his manhood—and the omission, once she had been separated from Caleb, was triggering a secret curiosity that would allow her no peace of mind. She wanted to know what he looked like. Not just most of him, but all of him—every last mysterious inch of him. But why?

"What happened?" Natasha asked.

She was suddenly painfully aware that she came from a very different social milieu than Anastasia, and that there was the distinct possibility that the princess was easily disturbed, whereas Natasha, who had been fighting to retain her dignity virtually every day of her life for the past several years, would be relatively unaffected by it.

"This man was rude to me," Anastasia said, quite

129

well aware of the fact that she was leaving several major factors out of her statement, and pleased that she had.

She couldn't confide completely in Natasha Stantikoff. Not yet, anyway, and it was simply too embarrassing for her to admit to being so flustered because she'd seen a naked man.

Besides, hadn't she perfected the persona of the flamboyant, wealthy princess of malleable morals and unquenchable desires? Hadn't half the rumors of her having this lover or that one — or even several lovers tucked away in small apartments scattered throughout St. Petersburg — hadn't they all been started by her? And all because the rumors of her wild ways actually helped to protect her against a male population that she did not trust at all, and was quite frankly intimidated by, even though she would go to her grave without ever admitting she was intimidated by anything or anyone.

"Men!" Natasha said after a brief silence. "All they do is complicate a woman's life! But I hardly need tell you that."

The women looked into each other's eyes, each silently asking questions of the other, neither one wanting to reveal too much of herself while learning everything there was to know about the other. From Natasha's off-the-cuff comment, it was clear that she knew of Anastasia's reputation. But did Anastasia want to do anything to correct Natasha's misconception?

"What have you heard about me and men?" Anastasia asked, forcing a smile upon her lips. She saw Natasha's expression instantly change into an apologetic one, and she reached out to pat the seamstress's hand. "Don't worry. No matter what you say, you won't make me angry. I'm just curious about what you've heard about me. Apparently in your eyes I'm something of an expert on men."

Natasha cleared her throat, suddenly finding it very difficult to meet the princess's gaze. She wished now that she'd shown the good sense to keep her mouth shut, and kept the relationship with Anastasia on a purely professional level.

"Nothing much, really."

Sharply, Anastasia said, "Be honest! How will I ever know what is being said about me behind my back unless you tell me? I'm counting on you now."

For a few moments, Natasha tried to avoid the subject, but Anastasia never let her get far. Then at last, realizing she no longer had any option but the truth, she said, "I have heard—and I'm not saying I believed what I've heard, mind you—that you have—" she searched for the right word to use, blushing furiously as she did so "—*known* . . . several men in your life."

"Anyone in particular?" Anastasia asked, really quite amused now by her new friend's obvious embarrassment in discussing the subject of sex.

"There's supposed to be a prince . . . a *married* prince in Moscow, that you've known intimately since you were fifteen or sixteen." Natasha was staring at her hands in her lap, cursing herself for ever having even thought she could keep a job at Castle Talakovich as the princess's personal seamstress. There was no doubt in her mind that when she finished speaking, the princess would inform her that she was no longer employed, and should leave her presence immediately.

"What else have you heard?" Anastasia asked, leaning closer, not wanting to miss a single word, not even the slightest nuance or inflection in what Natasha had to say.

"This prince is supposed to have some power over you. Nobody really knows what it is supposed to be, only that you keep trying to break off your relationship with him, but he keeps drawing you back. And that even though you are always seen with other men, the prince in Moscow doesn't care. He has you under his power, and he summons you whenever he wants."

"Wants *what?*" Anastasia asked teasingly.

"You *know* what he *wants*," Natasha shot back, so embarrassed by the subject that she missed the teasing quality in Anastasia's voice.

It wasn't until Anastasia laughed aloud that Natasha realized she was being gently teased. And even though she was angry with Anastasia, she couldn't keep from laughing herself.

"I know that story well. I should — I made the entire tawdry tale up," Anastasia said. "Not one word of it is true, and that's the beauty of it."

"Why? Why tell such a story about yourself? It doesn't make sense to me."

Anastasia smiled weakly, and behind the humor in her lovely blue eyes there was an equal measure of sadness. "Every time a man looks at me, I have to wonder whether he's looking at me because I'm wealthy, or because I'm attractive, or because he wants something from my brother — some business deal, or what have you. I never can be certain what men want from me, and so, a long time ago — and I confess, I've always been a little wild — I started flirting with men. Lots of them. Every man who knew my brother was the target of my coquetry. But, you see, I never really did anything with any of them. The story about the jealous married prince in Moscow was just so that I could be with this man or that one, and when he tried to do more than I wanted, I could just say that I wanted to sleep with him, but I just didn't dare because my lover in Moscow would hire an assassin to have me killed if I did such a thing. Kill me . . . and the man I was with."

Natasha's smile slowly broadened as she began to understand the philosophy behind Anastasia's reasoning, and the more she thought about it, the more clever it seemed.

"So as long as you were willing to let people gossip about you, you were pretty much safe from men?"

"Precisely!"

Natasha laughed then, but behind the laughter lay sadness. She had thought that the Princess Anastasia Talakovich would lead a carefree life of uninterrupted happiness, and to discover that her wealth imprisoned her as much as it set her free was faintly disorienting, like discovering for the very first time that your parents are getting old, or overweight, or perhaps are not as intelligent and well-read as you once believed them to be.

"There, that's my great secret," Anastasia said, adding just a bit more wine to both their glasses. "Now it's your turn, and don't try to hold anything back. Is there a man in the countryside somewhere who's gotten your heart? Something put a blush in your cheeks, and I'm not going to let up until I find out all the juicy little details."

It was a struggle to keep the smile on her face, but Natasha managed to do just that. What could she do, tell Anastasia what had really happened in the carriage that morning? That didn't seem likely. To make matters even worse, Natasha herself didn't really understand all that had happened. What was it that had gripped her body with such intensity that she felt pleasure so exquisitely, so intensely, that it bordered on pain? What sorcery was it that Anton had used to make her allow him to do all the things proper women were not supposed to let men do?

Seconds ticked by. Anastasia grew impatient for Natasha to begin. It was only fair for Natasha, now, to reveal some deep, inner secret. If she would not, it would surely be a sign that she was not a woman who could be trusted, nor be able to throw open the doors of friendship.

"Well . . . ?" Anastasia prodded.

Natasha felt her ears burning, her cheeks turning

crimson as, once again, she twisted a small, perspiration-dampened hanky into a knotted cord of cloth between her hands.

For only a second she looked up into Anastasia's eyes. That was all the time she needed to convince herself that giving an honest answer as to why she had been absent-minded and flushed since her arrival at Castle Talakovich was not an option. How could she possibly find the words—mere sounds!—to adequately and accurately express the wickedly exciting things she had done, the cataclysmic, soul-wrenching feelings that had jolted through her with the force of a lightning bolt?

"Well?" Anastasia urged again, and this time there was no mistaking the impatient and mistrustful edge to her tone.

At precisely the same moment that Natasha opened her mouth to speak, having absolutely no idea of what she was about to say, she was spared the abject horror of having to confess her own passionate weaknesses when the door to the bedchamber opened, and Marta, the old servant, poked her head into the room.

"Pardon me, but Prince Anton will want to be seeing you soon in the library," Marta said. "That American fellow has been with him for a while now, so I suspect that they'll soon be finished with old stories and want to get down to business."

"Yes, I'm sure you're right, Marta," Anastasia said. When the door was closed again, she sighed theatrically. "Sometimes I wish she wasn't so awesomely efficient," she said, rising to her feet, kicking off her comfortable slippers as she pulled loose her dressing gown and let it slide down her arms. "I'm sorry, Natasha, but I really must sit in with Anton. He'll never admit it publicly, of course, but he really does need me."

Natasha was monumentally relieved that she did not have to open her heart to Anastasia's inspection and that her passionate abandonment of her senses in Anton's arms would still be a secret, but she was also curious.

She had heard that Anton and Anastasia were partners in running the vast business enterprises of the Talakoviches, and she had heard that the prince relied heavily on advice given to him by his sister. But Natasha, along with virtually everyone else in St. Petersburg, did not really believe the stories because, as everyone knew, women simply did not have the mentality or the personality it took to be a leader in the ever changing and always cutthroat world of business.

"You can quit for the day any time you like," Anastasia explained as she stepped into her dress and worked her arms through the tight, narrow sleeves. "I'll have a carriage waiting for you just outside the front entrance." The princess smiled as she laced the deeply plunging bodice of her dress. "Next time we meet, you can give me the answer you've been trying so hard to swallow."

"I will," Natasha said, picking up on the light-hearted tone that the princess now used. "Is the American with your brother? The one who is so rude?"

"Yes. And when I see him, I'm going to give that hideous ruffian a lesson he will never forget!"

As Anastasia prepared herself, pulling up her stockings, fastening her dress and adjusting the sleeves, Natasha wished that she herself was daring enough to wear the Empire fashion so popular in St. Petersburg, and indeed, in all the capitals of Europe. She was much more voluptuous than Anastasia, and while the low, U-shaped neckline looked beautiful and feminine on the princess, Natasha doubted her own fuller figure would be so attractively highlighted by the show of skin.

Natasha noticed how the princess had suddenly become very animated, and how her blue eyes were bright and alive with mischief, and with another emotion that Natasha was unable to identify.

"Don't work too hard. We've already made great progress. Stop for the day any time you like, in fact," Anastasia said, a bit breathless as she hurried to leave her bedroom. She sat down on the little bench in front of her dressing table to inspect herself in the mirror, checking to see that her coiffure was still properly in place. "If you're hungry, or you need anything at all, just ask one of the servants to get it for you."

Anastasia rose like a whirlwind from the small chair. "I probably won't see you before you leave," she said, turning briefly to give Natasha a smile before exiting the bedroom with a rustle of fine fabric, trailing the scent of lilac water.

Alone at last, Natasha was grateful that she hadn't had to open her heart to Anastasia, or to lie to her to protect herself. But now that she was alone, she couldn't help but wonder why the princess had gone to such a fuss to look her absolute best when, ostensibly, she was only going to see her brother, and another man she claimed to loathe.

The moment Anastasia entered the library, Caleb stopped speaking and smiled at her indulgently. He was entirely willing to wait until she had left the room again before he continued speaking to Prince Anton. When Anastasia smiled, nodded silently in recognition of both men, then sat in the third wingbacked chair to complete the triangle, Caleb cast a sidelong glance at his old friend as if to ask: Is she really going to sit in?

"It's been many years since you've been here," Anton said. "You must understand, my sister is no longer a little girl, as she was when last you were here. She's like my right arm. I don't know what I'd do without her wisdom, her insight."

Anastasia smiled and nodded toward her brother then leveled her piercing blue gaze upon Caleb. She never really believed he'd challenge her right to sit in on these critical discussions after Anton's explanation.

"I can see that she's no little girl," Caleb replied, his face expressionless. "What I don't see is why she's here. Anton, what I have to tell you must be kept in the strictest confidence. There's no room for amateurs, or a woman who likes to gossip."

A momentary clenching of the teeth was Anastasia's only outward display of anger. She had dealt with men like Caleb before—men who believed she was nothing more than an ornament for a man's arm, or thought that her responsibility to the family business was just to play the role of a figurehead, and not to advise her brother.

"I'm sure it is difficult for you to accept the fact that you will be working with a woman," Anastasia said, pretending that she had no opinion of Caleb one way or another. "But I am sure that you'll surmount your shortcomings." Her eyes challenged Caleb to refute her. "I've seen quite a bit of what you offer, and while I grant that your skills are impressive, you still have to prove yourself."

Caleb's expression remained unreadable, but Anastasia knew she had scored a victory. Caleb apparently had not told Anton of their accidental and embarrassing meeting in the bathing chambers. Anton was making no effort to hide his confusion.

"Now, may we continue?" Anastasia asked. "I'm really quite interested in finding out what information our money's acquired."

"Of course," Caleb replied. "But before I continue, please let me say that I hope one day soon to see as much of what *you* have to offer, Princess Anastasia, as you've seen of me."

I despise this man, Anastasia thought with crystal clarity and absolute certainty.

She could hardly wait for the day when Caleb would leave Castle Talakovich, and she would never again have to look at him. Even if Caleb was Anton's oldest and only real friend, Anastasia knew in her heart that she had more influence over her brother's actions than anyone else. If she made it an important enough issue, Caleb would no longer have any association with the Talakoviches, or the Czar of Russia.

"Now that we are all gathered, let's get down to business, shall we?" Anton said, looking at Caleb.

Anastasia sensed that her brother had intentionally neglected to mention that she would be a part of all the negotiations, perhaps knowing that Caleb would find it unacceptable. The two men exchanged a look that lasted only a moment, and what was most surprising was the underlying humor, as though one man had tricked the other, and that such a thing was not an uncommon occurrence.

"I'll start with the banker in Bonn," Caleb said then, resigned to the fact that a woman had to be considered an equal, even though he'd never heard such a preposterous notion before. "The man there is corrupt and venal, but I think he can use his connections for purchasing sabres and cannons directly from a foundry within his province. I spent several days looking into the foundry and asking questions, and I'd guess that the banker is part owner, or at least a silent partner in the business."

"You investigated the cannons?" Anton asked.

"They're fine quality weapons, but the method for smithing them is surprisingly antiquated. Whether or not the bank will provide the financing, and whether the foundry can produce enough cannons and deliver them quickly and secretly, are issues that have yet to be answered."

"What's your opinion?" Anton asked.

138

"I'd pass on this one. The banker isn't offering favorable rates, and there's nothing about him to make me believe he wouldn't turn on us if Napoleon discovered what we're up to, or if he got a better offer from someone else." Caleb looked from Anton to Anastasia. "It's not like Czar Alexander is the only leader who is less than ecstatic about Napoleon's troops being armed and ready to march."

"The man from Bonn is out of it then," Anton stated. He looked down at a single sheet of paper he held in his lap. "From there you went to . . . ?"

"Switzerland," Caleb answered.

Anastasia watched the process, and what fascinated her was that her brother had completely dismissed the possibility of doing business with the Bonn banker simply because of Caleb's opinion. She had thought that Caleb was just a vehicle for the transmission of information to Anton, and now she realized that, like herself, Caleb was much more important in the Talakovich business and in the secret maneuverings of the Russian government than outsiders might think.

"What happened in Switzerland?" Anastasia asked.

Caleb glanced at her. So far, he had directed all his comments straight at Anton. Now, after a moment of hesitation, he turned in his chair so that while he was still facing more toward Anton, he was at least somewhat turned toward her. It was not a full acceptance, but from what she could guess about Caleb's personality, winning any acceptance represented a major victory.

"If we get our financing there, we'll have no problems with confidentiality. But it is equally true that we'll have serious difficulties transferring the capital to wherever we choose to buy our cannons. The Swiss are sticklers for details, and they don't trust Napoleon any more than we do. They know enough to stay clear of the little madman."

Caleb leaned forward, placing his elbows on his knees. As he spoke, he stared at a spot on the floor, not really looking at anything or anyone, going backward in time to another place to recall it perfectly.

"In London, I met with a man named Parker Windom. A cagey fellow, he came straight out and said he didn't trust me, and that he wouldn't be inclined to do business with me since he knew I was the front-man."

Anastasia's brows pushed together. "You sound as though you like him. Why, when he clearly does not trust you?"

"Because he was honest enough to come right out and say what he thought. None of the others trusted me either, mind you. There is no way they could trust me with what little information I could give them."

"Did Parker Windom suspect our association?" Anton asked.

"I let him believe that I am working for a small but influential group of second-generation American businessmen who are, as their fathers were before them, still loyal to England and the Crown." Caleb smiled, pleased with his deception. "I believe he found it appealing to help others fight the United States government."

"Let's keep him as an option. Who else did you see?" Anton asked, making a notation on a sheet of paper.

Alone in Anastasia's bedroom, Natasha suddenly felt very much like a thief — like the thief that her aunt and uncle wanted her to be.

She had learned a secret about Anastasia, and she wished she hadn't. The more she learned of her new employer, the more she liked her . . . and liking the Talakoviches was not something she should do if she was to do the hideous things that her aunt and uncle demanded of her.

Horribly uncomfortable, Natasha went to the chest of drawers in the corner of the bedchamber. Upon its gleaming surface were several bottles of perfume, a small leather-bound book that might well be a diary, a large gold tray that held several hair combs, and a mahogany box that contained the princess's jewelry.

She used just the tip of her index finger to touch the jewelry box, as wary and tentative as if it were a dangerous animal that might snap at her at any moment. Natasha opened the lid slowly. Inside, there was an extensive assortment of ear-bobs, made from every jewel that Natasha could think of—ruby, emerald, diamond, opal, and more.

Different colors for different gowns, Natasha thought, shaking her head in amazement. Such wealth was unimaginable to her, even though she was surrounded by it now.

All I have to do is take one ear-bob, and that'll satisfy Aunt Aggie, Natasha thought, pushing the ear-bobs around in the box.

She stared at the jewels, hating herself for even thinking about stealing one of them. If there was any truth to what Aggie had said, it was that Anastasia had so many jewels that she probably wouldn't notice a missing set of ear-bobs.

Even if Anastasia didn't notice the ear-bobs had been stolen, would that make it any less of a crime? Natasha wanted to think that it would make a difference, but in her heart she knew it really wouldn't. Stealing is stealing, whether or not a person is caught.

And what would her fate be if she did get caught stealing from Princess Anastasia? Aggie and Ivan had told her countless stories of how cruel and greedy the Talakoviches were, so how could they possibly expect her to steal from people who would punish her beyond her imagination?

To think that Anastasia would not notice a missing set of ear-bobs was ridiculous, Natasha realized. The princess was much too intelligent, much too aware of her responsibilities and all that was expected of her, for her not to realize an expensive part of her wardrobe was missing.

Following close on the heels of this thought was another, even more disturbing one. Had the jewels been arranged in a pattern that only Anastasia was aware of? Had she made it look as though the jewels had simply been tossed into the box at random, when in reality it was only made to look that way so that she could tell if someone—someone exactly like *Natasha*—had gone poking about in her jewelry box?

How had the ear-bobs been arranged when she'd first opened the lid? Natasha desperately tried to remember, but couldn't.

Icy fear crept into Natasha's veins, and she cursed herself for ever having thought that she could be a thief. She simply didn't have the heart for it, and even now, though she had stolen nothing at all, she felt monumentally guilty.

Resolutely closing the lid on the jewelry box, Natasha grabbed her cape and tossed it over her shoulders, then left the princess's bedchamber, hoping and praying that Anastasia or Marta hadn't been spying on her from some secret vantage point.

Eleven

Natasha felt dead on her feet, though she had just now awakened, and should feel refreshed. Since the carriage ride with Anton, when she had allowed him to touch her and kiss her in ways too intimate and exciting to think about, she hadn't been sleeping well. To make matters even more unsettling, her aunt and uncle had been hounding her to steal something—anything—that they could use or sell for money.

Alone in the bedroom she shared with Aislyn, Natasha finished making the bed, then she sat upon it and buried her face in her hands, sitting quietly in the predawn dark. What had happened to her life? A week earlier she had shared something special with Prince Anton, but since that time, she had hardly spoken to him, and even then it had been while Anastasia and the American were there in the hallway with them.

Had Anton tired of her because she had left his passion unsatisfied?

It was a troubling thought for Natasha. She did not want to believe that what she had shared with Anton was merely physical. To her, it was much more than just two people allowing their bodies to feel pleasure. However mindless his caresses had made her, that still didn't counter the fact that Natasha had felt confident enough with Anton to let her senses—let the passion

143

that had been dormant within her for a very long time — explore the new realm of esthesia that Anton seemed so happy to reveal to her.

What would happen if he felt betrayed by her because she'd left him unfulfilled? She would lose her job, and with it, the income that was greater than any she'd known before. She'd feel the increasing pressure from her aunt and uncle, and perhaps — or was it *probably?* — have a more difficult time escaping from Uncle Ivan's hideous sexual advances. And what about Aislyn? Would she be able to keep Ivan at arm's length?

Natasha heard the bedroom door open, and she took just a second to force a smile on her lips, then raised her face out of her hands. She didn't want Aislyn to know how depressed she had become in the past week.

Only it wasn't Aislyn who had come into the bedroom without knocking, it was Uncle Ivan. His hair was uncombed, his robe only loosely tied closed to allow his gray-haired chest and belly to show. There was an angry look in his eye, and Natasha wondered if it was just his daily morning hangover that put him in a foul mood, or if she had unwittingly done something to rile his testy temper.

"Good morning," she said, trying to keep the smile on her lips, though smiling for her uncle hardly seemed worth the effort.

"Good morning yourself," Ivan said. He walked up close to Natasha, making no effort to close his robe, quite well aware of how much of himself was showing.

"What do you want?"

"Someday I'll show you," Ivan replied, grinning crookedly despite the drums of intemperance that pounded inside his skull. "But that's not my first concern at the moment. Right now I want to know when you're going to bring your uncle something he can sell?"

"What do you mean?"

"You know exactly what I mean. When are you going to get your little hands on something. I can sell? I've been patient with you long enough, girl. You can't say that I haven't. You've been at the castle a week and still you haven't brought me so much as a single silver spoon."

"I gave you every ruble I made last week," Natasha said quietly, working to keep her anger in check, knowing that she could not win in an argument with her uncle when he was only wearing a robe. She didn't doubt that he would find some reason to stay in her bedroom longer than he had to, and if given half a chance, he would probably find some way to *accidentally* have his robe open up so that he would reveal himself.

The thought of looking at her uncle's naked body almost made Natasha nauseous, and she knew that she had to put an end to the conversation quickly.

"That wasn't enough and you know it! After all the Talakoviches have stolen from me, I deserve much more than just your pathetic servant's pay!"

Ivan rocked back on his heels, pushing his stomach forward toward Natasha. The loosely knotted sash of his faded old robe slipped just a little further open. Ivan chuckled when Natasha turned her face away so that she wouldn't have to look at him.

"You getting shy now?"

Natasha stood, her dark eyes bright with pent-up fury. "I'm not getting shy. I *am* getting out of here as soon as I can."

"That's fine. You just do that," Ivan said, his breath strong and revolting as it hit Natasha with stomach-churning force so early in the morning. "And when you go, you take your friend with you. You see, the money you gave me and your aunt only paid for your rent here in this fine home we've provided for you. Aislyn . . . she hasn't given me nothing, and she'd better make me happy soon because my patience is running real low and some night soon it's going to be empty."

Natasha had always loathed violence of any sort, but as she looked into her uncle's bloodshot eyes, she understood at last how one person could consciously plan the murder of another. Uncle Ivan was truly evil—evil in every sense of the word. Sooner or later— probably sooner—he would not be satisfied with just stealing an occasional glance at Aislyn. Sooner or later, he'd steal much more than that from the poor girl, and he wouldn't hesitate to use violence to get what he wanted, even though she was pregnant.

"I'll get you something soon," Natasha heard herself whisper. "Something that will pay for Aislyn staying here."

"It'd better be soon," Ivan growled, then left the bedroom.

When Natasha was finished with her morning chores, she pulled Aislyn aside and warned her to be especially careful that day. Such warnings were always difficult because Natasha never could be certain if she was merely frightening her friend needlessly, or giving her a warning that might prevent a tragedy from happening.

When the carriage arrived for Natasha, she was disappointed but not surprised to find that the coachman was again travelling alone. Not since that first day, when she had experienced such happiness in Anton's arms, had the prince deigned to accompany her on the trip to the castle.

Alone in the closed carriage, Natasha stretched out as best she could on the seat and closed her eyes, trying to keep from thinking about Anton, and whether she had done something to make him stay away.

She wanted to believe that her only concern was to ensure her continued employment, but Natasha knew

146

that wasn't quite true. Anton meant more to her than just sexual pleasure, more than just employment. He meant a thousand strange and mysterious things, only a few of which Natasha really understood, and even if she didn't want to admit it, she knew her peace of mind would never be realized until she was able to speak with the prince privately. She had to know one way or another what he felt about her, and though she was certain her heart would feel ripped asunder if Anton held no dear feelings in his heart for her, she also knew that his contempt for her, or even his noncommittal attitude, would make it infinitely easier for her to steal from him.

"I'm telling you, that man has been a thorn in my side since the first moment I saw him," Princess Anastasia said as she studied her reflection in the full-length mirror.

Natasha was making the final adjustments to the bottom trim of the gown. The gown was egg-shell white, made of exquisite, almost translucent cloth, and it draped her body beautifully. Anastasia was talking of Caleb Carter, which was a topic she hadn't strayed far from in many days now when she was alone with Natasha working on the fittings.

"Aren't you exaggerating just a little?" Natasha asked. She had met Caleb only a few times, and even then it had always been very briefly. Natasha did not like Caleb. There was something distinctly dangerous about him that frightened her, and made her think that Anastasia would do well to avoid taunting the man so openly, and so frequently.

"Every suggestion, I make, he counters with something else. And Anton listens to every word he says!"

"Anton also listens to every word you say," Natasha pointed out.

"Of course he does! I'm his sister! But Caleb—he's

an American! He's just a man hired to—" Anastasia bit the words off. It wouldn't do to be telling Natasha family secrets, and certainly not secrets of state.

"Hired to do what?" Natasha asked.

"Perform vital services," Anastasia said with a casual shrug of her slender shoulders, belying the importance of her words. "He's naught but an errand boy, a hired servant."

"Like me?"

"No! Nothing at *all* like you," Anastasia said quickly. "*You* are exquisite at what you do, as witnessed by this gown that is *exactly* as I had envisioned it. *You* are entertaining to speak with, and *you* make me laugh. Caleb, on the other hand, sets my teeth on edge, and confronts me at every turn. No, dear friend, while it is true that both of you receive your pay from the Talakoviches, you are worlds apart."

"Are you sure there isn't anything more that you're not telling me? Or yourself?" Natasha asked, looking up into Anastasia's eyes, about to put the final few stitches in the gown's hem.

"If you're insinuating that I'm harboring feelings for Caleb, you're as wrong as you could possibly be. It bothers me that I used to have Anton's full attention, and now that attention is divided, and yes, I am being petty about it. But to think that that American *means* something to me—really *means* something—is beyond any stretch of the imagination. He's a rude man, and he has no sense of—"

Anastasia again bit her lip, stopping the word *hierarchy* from leaving her mouth. Caleb didn't know anything about social hierarchy, and it infuriated her, but she couldn't speak of this to her seamstress, even if they were quickly becoming very good friends.

As Natasha went back to work on the hem, Anastasia thought about the questions that had been asked of her.

How much of her anger toward Caleb was really

anger, and how much of it was fascination? She couldn't deny that the dangerous allure, the man-of-mystery element to Caleb's character fascinated her, and sparked in her a taste for intrigue that she hadn't thought she possessed.

His refusal to bow to her superior position within the castle, though infuriating, also intrigued Anastasia, since she couldn't help but take up the unspoken challenge and see if she had what it took to make Caleb fall in line with all the rest of the people hired by herself and Anton.

Anastasia and Anton had joked with each other for years that they were both such strong personalities that they might never find another person strong enough to be a partner in life with them. Caleb was certainly strong . . . but was there any tenderness mixed in with that strength?

"Anastasia, are you listening to me?"

It took a moment for her to shake away her internal questions and realize that Natasha had been talking to her. She smiled down at her seamstress.

"I'm sorry. I was thinking about something that Anton said to me."

"Something Anton said?" Natasha asked, one brow arched as though she suspected it might be someone other than her brother that plagued the princess's thoughts. "Anyway, what I wanted to know is whether you like the way I've done the neckline?"

Anastasia turned to face the mirror again. The gown was all loose, flowing muslin fabric that moved with her when she moved, simultaneously showing her body and yet concealing it. It was the current Empire fashion, taken from the fashions of the Holy Roman and Greek empires, and Anastasia positively adored the work Natasha had done.

The neckline dipped low in a deep "V" to display the soft, pale inner swells of her breasts, and the waistline, like in the old Roman days, was very high, with an ornamental brooch at the deepest point of the V, where the cloth sash belt surrounded Anastasia. The overall effect was one of simplicity, elegance, femininity, and yet strength and grace.

She turned to the side and raised an arm, inspecting how much of herself could be seen. If she should reach overhead for anything, just a hint of her breast would be revealed, though nothing more than a hint. As far as Anastasia was concerned, it was perfect.

"What do you think?" Natasha asked, nervously nibbling on her lower lip.

"I think it's the best work you've done so far, and I think you're an absolute miracle worker!"

Natasha tried to repress her sigh of relief. She wanted to appear confident enough that she never for a moment suspected her employer might be unhappy with her work, but she sighed anyway.

"What should we work on next?" Natasha asked. "Another gown? Perhaps something soft and pretty to wear beneath something less formal?"

Anastasia wondered if this was the time to tell Natasha that several of her old gowns were currently being altered to fit her. Though Anastasia had actually wanted to have entirely new creations made for Natasha, she also knew that to do that would have been an act of charity, which would not have been easy for the proud seamstress to accept. However, altering existing gowns, Anastasia figured, balanced the line between charity and kindness.

"I think something nice to wear next to me," Anastasia said at last. "Something that feels nice touching my skin."

There was a knock at the door that surprised both women. It was harsh, quick, three solid raps of knuckles against wood, then silence. Clearly, it was not one of the servants, and another meeting between Anton, Caleb, and Anastasia wasn't scheduled until after the evening meal.

"Yes?" Anastasia called out after some hesitation.

The door opened and Caleb stepped in, his animal grace and power never more apparent. He wore knee-breeches, shiny black boots, an ornate white frill shirt, and a shimmering blue-green jacket. His hair was combed back, parted on the side, and if Anastasia didn't know better, she'd think he looked like a wealthy, successful businessman instead of a man hired to do dangerous and secret work that could never be openly discussed in polite company.

"I have to speak with you," Caleb said. His eyes, dark and fathomless, darted from Anastasia to Natasha, then back again. "Privately."

For only a second Anastasia shot Caleb a look that said she did not at all appreciate the intrusion, or his abrupt manner. Then she bent toward Natasha and whispered, "You'd better leave. It's time I tell this American barbarian exactly what he can do with that attitude of his."

"You shouldn't be in a bedchamber alone with him," Natasha whispered. "It doesn't look right."

"Don't worry, I know how to handle his type."

Natasha nodded and left the room, though she did not like leaving her friend alone with Caleb. As she had felt so many times before whenever he was near, she sensed that Anastasia would need protection.

When she was alone with Caleb, Anastasia waited for him to say something about how she was dressed. She felt certain he would notice the new gown, especially since it was not yet late enough in the day to dress so formally. But he hardly glanced at her clothes, his eyes instead boring straight into her own, harsh and unflinching.

"I've come here to find out how long you intend to thwart me," Caleb declared, moving closer.

Anastasia smiled because Caleb had pronounced "thwart" incorrectly. In the days that they had spent together, she had changed her mind about his accent,

151

and now she found it appealing, and sometimes—like when he mispronounced a word—rather amusing.

"I don't know what you're talking about," Anastasia replied, though she knew full well that she had opposed Caleb at every opportunity, just as he had with her.

"I'm talking about letting your emotions get in the way of that brain of yours," Caleb said, moving very close now, glaring at the princess. "I'll admit that it took some time for me to accept that you're partners with your brother. I've never worked with a woman before. I admit to that, and I apologize for it. Now it's your turn to accept the fact that you've got to work with me whether you want to or not. I'm here, and I'm staying. Your brother counts on me; even your damned czar counts on me. So why are you fighting everything I try to propose?"

Anastasia had to resist the urge to step back to put a bit more distance between herself and the American. She couldn't let him think, even for a moment, that she was intimidated by him—even if she was.

"I oppose you because I don't like you," Anastasia said calmly, despite the suddenly riotous emotions racing through her. "I don't like you because you don't know your place."

Caleb issued a short, contemptuous laugh. "You don't like me because I don't know my place? What a joke! What a lie! You don't like me because I won't bow and bend to your wishes, and you know it! You don't like me because you only can feel superior with weak, fawning glassy-eyed boys surrounding you! With a real man—a man like me—you're trembling and frightened right down to your slippers, and that's why you insult me and refuse to give my ideas fair consideration!"

Each word he spoke struck home with Anastasia, though she did her best to deny it. She *was* trembling, just as he had said, but she refused to admit it, just as she refused to be intimidated by Caleb, which she suspected he also wanted.

"If you'll look very closely, my American friend, you'll see that I'm not wearing any slippers." She took a step backward and raised the hem of her gown, showing her feet sheathed in pale white stockings. "And I'm strongly inclined to doubt that there are any other men quite like you. You're unique . . . one of a kind, and for that I am endlessly thankful."

He smiled crookedly, and Anastasia cursed herself silently. She had meant for the statement to be an insult, but it hadn't come out that way at all. She let the hem fall around the floor again, her pale eyes locking with his ebony ones.

"I don't think you understand exactly what I mean," she said, and now there was no missing the faltering quality in her voice.

"That's where you're wrong. I understand *exactly* what you mean. You're the one having a difficult time understanding your own words." With two strong strides, Caleb closed the distance that separated them. "I understand you much better than you understand yourself!"

"You're arrogant!"

"You're right," Caleb said in a deep voice resonating with confidence. He took her by the upper arms, his fingers burying perhaps a bit more deeply into her smooth, tender flesh than necessary. "I am arrogant, but only because you bring it out in me."

Anastasia felt herself being slowly drawn to him, an inch at a time. His hands were tight around her biceps, and she wanted to protest, but she did not. After having lived her adolescent and adult life with men who were frightened of her intellect, her wealth, or her social position, there was something frightening and yet exciting about a man who had never bowed to anyone for any reason. Every day of her life, she had been looked after by servants, and someone always

153

knew where she was and what she was doing. Caleb had lived his life in secrecy, and it showed in his attitude toward life, and in the way he moved, thought, and behaved . . . and all of it was powerfully exciting to Anastasia.

Caleb bent low, so that his mouth was scant inches from Anastasia's, and she could anticipate his kiss. But he stopped before their lips met, and whispered, "Perhaps it's *you* who has to be put in her place."

Anastasia's body stiffened at the comment. Put in *her* place? No man had ever dared speak so demeaningly to her, and her eyes blazed with an inner fire of defiance.

"No man is so much of a man to be able to put me in my place," she whispered, just about to slap Caleb's hands from her arms.

She did not slap him because instead of backing away he pulled her even closer, his long arms looping swiftly around her. Then he kissed her hard, his mouth capturing hers, claiming hers. Anastasia squirmed, trying to get away, but Caleb held her fast, refusing to release her.

When Anastasia pushed hard against Caleb's chest, he released her. She stumbled several steps backward, wiping her mouth with the back of her hand as though to wipe off a kiss that had been unbearably foul. Rage and excitement battled for supremacy within the princess's heart as she glared at the handsome rogue who had dared behave so brazenly with her.

"You . . . you kissed me," Anastasia said in a breathy whisper.

Caleb placed his hands on his hips, pushing back his jacket, not realizing how the move made him look even leaner and more hungry.

Just looking at him, Anastasia wondered if he would devour her with his desire, and a little voice inside her head whispered that it wouldn't be altogether

154

bad if that should happen.

"Yes, I kissed you, but from what I've heard, I certainly haven't been the first," Caleb said after a moment.

He's heard the stories, and he thinks I'll just fall into bed with him.

For perhaps the very first time in her life, Anastasia regretted the stories of casual behavior that she had seeded and oft-harvested. She tried to tell herself that Caleb's opinion meant nothing to her, nothing at all . . . but if that was true, then why had she been disappointed when she hadn't seen pleasure or appreciation in his eyes when he looked at her in the attractive and daring new gown? Why had she allowed herself to be alone with Caleb in her own bedroom if his opinion meant nothing to her?

Very slowly at first, then with increasing conviction, Caleb shook his head. Then he turned toward the door, about to leave. "I've just got too many important things to do to concern myself about what bizarre things go on in your head."

As he started toward the bedchamber door, Anastasia's first emotion was one of relief. He was going to leave her, and very soon she would be free from his rogue behavior and all that dangerous charm that seemed to hover about him and seeped into her soul.

But following close at the heels of this emotion was a second one, infinitely more troubling and no less deniable. She didn't want him to leave.

For the first time since she'd burst in on Caleb when he had been in the bathing chamber, she was alone with him. She was alone with him, and she didn't want the time they spent together to end so soon, just as she didn't want that one harsh, demanding kiss she'd received to be the only one her lips would taste from Caleb Carter.

"Don't think you can get away that easily!" she whispered, angry with Caleb because he had made her want another of his kisses.

She rushed at him, furious with him for a thousand chaotic feelings that she had not wanted to ever be aware of, her small fists windmilling as she charged.

Twelve

Caleb spun on his heel to face her. There was a cruel smile on his face when he caught her fists before they came close to striking his face, and as she struggled, he folded her writhing body into his strong arms until no space separated them at all.

She tried to stomp on Caleb's foot, but he moved out of the way while retaining his tight hold on her. Anastasia was distinctly aware that she had forced Caleb to take her into his arms, and when she saw his face coming closer to her own, she closed her eyes in sweet anticipation.

His kiss made her spine melt. When their lips were pressed firmly together, Anastasia traced his lips with the tip of her tongue, then boldly explored his mouth. She had never wanted to kiss a man this way before, but Caleb was different in so many ways that she felt at that moment as though she'd never been kissed before. She wrapped her arms around his neck, holding him to her, arching her back so that her breasts could press against the hard-muscled surface of his chest.

He kissed her in a manner that was new, frightening, and erotic. His kisses were adamant, characteristic of the man, who lived at the edge of pleasure's chasm, taking sensation to its pinnacle, hinting at a feeling beyond pleasure but not treading into that as yet unwanted territory.

157

His hands moved down her back slowly, touching her through the sheer muslin gown, following the hollow at the small of her back, then the tautly rounded curve of her buttocks, forcing her body toward him so that she had no choice but to feel his arousal and be aware of the reaction she was igniting in him.

When the kiss finally ended, Caleb released Anastasia, pushing her to arm's length. His eyes were smoky with passion, his breath inhaling and exhaling deeply, rapidly as he looked down at her. It was clear that he had not really intended for this to happen, and that he was not pleased with his own lack of self-control.

"You'll be the death of me, princess," Caleb said harshly, his fingers once again burying into her tender shoulders. "You're my best friend's sister!"

Anastasia did not know what to say. She was even unsure of what it was she truly felt. Never before had she felt so emotionally adrift, so alone and insecure, so horribly uncertain. She had followed Caleb out into an emotional region that she did not understand, and she wished now that she'd never left that safe but false and boring land where men were frightened of her and thought falsely that she was a woman of loose morals who could not sleep with them only because of some dangerous lover living in Moscow.

Anastasia shivered, moving forward so she was once again in Caleb's arms. She had kissed many men before, but for all the kissing that she had done, she had only rarely allowed anyone to touch her body, and even then it was little more than a furtive squeeze of her breast.

The touches then had been light, clumsy, unsure, eliciting little reaction from her mind, and none from her body. Caleb's touches were firm, masculine, supremely confident. His strong hands not only touched her body, they touched her mind as well, and forced her body to respond favorably to the stimulus, as a flower opening to the sun.

She kissed his cheek, then his throat, inhaling deeply, enjoying the fresh, clean, earthy scent of the American man who frightened and excited her so. The silk cravat about his throat was smooth against Anastasia's cheek, but she hated the sartorial accessory because it kept her from kissing further on Caleb's neck. Baring her teeth, she bit him on the neck, drawing a flinch and gasp of surprise from him.

Caleb took Anastasia by the shoulders and pushed her backward again, his eyes blazing, his heart racing. He had not been able to get her out of his mind since the first time he had held her in his arms, and though she had seen him without any clothes on, he had not seen the sweet symmetry of her body, and the images his mind had created had haunted him every day he'd been in the castle.

"You're Anton's sister," Caleb said, his voice a gruff, angry whisper.

Of all the women who had shared his bed, he'd never seduced any friend's sister . . . but then, he was a man who had only one friend. His loyalties were few, but deeply felt.

Anastasia ran her hands over Caleb's forearms, touching him through the fine fabric of his jacket. She wanted to kiss him, to feel his strong arms surrounding her, his powerful, caressing hands touching her in places she'd never let any man touch before. She was aware that her passions had been aroused by Caleb, and that this was something that had never happened before to her.

For all her experience with kissing men in the darkened hallways during debutante balls and royal functions, Anastasia had never felt the pleasure that the more promiscuous young women giggled about. Now that she had discovered she could, in fact, feel pleasure in a man's arms—at least in Caleb Carter's arms—she did not want that pleasure to end, certainly not because she happened to be someone's sister.

"I am Princess Anastasia Talakovich," she said slowly, enunciating her words carefully and with greater confidence than she felt. "I am Anton's sister, yes . . . but I am my own woman!"

Caleb watched his hands as though they belonged to someone else. They moved from Anastasia's shoulders toward her throat, to the slender gatherings of cloth that constituted the shoulder straps of her new gown. He curled his fingers into the cloth and pulled apart slowly, opening the deeply plunging neckline even more, pushing the cloth over Anastasia's shoulders, hesitating only a moment, then further down her arms.

The high, firm mounds of Anastasia's breasts were at last revealed to him, the areolas soft pink, capped by erect nipples. A deep, rumbling groan of ecstasy worked its way from Caleb's throat as he looked first at the princess's naked breasts, then into her shimmering eyes of sky blue.

"I am . . ." Caleb said, then stopped, unable to make his throat form the words that he suddenly felt needed to be said.

He hadn't completely reconciled in his own mind the fact that the woman who fascinated him also happened to be his best friend's sister. Whether this constituted some hideous act of disloyalty — whether he was being a traitor to the only man in the world he considered a friend — he had yet to make up his mind.

"What are you, Caleb?" Anastasia asked, and with the question she hoped to receive a thousand answers, though she doubted she would receive even one.

"I am a commoner, an American . . . and you are a princess."

Anastasia found it difficult to look into Caleb's eyes. He was looking at her breasts now and then, and she felt exposed and vulnerable. She wished that she had large breasts, like Natasha, and then perhaps she

160

would not feel, as she did now, horrendously unsure of whether Caleb found great pleasure in looking at her or not.

"You are an American, but nobody would ever dream of thinking of you as a commoner," Anastasia said quietly, honestly, letting her heart speak words to Caleb that her better judgment thought should remain unvoiced. She fought against the urge to cross her arms over her breasts to cover herself. "There is nothing about you that's at all common."

She took her hands from his arms, then stepped further backward so that he could see all of her. Her heart was racing in her chest, her hands trembling, but Anastasia was determined that she would not let her own lack of courage prevent her from experiencing the mysteries that Caleb seemed to have the answers to.

"Do you like what you see?" Anastasia asked, easing her arms out of the gown.

The gown, now freed, slithered down her body, catching at the faint curve of her hips. Part of her wanted to push the gown off completely, to reveal herself to Caleb with as complete a detail as he had been revealed to her, but her hesitant courage would not allow her to act that brazenly.

She took a faltering step toward Caleb, and the gown slipped a little lower on her hips. She grabbed for it quickly. The sudden, hurried move completely destroyed the image of confidence and sensual ease that Anastasia had hoped for, and now, feeling exposed, vulnerable, and no longer in the least bit sexually adventurous, she wanted to run from her bedchamber and hide, or chase Caleb from it and never see him again.

She crossed her arms over her breasts, tilting her facedown so that she would not have to look at Caleb.

If he had not seen it with his own eyes, he never would have believed it. Princess Anastasia Talakovich, as absolutely everyone knew, was a woman of considerable experience with men, and with the activities that take place in bedchambers.

But all Caleb had to do was look into her eyes to know that such was not the case. The *rumors* might say that she was the cool, cunning seductress, flitting about from man to man and bedchamber to bedchamber, seeking pleasure wherever it was to be found. But no woman was actress enough to be as suddenly shy, modest, and frightened by what it was she had started. Anastasia's sudden loss of courage was not an act to heighten the passions of the man she was with, it was the genuine emotion that she felt, and because it was — because she was not the sexual adventurer Caleb and everyone else thought she was — Caleb's desire for her intensified tenfold.

"Come to me," Caleb said, his voice soft, his tone powerfully commanding.

"I can't. I'm sorry. I shouldn't have ever . . ."

Anastasia started to work her arms back into the straps of her gown. It wasn't too late, she told herself, to prevent this minor mistake from becoming an even larger mistake. As she tried to get her gown back into proper position, she found it impossible to both keep herself properly concealed and yet work her arms back into her gown.

"Don't do that," Caleb said, his voice a low growl, like that of a threatening wolf.

Anastasia froze. Her heart stopped beating, and her breath caught in her throat. She could not look up, and she could not make her arms move the way they needed to if she was to get her gown back into proper position. Her legs trembled, and she realized that Caleb's danger — the threat that she had been aware of from the very first moment she'd set eyes upon him — was that he took control of the world around him, and all the people in it.

She might be standing in the middle of her own

bedchamber, but she was in Caleb's world now, and he was the unquestioned ruler of it.

"Come to me, Anastasia," he said softly, reaching his hands out to her. "There's no need for you to be afraid. I understand."

How could you possibly understand? she thought a bit angrily. *I am not the woman you think I am! That promiscuous woman is my creation, my protection! I've never let any man look at me!*

In a deeper voice, one that suggested perhaps he did not understand all that he claimed to, Caleb repeated, "Come to me, Princess Anastasia."

She looked up at last, shivering with the conflicting emotions that waged battle within her soul.

"I never have . . ." she began, then her words died out as the torn threads of her courage vanished altogether.

"I know you haven't," Caleb replied, his dark eyes fathomless. Anastasia could not tell if he was furious with her for having been tricked as to the type of woman she really was, or whether her innocence excited him. "But you will today . . . with me . . . because you must."

"I can't!"

"It is your destiny. Now come to me, princess."

"No!"

She saw his expression, that one of steel resolve that would not be altered or swayed by anything short of divine intervention, and Anastasia knew that Caleb was telling the whole, damning truth; it *was* her destiny to be with him. She had been waiting for a man like Caleb — strong, independent, defiant of life, and living only by the rules that he wrote for himself, determined to take what he wanted without either creating victims or being a villain.

Whether she'd known it or not, she had been waiting all of her adult life for Caleb to come by and take command, thoroughly and completely, so that for

163

once in her life she would not have to feel the burden of responsibility, so that she could simply *be* rather than having to *be in control.*

"Come to *me!*" Caleb commanded, louder than before.

She would not give in to him, and she did not want to. What she wanted, what secret fantasy she never before knew harbored within her soul, was to be possessed by Caleb, to be thoroughly and completely conquered by him.

She needed a man at least as strong as herself, and though she had never before found such qualities in any man—any man other than her older brother Anton—she was certain she had found it in the mysterious American mercenary whose background she knew nothing of at all.

She waited, unmoving, frightened of the desire she had inspired in Caleb, awed by the ethereal hunger for passion within her own soul. Very slowly, Anastasia tilted her head up to look squarely, defiantly into the American's coal black eyes, and as she met his fiery gaze, she let her hands fall to her sides to reveal her soft, pale breasts in all their petite perfection.

"No, Caleb, I *won't* come to you," Anastasia said softly, with more than just a hint of an imperious awareness of the differences in their social stations.

Caleb knew he was being challenged, and he knew that if he had any sense at all, he would turn on his heel and walk out of the princess's bedchamber, where he shouldn't be under any circumstances, and certainly not when she was naked from the waist up, and her small, exquisite breasts were there as a temptation that no man—at least no man whose blood was as hotly passionate as Caleb's—could resist.

Looking into Anastasia's eyes, he saw both the fear and the courage that battled within her, and he sensed that she was clinging desperately onto something—some idea or belief—and that alone was preventing her from following his command.

"If you want me, Caleb Carter," Anastasia said coolly, her tone blatantly sensual and challenging, "then you'll have to come to me."

He knew then what she was clinging to—her damned superiority—and her challenge was much more than Caleb could take. He was at last confronted by a woman at least as strong-willed as he was, and even as he rushed across the small space that separated him from Anastasia, he realized that he had lost the struggle. Anastasia had forced him to come to her, and it would do no good at all to pretend that he hadn't lost the battle of wills.

With his big right hand he caught Anastasia's gown and pulled down hard. Her gown rumpled in a heap about her ankles. Caleb hesitated only a moment to let his eyes feast upon her finely tapering legs sheathed in fine, sheer white stockings, and her shimmering creme-colored silk pantalets. Then he scooped her into his arms and carried her quickly across the room to her large bed with the enormously thick goose down mattress.

Anastasia wrapped her arms tightly around Caleb's neck. She felt overwhelmed by Caleb, and his forcefulness was rather intimidating, and perhaps she would have been more frightened of it if she hadn't intentionally sought such extreme, commanding behavior.

He nearly threw her onto the bed, his heavy body covering her own. Twisting upon her, Caleb forced his knee between Anastasia's, then quickly insinuated his hips between her thighs, pressing his clothed pelvis firmly against hers. One hand slipped beneath the princess to tightly squeeze her buttocks while his other hand wedged between their bodies to crush Anastasia's breast.

When he kissed her, Anastasia felt as though she was simultaneously all-powerful and completely helpless. Caleb's weight was completely upon her, pressing her into the mattress, but Anastasia did not at all mind the pressure. Just the opposite was true. His broad, lean chest covered her, and seemed also to protect her.

As he moved, his hips rocking intimately from side to side, she felt the long, hard line of his manhood throbbing, straining against her and the fabric of his breeches. She wanted to touch him there, to explore with her hands with careful detail so that she would know his body as well as he seemed to know hers, but she could not make herself be that bold, and even if she had wanted to, she highly doubted she could push Caleb off her to make such an exploration possible.

His hands seemed to touch her everywhere, alternately with strong caresses, at other times much more tenderly. He pinched her nipples, drawing a little cry of ecstasy from Anastasia, and a second one when he bit her on the neck. She clung to him, no longer really sure of what exactly was going on, happy and confident that Caleb knew what needed to be done, and would not stop until all the mysteries that had danced in the shadows of Anastasia's mind would be revealed in majestic splendor.

When he forced her arms from around his neck, then rose to a kneeling position on the bed, Anastasia was confused, and she reached for him, but he only batted her hands away impatiently. A moment later he pulled free the drawstring of Anastasia's pantalets, and jerked them sharply down her legs, taking her stockings down at the same time.

Without her pantalets, Anastasia felt suddenly very cool down low, and only then did she realize how moist and heated Caleb had made her. And when he placed his hand there, boldly touching her with a firm, circular caress, the tip of one finger slipping between tender folds of pink flesh, the princess trembled with rapidly escalating desire.

She reached for Caleb, and he stretched out beside her, only some of his weight pressing down upon her now, allowing his hands free access to explore Anastasia's porcelain-perfect body.

So enraptured was Anastasia that she did not hear the knock on her bedchamber door.

She didn't, but Caleb did. He pushed himself away from Anastasia, and the expression on his face told her that something was terribly wrong.

"Anastasia, are you in there?" Anton called from the hall. He rapped his knuckles impatiently against the thick oak door again. "Anastasia, are you in there?"

Her heart stopped beating.

Caleb bolted from the bed and made quick strides until he was behind her dressing curtain.

"J-just a moment," Anastasia called out in a quavering, cracking voice. She realized she'd need some excuse for not hearing her brother right away, and when she said, "I was sleeping," she knew it was a feeble lie.

Thirteen

It had been a week since Anastasia had come to Natasha, her face pale, her hands trembling slightly, and asked her to move into Castle Talakovich. At first Natasha had wanted to resist. She didn't like the thought of leaving Aislyn alone with Uncle Ivan, but looking into Anastasia's eyes, Natasha realized it was not just a frivolous request.

"What happened?" she asked. "Did that American say something, or do something? I *knew* I shouldn't have left you alone with him."

Though Anastasia repeatedly assured her that Caleb had done nothing to frighten her, Natasha was still skeptical. Eventually, when Anastasia stated that she needed Natasha's "good judgment" to lean upon, Natasha relented and agreed to the move, but only on the condition that she was allowed to use a horse every other day to travel back to her home to see how her aunt and uncle were faring in her absence.

Actually, she didn't care a whit how Aunt Aggie and Uncle Ivan were; though she was greatly concerned about Aislyn.

Natasha had just finished making her bed—a task she continued to do herself, even though Anastasia had assigned a maid to handle such chores—and had just sat down in her chair, the one near the east-facing window that she sat in so she could do her most intricate needlework first thing every morning by sunlight—when the butler handed her the envelope.

"This just arrived for you," he said in his expressionless tone, placing the envelope on the small table beside Natasha. "The messenger was a shoeless boy badly in need of a haircut, a bath, and lessons in manners."

Natasha glanced at the envelope and recognized instantly her uncle's scratchy, almost illegible script. Her throat constricted at the possibilities of what Ivan might want. However, Natasha did not want the butler to see her fear. The hired servants at Castle Talakovich had all taken notice of how quickly Natasha had become the princess's favorite, and though they never let Anastasia see their jealousy, they made no efforts to hide it from Natasha.

"Thank you," Natasha said nonchalantly, turning her attention back to the soft, flowing muslin gown she was trimming with aqua blue lace. She was careful to not let her eyes stray to the envelope.

It wasn't until the butler left and closed the door that Natasha tossed the gown aside and picked up the envelope. The outside was smudged with dirty fingerprints, making Natasha conclude that her uncle had bribed one of the numerous boys who lived near him to be the messenger. Though the boy's efforts would undoubtedly come cheap, it would still be money which Ivan would surely much rather spend on liquor. That wasn't a good omen, Natasha decided, pausing just one more second to summon all her courage before she ripped open the envelope.

Uncle Ivan had always considered a formal education a waste of time, and not a manly trait to acquire, so it was difficult for Natasha to figure out exactly what he meant with his horrendously misspelled words. This problem was exacerbated with Ivan's transparent attempt to disguise the real meaning of his words. He, apparently, was worried about the letter being intercepted and read.

Natasha had to scan it three times before she was absolutely convinced that she had not missed any of her uncle's veiled threats.

In so many words, Ivan had made it known that he had shown great patience in the past, but that his patience was running out. He reminded Natasha of her "agreement," with him, and of her "family duty." Uncle Ivan was looking for Natasha to see to it that he would not have much longer to wait before he saw "good results" for his "good actions." If he did not hear from Natasha soon, he would visit Castle Talakovich personally so that she could inform him on all the wonderful ways her life had changed. He assured Natasha that Aislyn was in good health, and he would make it his personal responsibility that she was happy both morning and night.

The thought of Uncle Ivan's grimy hands upon Aislyn's pregnant body chilled Natasha's blood, even as it flooded her with explosive rage.

Ivan was very nearly illiterate, but he was still able to frighten Natasha to the center of her soul. He had made it very clear that unless Natasha provided him very quickly with something of great value, he would force himself upon Aislyn . . . and what actions Ivan might take after that Natasha didn't want to contemplate.

She had to provide Ivan with something. But what? On three different occasions Natasha had looked at Anastasia's jewelry, and every time she did, she felt hideously guilty for even *thinking* about stealing one of the pieces. When she made a comment about what type of jewelry would look best with a particular gown, Anastasia rattled off the choices she had quickly, which made it abundantly clear to Natasha that though she owned many pieces of exquisite jewelry, she didn't have so many that she wasn't aware of precisely what she had.

Sitting in her chair with her morning tea growing cold on the table beside her, Natasha stared out the window at the workers out in the fields far beyond, and decided that she simply couldn't steal from Princess Anastasia. She couldn't because it was morally wrong, and because she was certain that her own rampant sense of guilt would get her caught even before she left the castle.

That meant that she had to figure some other way of satisfying Uncle Ivan's greedy demands.

Natasha took a sip of her tea and grimaced. It had gone cold. She looked out the window at the green, rolling countryside. She needed to go for a walk. That would clear her mind and allow her to look at her situation with new eyes.

She set her sewing aside. The truth of it was that Princess Anastasia had many gowns, and whether Natasha finished this particular one today or tomorrow really couldn't make that much difference.

She made her way down the hallway and to the stairs without being noticed. As her flat-heeled slippers tapped softly against the marble floor, she passed a shuffling old maid who barely paid her any attention at all. Only the most fleeting and unveiled contempt passed across the old woman's features to let Natasha know that her presence in the castle was not appreciated.

Natasha made her way outside where she could breathe fresh air, without giving the woman a second thought. In the time that she had been in the castle, Natasha had discovered that a small handful of the servants did the vast majority of the work, and the rest of the servants spent the bulk of their time complaining of their lot in life. She didn't care what the lazy old woman thought of her.

To the east was the stables, but Natasha didn't want to go there, even though she had always felt a kinship with horses. There were too many stable hands moving about, handling their daily chores, for Natasha to have any sense of privacy if she went there. To the west was the smokehouse, where men were making repairs from a fire the previous week that had gotten out of control.

At last, feeling a little frustrated, Natasha followed the castle wall westward, then turned north as soon as she could. There wasn't much of anything besides pasture and farmland in that direction, which would almost guarantee Natasha privacy.

It was as Natasha was passing beneath the library window that she heard the familiar though disquieting sound of the American's voice. Caleb Carter, in his mildly accented Russian, was saying something about an arrival, and Anton was questioning whether more guards should be employed.

Natasha flattened herself against the stone wall of the castle so that she could not be seen by anyone in the library. She had already determined that theft from either Anton or Anastasia was out of the question, but Natasha felt no great loyalty to the mysterious American with the eerie aura.

"The strongbox is coming by normal coach, and will arrive exactly one week from today," Caleb was saying from inside the library, his voice carrying through the large windows opened wide to let in the morning breeze. "I haven't put on any extra guards because I figured they would only draw attention to the carriage. There are enough spies in St. Petersburg without helping them."

Anastasia asked, "Are you sure that's wise?"

Natasha smiled, assuming that at any moment now her friend would begin shredding the spooky American.

"No. I'm not sure of anything," Caleb said.

His admission of ignorance surprised Natasha, and she wondered if she knew the American as well as she thought.

172

Anastasia asked, "Is it too late to send guards to escort the carriage?"

"It'll be here on time," Caleb said sharply, impatience showing in his tone.

Natasha had never heard anyone speak to Anastasia in that tone of voice before.

"If you're looking to follow the rules," Caleb continued, "you'll just have to keep looking. There are no rules for what we're doing. We just have to follow our instincts and hope they lead us to where we're supposed to go."

Natasha recognized Anton's deep chuckle, and she wished that she could be with him now. And for the hundredth time she wondered why Anton and Caleb were such close friends.

"If there were rules, you can bet Napoleon would have broken them all by now," Anton said.

"He doesn't trust us any more than we trust him. That's why we need what's in the strongbox as much as we do," Caleb added.

They said more, though since Natasha was listening from outside the room and hearing only some of what was said, and taking even that out of context, she couldn't understand what they were discussing. The longer she waited the more likely it was that someone would see her standing with her back to the castle wall, and finally Natasha moved on, walking swiftly with her head down in thought.

What was arriving by coach?

The question haunted Natasha. She knew it had to be something to do with the French emperor, Napoleon Bonaparte, and that despite the apparent friendly relationship between France and Russia, neither Caleb nor the Talakoviches trusted Napoleon.

With her thoughts in a whirl, Natasha walked on, wondering if Ivan would be satisfied with what she had to bring him, certain it wouldn't be enough for her greedy uncle.

At least it was something, she told herself. And until she could get Aislyn safely away from Uncle Ivan and into Castle Talakovich, she had no choice but to do things she found reprehensible.

A slow, building sense of dread came over Natasha. She was about to do something wrong, but she didn't see any other way of protecting Aislyn, or her unborn child.

"How has it been around here since I left?" Natasha asked Aislyn as they sat in the small bedroom they once shared. The room had never seemed large to Natasha, but compared to her current living conditions, it suddenly seemed smaller than a walk-in closet.

"The same as always," Aislyn replied, putting a brave smile on her soft lips. The smile didn't fool Natasha for a second.

For a moment Natasha deliberated on whether she should ask the next question. She waited only a moment before deciding that under no circumstances is ignorance bliss.

"Be honest now . . . how has my uncle been treating you?"

Aislyn's smile broadened, as though the effort to keep it there magnified it. It wasn't until the smile reached its full breadth that the strain of it began to show. Then it crumbled quickly, and unshed tears glistened in the brave young woman's eyes.

"He . . . he touched me here," Aislyn said in a weak, faltering voice. She crossed her arms over her breasts, as though to shield herself from an invisible, unspeakably foul touch. "He said I owed it to him, and that if he ever crawled into my bed, I needn't be too worried about it since I'm already with child."

Natasha didn't know what to say. She had been forced to suffer from her uncle's despicable behavior, but she never had to worry about a child. Being responsible only for herself had given her the confidence that if things ever got too bad, she could always leave and take her chances on her own. That was not an option afforded to Aislyn, who in the autumn would have a newborn baby to care for.

"Just be strong," Natasha said, painfully aware of how ridiculously inadequate her words were. "Very soon I'll get you out of here."

"You will?" Aislyn asked, desperate hope shining in her countenance.

"How would you like to live in the castle with me?"

"Castle Talakovich? But how? I can sew, but I'm no artisan with a needle and thread — not like you."

Natasha patted her friend reassuringly on the cheek and rose, realizing that if she was to maintain her friend's confidence, she couldn't allow too many questions . . . because she didn't really have too many answers.

"You let me worry about that," Natasha said. "I've got everything taken care of."

Actually, she had no idea of how she was going to convince Anastasia to allow Aislyn to move into the castle, though there didn't seem to be any good reason to let Aislyn know this.

Aislyn, of course, was filled with hope and questions. Natasha tried to fuel her friend's hope while deflecting her questions.

She stepped out of the bedroom and into the small home's main room, where Ivan and Aggie sat in their chairs near the single off-kilter table.

"Uncle Ivan, how have you been?" Natasha asked, her smile as false as the one Aislyn had sported earlier.

"Why do you want to know? You've never cared before."

Natasha pouted as though she'd hardly ever argued with her uncle. Then, with just the slightest nod of her head toward the door to silently indicate that she

175

wanted Ivan to follow her, she left the small house.

Ivan followed her quickly, and it wasn't difficult at all for Natasha to see the avarice shining in his eyes.

"What did you bring me?" Ivan wiped his palms on his shirt, then cupped them for Natasha to fill.

"I didn't bring you anything I can put in your hands," Natasha said. Ivan shot her a threatening look, and she responded with what she hoped was a placating smile. "I brought you information instead. Important information."

"What's it worth to me?"

Natasha explained slowly what she had heard, using what few theatrical skills she possessed to make the news she'd overheard seem worth thousands of rubles. Uncle Ivan eyed her suspiciously as she told her story. During the second telling, Natasha added fragments of made-up details that she hoped would add more mystery and perceived value to the story.

"What's in the strongbox?" Ivan asked, scratching a beard-stubbled chin with long and dirty fingernails.

"I don't know exactly, but it just has to be valuable, can't you see?"

"I can see more than you think," Ivan shot back, sharply offended at the slight to his intelligence. "I can see that you haven't brought me one solid thing I can sell! I can see into the future, too!"

She didn't want to ask, but she couldn't resist. "And what do you see in the future, Uncle Ivan?"

"I see Aislyn in bed all ready and naked, that's what I see," Ivan said, his words coming out fast with his anger, tumbling one over the next. He jabbed Natasha in the chest with his forefinger, striking her with such force she flinched. "And you'd better come back soon with something better for me than that, or I'll see you in bed stretched out naked for me, too!"

"Will you be needing anything else?" the old

woman asked without enthusiasm.

Natasha looked at the maid, then shook her head. The maid left Natasha's new second floor bedchamber without a backward glance. The household staff and servants in Castle Talakovich had already heard that Natasha had been moved to the second floor, where only Prince Anton, Princess Anastasia, and the revered old maid, Marta, had bedchambers. The rest of the staff lived on the first floor, and virtually all of them were contemptuous of the hard-working new seamstress who had somehow ingratiated herself to Prince Anton and Princess Anastasia when they themselves had not, despite long years of service.

Alone in her room, Natasha paused a moment to think both about her good fortune, and about Aislyn's continued jeopardy. It just didn't seem at all fair that only yesterday morning Aislyn had confessed that Ivan had put his hand on her breast, and this morning Natasha was moving into bedchambers very nearly as spacious as the entire house that she had moved out of.

Along the interior wall was a big fireplace, with ventilation that ran both up and down, so Natasha knew that in the rooms directly above and below hers there were also fireplaces. She had her own armoire for clothes, though she really had very little—most of her garments recent gifts from Princess Anastasia— and the scarcity was even more apparent when she hung up her four dresses, three chemises, and six petticoats in a closet designed for fifty times that amount of apparel.

Natasha was standing at the window, looking out at the workers within the castle walls, and the farmers working outside the gate, when she heard the scrape of a boot heel against the polished wood-slat floor. Natasha smiled without turning, recognizing the sound. On two previous occasions she had been startled by Prince Anton, since when he walked he seemed to make no noise. After that, he had promised to be "more noisy afoot," to warn her of his presence.

"Good morning," she said, absurdly pleased that the prince had fit it into his busy schedule to greet her in her new room.

"How do you like it? Will it suit your needs?"

She loved his voice, even if she didn't always like the things that Anton said. Even when he was making no effort at it, each word he spoke rang with confidence. Confidence . . . and a warm, sensual quality that touched Natasha's skin with the warmth of brushed flannel on a chilly autumn evening.

"It would be hard not to like this room," Natasha said, turning slowly to face Anton. She had thought he'd already entered her bedchamber, and she was surprised to see him leaning negligently against the door frame, waiting for an invitation to enter.

"May I enter?"

"Of course. You own the room."

Natasha hadn't meant the comment negatively, but she saw instantly from Anton's reaction that he'd taken offense.

"I also own the houses of the villagers who work in my fields, but I wouldn't presume to walk uninvited into their homes, either."

Natasha murmured an apology. The prince was a difficult man to understand, at one time forceful and domineering, and the next thoughtful and considerate.

"I haven't seen much of you lately," Natasha said, then instantly regretted it. So much time had passed since she had been in Anton's arms that she'd tried to pretend that the entire thing had only been a bizarre, vividly erotic dream.

"Work, I'm afraid. You can't see them, but there are a thousand little strings attached to me, and even as I speak, someone somewhere is pulling at a string, demanding my immediate attention."

He smiled, and Natasha felt as though one of those little strings was attached to her heart.

"You don't really look like a puppet, and if you want to know the truth, I really can't imagine anyone but yourself pulling your own strings."

Anton laughed softly, and Natasha tried to pretend that she didn't really want to throw herself into his arms.

"A nice view from this room," Anton said calmly, moving closer, his hands clasped nonchalantly behind his back. "You get the morning sun from this room. My room is just two down from here, and I've always loved taking my morning meal while looking out at the sun."

His bedchamber is just two rooms down from mine? she thought. She said, "I didn't think you were so sentimental."

The revelation could mean nothing at all. That's what Natasha told herself. Just the same, her heart clenched in alarm at the thought of a slumbering Prince Anton so near each night.

He moved closer, everything about him well orchestrated, from the immaculate part in his hair to the pristine cut of his stunning white silk shirt beneath the aquamarine jacket, all speaking silently of wealth, style, sophistication, and confidence.

"I've been wanting to talk to you," Anton said, his voice dropping just a little lower, taking on an intimate quality that had not been there earlier.

Natasha turned more so that she faced Anton directly. Her mouth quite suddenly felt dry, and she moistened her lips with the tip of her tongue, oblivious of the tempting portrait of innocent seduction that she presented to the prince, unaware of how thoroughly her every gesture captivated all his senses.

"What . . . what about?" Natasha said, breaking the brief silence that had developed between them.

"You *know* what about." He raised his eyebrows for

only a moment, and Natasha was amazed at how his cool gray eyes, which so often were completely expressionless as they darted here and there to take note of everything simultaneously, could shimmer with faint amusement. "We haven't really talked about what happened, and I didn't want you to think that I usually . . ."

His words died away, and Natasha just stood there looking up into his face, waiting for him to continue, telling herself that it really shouldn't matter what he said, but desperately wanting the prince to tell her that she was special, that she wasn't just another of his many sexual conquests.

Natasha closed her eyes for only a second and inhaled deeply. *Think about Aislyn,* she reminded herself.

She was just about to ask Anton whether Aislyn could move into the castle when he reached out to take a curling strand of hair near her temple and twirled it around the tip of his index finger.

"Natasha," he said softly, bending low.

It was just her name. She'd heard it said countless times before, and by many, many people. But when Prince Anton said her name, he uttered it like a one-word prayer, and the effect of it upon Natasha's better judgment was startling.

She closed her eyes, tilting her mouth up in offering, and when she felt Anton's lips, sweet and arousing, pressing against her own, she moaned and leaned into him, deepening the kiss.

She had expected the kiss to last longer than it did. Anton straightened suddenly, his gaze snapping around toward the doorway.

When Natasha followed the direction of his gaze, her heart sank and hot embarrassment darkened her cheeks. It was the old maid who hated her so much, standing at the doorway, looking at Natasha now as though she were nothing more than a professional woman, a prostitute, and that was why she had been given a large bedchamber on the second floor of the castle.

"Excuse me," the old woman said, pretending that the prince was not standing right beside Natasha. "I brought you the fresh linens that Princess Anastasia wanted you to have."

She set several towels down on the table beside the pitcher of water and the basin, then left the bedchamber. Never once during the time that she'd been there had she ever made eye contact with Prince Anton, but Natasha had no doubts that before the day was over all the household staff would know that she had been caught kissing Prince Anton.

"I'm sorry," Anton said, sliding his arm around Natasha's shoulders. "I didn't mean for that to happen. I should have closed the door."

Natasha shook her head. *No, you shouldn't have closed the door, you shouldn't have come in here at all*, she thought, though she only half-believed this.

"By tomorrow at this time, everyone in this castle is going to think I'm a—"

She wanted to say the word *whore*, but she could not. It didn't matter to her that Aunt Aggie thought nothing of sleeping with a man for financial gain, and it really didn't matter to her that the servants might think she was a woman who had slept her way to the plush second floor of the castle. What mattered to Natasha was that *she* didn't think of herself as a whore.

"They'll only think what I tell them to think," Anton said, taking Natasha by the shoulders and bending low so that he could look straight into her eyes. "And if that bitter, lazy old woman says one word about you, I'll have her thrown out of here before she can take a second breath."

"No, don't do that," Natasha replied quickly. "I don't want to be responsible for—"

"She's responsible for her own problems. I've been wanting to be rid of her for years. If she says one word about you, if she does anything at all to make you unhappy, I'll see to it that—"

"Don't!" Natasha snapped.

She placed the pads of her fingers against Anton's mouth, silencing his words. She did not want to know what he would do. She knew that he held extraordinary power in his hands, and that if he decided, he could turn a person's life into a nightmare existence. Natasha knew all these things about Prince Anton, but she didn't want to hear it from his own lips—not the lips that kissed her with such passion, and unlocked a secret part of herself that he had taught her existed.

"Can we go for a walk? Do you have time for that?" Natasha asked, not wanting to be separated from Anton, but knowing that it wasn't proper to be in her bedchamber alone with him.

"Of course." He smiled down at her, his palms sliding up and down slowly over her upper arms and shoulders, warming her to feelings that Natasha was hardly aware existed. "Where would you like to go?"

It seemed a bit too good to be true, especially after the crucifying looks Natasha had received from the old maid. "How much time do you have?" she asked suspiciously.

Anton grinned sheepishly and rolled his eyes with a long-suffering sigh. "At noon Caleb and I are meeting with a weapons . . . with a gentleman from Austria. But that's hours from now."

The truth of it was that spending three uninterrupted hours alone with Anton was more than Natasha had thought she could hope for.

"Tell me where you'd like to go, what you want to do."

I want to kiss you again, she thought. "I want to see your stables. I've always loved horses."

"You need only wish it, and it will be so!" Anton declared, taking Natasha by the arm and leading her out of the room, his long legs setting a pace so swift she nearly had to jog to keep up with him.

Fourteen

He was so beautiful, it nearly brought tears to Natasha's eyes.

"He's six weeks old today," Anton said, sounding every bit the proud father.

The colt was all legs and awkwardness and energy in the stall. He tried to feed from his mother, then stopped midway through to investigate Anton and Natasha, nuzzling both of them, snuffling their hands and their clothes before returning to his mother.

"My current pride and joy," Anton said, leaning against the stall. "I can trace his bloodline back five generations."

"That's important to you, isn't it? To be able to trace your lineage?"

Anton glanced at Natasha. "Are we talking horses here?"

"Horses, and people, too. You come from the aristocracy. You are, after all, *Prince* Talakovich."

Natasha watched as the young stallion nursed, and she felt a small emptiness inside. What would it be like to be a mother? To hold a small child in her arms, knowing that the child had come from her own womb? And what would it be like if the father of that child was dead, just as the father of Aislyn's child was dead, even before the child had been born.

"What's wrong? You looked sad suddenly," Anton said.

It bothered her occasionally that he was so perceptive. She wished that he wouldn't foist himself into her thoughts and troubles as easily as he did.

"It's nothing," she said finally "Just a stray thought that shouldn't have been in my head. Nothing to trouble yourself over."

The young foal finished nursing, then went back to see the guests, drawing chuckles of approval from Anton and Natasha. Natasha petted the colt's mane and neck and nose, which was velvet soft. She inhaled deeply, loving the smell of well-kept stables, of hay and horse and new life.

"You still haven't answered my question," Natasha said, not looking at Anton, but feeling his close scrutiny. "Is bloodline that important to you?"

"I'd be lying if I said it wasn't. From the time I was old enough to listen I've been told who and what I am, and what is expected of me. One does not have the name Talakovich without understanding all the Talakoviches that have come and gone before."

"Let's walk," Natasha said suddenly, trying hard to smile but not really managing one.

She was a commoner, a young woman born into the middle of Russian society, neither rich nor poor. It made Natasha feel almost nonexistent.

Anton had told her what she needed to know about himself, even if it wasn't what she wanted to hear. She saw no need in prolonging the subject, or continuing the conversation.

She started toward the doorway, but Anton caught her hand, turning her so that she faced him.

"What's wrong?" he asked, his eyes searching Natasha's face for an answer that held more than mere words.

"Nothing is wrong."

"You're not telling me the truth," Anton said

sternly. "You asked me something, and I told you the truth. The least I deserve is the same from you."

Natasha looked straight into Anton's eyes, willing herself to tell him the truth. But what was that truth? That he had touched something deep within her heart, but that she mustn't accept this, since she had always been taught that he was the devil incarnate, and was the oppressor to her family? That she had a friend that she was struggling to protect, and the only way she could protect that friend was by betraying her friendship with Anton's sister?

She wanted to tell Anton that she never knew who her grandparents were, much less her great-grandparents, and that she'd never really considered this truly significant in her life. But talking to Anton, she felt inferior somehow. He knew exactly where he came from. She did not, and though she could accept this, she doubted that Anton could.

She took a step backward so that she was out of Anton's reach and asked, "Are you keeping the colt for yourself, or is he going to be a gift?"

Anton eyed Natasha, accepting the change of subject without comment.

Everyone in St. Petersburg knew that Anton liked to give away colts to help smooth the way for profitable business ventures. A colt from the Talakovich stables was highly valued by men who appreciated high-quality horses.

"As a matter of fact, this little one has been promised to Czar Alexander. Apparently, Alexander's going to give him to the nephew of someone important in Oslo. It's all very complicated, but everyone will be happy in the end."

"Everyone except the colt, who gets taken away from his mother."

"You can't stay at your mother's side forever."

It all seemed so unfair to Natasha. She didn't believe that the colt, so young and innocent and curious about life, should be used as a pawn for the continuation of power, prestige, and wealth of men who already have more of all three of those things than they really needed. It bothered her, too, that Anton understood and helped further all the cabalistic traditions that were necessary for these rich and powerful men to retain and increase their wealth.

"Can we go back to the castle now? I've really got quite a bit of work to do, and your sister doesn't pay me to take walks with you."

"Are you angry with me?"

"No." She turned away from him. "I'm angry with myself."

"For what happened in the carriage?"

"No. Yes. I don't know."

Natasha sighed, letting her shoulders droop for a moment, oblivious to how the move made her breasts rise and fall appealingly within the bodice of the gown that Natasha had given her. Though the gown had been altered to fit Natasha's more voluptuous figure, the neckline was still in keeping with the style Anastasia favored, which was considerably more revealing than what Natasha preferred.

She said, "I'm angry with myself. Can't we just leave it at that?"

"I've never been one to leave well enough alone."

He closed the distance that separated them, but Natasha moved away. She did not want to be taken into his arms, and she did not want to taste his kisses. She'd done all that before, and though at the time she felt heavenly, she was left with regrets and remorse over what she'd done. The pleasure that being in Anton's arms gave her simply was not worth the price she had to pay for it later.

The twinkle in Anton's eyes, the mischievous glint that was so incongruously boyish in his usually stern countenance, let Natasha know that he was feeling playful. She did not want playfulness from him. Not now, anyway.

"Don't," she said, turning, walking backward with her hands in front of herself as though to ward off an attack, though she knew fully well that Anton would never hurt her. "What you're thinking of isn't the reason why we're here. In fact, that's the reason we're here instead of back in my bedchamber."

"You mustn't be afraid to be spontaneous. Life is sweetest when it's not . . . preordained."

Natasha took another step backward, then felt the top rung of the wood plank stall against her shoulders. She couldn't move away from Anton any further. When she glanced toward the doorway to the stables, she saw that it was closed. She was alone with Anton in this sectioned-off area of the stables.

If she ran for the door, she would be free from Anton's allure. If she simply told him sternly to leave her alone, she would not be tempted by the ecstasy that she knew all too well was possible the prince's kiss and touch would bring.

She could escape, but she did not want to. In a deep and honest place within herself, she realized that she might run from Anton's physical presence, but in reality, she would only be running from herself.

As Natasha looked into Anton's cool gray eyes, she decided that she had run from him, and from herself, long enough. Once before, in the early morning hours when she had been with Anton, she had let her instincts have free rein . . . and she would once again let destiny take its course.

She held her hands straight out in front of herself, with the fingers splayed. Anton placed his palms against hers, lacing his fingers together with hers almost as though in prayer. As he moved closer, he pulled her arms apart.

Natasha, in anticipation of his kiss, moistened her lips with her tongue. She had no idea at all of how she excited Anton with almost everything she did.

188

Her arms were wide apart when Anton's mouth came down to cover her own. Natasha shivered as Anton leaned into her, pressing her backward against the stables, forcing her full, round breasts to become compressed within the daring decolletage of her gown.

Her nipples felt tight, hard, erect; her breasts felt swollen, over-full. She squirmed, twisting her shoulders just slightly as she danced her tongue against Anton's, forcing her breasts to rub against his chest, heightening the dizzying tingles that came from her passion-hardened nipples.

They had denied themselves the passion that was so mutually felt for so long that the kiss, though not the first one they'd shared, took on a completely different meaning than any of the others.

She had kissed the prince before, and she was prepared for the slow, enticing flow of warmth and excitement to go through her as his lips and hands and spirit aroused her. Natasha was ready for that slow progression, not for the hurricane storm of sensation that gripped her with a fierceness that took her breath away. Her arousal was so rapid and so intense that it was like a madness in the blood that compelled her beyond any sense of reason.

For Anton, it was as if a fire suddenly raged within that would not be dampened. He felt Natasha's response to his kiss, felt how she thrust her tongue between his lips boldly, how she leaned into him to press her breasts against him, and the recognition of her passion multiplied his own many times.

He released her hands, reaching inward to cup her breasts, squeezing them tightly through her gown. He felt the hardness of her nipples, and the way she shivered when he rubbed his thumbs over them.

"Anton! Oh, Anton!" Natasha gasped, pushing her fingers into his dusty-colored hair, her mouth never quite leaving his as she spoke.

189

He lifted her into his arms, carrying her across the narrow walkway to where fresh, clean hay was mounded for the colt's mare. Anton set Natasha down gently on the crest of the hay, attempting to kiss her constantly throughout, and succeeding almost completely.

"This is madness . . . here," Anton muttered, his face buried in the smooth arch of Natasha's neck.

He kissed her throat, his tongue gliding delicately over her, tasting the sweetness of her. In the back of Anton's mind, he tried to remember the last time he had been with a woman as beautiful as Natasha, seeking the pleasures of the flesh in the stables. But even in his passion-addled state, Anton realized that he had never been so excited by a woman as he was by Natasha, and the last time he had forgone the comforts of a plush mattress beneath him, with servants waiting in the hall outside the bedchamber should replenishments of wine or caviar be needed, was when he was a teenager, and sex was new and mysterious.

He touched her knee, pushing it aside, feasting upon Natasha's mouth as he pulled up her gown. When at last he was able to press his hand between her thighs, he felt the heat and moisture of her excitement through her pantalets.

Relief and passion surged through him as he was given the irrefutable proof that she was as aroused as he was. She was excited as she seemed, not just pretending to be passionate because he was a wealthy prince, and she wanted access to some of that wealth.

He had imagined what it would be like to at last make love to Natasha, but none of the scenarios that had gone through his mind were at all like what was happening now. He had pictured candlelight and a fine Bordeaux wine with just enough body to it to relax the inhibitions without in any way dulling the senses. He had imagined a delicate meal of pheasant or duck, and an evening breeze that carried the scent of spring flowers on it. He had imagined a thousand times how their first lovemaking would be — silk sheets and the quiet giddiness of afterplay.

None of the scenarios involved the scratchy texture of hay beneath him, nor the earthy scene of horse stables.

If Anton was disappointed with the ambience, Natasha was oblivious to it. It did not matter to her that hay was spearing her skin through her thin muslin gown. The hay beneath her was not scratchy; rather, it was a feather-soft cushion enabling her to accept Anton's additional weight.

She clung tightly to Anton, her hands beneath his jacket, fingers pressing into the solid muscles of his back and shoulders, caressing him through his exquisite silk shirt. Her lower body was angled away, thighs apart, bestowing herself upon Prince Anton and the sweetly arousing, intimate caresses that pleased her so.

It was a blind fury of passion that could not be slowed, hindered, inhibited in any way. Natasha was aware of how wantonly she was behaving, and she did not care. Nothing mattered to her as she pulled at Anton's clothes, nothing but to leave the frustrations and turmoil of her life, and escape into Prince Anton's arms. She was weary of making decisions, tired of feeling responsible and carrying the burden for problems and troubles that were none of her own making.

"Take me, Anton!" she gasped as he pulled out of her grasp just long enough to draw her pantalets down her shapely legs. "Teach me! Take me there again!"

He opened his breeches just enough to free the engorged length of his masculinity. Natasha gasped when she saw him. He looked huge, intimidating. A shiver of apprehension worked its way rapidly up her spine, and she pushed away from Anton slightly.

"Don't be afraid," he said, leaning over her, kissing

her cheek and ear. "It will be beautiful."

But Natasha wasn't quite so sure anymore. The passion she had felt when he touched her down low, when he kissed her mouth or caressed her breasts—that was pleasure without fear. The sudden reality of having to cope with *his* excitement was a two-edged dagger, eliciting equal measures of passion and fear.

"Anton, I don't know if I can," she whispered, and the sincerity in her deep brown eyes touched Anton in a way that made him pause. "I've never . . . before . . . ever.

He smiled at her then, leaning over to kiss her lips quickly, lightly. "Don't be afraid," he whispered, sliding one arm around her shoulders, cradling her head in the crook of his elbow. "I would never hurt you. You must believe me."

Natasha closed her eyes and thought, *Don't be afraid! He's telling you the truth!*

And following close at the heels of this thought was another one. *He's a Talakovich, and he's seduced dozens of foolish virgins just like you! Haven't you heard all about the lives that he's destroyed?*

"You're thinking too much," Anton said, his voice now a sultry purr that touched her with as much seduction as his fingertips. "There's a time for thinking and a time for feeling. This is a time for feeling."

All Natasha's emotions were a chaotic, jumbled mess. She kissed Anton, feeling the tip of his tongue fluttering briefly, invitingly between her lips. She hesitated, then touched her tongue to his. It was a sign of acceptance, of capitulation to the passion that both of them felt.

Anton rolled onto Natasha, his slender hips moving between her parted thighs. He cradled her head upon his arm. He felt the heat of her naked thigh against his throbbing manhood which pulsed with the fire of his passion.

"Touch me," he whispered, his lips brushing against

Natasha's as he spoke the feverish words. "Guide me, Natasha. I need your help."

He had said exactly the words that would touch Natasha the deepest. The next move was hers, and she knew that if she refused Anton this last request, he would press the issue no further.

She reached between their bodies with a trembling hand, touching him first only with the tips of her fingers, as though afraid he would strike out at her. Then, with slowly increasing boldness and curiosity, she took him into her hand, curling her fingers around his thick, pulsing length, twisting her body at the same time so that the flaring crown of his passion touched the moist, inflamed entrance to her womanhood.

Natasha raised her knee, sliding it against Anton's hip. His face was so close to her own, his gray eyes wildly intense with the strain of his self-control.

"I'm not afraid," Natasha whispered, as much a declaration to herself as to Anton. "I'm not afraid . . . but be gentle with me."

"I will," Anton replied, pushing down into her, feeling her opening to him. "Always."

Fifteen

Natasha sat in her bedchamber, staring out the window. The sky had become overcast late in the day so that now, with sundown, not even a single star could be seen in the ebony sky.

She felt lonely. Lonely in a way that she never had before. She wanted to talk to Aislyn, to ask her friend how she had felt after having made love for the first time, and whether or not this emptiness she felt in her heart was common, or unique to just her.

Losing her virginity had not been without pain, though the pain was short-lived, and had quickly yielded to a vast pleasure. The sensation of Anton inside her, thrusting, charging, his great heart beating furiously near her own, his body propelling him in long, filling thrusts—it had all been much, much more than Natasha's romantic fantasies had imagined. Though she never reached that pinnacle of sensation that Anton had brought her to with his intimate kisses in the carriage, the lovemaking was supremely satisfying nevertheless.

But then, shortly after Anton shuddered and gave out that great heartcry of pleasure, driving into her as passion rushed through him, the sound of stable boys laughing outside could be heard. Though Anton assured Natasha that the boys had heard nothing of their lovemaking, and were no doubt laughing about something entirely unrelated to what he and she had just done, the sound of their adolescent laughter put an enormous damper upon Natasha's spirits.

She did not know what to say immediately after Anton had slipped out of her, ending the lovemaking. He wanted to "take her to the summit," once more, to bring her to a climax, but Natasha insisted against it. More than ever, she needed to think, to come to some understanding of what she had just done and experienced, and why she had done it.

What was the appropriate thing to do after making love frantically? Talk softly about it afterward? she mused. And how did one go about putting one's pantalets back on? Were compliments in order? To her from him, or the other way around? Natasha didn't have any of these answers, and the insecurities flurrying about in a mad chase were terrorizing her emotions.

Anton tried to assuage her fears. He held her hand and stroked her hair, and even made a few jokes while plucking errant strands of hay from her auburn hair. He told her that she was beautiful, and inquired whether she was sore. She was, in fact, uncomfortable, though she did not admit to this. It seemed that to make such an admission would diminish Anton's pleasure—he had, after all, made a solemn declaration that he would not hurt her.

They'd hardly stepped foot outside the stables, moving into the glare of the morning sunlight, when a young boy dressed as a house servant came rushing up to Anton, stating that the Princess Anastasia needed to see the prince immediately.

"I'm sorry, but I really must leave you," Anton had said, his eyes searching Natasha's face, trying to see into her heart. "Anastasia wouldn't have sent the boy to hunt me down unless it was important."

"I understand," Natasha said, though she really did not. "Heed your sister. I'll be fine."

But she wasn't fine. She felt abandoned. She felt cheated out of her time with Anton. She felt certain that if she had been able to have more time with the prince, he would have been able to allay her fears. He would have been able to convince her that she'd been a satisfying lover. Even if it wasn't true—and Natasha was absolutely certain that she wasn't a satisfying lover, reasoning that if she was, Anton would still be with her—she wanted to be told that she had given him great pleasure, and that the compelling emotions that had driven them inexorably into each other's arms had much more to do with what was in their hearts than the unsatisfied longings of their bodies.

Those were the words and emotions she longed to hear from Anton.

The knock on the door was soft, hesitant. For only a moment Natasha felt a burst of elation, believing that perhaps at last Anton had come to her, though this relief was short-lived. Anton *never* did anything so timidly as to knock like the proverbial church mouse.

Anastasia opened the door just enough to see out into the hallway. Standing there was the young man who had shattered Natasha's happiness by bringing the message summoning Anton earlier.

"I'm sorry to disturb you, miss," the young man said, standing nervously in the hall, shifting his weight from one foot to the other. "I hope you weren't sleeping."

Natasha's heart went out to the young man. She hoped that Anton hadn't taken his anger out on the boy, who she could see was very nervous.

"I wasn't sleeping. What is it?" she asked, forcing a small smile to her lips to ease the boy's nerves.

"Prince Talakovich gave me this to bring to you right away." The boy extended his hand, presenting Natasha with an envelope sealed with wax with the royal crest pressed into it.

"Thank you," Natasha said.

Leaning against the bedchamber door, she took a moment to look at the envelope. The last time she had received something like this, it was from her uncle, and it had contained a less-than-veiled threat. For a second Natasha thought of simply tossing the envelope in the fireplace. Good things did not come in packages like that.

Steeling herself, she broke the wax seal and pulled out the single sheet of paper.

Prince Anton's handwriting was tight, the letters crisply compressed, as though he had a lot to say and did not want to stretch anything out longer than was absolutely necessary. He kept his handwriting under as tight control as his emotions.

The letter read simply, "The honor of your presence is requested in the wine cellar at your earliest convenience. Respectfully, Prince Anton Talakovich."

Natasha's heart quickened momentarily before she tamped down emotions that she knew were best restrained, if not ignored. She'd let gentle emotions lead her astray in the past when Anton was added to the equation, and without exception she had regretted her lack of self-control.

First she'd let herself become swept away by Anton, and allowed whatever it was that had happened in the carriage to occur. Natasha still did not know quite exactly what it was that had happened in the carriage with Anton, except that she had felt sensations more intensely than she had ever before thought possible, which must surely be terribly wicked.

Then, after she'd convinced herself never to behave in such a way again, she'd abandoned her better judgment to Anton again—only this time losing her virginity as a result of her weakness, in a manner more befitting a trollop, with pantalets flung aside and gown raised for expediency's sake while laying on a mound of hay. That apocalyptic moment ended abruptly when Anton abandoned Natasha to rush off to his sister, no doubt needing to make some critical decision concerning something that would make the Talakoviches even wealthier than they already were.

Natasha was absolutely certain that there wasn't a rational soul in the world who could criticize her if she turned down the prince's request and simply stayed in her bedchamber, where she was alone, but gloriously safe from both Anton and her own weakness that mysteriously never really manifested itself unless the prince was nearby.

On the other hand, there wasn't a strong-willed woman in the world who wouldn't agree with Natasha's belief that she had to confront Prince Anton, and tell him that he simply should not treat women so cavalierly. Until some woman of great courage stood up to the prince and told him that he simply had no right to treat women that badly, then he'd never change.

With a moral sense of mission filling her, Natasha tossed the invitation upon the small table beside her, and rose quickly to her feet, quite determined to take the too handsome prince to task for his behavior.

Natasha walked swiftly out of her bedchamber, her legs scissoring as she moved down the hall, thinking it was long past due for Anton to hear a few things about himself that his wealth, power, and good looks had prevented him from hearing . . . and it would have been much easier for her to concentrate on this if she wasn't still a little sore down low from the last time she'd found herself face to face with the infuriating and enigmatic Prince Anton Talakovich.

Anton paced nervously the length of the wine cellar, his keen senses alert for the sound of approaching footsteps from the hallway.

He was nervous, and this little fact did not please

him in the least. After all, it wasn't exactly like this was the first time that he'd planned to meet a woman after making a too-hasty exit after their first lovemaking. However, it *was* the first time that the woman's continued good opinion of him truly—and astonishingly—meant something to him. As was his habit, he viewed the situation in financial terms and realized that he had made an emotional investment in Natasha, though he wasn't entirely comfortable in accepting this knowledge.

It hadn't been easy keeping what he was doing a secret. The old servant Yatzka helped Anton carry down the table and the two fine chairs to the wine cellar. When Yatzka offered to find other servants at the castle to help move the furniture, Anton instantly squashed the idea, and Yatzka was sage enough to avoid asking any further questions concerning the master of the castle's highly unusual behavior.

There was a perverse humor in what Anton was forced to do. Of all the women that had spent the night with Anton in the castle, he'd never once made any effort to hide anything from Anastasia. And though, on occasion, a comely servant girl might cast a flirtatious glance in Anton's direction, he'd never cast any glances in return, too well aware of his position of power to take advantage of it, too unwilling to go to the great effort necessary to hide the liaison from his sister. So here he was, a man of prodigious wealth and influence, known throughout the land as a remorseless rogue, hiding in the wine cellar, hoping the servants didn't become loose-tongued with Anastasia.

If any of the servants discovered him with Natasha, it would be unfortunate; if Anastasia caught the two of them together, it would be catastrophic. Anastasia could get absurdly protective, especially where the castle staff was concerned, and Anton really didn't want to justify all the hows and whys he found himself unable to stay away from a certain seamstress with a beauty mark just above the most kissable lips the world had ever known.

Anton's mind was on Natasha when, during a turn as he paced, he struck a slender, poorly balanced wine rack with his shoulder. The dusty wine bottles rattled dangerously, and Anton needed all his extraordinary reflexes to keep the rack from falling over.

And that was why Anton was in the less than dignified position of leaning against a dangerously teetering wine rack when a spirited and decidedly agitated Natasha Stantikoff entered and demanded to know, "Just who do you think you are to summon me like one of your stable boys?"

Natasha was three steps into the wine cellar when she first saw Anton looking for all the world like he was trying to hold a wall in place. A second after that she noticed the table with the exquisite white table cloth, the fine dinnerware, the gleaming silverware, the brightly polished candlesticks, and two things became instantly clear: none of this belonged in the wine cellar, and Anton had gone through considerable effort to be alone with her, and yet still be surrounded by — and offer her — the creature comforts that had always been a part of his life.

Anton was not a man easily taken aback, but he had never been muddle-headed about a woman before — certainly never so much so that he nearly knocked down a wine rack, coming obscenely close to destroying more than a dozen of the finest bottles of wine in the world. Added to this was the discombobulating reality of a young woman confronting him in full vitriolic dudgeon, and not in the least bit hesitant in venting it directly at Anton. All in all, it was no wonder the prince was struck speechless for several seconds.

Natasha turned away from Anton even before he'd released the wine rack, confident at last that it would stay in place, and not come crashing down upon the small round table he'd gone to such lengths to surreptitiously bring to the wine cellar.

"Flowers," she said in a voice barely more than a whisper. She leaned over the table to smell the three roses in the slender vase. "You brought me flowers."

Anton recovered his composure in an instant, his confidence bolstered by the response he'd received from the flowers. He felt almost guilty about Natasha's pleased response, since he'd picked them almost as an afterthought, never realizing the profound influence they would have upon the young woman's combative mood.

"Yes," Anton said, smoothing his blue velvet jacket into proper place. He moved beside Natasha, his eyes intent as he studied her, trying to judge her mood. "I brought flowers, and I've got a very nice wine chilling on ice, and very shortly there will be sauteed beef strips served. You did say you enjoyed beef, didn't you?"

Natasha nodded, still looking at the beautifully laid-out table with the centerpiece of three roses. She'd always thought herself to be too pragmatic to be taken in by dramatic gestures, but now she knew that wasn't the case at all. She *loved* Anton's dramatic gestures, like when he greeted her at her house with a carriage filled with fine food and wine; and now, hiding as they were in the wine cellar—

"Why are we here?" Natasha asked softly, voicing the question as it occurred to her. "Why hide down here? Aren't there twenty-some rooms in this castle?"

"Yes, twenty-some," Anton replied, his eyes narrowing just slightly as he looked at Natasha in profile. "We're down here, in the wine cellar, because I don't want Anastasia to know that we're . . ."

"Are you ashamed of me? Is that it?"

"No, it's not that at all. It's just that my situation with you is unique, and I don't want to explain it to

201

Anastasia at the moment. Not when she and I have so many other matters that absolutely must keep our attention."

"Is it embarrassing to have a common seamstress as a lover? I should think that being your lover is certainly no unique experience." Natasha's words were uttered with the calm detachment of a woman who was discussing someone she did not know at all, quite unlike a woman who was falling in love with a man rumored to have many lovers.

"You're anything but common, though the fact that you are my sister's seamstress is, in fact, the problem. It's the reason why we're down here in the wine cellar instead of having our meal upstairs in my bedchamber, which is where we really belong."

"That's where *you* belong," Natasha said calmly but quickly. "You're assuming that I'd have gone there to see you, which might be a bit presumptuous on your part."

Anton reached out to touch Natasha's soft auburn hair, and she let him caress her tresses momentarily before stepping out of reach. Sensing her mood, he motioned to the chairs.

"Please, can we sit, and I'll tell you everything?"

He held a chair out for Natasha, and she took it suspiciously, certain that she was making a mistake by letting Anton talk. Whenever he talked, she had a way of losing certain articles of clothing — like her pantalets, for example — and she had not come to the wine cellar to do anything other than tell Anton exactly what she thought of him, and of the way he treated women.

He poured the wine before taking his own chair. Beneath, the table, Anton's foot rested lightly against Natasha's, and though she moved her foot, he moved his so that they were once again touching. Natasha moved her foot again. Letting Anton touch her was another all-too-certain way of losing control over her better judgment.

Natasha looked at Anton as he adjusted the candle in the holder. He had gone to some effort to look especially handsome this evening, she noted. His hair was brushed so that not even the errant lock that curled at his forehead — always out of step with the rest of his hair — was allowed to mar the orchestrated look. His boots were polished to a mirror finish, making Natasha wonder which one of the castle staff had been given the chore of polishing them to such luster. Prince Anton always dressed fashionably, but Natasha suspected that the cut of his fine breeches, and the magnificent tailoring of his white shirt were just a little higher than even his usual high standards.

And she knew she'd be lying to herself if it didn't please her to realize that the prince had gone to some trouble to make himself look handsome to her.

She wished now that she had changed into something different as well, but she still wore the gown that she had worn when Anton had thrown her onto the hay and lifted her skirts and —

The thought sent a shudder through Natasha, making her close her eyes just briefly. When she opened them again, Anton was looking at her suspiciously.

"Are you cold?" he asked. She shook her head. "You're not feeling well?" Again she shook her head. "Try the wine. Perhaps that'll warm away the shivers."

Natasha sipped the wine, and as she had expected, it was magnificent, but she couldn't think long on the excellence of the wine because fresh memories of that morning were flooding through her.

Earlier, she had ordered a bath heated, but she hadn't taken it. When Natasha began removing her gown, she could smell the unmistakable scent of Anton upon her clothes . . . Anton, and lovemaking. She'd sat then and thought about her actions that morning, and before she knew it, she had forgotten all about the bath, and then the boy had arrived with the message that Anton wanted to see her in the wine cellar.

"Tell me what's wrong, and I'll make it right," Anton said, and there was the air of command in his voice that said he wasn't simply boasting.

Natasha smiled at him and sipped her wine. "You said that you were going to explain everything to me. To the extent that your life is a series of secrets, kept from me and everyone else who knows you, I'm inclined to be doubtful of your claim."

Anton half-smiled. "You're angry with me, and you've a right to be. I'm just hoping you'll understand that the events of this morning were not planned, and that I did not mean to leave you as abruptly as I did."

"But you would, even under the best of circumstances, have left me, wouldn't you?" Natasha raised an eyebrow, challenging Anton to refute her. When he did not, she shrugged and added, "I'm not the one to do the talking. Tell me this *everything*."

Anton leaned back in his chair, tilting it onto its back legs, looking at Natasha as though seeing her for the first time. She was different from all the other women he'd known. Hours earlier he had taken her virginity—the virginity that she offered, he told himself, though this seemed a minor point, and he still felt vaguely guilty about what he'd done—and now she was openly challenging him to defend himself.

In the past, he had told his sister that he was waiting for a woman who would stand up to him, a woman strong enough to stand straight upon her own two feet. Now that he was confronted with such an apparition, he wasn't so certain he was happy to have his wish fulfilled.

"The reason we're in the wine cellar is because you are currently paid by the Talakovich coffers. That gives me a considerable amount of influence over your life." Anton paused a moment, expecting Natasha to challenge him on the point. When she did·

not, he continued, speaking clearly, like he did when he had to explain difficult bargaining issues to Czar Alexander. "From the time that Anastasia and I were old enough to understand such things, we were told that we must never abuse the position that we were born into. The worst kind of abuse, I have always been told and which I believe to this day, is the kind of abuse that happens when fat, rich old men try to recover their youth with the young bodies of household servants who don't dare say no to the demands for sex for fear that they'll lose their livelihoods."

Natasha stared at Anton, wondering if she would be able to tell if he was telling her a lie, hoping that the words and the honesty that seemed to shine in his countenance were true.

Natasha asked in a whisper, "Then it's not just that I'm a commoner?"

Anton shook his head, then sighed, as though this whole subject were deeply troubling to him. "As I told you before, you're anything but common. If the situation was different . . . maybe if that madman in France wasn't preparing to march . . . maybe if the czar understood half the things about his own people that he thinks he does . . . maybe if . . ."

His words trailed off, and Natasha didn't try to make him continue. She believed him completely, and this was new for her. Usually, she believed *most* of what Anton said to her, but not all of it, always able to sense some avoidance, some omission in what he told her. This time it was different, and in a peculiar way, she felt closer to him now than ever—even when they had made love.

"What is Napoleon doing that worries you so?" Natasha asked. She'd never held much of an opinion on the French leader before, but now that Bonaparte seemed somehow responsible for hindering her own pursuit of happiness, she was quickly discovering that she detested the bold megalomaniac.

"It's nothing," Anton replied.

It was such a bald lie that he knew Natasha didn't believe him for a second. He smiled, looking into her eyes, silently asking her to accept his nonanswer.

For several seconds they looked at each other, each thinking that the conversation wasn't the "everything" that Anton had promised. Then there was a soft rattling sound and Anton smiled broadly, rising quickly from his chair.

He went to the far wall, pulling open a panel to reveal a silver tray laden with plates of food.

"How did that get there?" Natasha asked, rising to inspect what seemed to be a hole in the wall.

"There's a shaft that runs from the basement all the way to the top floor. This little box is connected to pulleys, which carry it up and down. That way, when Anastasia and I are entertaining guests, the butler can come down here, completely load this box with fifteen or twenty bottles of wine, then have someone upstairs lift it to the ballroom with the pulleys. It's faster, and there's never any risk of someone tripping and breaking irreplaceable wine. It's also awfully handy in the winter time, when we keep wood stored in the basement to keep it dry."

Anastasia was amazed at the contraption, but she didn't have much time to think about it because Anton was already ushering her back to her chair and serving up the scrumptious meal before she could ask many more questions.

"How is it?" Anton asked softly after the meal had progressed.

"Magnifique!" Natasha kissed her fingertips in the way that she had seen Anastasia do, speaking the single French word, hoping that she might seem more sophisticated than she felt.

Anton smiled indulgently, quite aware of what Natasha was attempting to do, thinking that she was much more impressive when she wasn't trying to be anything but what she was — a beautiful, talented, remarkable young woman who had emerged from an unremarkable background.

He watched her eat, taking delight in her hearty appetite, pleased that he had been able to make her happy. He made a promise to himself to make sure that the chef was suitably rewarded for his excellent work.

Natasha told herself that she really shouldn't top off her meal with the thick slice of cake topped with a sweet white frosting, but Anton was insistent that "you can never overdo the pleasures of the palate," so she relented, allowing him to serve her much more cake than she'd intended.

As she nibbled at the delicious dessert, she wondered whether there would ever come a time when she and Anton wouldn't have to hide the feelings they shared for each other, and wondered, too, whether their feelings were shared, or if she had allowed herself to fall in love with a known rake who did not share her feelings.

Natasha didn't want to think such disquieting thoughts. She was enjoying her time with Anton, and the troubles that Uncle Ivan and Aunt Aggie represented seemed worlds away. What would happen would happen. Right now, she was hiding away with Prince Anton Talakovich, and he was making efforts to ensure her every happiness. Anything Natasha wanted, she could have . . . and she wanted Anton.

Leaning back in his chair, tilting it dangerously upon two legs, Anton smiled at Natasha. "We seem to be doing everything backward. We make love in the morning, then have the seductive meal late that evening."

Natasha looked down at her plate. It embarrassed her to have him say such things, even if they were true. She had loved making love to Anton, but she didn't want to talk about it.

He came forward, the front legs of his chair striking the stone floor and echoing through the cellar. Reaching out across the table, he took Natasha's hands in his own, pushing the candlesticks and flowers aside with his forearms.

"I didn't plan for this morning to happen the way it did, but that doesn't mean that I hadn't dreamed about making love to you—no, *with* you. Since the first time I kissed you, the first time that I felt your body next to mine . . . I haven't been able to think of anything other than you."

Natasha met his gaze briefly, then looked down at his hands holding her own. Anton's eyes were much too intense, too fierce, for her to gaze into them long without feeling intimidated.

"I'm sorry it had to happen that way, but I'm not at all sorry it happened," Anton said quietly, giving Natasha's hands an occasional squeeze to heighten the impact of his words. "You should have felt cool silk sheets against your naked body, and known the pleasure of icy champagne after making love with me. It should have been a slow, tender, sweet time, and it wasn't. But I'll make that up to you, Natasha."

"You've said many things to me, and in a dozen different ways I believe that you're the most intelligent man I've ever met or am likely to meet. But this time you're wrong. For once, you're completely wrong."

Natasha turned her hands so that she could stroke her thumb against his. It was a small act, apparently nothing of great consequence, but she was taking charge, touching instead of just being touched, and it was important to her.

"You see, if we'd been in your bedchamber, I might not have gone through with it," she continued, finding it extremely difficult to talk about the one time she had made love, but persisting nevertheless. "I might have become frightened. I'm an impulsive woman. I never knew that about myself until I met you, but I realize that now. That's why I know that what happened—our making love in the stables—happened exactly the way it was destined to."

"But I didn't make you happy. Not *completely* happy."

Natasha smiled softly. Anton was thinking that because she had not achieved an orgasm, she hadn't enjoyed herself completely, but that certainly wasn't true. Actually, she had been able to feel Anton's passion, sense his excitement, much more clearly because she hadn't been completely concentrating on her own body and her own feelings.

"You're wrong again," she said, raising her gaze to meet Anton's. "You made me happier than you'll ever know."

And I want you to make me that happy again, right here. Right now, in the wine cellar!

Natasha wanted to put to words the erotic thought that had sprang into her head, but she could not. Simply talking about their lovemaking in the stables had taken as much courage as she had. Once again, she didn't need to say anything.

"Not now," Anton said.

Natasha blushed, part of her quite furious that he had once again been able to read her thoughts, and part of her happy that she hadn't needed to voice her desires to make them known.

"Why?" she asked, a niggling fear suggesting that she hadn't pleased him.

"Because I don't want it to be painful for you. Sometimes, so soon after the first time, it can be painful."

She knew then that Anton had seen through her earlier lie, when she'd denied being sore. What she wanted to tell him was that it was a delicious discomfort, and that throughout the day, when she felt that tiny pinch of discomfort, it had been a reminder to her of what she had done, and of the feeling of oneness she'd felt with Anton.

"But there will come a time, my dear Natasha, when you will hear a soft knock upon your door."

"Late at night?"

He nodded, his eyes twinkling mischievously. Natasha wanted to take him into her arms and kiss him. She wanted to do more than that, but there wasn't even the comfort of a mound of hay to be found in the wine cellar.

"And I will pleasure you slowly and thoroughly, and our time together will be everything that this morning was not."

Natasha tried to hide her smile. She mustn't smile with anticipation, she told herself. It wouldn't appear ladylike.

She didn't give a damn about being ladylike.

"When?" she asked, looking him straight in the eyes, and saying without words that if he wanted her then and there, right on the cold stone floor, she wouldn't resist.

Sixteen

It was several days later that Marlena said, "You must be the seamstress that we've all heard so much about," her voice treacly with malice and condescension.

"That depends," Natasha replied, not in the least bit put off by Marlena's implied threat. She'd already been told by Anastasia that she and Marlena were certainly not good friends, and that Marlena had a decidedly savage side to her personality.

"On what?" Marlena asked.

"On whom you're getting your information from. You'll find there are quite a number of people around with nothing at all in their heads who insist on talking all the time." Natasha looked into Marlena's eyes, challenging her to try another insult.

For several seconds, no one in the group of four women said anything, then Princess Anastasia moved forward, instantly judged the situation to be a tense one, and immediately turned the attention to herself, defusing the explosive tempers as well as barely hidden smirks.

Natasha moved away from the women, heading toward the long table filled with sliced meats, fruits, caviar, and countless other delicacies.

This was the first formal function that Natasha had attended at Castle Talakovich, though she had "socialized" with guests at the castle several times before. Almost without exception, Natasha decided she did not like the women that Anastasia called friends, though the princess didn't harbor much affection for her peers, and made only scant efforts to hide that fact.

From a corner of the ballroom, Natasha watched as Marlena swayed over to where Anton was standing with a small group of men, all of them older than himself, not one of them anywhere near as dashing or desirable as the prince. Even from the considerable distance that separated them, Natasha could sense Marlena's hunger for Anton. There were little signs, nothing terribly overt yet all of them unmistakable, letting Natasha know that she wanted Anton.

The other men, after giving Marlena a good long look, moved away politely. Natasha sensed Anton's power and realized that these men did not want to be an obstacle to Anton. It made her wonder if everyone in all of St. Petersburg bowed to the Talakovich charm and power.

He won't fall for a shallow witch like that, Natasha thought, then scolded herself for her cattiness.

She watched as Marlena touched Anton's hand, smiling up at him appreciatively, laughing softly when the prince said something. And Natasha watched as Anton smiled in return, and though he did not touch Marlena, his eyes did stray down to the plunging decolletage—the decolletage being considerably more revealing than anything Natasha preferred for herself—and suddenly she wasn't as confident as she I had been.

If she touches him again, I'm breaking all her fingers.

Marlena did touch Anton again, just seconds later, and she let her fingers linger on Anton's chest much longer than she had any need to. Natasha did not rush across the ballroom and break the woman's fingers, though there wasn't anything in the world at that moment that would have given her more pleasure.

Anton laughed, smiling down at Marlena, that absurd dimple in his cheek dancing merrily, and so easily visible to Natasha's affronted eye, even from across the room.

He's going to sleep with her, Natasha thought. *She's young and beautiful and she's no doubt considerably experienced in sex and she knows how to please Anton in ways that I don't . . . and I can't watch any more of this. I can't stop him from sleeping with other women, but I don't have to watch him being seduced.*

She stepped through the rear doors of the ballroom, into the cool night air of the courtyard, breathing in deeply in hopes of melting the avalanche of fears that had suddenly buried her, trying very hard not to think of all the magnificent moments of stolen, frantic passion she had shared with Anton in the past week.

Back in the ballroom, Anton was amused with Marlena's aggressive persistence. It had been more than two years since he'd spent one foolish and vastly unsatisfying weekend in her bed. He hadn't been to her apartment in St. Petersburg she kept for just such activities since then, and he'd left her with a bauble as a memento of their time together.

Periodically, Marlena let Anton know that should he be so inclined, she would gladly spend another weekend with him. Anton was not tempted. He found her vain and selfish out of bed, and even more so in bed.

"You're looking lovely as ever," Anton said, smiling at Marlena.

Out of the corner of his eye he noticed Natasha leaving the ballroom, and he felt it was an absolute travesty that his social position forced him to waste his time and breath on Marlena because she came from one of the wealthiest and well-connected families in St. Petersburg, when what he really wanted to do was lock himself away in his bedchamber with a low-born woman named Natasha Stantikoff.

"I'll thank you for the compliment," Marlena said, her gaze undressing Anton, her demeanor indicating she didn't care who knew it. "But we both know you haven't done much looking lately." Her expression took on a playful sternness. "At least not at me."

"Not at anyone, I'm afraid. Alas, duty calls. I don't have time to do anything but work and sleep. The only woman I've looked at in ages is my own sister, embarrassing as it is to admit that."

"I'd ask her about that, too, only I know that the two of you conspire together to keep your indiscretions . . . discreet."

Anton chuckled softly, pretending he hadn't caught the edge of raw malice that lay just beneath the surface of Marlena's words. Surely she had to know how annoyed Anton became whenever anyone brought up his sister's much-rumored, though unfounded, "indiscretions."

"Well, my dear, as we all know, you mustn't believe everything you hear," Anton said, wondering how on earth he'd ever managed to find anything appealing about Marlena.

She started to say something more, but Anton slipped from her grasp, murmuring something about seeing what it was his sister needed.

Out in the courtyard, Natasha was surprised to find Caleb sitting by himself in the dark. Only the glowing red ember of his cigarette signaled his presence, and when she looked at his shadow-shrouded figure, she got the distinct impression that he had intentionally puffed especially hard on his cigarette just so that she would notice him. His movements, like those of Anton's, were as quiet as a stalking cat's.

"Good evening," Natasha said, moving in his direction.

214

"You don't care for crowds either, I see."

Natasha moved closer before answering. She wished that she could see Caleb's eyes, but his face was swathed in a mask of shadows. Seated on a small bench, he appeared completely at ease seated alone in the dark, a nocturnal predator in spirit, if not in form.

Caleb was sitting on one side of the small bench instead of directly in the middle, making Natasha wonder whether he had been expecting her, and whether she should sit down beside him. She did not want to get too close to Caleb, though logic told her he presented no deep threat to her.

"It's unfortunate that you don't like me," Caleb said, speaking slowly and clearly, loud enough so that Natasha could hear him, but not so loud that his voice would carry into the ballroom.

"I never said I didn't like you. I've hardly said anything to you at all." Natasha was surprised with Caleb's bluntness.

"Which says quite a bit in itself," Caleb replied. "You've had an interesting influence on Anton."

"Anton? What has he said?" Natasha asked more quickly than she'd intended. She could imagine the two men talking about their sexual conquests, and she didn't want to have her name tossed about in such a scurrilous fashion.

"Very little. Like you, he often says the most when he says nothing at all."

Natasha's relief was palpable, and was quickly replaced by curiosity. What was Anton like when he wasn't with her? The prince seemed to have only one true friend, and that was the American, Caleb Carter. What was Anton like in the company of his friend?

"I guess I don't understand what you're hinting at," Natasha replied, trying to not sound as anxious for information as she really was.

"I'm not hinting at anything. But to answer the

215

question that is burning in your brain, Prince Anton has, most particularly since your arrival at the castle, been quite uncharacteristically absentminded. On several occasions I've found him thinking of something — or someone, though he'd never admit to anything when accused, you must understand — other than the problems at hand. For any man other than Anton, this wouldn't necessarily mean that much. But's he's not like most men. His powers of concentration are astonishing. It would take quite an extraordinary woman to play with his thoughts like that."

Natasha's evaluation of Caleb went up considerably then, though she knew she shouldn't alter what she thought about him just because he had said something that she enjoyed hearing. The truth of it was that Caleb hadn't changed a whit, and that she found him just as silently intimidating as she ever had.

"I hope that the complications don't overwhelm you," Caleb continued. "It can be difficult trying to fit in at Castle Talakovich, and even more difficult when your life becomes intertwined with Anton and Anastasia."

"You seem to have managed."

"But only because I don't waste my time in worrying about complications. My life *is* intertwined with both Anton and Princess Anastasia, but whether or not anyone else accepts that makes no difference to me."

Natasha looked quizzically at the seated man. Maybe her dislike for him was unfounded. Maybe it was just his position as foreigner, a permanent outsider, that she found so peculiar and threatening.

Slowly, Natasha's opinion of Caleb began to expand. She knew that Anastasia found him interesting. But *how* interesting? Anastasia was a woman pretending to be more experienced sexually than she really was; Caleb appeared to be a man pretending at nothing at all, who simply *was,* regardless if anyone found him intimidating or appealing.

"What about you?" Natasha asked. She moved slightly, hoping—but failing—to get a better view of Caleb.

She saw in the moonlight a slow flash of pearl white teeth. Caleb had smiled, but that was all he'd done. He hadn't answered her in the least.

"What's so amusing?" she asked.

"I believe Anton has come to see you."

Natasha turned to look at the ballroom doors. She saw that Anton was leaning against the wide doors, talking with Anastasia.

"No, he hasn't," Natasha said, turning back to the bench.

It was empty. Caleb was gone. He hadn't made a sound. A shiver of apprehension went through Natasha. She hoped that Anastasia had enough good sense to avoid becoming emotionally involved with the American. He might not be the unthinking, cold-blooded creature that she'd first thought he was, but he was still much too much—of exactly what, Natasha couldn't tell—for the pampered Princess Anastasia.

Several evenings later, Anton knocked softly on the upstairs bedchamber door. A moment later frightened eyes peered out through the crack.

"Good evening," Anton said, giving Aislyn what he hoped was a comforting smile. She seemed very frightened during the entire week that she had lived in Castle Talakovich. Anton hoped that living in the castle would calm her. He believed that nervous mothers gave birth to troubled children.

"Good evening, kind sir," Aislyn replied quietly. She opened the door just a little more, so that her entire face was visible to him.

Anton looked at her, thinking that she was trying to

summon courage to do what she felt she must. He could only guess at what trauma she had endured while living with Natasha's uncle.

"Would you like to come in?" Aislyn asked, taking a small step back into the room, opening the door more.

"No, it's your room and you deserve your privacy," Anton replied quickly, hoping to calm the woman's fears. "I just wanted to see if you had everything you need to be comfortable."

"Yes, good sir, I have everything—much more than I could hope for."

Anton hated the way Aislyn's eyes were so often cast down to the floor, and how her voice carried the hint of the defeated in it. He was hoping that in time her confidence would return, and that with it, her inner strength.

"If there's anything you need, either ask me, or if you'd feel more comfortable, ask Natasha."

The worst part of it, Anton thought later after the door had closed and Aislyn was again left alone in her bedchamber, was that she didn't seem to trust her own happiness. It was clear that she was joyous about no longer living with Natasha's relatives, but she couldn't take happiness in being free, for fear that something bad would soon happen, as though she did not really warrant something good happening to her.

Anton looked up and down the hallway, deliberating about which direction he should go. It was late, very nearly midnight, and he couldn't see any light coming from beneath any of the doors. Along this hall were Aislyn's and Marta's bedchambers. Further down, near the stairway, was his own bedchamber, along with Anastasia's and Natasha's.

Nobody knew he was awake. As ridiculous as it was, he still did not want anyone, especially not his sister, knowing that he was having an affair with Natasha. He still didn't want to try to justify his actions, and occasionally he wondered if this was because he really couldn't accept what he was doing. Was it so wrong to take pleasure in the arms of a woman under his employment?

He walked slowly down the west hall, telling himself that he was only taking a midnight stroll. The tension of trying to decide what to do about Napoleon's burgeoning military, and paging through the endless reams of documents from bankers both honest and corrupt throughout Europe, had left his powerful body feeling edgy and unused.

He reached the end of the hallway and turned north, moving with constantly accelerating steps, and when he saw the pale yellow light coming from beneath Natasha's bedchamber door, his smile stretched wide across his handsome face, and all pretense vanished.

He stood before the door, his fist just inches from the door, waiting, wondering, realizing that it was futile to assume that a man in his social position could ever have anything more than an affair with a woman from Natasha's position.

The sound of his knuckles upon the solid wood door let Anton know that the powers that compelled him forward were much greater than those which held him back.

"Yes? What is it?" Natasha called from inside.

"Nothing. Well, something, but nothing that I want to explain from the hallway." Anton leaned against the door jamb, his head against the cool, hard wood. "I've got to talk to you." An intimate whisper.

"Why?" Another intimate whisper, breathy and seductive, came from just on the other side of the door.

"Because I do. Isn't that reason enough?"

"Not for a man like you," she said, and it was clear that she knew exactly what kind of man he was, and she loved him for it. "Your motives are always hidden. Tell me what you want, or I won't open the door."

Anton smiled, and he checked up and down the hallway. This was not a conversation he wanted anyone else to hear.

"I want you. How's that for honesty?"

"How do I know you want me? Really want me?"

Anton grinned. Natasha had changed quite a bit since the first time they had made love, and he liked the change. She was allowing herself to be playful about making love. Before, each time they kissed, each time they made love, she went at it with the seriousness and concentration that suggested each and every moment was sacred.

"What can I do to prove my desire?" Anton asked.

He had several thoughts on the subject, though he wasn't feeling particularly inclined to follow through with any — at least not while standing out in the hallway, with his sister's bedchamber door only a short distance away.

The door opened just an inch. Natasha peered out, her expression one of thoughtful consideration, though the twinkle in her rich brown eyes suggested that she wasn't nearly as serious as she wanted to appear.

"I can think of a way you can prove your desire, Prince Anton," Natasha said, and the seductive purr in her voice had an even greater impact upon Anton's senses now that it was no longer being muffled through the door.

She opened the door just a little wider, and Anton was faintly disappointed to see that she had on a rather thick, concealing robe. Through the opening at the throat, he could see that she wore beneath it a nightgown, also of modest cut.

For a woman with the skill to create the latest fashions that were so flamboyant and daring that Princess Anastasia considered her invaluable, she wasn't a daring dresser in her own right, Anton thought, silently promising himself that with time he would get Natasha to change.

"Are you going to let me in?" Anton asked. Natasha's hair was down, falling around her shoulders in loose waves of shimmering auburn. He decided that she really must leave her hair unbound — at least in private, when she was alone with him.

"I was working," Natasha replied. She cast her eyes down for just a moment, the demure working girl speaking with her employer. It was all a ruse, an act, and it played havoc upon Anton's senses.

"It's nearly midnight. You shouldn't be working at this hour."

"What *should* I be doing?" She looked him straight in the eyes, challenging him to speak the sensual words, hungry to hear them.

"Let me in and I'll show you."

"If I must," Natasha replied with a weary sigh of resignation that was all pathos and long-suffering, with only the slight curl at the edge of her mouth and the light in her eyes to suggest that Anton's midnight arrival to her bedchamber was a dream come true.

Anton slipped soundlessly into the room. Natasha quickly turned her back on him, her nimble step allowing her to just slip away from Anton's reaching hand. She went quickly to the chair that she had been sitting in, her work on the floor beside the chair, a lamp burning upon the small table nearby.

"Natasha . . ." Anton said softly, amused and yet disappointed when she returned in a flash to her chair, picking up the garment that she had been working on. He hadn't come to her bedchamber at midnight to *talk* with her, or to simply sit idly by while she worked. "It's much too late for work. I'm sure my sister will understand if whatever you're working on isn't finished by morning."

"It's not for Princess Anastasia, it's for me." She turned her gaze briefly up to him. "I only work on my

221

own clothes late at night, after I've finished whatever I had planned to do for your sister during the day."

Anton remained standing, looking down at Natasha, thinking that this little game of coyness, of tease and run, had gone on quite long enough now, thank you, and wouldn't everyone be much happier if the nice, big, comfortable bed were now in use?

Natasha held the garment out in front of herself, showing it to Anton. It was a chemise, made of ivory fabric that shimmered, reflecting the lamplight. She was almost finished embroidering small flowers into the trim along the bottom hem.

All she had to do was take a look at Anton's face as he studied the garment to know that he was wondering what she would look like with it on.

"You look like you've a question in mind, one that you're not voicing," Natasha said, leaning back slightly in the rocker. She crossed her legs at the knee, and her thick robe parted, drawing Anton's attention. She made no effort to readjust the robe.

"I thought I was the one who could read other people's thoughts."

Natasha allowed herself a positively wicked grin. "You've taught me a few things since I've known you."

"Just a few things?" Anton asked, arching a brow above a cool gray eye.

It was all so absurd to be sitting and talking when they should be on the bed hugging and kissing, Anton told himself. But what was also true was that he *liked* this change in Natasha, even if it was currently driving him slowly and quite completely out of his mind. It shouldn't be necessary for him to seek compliments from Natasha concerning his sexual prowess, either, but he wanted to hear them from her lips just the same.

"Yes, only a few," Natasha teased, and the light in her eyes became devilish when she saw the disappointment on Anton's face. "But they were truly invaluable lessons, each and every one. I really don't know how I shall ever repay you."

Anton bit his tongue. The notion of payment was a touchy one for him since he was, at least technically, Natasha's employer, which was the reason he shouldn't be in her bedchamber at any time, and certainly not at midnight.

Natasha resumed her sewing, pretending that she couldn't sense the intensity of Anton's gaze upon her, or feel him removing her clothing hurriedly with his eyes.

"Now what is that question that has been at the tip of your tongue, Prince Talakovich? The one you haven't spoken?"

Anton moistened his lips and tried to clear his throat. This casual flirtation from Natasha was affecting him with much greater intensity than he'd thought possible. He looked at her knees, covered by an inexpensive cotton nightgown that had clearly been washed many, many times, and thought that Natasha's body, her flawless velvet skin, deserved to be touched by nothing less than by the finest fabrics money could buy—and he was just the man to make sure she got them, too!

"Well?" she asked, intent on the chemise.

"I'd like to see what you look like in that chemise," Anton said, and the tightness in his throat was only slightly apparent in his tone. "That's the question that I hadn't asked."

Natasha rose slowly from the rocker. "Very well then, Prince Anton, if that is what you desire . . ."

She started toward the dressing screen in the corner of the room, then stopped and turned to face Anton once again. "I assume you're thinking of purchasing a chemise for a friend. That Marlena woman I met at the ball, perhaps?"

Caught off guard, Anton didn't quite know what to say. He hadn't really thought that Natasha had seen

Marlena's open flirtation with him. Now he realized that Natasha was much more perceptive than he had previously given her credit for—and far more jealous.

"No," Anton said finally. "Actually, she hadn't crossed my mind. I was thinking of someone endlessly more . . . fascinating."

And someone who, though I've made love to her several times, I have never had all to myself, without time constraints, without wondering if we would be discovered at any moment, with the comfort of a bed beneath us, with . . .

Natasha spent several seconds just looking at Anton, weighing the veracity of his last statement, trying to discern his thoughts. The notion of any woman putting her hands on him made her grit her teeth in rage, which surprised her, since she'd never before thought herself a jealous woman—though she'd only recently met Prince Anton. That, she decided, explained much.

She went behind the dressing screen, and as she loosened the sash belt of her robe, she discovered that her hands were trembling just slightly. She smiled. She was just as excited now by Anton as she had been the first time he had made love to her. And at last, they had time to be together. He had come to her bedchamber, and their loving would not have to take place frantically in the linen room, with only a minimum amount of clothing removed (as they had made love the previous afternoon, between argumentative work sessions with Caleb and Anastasia), or upon scratchy, dusty hay, which had the most disquieting propensity for getting in exactly the wrong place at exactly the right time.

On the other side of the dressing screen, Natasha could hear Anton rocking in her chair. She could also hear him drumming his fingers against the arms of the chair. She knew that she could not hold him back much longer, just as she could not hold *herself* back

4 FREE BOOKS

TO GET YOUR 4 FREE BOOKS WORTH $18.00 — MAIL IN THE FREE BOOK CERTIFICATE T O D A Y

Fill in the Free Book Certificate below, and we'll send your FREE BOOKS to you as soon as we receive it.

If the certificate is missing below, write to: Zebra Home Subscription Service, Inc., P.O. Box 5214, 120 Brighton Road, Clifton, New Jersey 07015-5214.

FREE BOOK CERTIFICATE

4 FREE BOOKS

ZEBRA HOME SUBSCRIPTION SERVICE, INC.

YES! Please start my subscription to Zebra Historical Romances and send me my first 4 books absolutely FREE. I understand that each month I may preview four new Zebra Historical Romances free for 10 days. If I'm not satisfied with them, I may return the four books within 10 days and owe nothing. Otherwise, I will pay the low preferred subscriber's price of just $3.75 each; a total of $15.00, *a savings of the publisher's price of $3.00.* I may return any shipment and I may cancel this subscription at any time. There is no obligation to buy any shipment and there are no shipping, handling or other hidden charges. Regardless of what I decide, the four free books are mine to keep.

NAME

ADDRESS _____ APT

CITY _____ STATE ____ ZIP

TELEPHONE ( )

SIGNATURE _____ (if under 18, parent or guardian must sign)

Terms, offer and prices subject to change without notice. Subscription subject to acceptance by Zebra Books. Zebra Books reserves the right to reject any order or cancel any subscription.   ZB0893

much longer, and though she did not have much experience in the sexual realm, Natasha knew that this evening would be one that she would remember for the rest of her life.

She dropped the robe to the floor, then pulled the old nightgown over her head and discarded that on the floor, too. She was almost embarrassed to be seen in the old bed clothes, and she was enormously relieved that she had nearly finished the chemise when Anton knocked.

Quickly, she put three stitches into a final small embroidered red rose, then bit the thread to break it. The chemise came down to the tops of her thighs, hiding the triangular patch of curling auburn hair, but only so long as she stood perfectly still, and the chemise was pulled as low as it could possibly go.

She inhaled deeply for just a moment, summoning her courage, wishing she'd had the time to do something special with her hair before she stepped out from behind the dressing screen to show herself to her lover.

"Are you coming out, or do I have to come over there and drag you out myself?"

Natasha laughed softly, loving Anton's impatience. "Don't be in such a hurry. All good things come to him who waits."

It hardly seemed like a time to quote the Scriptures, but Natasha wasn't giving that a second thought as she stepped out from behind the dressing curtain, tingling from head to foot with excitement.

Seventeen

His breath caught in his throat, and he squeezed the arms of the rocking chair so tightly his knuckles turned white.

Could there be any doubt — any possible doubt at all — that Natasha Stantikoff was the most sensually alluring woman the world had ever known? Her luxurious auburn hair fell down the sides of her face, framing her loveliness, and her soft lips seemed to beg to be kissed. Her breasts, large and round, pressed against the chemise, filling it out and lending the garment erotic life. Through the light material, Anton could see the budlike tips of her breasts, and he wondered if they were erect from passionate excitement, or fear, or a combination of both. His eyes trailed slowly down her body, past the sweeping curve of her hips, to the bottom hem of the chemise. It hid her secret place — barely.

For an instant, Anton looked away. It was difficult for him to look away from Natasha, even for a few seconds. Her allure, her pull on his senses was such that it clouded his judgment and made all the other responsibilities in his life seem like insignificant distractions. He turned his heated gaze back to Natasha, feeling himself falling victim to her inexorable sensuality. His need of her was intoxicating, making everything else in his life superfluous, and Anton wondered whether his hunger to taste Natasha's charms was becoming an addiction.

Anton had known several men — wealthy men with time and money to be foolish — who allowed their weakness for thrills to become addictive, dominant, and ultimately, imprisoning. For them, the taste for vodka at first was enjoyed at the end of the day, only after the responsibilities of work and family had been satisfied. Then the need for vodka started at noon, and eventually, a small bottle in the bedside table was what the man reached for first thing in the morning upon waking, and the last thing at night before collapsing into bed in a drunken stupor. For other men, it was the allure of opium dens that became the one thing they could not resist, even when they knew it was killing them.

Was Natasha his addiction, his weakness?

Was this what her earthy sensuality was becoming for him? An addiction that in the early stages brought with it nothing but ecstasy of the finest sort . . . until the ecstasy came to an end, replaced by the mind-numbing, soul-destroying, misery of addiction.

Perhaps a few more torrid evenings with Natasha was all he needed to free himself from the pull of her sensuality, Anton thought. If he could sate himself with her charms thoroughly and completely, then perhaps he would at last be able to see her with the same detached objectivity that he'd been able to look at all his past sexual conquests.

Yes, Anton thought with tenuous confidence, once I have my fill of her, she won't have any power over me at all.

"Does the chemise please you?" Natasha asked, standing ten feet from Anton, feeling the heat of his gaze upon her.

Anton was looking at Natasha's legs, imagining the thrill that would be his to feel them surrounding his hips as he thrust himself deeply into her. Even the

227

sight of her bare feet excited him, and he realized that he really had gone thoroughly mad for this mysteriously enticing seamstress.

"The chemise is lovely," Anton said.

He was using all the strength of will he possessed to remain seated. Natasha, after all, had been the one who started this play-acting, and although every nerve in his body was demanding he rush over and take her into his arms, he would allow her to play this game through to its conclusion. At least he'd *try* to let her finish. His passion, escalating dangerously with each passing second, might not let him be so patient.

"Then you feel that the craftsmanship is suitable for you? I understand that quite a number of women have received gifts from you. I'm sure you wouldn't want to disappoint any of your lovers."

Natasha walked forward slowly, bent just slightly so that the chemise continued to cover her womanhood from Anton's hungry gaze. When she was directly in front of him, she knelt slowly, trying to rid herself of the image of other women — women more experienced in sexual matters and, she assumed, more skilled — touching Anton.

"Actually, I only have one lover at the moment."

"Only one? I've been given to understand that you require more than one woman to satisfy you."

"It depends upon the woman."

"You seem uncomfortable," Natasha said, pretending to dismiss the comment, though hearing that she was Anton's only lover made her heart soar. "Let me help you with your boots."

She cupped her hand around the back of Anton's heel, helping to ease his knee-length black boots off. On her knees, she leaned forward as she pulled off the boot, aware that by doing this Anton was able to see deeply into her chemise. She loved the way it felt to tease him, to flirt with his virility and try his patience.

When his boots were off, Natasha eased off his

socks one at a time. Anton leaned forward, placing his hand upon her naked shoulder, but Natasha did not allow herself to be drawn into his embrace. She at last had time to be with Anton, and she would not be hurried either by him, or by her own fears that what she was doing might not please a man as experienced and skilled in the art of sensuality as Prince Anton.

She rose to her feet, bending and turning to keep her womanhood hidden from Anton. She stepped behind him, and he tried to turn in the rocker to look at her, but Natasha put a hand firmly on his shoulder, stopping him.

"Let me help you get more comfortable," she said, playing her hands upon his shoulders near his neck.

She squeezed the sinewy muscles in his shoulders, and he sighed. After several seconds, she helped him remove his jacket, then leaned over his shoulder to loosen his cravat and shirt. Her fingers lingered much longer upon his chest than necessary, and down low, Natasha could feel that she was becoming heated, moist, and tinglingly ready for Anton.

But though her body was ready for him, her mind—the erotic imagination that she had only recently discovered even existed—was not yet ready for him, and instinctively she knew that the longer she delayed the consummation, the greater their fulfillment would be.

She helped him out of his jacket and shirt, standing at the side of the chair, and when Anton brushed the back of his knuckles across her breasts, the contact, though brief and separated by the sheer fabric of the chemise, sent a hot flush of excitement coursing through Natasha's veins.

She moved to the front of his rocker again, kneeling so that she was not quite directly in front of him. She placed her elbow upon his knee, leaning upon him, her eyes smoldering with sensuality.

Anton was holding onto the arms of the rocker, and

judging from the way the muscles in his forearms and hands were flexed, he was afraid that if he didn't hold tightly, he wouldn't be able to keep his hands from Natasha.

"Are you more comfortable now?" Natasha asked softly, her eyes taking in the planes of his chest and stomach. The muscles in his stomach were rippled, the circular ridges of muscle beneath his pectorals precise. His body was made for action, and the sight of it — as always — made Natasha shiver.

Afraid that his own voice would betray the wild emotions racing through him, Anton merely nodded. He had been teased before, flirted with and seduced, but never had he been so hungry for the taste and feel of a woman. Natasha was simply making up the rules as she went along playing the game, and her instincts were unerringly accurate, allowing her to tantalize Anton as no woman ever had.

"But you're not *completely* comfortable," she said, letting her gaze drop slowly from Anton's handsome face, which held a slightly strained expression.

He was erect, the long, rigid length of him trapped within the tight confines of his breeches. He stretched a considerable way down the leg of the garment. Natasha looked at him, and she could almost swear that she could see him throbbing with passion, even through his breeches.

"Let me help you," she said, pulling loose the closure of Anton's breeches.

She had never before been so brazen, so bold, and she dared not look up into his face for fear that what she would see was not complete acceptance of this game that they were playing, and which she was enjoying so very much.

Since he was seated, it was difficult to remove his form-fitting breeches. Anton raised his hips to assist her, disappointing Natasha momentarily, since she had wanted to be the one solely and completely in control of the situation. She wanted to be as competent in this encounter as Anton always had been with her in the past, taking care of absolutely everything so that all she had to concern herself with was her own pleasure.

She fumbled a bit more, then Anton stood and unceremoniously dropped his breeches to the floor, stepping out of them quickly.

Natasha averted her gaze briefly, suddenly afraid to see the naked arousal that had given her such pleasure in the past. When Anton attempted to lift her, she looked up at him, shaking her head in negation, patting the chair.

"You're more comfortable now, I'm sure," she said, the slight quavering in her voice an indication of her rapid heartbeat. Now that she had looked at his arousal, pale and fiercely beautiful, she couldn't take her eyes from it.

"Yes. Quite comfortable," Anton replied. His erection was flagrant, and the seeming casual nature of this conversation both infuriated and aroused him even further, heightening his anticipation for whatever delights Natasha might come up with next.

"That's good. I want you to be at ease. I know that you work very hard on matters of grave consequence to Russia, and I don't want you to be *tense*"—she touched the shaft of Anton's arousal with a fingertip as though to test it—"while you're with me."

"Yes, well, sometimes a man can appear tense, shall we say, even when he's perfectly . . . at ease."

Natasha crossed her arms upon Anton's thigh, letting her gaze roam slowly over him. His body was lean and solid, and because he was squeezing the arms of the rocking chair so tightly, extending every muscle to its fullest, his chest and arms looked all the more powerful.

His arousal, too, fascinated her. She'd never before really looked at him, not *really* looked, and seeing

231

him now filled her with mixed emotions. His manhood seemed powerful, vital, and overtly threatening. She tried to imagine it inside her, thrusting mightily, and somehow she just couldn't envision herself being able to accommodate such an enormous thing, at least not without hideous pain.

Slowly, Natasha uncrossed her arms and leaned away from Anton so that she sat on the backs of her heels. She looked straight into Anton's eyes at last, and the strain and struggle for self-control that she saw pinching at the corners of his eyes, and in the set of his wide, sensual mouth, told her that she had nothing to fear, and that Anton wasn't at all displeased with her play-acting.

She felt quivery with excitement, heated and wet. She squeezed her thighs together, wanting to dispel her thoughts which were currently centered down low, but by pressing her knees together she only increased her own throbbing, coiling hunger.

Later, later, Natasha thought. *My magic moment will come later . . . for now, it's Anton's time.*

"I wondered if you would ever come to see me here," Natasha whispered, her elbow upon Anton's thigh. She was looking at his face, but her concentration was elsewhere on his body.

Anton touched his fingertips lightly to her cheek. He could feel the heat and firmness of her breasts against his thigh, and he knew that unless something happened very quickly, he could not possibly control himself. He *had* to take Natasha into his arms!

She turned her head to kiss Anton's palm, and as she did this, she moved her hand from his thigh, moving just a few inches to brush the backs of her knuckles against his rigid arousal. Slowly, she brought her hand up and down, touching him lightly with the backs of her fingers. She watched him throb, able now to see his pulsing blood adding length and girth to this, the most glaringly visual embodiment of his

232

passion for her. She turned her wrist, and slowly, firmly, curled her fingers around his staff.

Anton sighed, his hands back on the arms of the rocker as he fought to control himself, as he struggled with the rising tide of passion that made him feel as though he needed to straighten his legs lest his entire body begin to cramp up in knots of agonized muscles.

This was the first time that Natasha had seen all of Anton, his entire body completely naked and magnificently aroused. The sight of his body dramatically heightened her own excitement, and this came as something of a shock to Natasha, since she had never really thought of a man's body as being arousing to a woman, and she'd never even heard of any woman finding pleasure in a man's naked form.

But she wasn't just any woman, and she really didn't care what anyone else thought. At least not at that moment, with her small fist moving up and down upon his unyielding length, and the surface of her skin tingling so deliciously.

"Nat-Natasha, you must know that if you continue to do that, you will perhaps get more of a response from me than you want," Anton said.

His knuckles were white as he squeezed the rocker's arms, a muscle twitching in his jaw with the strain of controlling himself.

Being passive in such a situation was not something he'd ever before experienced or even had thought of attempting, Natasha's game had progressed nicely — and erotically — he was now a thousand times more than just ready to feel her curvaceous body beneath his own as they lay in the center of her spacious, comfortable bed.

Natasha watched her own hand working upon Anton, judging with a strangely detached objectivity the response she was drawing. She ran the pad of her thumb over the very tip of his arousal, and Anton trembled briefly, his phallus throbbing powerfully

233

against her palm to tell her that her instincts had not failed her at all.

"Natasha . . . I . . ."

"Sh-h-h. You don't have to say a word," she purred.

She turned slightly so that she was almost at a right angle to the prince, leaning over his powerful, naked thigh. She bent low to kiss his thigh, letting the tip of her tongue flick out quick and light to taste his flesh. As she did this, her hand never slowed its continual caress and undulation of his manhood.

"But Natasha, I don't think you really understand," Anton hissed, the words being ground out through teeth clenched with the strain of withheld passion. "Damn it, woman, I'm not made of stone!"

Natasha purred, leaning a little further over Anton's thigh so that her breasts slid over him. Warm ripples of excitement washed through her, and her nipples literally ached with the need of Anton's caress and kiss. But it was not her passion's need that she was concerning herself with, and now that she had found the courage to continue on this long, she would see the game through to the end, no matter what.

"Not made of stone? You feel hard as stone . . . warm, vibrant, living stone," she whispered, placing her right hand lightly upon Anton's naked, flat stomach as her left hand continued caressing him. "Wonderful" — she kissed his thigh, inching just a little closer to him on her knees — "thrilling" — her breath was heated against the crown of Anton's erection — "stone!"

She kissed him lightly, tentatively. She heard Anton's surprised gasp and was not entirely certain that she had made him happy. She felt his thigh quivering with suppressed tension. The heat of him seeped through her chemise into her taut breasts. She kissed him again, and then again, and felt Anton's palm resting lightly upon her back.

"Don't stop," he whispered.

234

Natasha tasted him then, letting her tongue play lightly against the taut crest of Anton's arousal, circling slowly. She heard him moan, a deep, rumbling groan of passion, and whatever doubts that Natasha might have had about her own sexual prowess vanished — at least for a little while.

By the time she took him into her mouth, Anton's body quivered, and he had reached beneath her curled figure to cup her breast in his hand.

Slowly and tentatively, then with increasing depth, speed, and confidence, she pleasured him with her lips, her hands, her tongue, her heart and soul, and when at last he warned her that he could withstand no more, Natasha only paused long enough to look up into his eyes and wordlessly let him know that she would accept nothing less than his total abandonment to the pleasure she so willingly provided.

The chemise had been discarded long ago, and Natasha was a little sore once again, though it was the most exquisite discomfort she had ever known in her life.

Prince Anton's recuperative powers astonished even him and when he had carried Natasha to the bed and removed the single, superfluous article of clothing that she wore, he proceeded to convince her with words and deeds that she was the most beautiful, fascinating, erotic, conniving, devious, deceptive, enthralling, delightful, beguiling, and perhaps most of all infuriating woman in the world.

She was laughing softly when Anton pushed into her, easing himself in slowly, and his effortless, tireless pursuit of pleasure brought her to the pinnacle three times — and very nearly a fourth time — before the final groan of ecstasy rumbled through Anton's chest.

"I'll never have enough of you," he whispered, his

face and shoulders damp with the perspiration of his efforts, glistening in the pale lamplight as he rested upon his elbows, looking at Natasha beneath him.

She pushed his sandy hair away from his forehead and tried to stop smiling, but couldn't. She was sore — not just a little uncomfortable this time, but sore — and yet she wanted more, which baffled her somewhat, since she was quite certain that her body couldn't withstand yet another orgasm, and even if her body could, she doubted her mind could.

There had to be a limit on how much pleasure the human body could withstand in the course of a single evening, and she felt certain she'd come to that point.

Anton rolled away from Natasha with a groan. She curled up at his side, her head upon his chest, his arm around her shoulders.

"I didn't know that two people could do that so many times," Natasha whispered, feeling little-girl-naughty and worldly-woman-wise at the same time. The smell of sexuality pervaded the room, and every time she breathed in, she was reminded of how they had spent the last four hours.

"Frankly, I didn't know I was capable of that myself," Anton murmured.

His fingers were tracing circles on Natasha's naked shoulder. Her skin was damp, as were the sheets, and though Anton felt as though all the energy had been drained from him, in the back of his mind he wondered if it would be possible for him to once again make love to Natasha before he left her bedchamber.

"Are you telling the truth now, or are you just saying that to make me feel good?"

"I'm telling you the truth. Never before have I wanted a woman as desperately as I want you. I kept thinking that surely I would be satisfied, but then I only wanted more."

Natasha chuckled throatily, her tongue flashing out briefly to touch Anton's chest. He was salty. It was not a taste she particularly liked, but she did like the way he had become so heated, so she brushed her tongue over his nipple again.

Maybe she did like it, she decided.

Anton shifted his weight, moving his hips away from her. It was a preparatory move, unconsciously letting Natasha know that he had to get out of bed. He didn't know what time it was, but the sun most surely had to be coming up soon, and he couldn't get caught in her bedchamber.

"Tomorrow is going to be hell," Anton murmured.

"But tonight was heaven," Natasha countered, sliding her hand around his midsection. She pulled herself close to Anton again, easing her knee over his thighs to squeeze more of herself against him. After having spent so many frantic moments of lovemaking with Anton with very few articles of clothing removed, it was positively glorious now to be able to have all his naked body against her.

"Yes, tonight was heaven. Unfortunately, tomorrow is going to be very long, and unless I'm very much mistaken — and I am seldom very much mistaken — tomorrow is going to be here in an hour, or so."

Anton tried to ease out of the bed, a bit more purposefully this time, but Natasha's arm tightened around his waist, and she locked her leg around his.

"Don't leave," she whispered, and though she didn't want to sound as frantic, as needy, as she felt, her emotions betrayed her.

"I have to," Anton replied softly, compassionately. He rolled so that he was on his side, facing Natasha in the bed, their arms and legs entwined. "I don't want to, Natasha . . . but I must."

She squeezed her eyes shut, burying her face into Anton's neck just beneath his chin.

I'm not going to cry. I'm not! I'm not going to cry! I knew that Anton had responsibilities to people other than myself from the very beginning! I'm not going to

237

cry, damn it!

Anton stroked Natasha's hair, making soothing noises in her ear. His eyes were squeezed tightly shut as well. He, too, did not want to leave, but for him, the irony was so much greater. How absurd it was, he told himself, that his title made it impossible for him to spend the night with a beautiful woman in his own home! If she were a member of the decadent St. Petersburg aristocracy, landed and wealthy, he would not hesitate a moment to spend the evening with her — except the evening would be spent in his own bedchamber, which was always stocked with such niceties as cold champagne, which Anton particularly appreciated after making love.

But she wasn't a princess. She didn't have a title. And because she did not, he couldn't afford to let anyone — not his sister, and certainly none of the servants in Castle Talakovich — know that he had spent the night making glorious love with her.

Men in his position of wealth and power had for hundreds of years abused the power they held, using that power to coerce servants into bed. If the rumor got out that Anton was no different than so many of the other men in St. Petersburg who did just that, it wouldn't be the end of the world for Prince Anton Talakovich, but people would think of him differently than they did now. They would see that the code of conduct that he ascribed for himself was not cast in stone, as everyone always believed. They would see that Anton, contrary to the reputation that he had done everything to foster and everything to maintain, did have a weakness. His honor and integrity were malleable, it would be said, and from that point forward, no one would ever again look at Prince Anton Talakovich in quite the same way, and his enemies would not fear him quite so much, and his allies would not trust him quite so much.

"I have to leave," he whispered. "I'm sorry, my darling, but I truly must."

Natasha nodded, her face still buried in Anton's throat. She did not speak because she didn't dare, afraid the tears would start flowing. She was certain that once they started, they wouldn't stop until she had cried herself completely dry. The moment Anton would leave the room they'd begin—she accepted this. All she really wanted to do was postpone the tears so that Anton wouldn't see them.

She forced a brave face on, then pushed herself away from Anton. It was a weak and faltering smile that she gave him, but it said that she understood, and seeing that Anton wasn't happy about leaving either made it easier for Natasha to accept.

He got gingerly out of bed, surrounded by the heady perfume of their loving as the bedclothes shifted.

Never had he ever had a night like this! Never had he felt so inspired to passion, so driven by a need that Natasha ignited within him, like a fire that blazed white-hot without consuming that which fed the flames.

He retrieved his clothes from where they'd been left on the floor near the rocker. He knew there was something that he should say—but what? The glib conversational banter that had always served him so well in the past would not do with Natasha. She wasn't in the same league with the other women that Anton had shared his passion with.

But had he shared something more than just his body with the seamstress?

It was an unsettling thought. He'd never before given a great deal of consideration to women he slept with—not the kind of consideration that walked hand-in-hand with an involvement of the heart. Sure, there were moments when he wondered what gift was appropriate for what woman, and when he thought that this particular woman or that one had been really quite entertaining out of bed as well as in it. But never before—not until he was bending to retrieve his own clothes from the floor so that he could sneak back to his own bedchamber unseen by his sister or servants—had he ever thought about whether his heart as well as his body and his relentless passion had been involved with his bedchamber activities.

Was this what it was like to be in love? Anton did not know because he'd never been in love—or in any approximation of love—before. He felt as though he could never get enough of Natasha, as though he could never be so completely satisfied that he would be sure that he had ascended the heights of pleasure as high as possible with her. Once he was certain that he had experienced it all, then it would be time to move on, just as he'd always done before, to leave Natasha and find a new woman to experience and explore.

The thought of leaving Natasha brought an immediate pang of remorse to Anton, powerful enough to make him outwardly flinch. But what option did he have? Even if the feelings he held in his heart for Natasha *were* love—and he was becoming more convinced all the time that he *was* in love—there were only so many options available to him. He was, after all, Prince Talakovich, with all the responsibilities and obligations that went with the title and the position. And Natasha was a commoner, plain and simple.

But Prince Anton Talakovich couldn't marry a commoner, could he? Though, truth be known, Natasha Stantikoff was anything but *common*.

He had never really thought of it before. He had always assumed, of course that he would marry a peer. The fact was, with very few exceptions, the people he knew at all well were members of the Russian aristocracy, as their parents had been before them, and their parents before that.

Anton forced such questions from his mind. There

would be time enough later, when all his thoughts were lucid, to contemplate his personal future, and what role Natasha might play in it.

He straightened and turned to look at Natasha. Her head was on the pillow, auburn hair spilling out dark against the white linen, shimmering with the fading moonlight that streamed through the window.

He could not see her eyes, and he wished he could. Were they sad? He knew they were, and it baffled him that he wanted to see her sadness. His history had always been to avoid women who became sad when he left them after sex. The women were supposed to know that he wouldn't be staying the whole night. But Anton didn't want Natasha to be anything like the women he'd once sought out.

"I'm sorry."

The words were out of his mouth, their velvet-soft sound surprising him. Prince Anton Talakovich apologizing for leaving a woman's bedchamber? It was unheard of!

"I understand," Natasha replied softly.

Anton paused, holding his breeches in one hand, his white shirt in the other. He had no real knowledge of what he had just apologized for, just as he wasn't at all certain what it was that Natasha had understood.

"You look so beautiful like that," the prince whispered, feeling compelled to say something, though what exactly it was that his heart wanted to say, he could not be sure.

Natasha was on her back, the sheet pulled up to her underarms. Her hands were at her stomach, fingers laced together loosely. She was looking at him, watching his movements as though to keep a part of him with her in his absence. Such sentimentality should have rankled Anton's nerves — it always had in the past, he told himself — but instead it pleased him enormously that she would be thinking about him, even when they were no longer together, sharing a passion that was shocking in its intensity and its enduring unsatiable fervor.

"Don't leave me tonight," she whispered.

The words tore into Anton, ripping huge holes in the protective armor that surrounded his heart and soul.

She's just a woman. Not the first one I've left after sleeping with, nor the last. I don't have time for a long-term affair with a commoner.

The thought was forced forward from the deep recesses of his mind that demanded there be no change in his life, that he simply continue on, moving from this woman to that one, leaving behind him only memories and the gift of jewels to mark a path of yesterday.

It was a self-delusional wish. The difficult aspect of Anton's brilliant mind was that it worked magnificently well to delude others, but rebelled mightily at the notion of allowing himself to be deceived.

"I must."

The words were torn from his throat, and he turned his back on Natasha so that he wouldn't have to see her out of the corner of his eye as he dressed.

He hoped that when she started crying—and his confidence told him tauntingly that she would cry because of him, and that the guilt would weigh heavily upon his shoulders—she would be silent about it. He thought she would be. Natasha was a strong woman in many ways. She would cry, but her pride wouldn't allow her to let him see the tears, and for that he was thankful. He *needed* her strength because he wasn't so sure how much of his own strength he had—the strength he needed if he was to leave Natasha, as logic and propriety dictated he must.

In quick order Anton put his clothes on, leaving his boots off so the heels wouldn't click against the floor as he returned to his bedchamber. He turned toward the bed again, and was surprised to see the tears glistening in Natasha's eyes, the moonlight playing in the crystal pools.

Only a bastard would leave Natasha now, Anton thought, unconsciously using an epitaph hideous to a man able to trace his genealogy back as far as he could.

He went to the bed, bent low, and kissed Natasha first on the lips, then on the forehead. He straightened before she had the chance to slip her arms around his neck.

"I'll make everything better next time, I promise," he said.

She nodded, her head never moving from the pillow, her eyes filled with sorrow. For an instant, as he stood there at the side of the bed looking down at her, Anton wished that Natasha would beg him to stay. He wanted some weakness to be shown, some silly, maudlin display of emotion so characteristically feminine so that he could lump her together with all his past sexual conquests.

She said nothing. She didn't even accuse him of wrongdoing with her much-too-expressive eyes.

He turned and walked out of the bedchamber without a backward glance, and it wasn't until he closed the door silently and was standing in the hallway alone that he realized he'd be the most repellent cretin to ever walk upon Russian soil, to say nothing of the least intelligent man God had ever seen fit to allow to live, if he left Natasha Stantikoff.

He opened the door, slipped soundlessly back into the room, and whispered hotly, "I can't leave you! Damn it, Natasha, I tried, but I just can't leave you!"

She flew from the bed into Anton's arms, and when he carried her to bed, the tears that she shed were tears of joy.

Eighteen

It was before dawn, but Anastasia had not been able to sleep. She hadn't been sleeping well since the incident, since that silly, foolish moment of weakness, when she and Caleb had embraced, and for reasons she did not understand at all, she had not stopped his questing hands.

In her heart, Anastasia knew that she had more than simply allowed Caleb to touch and kiss her. She had invited his kisses and caresses, and there hadn't been a single moment during the incident — and that's how she thought of it, *The Incident* — that she hadn't loved with every ounce of passion she was only now realizing she possessed.

Thank God that Anton had showed up at the door when he had!

From that moment, Anastasia had avoided Caleb whenever possible. Twice she'd found herself alone with him, and once he'd even tried to kiss her, but she had managed to elude him without being too terribly rude. His dark eyes seemed to remove her clothes, just as his hands had previously, and if Anastasia was certain of anything it was that if she allowed Caleb to touch her again, she would not have the strength to keep his passion at bay.

So she avoided him, and pretended that nothing had

ever happened between them, and that was the way it positively had to remain because she was Princess Anastasia Talakovich of Castle Talakovich, and he was Caleb Carter, an American of extraordinary abilities, dubious history, and at best a peripatetic and uncertain future.

The castle was silent as Anastasia walked down the hall, the single candle casting pale, flickering light out in front of her.

She passed Aislyn's bedchamber and saw that a thin trickle of weak light came from beneath the door, but she knew that Aislyn was sleeping. Since arriving at the castle, Aislyn had slept with an oil lamp turned down low. Anastasia didn't know exactly what made the young, pregnant woman so frightened of the dark, but she suspected it had to do with whatever or whomever she had moved away from.

When Anastasia had first asked if it would be possible to allow Aislyn to move into the castle, Anastasia had almost refused. After all, though the castle had many rooms, it certainly wouldn't do to just let everyone who felt that life had not treated them well move in. So she had put Natasha off by saying that she would consider the request and discuss it with Anton. After making a few discreet inquiries, she discovered more about the unsavory character of Ivan and Aggie Pronushka, and that made Anastasia's mind up for her.

She told Natasha that her friend could move in, but she would be required to work around the castle, doing light jobs that would not endanger the baby growing within her womb. It was a requirement that both Natasha and Aislyn happily agreed to.

Anastasia could hardly wait until Caleb left the castle. He had already told Anton that he would be going to the hunting lodge for several days, and Anastasia felt certain that if she could just be free from his presence for a couple of consecutive days, she would at last be able to forget about *The Incident,* and about Caleb as well.

When she reached Anton's bedchamber, she knocked lightly on the door, then opened it. She expected to have to shake her brother's arm lightly to awaken him, and she expected to get a dark look from him because he never liked being awakened, especially not without very good reason, and she doubted that her reason — she just needed to talk — would qualify as a sufficient reason.

What she did not expect to see was his bed squared away and neat, and clearly not slept in.

For a moment Anastasia wondered if her brother had left that early in the day to go to the library to start work. She dismissed this notion immediately. Even if he had, he wouldn't have made his own bed. She and her brother had had servants to handle that chore from the day they were born.

Which left only one conclusion: Anton hadn't gone to bed last night.

And yet he was in the castle. Anastasia had been working with him almost to midnight.

So where was he?

The swine!

Anastasia rushed to the room that Natasha now occupied. Earlier, when Anastasia had noticed that the other servants didn't care for the special treatment that Natasha had been receiving since moving into Castle Talakovich, she moved the seamstress up to the second floor to protect her from painful comments. Now she thought how absurd it was for her to think that she would *protect* Natasha by putting her in a room *away* from the other servants, but *closer* to her own licentious brother!

She hardly paused at Natasha's door before rapping her knuckles on it, asking quietly, "Natasha, are you all right?" and then opening the door and stepping in.

It took only a moment for Anastasia's eyes to adjust

to the dark room, and what she saw took her breath away.

"You licentious, scurrilous, inexcusable swine!" Anastasia hissed, seeing her brother in Natasha's bed.

She took a step toward the bed, then caught herself and turned sharply just as a surprised Anton and Natasha opened their eyes. Anastasia rushed to the fireplace, and quickly withdrew a fire iron from its holder. Wielding the poker with both hands, Anastasia rushed back to the bed, holding her bludgeon high overhead.

"You swine!" Anastasia hissed through clenched teeth, keeping her voice down so that she wouldn't alert any of the servants. She didn't want this family shame to be gossiped about. She'd teach her older brother a lesson, but do it quietly.

"Anastasia, wait a minute!" Anton said, clutching onto the sheet as he rose onto his knees, pushing Natasha behind him to protect her as he moved to meet his sister's attack.

"Animal!" Anastasia hissed, then brought the poker down hard, trying to hit her brother on the shoulder. She would have aimed for his head, but she only wanted to teach him a lesson and protect the dignity and honor of her new friend, Natasha, not kill her worthless brother.

The fireplace poker smashed hard against Anton's forearm, and he groaned and tried to snatch the weapon away from his sister, but she moved very quickly, nimble on her feet. He wished now that their aunt had not insisted that both he *and* Anastasia receive fencing lessons. The practice Anastasia had done with a sabre was showing now in the way she moved expertly out of the way of his counter-attack, then moved in again to bring the iron head of the poker down hard against his vulnerable shoulder.

"Stop it, damn you!" Anton hissed, his body coiled now, like a cat about to pounce.

Anastasia took several steps back, continuing to

hold the poker with both hands. She was breathing hard, though it was more from anger than exertion. It had shocked her to hear Anton swear at her. As protective as he was, he had never allowed anyone to use strong language in her presence, even though he, like almost everyone else, believed that Anastasia was free-spirited with men in private.

Natasha was on her knees, mortified, hiding behind Anton, trying to find enough sheet to wrap around her naked body. She was wildly embarrassed at being caught by Anastasia, and she was certain that Anastasia would ask her to leave the castle immediately.

"Listen to me, Anastasia, this isn't—" Anton said.

"Silence!" Anastasia snapped.

Natasha gasped. She could not imagine anyone, not even Anastasia, speaking that way to Prince Anton Talakovich.

To Natasha, Anastasia asked, "Are you all right? Did this animal hurt you? Nothing like this will ever happen again. I promise you that. I'll have Marta keep an eye on him day and night from now on."

At that, Natasha smiled, though she ducked behind Anton so that Anastasia wouldn't see it.

Anastasia stood there, holding the poker in both hands, ready to strike her brother again if she thought it was necessary. She looked at Anton, the man she trusted completely, and couldn't imagine him being so crass—so bourgeois, so common—as to use his wealth to lure or foist a young woman like Natasha into his bed.

"There is an explanation for all this," Anton said, rubbing his biceps where the curved head of the fireplace poker had struck him. A deep bruise was already beginning to form, showing purple-blue against his pale flesh. "However, none of us want to explain any of this to Marta, now do we? Since we don't, let's all discuss this downstairs in the kitchen, over coffee and tea."

Anastasia lowered the poker, but made no move to put it away. "Natasha, let me see you."

Natasha looked over Anton's shoulder. Her deep brown eyes were filled with a mixture of embarrassment, chagrin, and humor—but there wasn't even a hint of defeat or sorrow in them.

For several long seconds, Anastasia simply looked into Natasha's eyes. She was certain that if she looked into her friend's eyes, she would know the truth about what had apparently happened. And then, at last, though she still had her doubts, she believed that if Anton was in Natasha's bedchamber, it was with the occupant's consent. Exactly how much coercion Anton had used to gain entrance had yet to be determined . . . but if Anastasia was certain of anything, it was that she would learn the entire truth from someone now in the room.

"I'll see both of you downstairs," Anastasia said finally, now feeling just a little foolish at her brash behavior. "Don't keep me waiting long."

When she closed the door behind her, Anastasia heard her brother's rumbling laughter, and Natasha's much softer laugh, along with Natasha's muffled statement that what had just happened wasn't at all funny, so there was nothing to laugh about, and should Anton *continue* to laugh, he would never again be invited back to the bed he was now warming.

"Stop that now," Natasha chided, pushing Anton's hand away from her thigh as she pulled up her stocking. While she was busy trying to put her clothes on, Anton was busy trying to remove them. While Natasha was "getting furious" with Anton for his "lustful ways," she was loving every minute of the play.

Even though she hadn't gotten very much sleep, Natasha felt magnificent. To have Anton in her arms as she slept, to feel his strong body warm beside her—it was everything she had ever hoped it would be. And even though the awakening had been harsh, with Anton receiving a bruise on his arm from his own sister, Natasha wouldn't have changed a single second of the time she'd spent with the prince.

"Are you about ready to face the enemy?" Anton asked, running a brush through his sandy hair, inspecting his appearance in the dressing mirror.

"Your sister is *not* the enemy," Natasha asked.

She, too, peered at her reflection in the mirror. Did she have the look of a woman well-loved? She thought she did, and she certainly *felt* well-loved, though whether or not it actually showed was a matter of interpretation.

"She's not? Then why is there a bruise on my arm that's not so mysteriously in the same shape as the fireplace poker in this bedchamber?"

Natasha punched Anton on the arm—careful to hit his uninjured appendage—and laughed when he accused her of being abusive.

"Every man should be abused the way you have been," Natasha said, wishing her cheeks didn't color every time she thought about everything she and Prince Anton had done to each other only hours before.

They found Anastasia waiting for them in the dining room. It had taken nearly an hour for Anton and Natasha to get ready, and the coffee, tea, and pastries were on a tray waiting for them. Anastasia had an impatient look on her face as she sat at the long table. Natasha noticed immediately that the servants were not in the dining room, so they'd been excused in the name of privacy.

"You don't need to have that look in your eyes," Anton said to his sister as he pulled out a chair for Natasha. He poured her tea, and Natasha wondered if she was in a dream, or if she was really being served by a flesh-and-blood Russian prince.

Anastasia looked at Natasha and asked, "Just tell me this: did you want it to happen?"

250

Natasha nodded, looking straight into her friend's eyes. She would never deny that she had wanted Anton, just as she would never again think of herself in the same way after last night.

"Very well then," Anastasia said. "What the two of you want to do is your own affair—pardon the expression. I just needed to know that whatever decisions were made were *freely* made."

"I assure you, darling sister, I'm not the barbarian you think I am."

"I didn't call you a barbarian, I called you a swine."

Anton and Natasha chuckled softly, but Anastasia did not even smile.

"What's wrong?" Anton asked. "Both Natasha and I have told you that the evening shared together was . . ." His eyes narrowed, and Anton felt a hideous dread coming to life in the pit of his stomach. "Anastasia, out with it! What happened?"

"It's the documents," she said, her face becoming pale, drawn. "The messenger arrived just a few moments ago. The carriage was attacked. Only one man survived. It was carnage." Anastasia bit her lower lip and looked away for a moment, composing herself. The news she'd received had shaken her deeply. "A man was lying in ambush for the carriage. He had a gun with him, and he shot without warning."

Natasha understood very little of what Anton and Anastasia worked on during the day, so she maintained a respectful silence as they spoke. She realized that whatever had to be done next probably wouldn't involve her. She didn't want to be a bother to the prince and princess in this time of apparent crisis.

"What was taken?" Anton asked.

"The strongbox."

Anton cursed. "That means that he knew in advance. Somehow, he knew in advance about the carriage, and what it was carrying." Anton exploded to his feet, too restless and angry to remain seated.

"Where's Caleb? He should be here."

"You don't suspect him of betraying us, do you?" Anastasia asked, the shock she felt at such an accusation clear in her voice.

"Of course not!" Anton snapped, annoyed that the question would even be given voice. "I just feel better in a crisis situation when he's near. He's a good man to have at your side when the shooting starts."

"Shooting?" Natasha asked, unable to keep the single word to herself.

"If Napoleon gets wind of what was in that strongbox, he'll invade tomorrow."

"But he's our friend! Didn't the czar and Bonaparte just agree to—"

The look that Anton gave Natasha told her that she knew nothing at all about political realities. She took a sip of her tea, and promised herself that she wouldn't ask another question of Anton until the crisis had passed.

"So where the devil *is* Caleb?" Anton asked, starting for the door to have one of the servants summon the American.

"He's not in the castle," Anastasia said, and the slight hesitation in her voice said she knew more. Anton's fierce look silently demanded she tell all. "He went to the hunting lodge for a few days. He left late last night."

Anton cursed again, shocking Natasha, as well as Anastasia. He was not a man given to freely using strong language in the company of women.

"He told you what he was doing, but he didn't tell me? That doesn't seem like Caleb," Anton commented, his gaze, silver-gray and cold as ice, narrowing upon his sister.

"We . . . had an argument," Anastasia explained, trying to sound light and flippant, and failing. "He got angry with me and he said he wanted to spend some time alone. You know the way Caleb is."

252

"Yes, I do. And sometime you can tell me what you two were arguing about."

He went to the door and opened it. A servant was waiting outside in the hall and Anton issued orders that a rider, on the swiftest horse in the stables, was to ride to the hunting lodge to inform Caleb that his presence was needed immediately.

Anton returned to the table and forced himself to sit. His gaze took on a distant quality as he attempted to picture the scene of what had happened to the carriage, and what possible damage the theft might cause.

"In the strongbox were the best proposals for weapons," he said in that dreamy tone that indicated he was thinking aloud, as he often did when he was trying to clarify an issue to himself as well as to Anastasia. "There also were production schedules for the forging and delivery of cannons."

"And bribes," Anastasia added, her voice soft and dreamy, like a higher-pitched version of her brother's. "There was a list of all the bankers that Caleb contacted, and how much money had secretly exchanged hands."

"Damn . . . damn it a thousand times," Anton muttered, trying to imagine what Napoleon's reaction would be when and if he discovered that the Czar of Russia did not trust the French emperor, and was making preparations to defend his country against invasion from the west.

Sitting quietly, Natasha stared at the tea in her cup. Though she appeared impassive, her heart was racing, and her hands were trembling so much that she placed them in her lap so they wouldn't be seen.

The carriage . . . attacked as though the assailant knew in advance that it was coming . . .

"Natasha, what is it?" Anton asked. "You know something, don't you?"

She looked into his eyes, then looked down. If ever

253

she wished that Anton could not read minds, it was at this very moment. Guilt and shame turned her cheeks crimson. Anton bolted to his feet, moving so that he stood very near, looking down threateningly at her.

"Tell me, Natasha!"

"I never thought . . . I didn't want anyone to get hurt," she stammered.

Slowly, with growing awareness, she realized that innocent people had been killed—murdered in cold blood—and at least some of the blame for their deaths had to rest upon her own shoulders. She started to cry. Anton put his hand on her shoulder, his fingers like the jaws of an animal biting into her flesh. She flinched in pain, and he shook her.

"Tell me, Natasha! Tell me what you know!"

Guilt overwhelmed Natasha. She told them everything she knew, and tried to give the reasons for telling her uncle what she had overheard when she stood outside the library windows.

When she was finished, she turned to look at Anastasia. What she saw there was a mixture of horror and sympathy. At least to some degree, Princess Anastasia could understand why Natasha had told her uncle about the carriage. But when Natasha looked at Anton, all she saw was contempt in his expression. She had betrayed him, been a traitor to him in his eyes, and there was nothing that she could do to change the way he felt.

"I'm sorry," Natasha whispered, the tears running down her cheeks, salty against her tongue as she spoke. "I never meant for anyone to get hurt."

"Well, somebody did get hurt," Anton said, his eyes filled with hatred, shredding Natasha's soul. "Three men are dead and a fourth is wounded. Five thousand rubles has been stolen, and documents that could lead to war with the most powerful military force in the world is missing. If we *do* go to war with Napoleon, as unprepared as we are now, there won't be three dead, or three hundred, or even three thousand! There'll be three million dead men, and all because you believed some lazy drunkard who convinced you that life had been unfair to him, and that he was some victim of my greed."

Natasha reached out to take Anton's hand. He pulled away from her as though she were poison.

"We took you in, befriended you, trusted you, and this is how you repay us," Anastasia said softly, shaking her head in utter disbelief.

Nineteen

He hated her. There really couldn't be any doubt about that now. There was no mistaking the way Anton was looking at her with such loathing, such contempt.

Natasha wanted to die. She wanted to curl up, wrap her arms around her knees, close her eyes, and never again have to open them.

She sat next to Anton in the carriage, though from all that he had said to her, she could have been alone. They were rushing to Uncle Ivan's, where Anton intended to take justice into his own hands, swiftly and decisively.

Anton cracked the whip against the horses' flanks, adding speed to their gallop. At one point, Natasha nearly fell out of the carriage when the wheel hit a rut in the road, and the carriage careened dangerously.

"You don't have to be cruel to the horses," she said to Anton above the pounding of the hooves. "You're angry with me, not them. Why not take the whip to me?"

Anton shot her a glaring sideways look. "I ought to," was all he said.

A few seconds later, he tugged lightly on the reins and the two horses gratefully slowed their pace. As angry as Anton was, he couldn't vent his frustration on the fine animals who had never betrayed him, his family, or his country—which was more than he could say about the woman who sat beside him in the open carriage.

He'd put four miles behind them before slowing the horses. That was enough time, he told himself, to let his anger flow freely. Now it was time to think clearly, logically, decisively.

After learning what he could of the attack on the coach, Anton had no doubt that Ivan Pronushka was responsible. From all that Natasha had told him about her uncle, and what she'd told Ivan, there could be no doubt that he was responsible.

But how much could Ivan understand of what he'd stolen? If he took only the rubles, it would only be a minor loss—an expensive mistake on Anton's part, but certainly nothing that couldn't be overcome. But if Ivan was smart enough to understand what the documents meant, then the loss of the strongbox was catastrophic.

To make the situation even more untenable, Caleb was at the hunting lodge, and if ever there was a time when Anton wanted his friend at his side, it was now. Anton dared not take any of his men with him to Ivan's. There could be no doubting that Czar Alexander had spies within Napoleon's camp; it was only safe to assume that Napoleon had spies within Alexander's camp. Everyone who mattered knew that the Talakovich family was intractably linked both politically and financially to the czar. It would only be intelligent to have spies within Castle Talakovich, and though Anton loathed Napoleon Bonaparte, he never doubted the Corsican's brilliance.

So he had to go after Ivan all by himself. To take men with him—anyone other than Caleb—would signal that something was desperately wrong. Men talk, especially soldiers. Even if he didn't tell his men why they were hunting Ivan Pronushka, word would get

257

around, and sooner or later that word would grow wings and fly back to Paris, where Bonaparte might be able to make sense of it.

Anton tried to plan what his next step would be if Ivan wasn't at his home. Unfortunately, he could think of nothing. For an instant, he closed his eyes and imagined the consequences of those secret documents getting into the wrong hands, and no matter how he looked at it, the end result always came down to one thing: war.

And that just couldn't happen. Not now. Not yet. Not when the entire Russian military was so poorly equipped and trained, not when the conscripted soldiers were unmotivated, not when Bonaparte's men were so well trained, disciplined, made confident by the victories they'd known thus far.

Anton could picture the damage Bonaparte's heavy cannons would do, see in his mind's eye the French troops in their fine uniforms and good boots ideal for marching, advancing upon the ragtag defense lines formed by the Russian soldiers.

The ghastly image made Anton shiver. It would be carnage. A nightmare of death and destruction, and Mother Russia would burn.

"I'm sorry."

Anton turned to look at Natasha. He wished she would stop apologizing. Every time she did, he was forced to look at her, and when he did, fresh anguish burst anew in his chest. She looked so defeated, so thoroughly and completely defeated.

He knew that she had never dreamed her lazy, alcoholic uncle would go to such violent lengths to steal, but that couldn't diminish what she had done. She had betrayed him, and he discovered this the morning after sharing himself with her. Their night of lovemaking had been more than just sex, more than just a release, and complete fulfillment of all the carnal impulses that drove them. It wasn't just lust, and because it wasn't, Anton felt doubly betrayed by her.

He turned his attention back to the road, ignoring Natasha's apology, forcing himself not to think either about her pain, or the pain he felt inside from her deception. At the moment, there were more important problems to address and avoid, like a war with the most powerful military on the planet, than concerning himself with his own petty problems.

When they reached Ivan's, Anton approached slowly, a pistol in either hand, each cocked and ready to shoot. He kicked open the door only to find Aggie sitting near the fireplace, her face bruised and swollen.

"Kill him!" Aggie screamed later. "Kill my husband when you find him! He left me! The first time he ever had money in his whole life, he leaves me!"

Anton looked at the old woman, shaking his head slowly in disgust. Apparently, Ivan had quickly figured out the potential value of what he'd stolen, returned home just long enough to pack a few things, then left again. When Aggie tried to stop him, he beat her for her efforts.

"Who's going to take care of me?" Aggie demanded, rising from her chair, flinging her arms about wildly. "Where's Aislyn? At least she made sure my breakfast was cooked and my laundry washed!" She waggled a finger at Natasha. "And you, you ungrateful wench, you left me, too! Spreading your legs wide for a prince while your poor aunt hardly has a morsel of food to eat! How could you do that to me?"

Natasha was ashen-faced as she listened to her aunt's diatribe. For an instant, Anton was convinced that if he raised his pistol and shot the old woman, Mother Russia would be the better for it. But he would not play that role, not even though the power of life and death did rest in his own hands.

Even if he did kill Aggie Pronushka, her kind would still continue, still demand that someone take care of them, still accuse the world of being unfair, still blame all their problems upon others. And in the end, when even those closest to her abandoned her, as Ivan had, she would scream for them to be killed for having more greed and less loyalty than she herself possessed.

"Where did he go?" Anton asked, his voice soft as a whisper but sharp-edged as the dagger in his belt.

"I don't know," Aggie replied, slumping back into the chair. "All he said was that he was through with me. That's all I know."

Anton stepped forward and touched the muzzle of his pistol against Aggie's forehead. She trembled, her eyes crossed as she stared up at the weapon.

"Tell me the truth. If I think you're lying, I will squeeze the trigger."

Natasha looked away. She was certain that her aunt would lie. She always lied, and Natasha thought certain she would lie to protect her husband, even if he did abandon her.

"I don't know where. All he said was that he had something that Rosto would pay for."

"Rosto?"

"Rosto Rapp. That's Ivan's cousin."

"Where does he live?"

Aggie turned away. She couldn't stare at the pistol any longer, and she was certain that as soon as she finished telling Anton all that she knew, he would kill her. Her only comfort was that when Prince Talakovich eventually found her husband, he would kill Ivan, too.

"I asked you where he lives."

"In Paris. He's an important man, Ivan says. Ivan's talked about him now and then."

Anton felt the stab of fear go straight through his heart. The papers, all those damning documents, were headed for France. If they ever reached that country . . .

He ruthlessly squelched the thought. Now was not the time to let his fears of what might happen prevent him from doing everything in his power to stop it.

260

Carefully, Anton lowered the hammers on both pistols, disarming them, his mind in a whirl. He had to get back to Castle Talakovich, explain to Anastasia what had happened, collect weapons, supplies, money, and Caleb, then head out after Ivan. When he found him, there would be no court tribunal to determine guilt or innocence, no thoughtful discussion of what the appropriate penalty should be for the crimes that Ivan had committed. Justice would be swift and sure.

Until Anton held those documents in his own hands—until he personally delivered them to Czar Alexander's hands—he could not rest, and the only man he would trust was Caleb.

He turned and started for the door, and Natasha got in step with him.

"Not you. You stay here," he said coldly.

Natasha stopped. The implacability she saw in Anton's eyes told her that arguing with him was useless. She was no longer concerned for her own happiness and safety, but she did not want her friend to suffer.

"Can Aislyn stay with you? She's pregnant." She waved her hand around the house, and nodded in Aggie's direction. "This is no place to have a baby."

"Of course Aislyn can stay in the castle," Anton answered, not a hint of warmth in his tone. "She's never betrayed me. But you . . ."

By leaving the sentence unfinished, it was much more damaging to Natasha than if he'd actually simply said what he felt. She turned away, unable to withstand the hatred she saw in his cold gray eyes.

"He can't get far," Natasha said softly, hoping that she hadn't caused as much damage as it appeared.

"There were travel permits in the strongbox, carrying the czar's seal. Whoever possesses those documents can travel throughout Russia without being stopped. That one document will get a person through most of Europe. He *can* get far, Natasha. But when I find him, he won't get one step further."

Anton stood at the door's threshold, knowing that when he left Natasha behind, he'd leave part of himself behind. He knew, too, that when he left her, he would leave her for all time. He'd never again allow himself to look at her, because to do so would only cause him to feel the pain in his heart that he was feeling now, and he never again wanted to experience such wrenching torture.

"You won't find him," Natasha said. "He's lazy, but he's shrewd. He's smart like a fox."

Anton grinned crookedly, without humor. "I'll match intellects with that fool in a heartbeat."

"You don't think like he does. It's not a matter of intelligence, it's a matter of craftiness."

Again Anton scoffed. "He's an idiot. I've met and defeated foes a thousand times more competent than he."

"You know how to fight men in politics, men in business, bankers and the like. Do you know how to go against a man like my uncle?"

"And you do know, I suppose."

"You're a prince. I spent years living here," she said, spreading her hands out to encompass the living area of the small home. "Which one of us, do you think, better understands how Ivan's mind works? He's lazy, violent, abusive, and he drinks too much . . . but he's managed to always have a home, and always have food, and he's done this without ever having to work. Does it sound like he's a stupid man, Anton?"

Anton's teeth were clenched in rage as he stared straight into Natasha's eyes, listening carefully to every word she spoke, trying desperately to find the flaw in her logic. But there was no flaw. Everything that she said rang with the clarity of truth that was both infuriating and undeniable.

"The minute you slow me down, the first time you complain about anything, I'm throwing you into the road, and you can stay there, for all I care."

Natasha said nothing. There was nothing to say. Anton hated her, she was certain. Her only hope for redemption was to help him catch Uncle Ivan, and return the stolen documents.

He left then, and Natasha ran after him, leaping into the carriage. Behind her, she could hear Aunt Aggie screaming, accusing Natasha of abandoning her in her time of great need.

It wasn't the finest inn, but it was better than any that Ivan had stayed in before, and the prostitute beside him was easily the youngest, most attractive, and most expensive woman he'd ever paid for.

"Are you going to be staying around long?" the prostitute asked, leaning against the headboard while Ivan absently pinched her nipples.

"Maybe I will. Maybe I won't. Why don't you show me a good time again, and I'll tell you? Make it worth my while and I might stay," he said, grinning.

The prostitute was young, but she wasn't foolish. "I've already tried to get you going again, and you can't," she said. Clearly, the memory of her efforts to make it possible for Ivan to enter her body had not accomplished anything more lasting than a bad attitude on her part. "Maybe if you didn't have that bottle to your lips all the time you wouldn't be—"

The stinging slap surprised her more than it hurt her. The prostitute knew better than to let Ivan see the hatred she had for him. She rubbed her cheek, pretending that it hurt worse than it did so that he wouldn't hit her a second time.

"It was my fault," she said quietly. "I know that. I know that if I was better at it, you'd be like a stallion now."

"That's it! You're right!" Ivan snapped, sitting on the edge of the bed, looking at the woman's breast, at the fear that showed in her eyes as she rubbed her injured cheek.

He had money in his pockets now, and that meant that he didn't have to accept insults from anyone — certainly not from a whore. Sometimes it seemed as though women were the worst things that had ever happened to him, Ivan thought then. If it weren't for women holding him back, keeping him down, he would be living like the czar right now.

"Get out of here, but come back later. And wear something new. I don't want to see you in the same dress again."

The prostitute dressed quickly and was out of the room in minutes, and though she promised Ivan that she would be back, she lied. He had paid her more than her usual fee, but there was something about him that made the prostitute's skin crawl, that made all the warnings ring in her ears. He liked hurting women, even if he lusted after them, and even though he carried with him gold coins and Russian rubles, his clothes were old and grimy.

What made a man with that kind of money wear old, dirty clothes?

The prostitute forced the question from her mind as she left the inn. It was best not to think about certain things.

Back in the room, Ivan was throwing his things into the small bag, which was all the luggage that he had brought with him. He had told the prostitute to return, but even if she did, he wouldn't be at the inn. He had a long way to travel, and though he couldn't be sure if he was being followed, there could be no doubt that sooner or later, he'd have men chasing him.

After what he'd done, it could only be a matter of time before Prince Anton concluded who was responsible for the theft and murders.

Ivan smiled as he left his room. He'd been waiting all his life for this single moment in time. He at last

264

would have the world by the throat, and he intended to squeeze as tightly as he could. All he had to do was get to Paris and track down his cousin, Rosto Rapp, and the world would be his!

Anastasia was worried. Never before had she seen her brother quite so furious. It wasn't that he had been ranting and raving. Quite the contrary, he had kept all the roiling emotions inside, and that's what made Anastasia so nervous.

They had only been gone an hour, on the hunt for Ivan Pronushka, but already Anastasia was wishing that Anton had waited long enough for Caleb to return from the hunting lodge. Whatever misgivings Anastasia had of the American herself, she never questioned his deadly skill, and something — an intuition, an indefinable feeling — warned her that Anton and Natasha would need Caleb with them.

She paced the spacious confines of the castle's library, trying to stop worrying about her brother. Anton had been through a dozen situations much more dangerous than this, she told herself.

It didn't do any good. He was her brother, and she worried about him, just as she would always worry about him, even when they were both old and gray.

And then there was Natasha to think about. Part of the time Anastasia wished she had come forward, put her arms around Natasha's shoulders, and told the frightened and shamed woman that all would be well in the end. Natasha had looked so helpless and defeated sitting there in the hallway while Anton prepared himself for the road, packing bags and arranging the necessary equipment.

But though Anastasia sympathized with Natasha, and realized why she had done what she'd done, there could be no getting away from the fact that men were dead because of the things that Natasha had divulged to her uncle. There could be no denying that because of what Natasha had done, Russia could quite possibly soon be at war with the strongest military in the world.

And yet how could something like that be forgiven? How could Anastasia *not* forgive Natasha, who never meant harm to anyone, and had only acted badly because she had merely tried to protect her own pregnant friend from the cruelties of her uncle?

The thoughts kept going round in a mad hurly-burly in Anastasia's head. She wished that she could silence the questions, block them from her mind so that she could concentrate on other things, but they wouldn't leave her, not even for a second.

The knock at the library door startled Anastasia. She stopped her pacing, and called out. The butler stepped in.

"A messenger is here to see the American," he said in his funereal tone that never seemed to vary at all, no matter what the circumstances were.

"It's not Caleb? He hasn't come back from the hunting lodge?"

"No, miss. It's a man to *see* the American. Shall I send the gentleman away?"

"No, I'll see him."

Anastasia forced herself into a wingbacked chair, making herself appear calm, even though she was anything but calm.

The messenger was a tall young man, very slender and well dressed. He had the look of a man who'd spent much of his life in a saddle.

"I was paid to deliver this message to Caleb Carter, at his hotel in Moscow," the young man explained. "When I got there, the hotel told me that he'd moved here. I'm hoping you're going to tell me that's true." He grinned then, and Anastasia decided she liked the young man. He seemed honest and hard-working, and lately she hadn't found those traits in abundance in many people.

"Yes, he's staying in the castle for a while. He's been a very busy man, and he needs an extended holiday to recover his strength."

Anastasia kept the smile to herself. She couldn't imagine a situation where Caleb wouldn't be strong. He struck her like a gray wolf that could run tirelessly for hours and hours.

"You won't mind if I stay then, just until he returns?"

Anastasia rose from her chair, placing her hand lightly upon the young man's arm. Under the circumstances, she did not want any unnecessary persons in the castle any longer than absolutely necessary. There was no guessing what might happen next.

"There's no need for that. I can take the letter."

"But I was told to give it to Caleb Carter personally."

Anastasia smiled gently, looking straight into the young man's eyes, exuding that strange mixture of flirtatious sensuality, steelish intractability, and royal authority all at once. "I am Princess Anastasia Talakovich. On a dozen occasions I've entertained the czar in this room. Don't you think that you can trust me with a letter for one of my own guests?"

There wasn't a negative answer that the young man felt he could give to such a statement that wouldn't in some way be insulting to the princess. He handed Anastasia the envelope, and she personally escorted him back to the front doors of the castle.

"If you're hungry or tired, the worker's quarters are in the back. Tell them I sent you, and you'll be treated properly."

"Thank you, miss," the messenger said gratefully. "I could use a cold drink and a warm meal."

"Then you shall have them."

Even before the door had been closed, the smile vanished from Anastasia's face, and she rushed with undignified haste back to the sanctity and safety of the

267

library, clutching the envelope in hand.

As her brother had taught her, she inspected the quality of the envelope before ripping it apart. It was fine quality, egg-shell in color, expensive. For an instant she wondered whether she should wait for Caleb to return from the hunting lodge. He *was* the owner of the letter, after all.

This wasn't the time to worry about minor issues like ownership and privacy, she told herself. She opened the letter, realizing she'd likely have to deal with Caleb's anger later.

The letter was from Parker Windom, a London banker that Caleb had seen. Anastasia remembered that Caleb had been guardedly enthusiastic about Windom and his bank.

She read the letter quickly, three times over. Caleb had led Parker to believe that the munitions and weapons would be used by soldiers loyal to England against American colonialists. It was clear, too, from what Parker had written, that he had discovered that the Talakoviches were the real power behind Caleb.

"For the loan to be completed," Parker wrote, "I will require a signature either from the prince, or the princess. Their identity in this matter will be kept in the strictest confidence, I assure you. As you can well understand, being in the middle of the internal squabbles of other countries is not what this banking institution was created for."

She read the letter once more, being very careful with each word. Anastasia's English wasn't nearly as good as her French. When Caleb returned to the castle—if he'd even speak to her after all the fighting they'd done in the past, and now with her opening his mail—she'd have him look carefully at it, too.

She closed her eyes and thought carefully about what the next step would be.

Parker Windom wanted a signature, either from her or from Anton, before he'd allow the loan to go through. And since Anton was God-knows-where, and would be gone for God-knew-how-long, that meant it was up to Anastasia to travel to London.

It was important now for the loan to go through quickly, and for Caleb to set up the figurehead companies that would transport the weapons to Russia, and hide their actual destination from prying eyes. All this had to be done *before* Napoleon got his hands on the documents stolen from the carriage strongbox.

The smile that curled her soft pink lips was a naughty one. She hadn't been to London in several years, and she'd always enjoyed the city. It would be enjoyable to see it again. Even better than that, she would at last be in the forefront of Talakovich business. This time, she wouldn't simply be assisting her brother, working with him when they were together in the library, then pretending that she was just a flighty debutante whenever businessmen were around.

And there was one last factor about this venture that made Princess Anastasia Talakovich feel all warm, nervous, and trembly inside. If she was to travel immediately to London, as Parker Windom had insisted and circumstances dictated, then she would need a bodyguard, and there wasn't a man in the world more capable of that than Caleb Carter.

The prospect of being near Caleb sent shivers racing up and down her spine because Anastasia had never forgotten what it had been like to be in his arms, tasting his lips pressing hungrily against her own, feeling the great strength and forcefulness of his character consuming her better judgment so that all she felt was passion and desire.

Did she want to be with him for so long? Anastasia wasn't sure. She liked the idea of flirting, but Caleb wasn't a man that she could control with a stern look. He wasn't a silly man whose will she could bend to suit her own whims.

And just as she had never quite been able to forget

the pleasure she had felt in his arms, so, too, she had not forgotten the fury she saw in his eyes when she left him unfulfilled, or when she pretended that they'd never touched each other, never kissed.

Wasn't that the very reason that Caleb, his anger escalating, decided that he needed to go to the hunting lodge? Hadn't he gone there just so that he wouldn't have to be near her?

There was another knock on the library door. The butler stepped in.

"Miss, you asked to be informed when the American arrived. He has."

Caleb pushed the butler aside as he rushed into the library.

"Now just what in holy hell is going on around here?" Caleb asked, looking down at Anastasia like he wanted to tear her limb from limb . . . or maybe just tear her clothes off.

Twenty

Caleb was almost trembling with rage. It wasn't the fact that Anastasia had opened the letter from Parker Windom that made him so angry, it was that his friend had gone on the hunt for the thief of the stolen documents — without him!

Caleb cursed himself for letting his anger at Anastasia cause him to go to the hunting lodge. If he hadn't needed the time to be alone so that he could think clearly and lucidly, then he would have been at Castle Talakovich when Anton needed him. As it was, Prince Anton was travelling with Natasha, and while she was exceedingly beautiful, she was also the cause of their current problems, and she most certainly couldn't protect Anton like Caleb could.

He didn't like anything about what had happened. Anton was a capable man, with his fists, a dagger, sabre, or a pistol, but he was still nowhere near as good with weapons as Caleb was. Essentially, Anton was a boardroom warrior, and that's where he did his best fighting. That was why he needed Caleb — to do the dirty backroom deeds that were necessary if things were to operate smoothly.

Caleb cursed again and then went to the cabinet in his bedchambers, where he kept the whisky that he sometimes drank. He looked at the bottle with the amber liquor inside and wished then that he was back

271

home in America, where everyone spoke the same language as he. He wanted to be back in America, where he had few problems, and where the ones he did have were all small. He wanted to be in a place where the end result of failure was not a war between massive armies.

And he was lying to himself.

Caleb Carter wanted to be in the middle of it all. If he was painfully honest with himself, he was right where he wanted to be, and the only thing that bothered him was that he was not in on the hunt for Ivan Pronushka.

With a weary smile of resignation, Caleb closed the cabinet door. He didn't want anything to dull his senses. Not now, when so much was at stake.

So what was the next step?

He sat in the leather-covered chair in the corner of his room, placed his feet up on the stool, steepled his fingers, and closed off everything from his mind except thoughts concerning the problems at hand.

He could probably find Anton and Natasha. If he followed them, there was the real chance that he could help them find Ivan Pronushka. But to follow Anton meant leaving Anastasia alone. Caleb was certain the moment he left her alone, she'd be on her way to London to see the banker, Parker Windom. And even doing that wouldn't be such a bad move, since the banker's loan did seem to be the best one that had been offered, and if the czar's army was going to equip itself without alarming Napoleon, a loan from an outside country, and the discreet purchase and delivery of high-quality weapons had to be made.

What would Anton want me to do? Caleb asked himself.

And there was only one answer to that question. Anton would want him to stay with Anastasia to make sure that she was safe.

But safe from whom? What would Anton think if he

knew that Caleb had held Anastasia in his arms? What would the good prince think if he knew that Caleb had touched Anastasia's golden, slender body, and made her tremble with desire?

He'd be angry, that's what he'd be, Caleb decided.

He promised himself that he'd keep his hands to himself during the entire time that he was with Anastasia. He left the privacy of his bedchamber to tell the princess that they would be leaving for London as quickly as possible.

As much as Anton hated to admit it, Natasha had proven herself invaluable in the week that they had been hunting for Ivan Pronushka. It had taken three days for them to find the first trace of Ivan, and once they got it, Anton followed his instincts, even though Natasha disagreed with him.

"That isn't the way that Ivan's mind works," she complained. "You're thinking like a rich man."

"He's got five thousand of my rubles in his pocket," Anton had shot back. "Don't try to tell me he's not a rich man."

He refused to listen to Natasha's protests, and because he hadn't, they'd lost track of Ivan and a minimum of two full days as well. It was Natasha, working on a hunch, who suggested they find a tavern keeper who allowed prostitutes to frequent his establishment. Anton thought it would be a waste of time. He was wrong, Natasha was right, and because of her instincts they had once again found signs of Ivan during his westward travel.

The inn that Anton had chosen to stay in was not nearly as plush as he would have liked. In fact, he'd never before stayed in a room in Russia that he actually had to rent. But then, never before had he travelled without a retinue of men surrounding him.

"If you can write your name, we'd appreciate it for

the register," the innkeeper said, dipping a quill into ink.

Anton made a face. "Never learned," he said.

The innkeeper was used to illiterate guests. "And the names? I'll write them for you."

"Peotyr Bodzinsky."

The innkeeper waited, looking at Anton. "And the lady's name?" he asked at last.

"Whatever you want it to be," Anton said.

The men shared a smile, and Natasha turned away. Anton had treated her like she was his prostitute. She felt a pain deep down inside, but she didn't cry. She'd stopped crying after the second day with Anton. There simply weren't any more tears left in her. She'd felt as much acute pain as she could possibly feel. Now all that was left was a dull, throbbing ache, like a toothache where the nerves had become so raw they'd become forever numb.

She followed Anton to the room, carrying the single bag that held all her clothes and traveling items.

"Did you have to make it sound like you bought me?" she asked when they were alone in the room.

"No, I didn't have to, but I thought it would suit our purposes best. We don't have the look of a husband and wife. I don't want to show anyone my traveling papers unless I have to. By having the innkeeper think you're a . . . think that this evening is a business arrangement between us, he won't be inclined to ask any questions. He thinks he already knows what the truth is."

Anton threw his luggage on the bed and groaned. The bed did not seem at all comfortable. He was not accustomed to living like this, and for the hundredth time he wondered how Natasha had maintained her spirit when she'd been forced to live with Ivan and Aggie Pronushka for so many years.

Hardly had the thought entered his head when he chased it away. He refused to question anything con-

274

cerning Natasha. Every time he did, he began feeling sorry for her, and he couldn't allow himself to do that. It had been his own weaknesses, his hunger for her body and his desire to crawl inside her mind and share her thoughts and feelings, that had gotten him into so much trouble in the first place.

They had gotten a ritual down since the hunt started. Whenever they stopped at an inn, Natasha turned her back to Anton, undressed, then slipped quietly into bed. She stayed as close to the edge of the bed as she possibly could, and once in bed, she never moved a muscle. Anton did exactly the same thing, and though the two shared a bed, they never touched, never spoke.

Anton had pretended that they were husband and wife, but that hadn't happened again. To say that they were husband and wife, and pretend they were married for the innkeeper's benefit, was much too painful for Anton.

Anton removed his jacket, then sat on the edge of the bed and pulled off his boots, which now were scuffed and in need of polish. A grim smile pressed against his lips. This time he wouldn't be able to ring for Marta to have one of the servants polish them.

The soft knock at the door surprised Anton. He'd thought the innkeeper understood that he didn't want to be disturbed. For an instant, Anton and Natasha exchanged silent, questioning looks. Then Anton pulled the small pistol from the pocket of his coat and went to the door.

"Yes?" he asked, easing back the hammer of the weapon. He didn't trust anyone—certainly not the innkeeper.

"I brought you some hot water and clean rags . . . for afterward," the innkeeper said quietly, just loud enough to be heard through the door.

"Just leave it on the floor. I'll get it later," Anton replied.

There was a pause. Anton glanced at Natasha, and she was shaking her head slowly, amazed at Anton's lack of understanding.

The innkeeper said, "Slip your coin under the door. The soap and water come dear to me."

Anton understood finally that the innkeeper had hoped to increase his profits. He dashed back to his belongings on the bed, took a coin from his small leather pouch, and pushed the coin under the door. A moment later he heard the rattle of a pitcher and basin being placed on the wooden floor. Anton waited a few seconds, then checked the hallway. Finally, he took the water and pitcher into the room, smiling. It would be good to wash before seeking the barren comfort of sleep.

"Did you really think that he had gone through the trouble to heat the water just because he wanted you to be comfortable?" Natasha asked, sitting on the edge of the bed, watching Anton.

"Yes, I did. It seemed like a nice thing to do."

"Nice doesn't pay the czar's taxes. Out here, you've got to pay for everything, and everything has a price."

Natasha looked away then. It wasn't true, of course, that poor people didn't do anything nice for anyone else, and she knew this. But she also knew that Anton didn't know it, and she wanted to remind him of how out of his element he really was. He simply had no understanding of the innkeeper, or men like him.

Anton looked at Natasha as she eased out of her traveling dress. The spirit seemed to have been drained out of her since those hideous moments in the library, when she confessed to having told Ivan about the carriage. It burned in Anton's stomach to see her so unhappy, so defeated, yet he knew that he must not take pity upon her. He had already allowed his emotions to become involved, and because he had, he was now traveling incognito, living in conditions he found substandard, unable to reach out and touch the one woman he had once wanted more than anything else to touch.

"Natasha . . ."

She looked up at him, her fingertips toying with the straps of the chemise, unaware of how appealing she looked.

"Yes?"

Anton struggled to keep his gaze fixed upon her face. "Why don't you use the water first, while it's still hot?"

"Go ahead. He brought it for you. You paid for it."

"No, I want you to." Anton looked away. He tasted words upon his tongue, and knew they had to be spoken. "You've been quite helpful since we left Castle Talakovich. You understand how your uncle thinks, and I don't, and it is as simple as that, just as you said. If I'm going to catch Ivan before he makes it to Paris, I'll need you with me . . ."

He walked to the window and looked out. The night was starless, but the moon was full, shining brightly, sending moonlight into the room. He said, "Think of this as my way of saying I'm sorry that everything has . . . has been the way it has."

"Why not simply say you're sorry? I'd appreciate that more than the hot water."

Natasha looked at Anton's back, wanting him to turn so that she could look into his cold gray eyes. Even if she couldn't read his thoughts through his eyes the way he could with her, she wanted to see his face and just maybe find out what he held in his heart for her.

She waited for him to speak, but he did not, and finally Natasha accepted the fact that he would never forgive her for what she had done. Allowing her to use the water while it was clean and hot was a reward, payment for the work she'd done so far in tracking her uncle. It was payment, nothing more than that.

She went to the basin and poured the steaming water

277

into it. On the tray beneath it was a slender piece of soap, along with one small towel for washing with, and a larger one for drying.

What difference does it make if he sees me? Natasha thought with resignation. He doesn't care about me at all.

She grabbed the bottom edge of her chemise and pulled the garment over her head. Naked now from the waist up, dressed only in the pantalets that she had made for herself during the brief time that she had been living at Castle Talakovich when everyone was happy, Natasha bent over the water basin and picked up the soap, working up a rich, foamy lather in the wash cloth.

Anton heard the splashing of water, and he smiled, looking out at the ebony night. It pleased him to think that Natasha accepted his gift. During their time together chasing Ivan, she had been as cold and stoic as he had, never once complaining about the conditions that they were forced to live in.

Let her wash her face and feel refreshed, he thought as he turned slightly to look at her.

And then his breath caught in his throat, and his heart stopped beating in his chest.

She was leaning over the basin, washing her face, soapy from her stomach to her forehead. To see her breasts in profile, glistening with water and soap, moving gently as she washed her face, was supremely erotic to Anton. He caught his lips between his teeth and bit down hard to keep from gasping at the shock he felt. Down low he responded immediately to the sight of her, his manhood flaring to life spontaneously.

In a heartbeat, a thousand memories came flooding back to him, memories of the long, exhausting, erotic night that he had spent in Natasha's bedchamber at the castle, exploring again and again every inch of her curvaceous body, touching her, tasting her, burying himself deeply in her until he felt like he was a part of her,

278

continually driven forward by a desire that he did not fully comprehend but could only obey.

He watched as she placed the wash towel aside, then cupped the warm water in her hands, rinsing the soap from her face.

I've got to turn toward the window, Anton thought then, feeling as though he were being sucked into a vortex of desire from which there was no escape. I must turn around now or she'll catch me looking at her.

He did not turn away. Not even Anton's great strength of will was sufficient to make him turn away from Natasha.

When she had finished rinsing clean her face, she rinsed clean the wash towel, then began wiping the soap from her arms, shoulders, neck, and chest. Anton watched her, his eyes taking in every move of her hands, unable to deny himself the vision of her beauty.

And then, when Natasha was finished, she rinsed clean the towel, wringing as much water from it as possible. She turned toward Anton, making no effort at all to hide her bare breasts with the soft, dark nipples that glowed with the healthy clean sheen.

"I won't use the towel to dry myself," Natasha said calmly, looking Anton straight in the eyes. "At least you can use that first."

She turned away from him then, picking up her chemise and pulling it over her head. Then she slipped into the bed and curled up on the side, taking up as little space as she possibly could.

Natasha squeezed her eyes tightly shut, hoping and praying that the tears wouldn't start, and if they did, that she would be able to hide them from Anton.

She had thought that she couldn't hurt any more, and she was wrong. A knife in her heart wouldn't hurt as much as this. To have Anton look at her, wanting her, but refusing to touch her because of what she had done—it was the worst torture that Natasha could

279

think of.

She felt the mattress rock slightly as Anton got beneath the blankets beside her.

She thought that maybe tonight he would reach for her, touch her like he had when they were together in her bedchamber. If he touched her, Natasha knew that she wouldn't hesitate to give Anton whatever he desired. In this time of trouble, she wanted to feel Anton's hands upon her, feel his arms surrounding her. When she was in his arms and his body was strong and warm beside her own, she felt safe and secure as she never had before.

She lay awake, hoping Anton would reach for her . . . but he never did.

They were three days out from port, and Anastasia was finally feeling comfortable at sea. Whenever she sailed, there were always some uncomfortable days at first, but then she got used to the rocking of the boat, the snap of the sails overhead, and the splash of water against the hull, and she could then relax and enjoy herself.

She was glad now that she had chartered the boat, buying nearly all the passenger tickets so that the ship wouldn't be too crowded. The captain was happy to have her aboard, and profits would be considerably higher than normal, since there were many fewer mouths to feed.

She was standing on the deck when one of the crewmen approached.

"Princess Talakovich, please step away from the edge," the young man said respectfully.

Anastasia smiled at the sailor. He had the look of a man who'd spent his life at sea, his face lined and weathered, his countenance friendly and competent.

"Don't worry, I won't fall overboard," she said, smiling at the man. "I've travelled quite a bit."

"Yes, Princess Talakovich, I'm sure that you have," the sailor continued. "But you've never traveled aboard this ship, and if you would please step away from the edge, I would be very grateful."

"You're afraid that if I fall overboard, you'll have to answer to my brother," Anastasia said with a smile. She moved away from the edge of the boat though, having no desire to torment the kindly sailor.

"I simply do not want such a fine woman to have an accident," the sailor commented. He smiled finally, adding, "And I really do not want to answer for an accident when Prince Anton comes to call. His reputation is formidable."

The sailor left then, and Anastasia inhaled deeply. The sea has a special scent to it, a scent that can only be enjoyed aboard ship and far from land. Standing on shore, a person can't breathe the same scent, the scent that Anastasia had always loved. She associated freedom, excitement, and adventure with the scent of the sea.

If only Caleb wasn't in such a surly mood, Anastasia thought, then everything would be much better.

From the time they had left port, Caleb had been even more quiet than he normally was, withdrawn and somewhere faraway in his thoughts. Several times Anastasia had tried to draw him out, but he was unwilling to allow her to do that.

At first she thought that he was still angry that she hadn't fulfilled his desires in the same way that he had satisfied hers, but then she decided that he was probably just wishing he was with Anton, on the hunt for the missing documents. That's where the real excitement was, and Anastasia had no doubts that Caleb was anything but a man of action who always sought the fiery thrill of danger.

She wanted to flirt with Caleb, to say naughty things and to feel the heat of his eyes upon her. It would be fun to toy with Caleb the way that she had toyed with so many men from St. Petersburg and Moscow . . . except Caleb was much too dangerous a man to toy with, and Anastasia knew it.

She suspected he saw through the charade she presented. He knew that behind the flamboyant spirit, beneath the veneer of daring and adventurousness, there was a young woman frightened of being hurt, of being touched, a young woman who was supposed to be accustomed to knowing the pleasures of the flesh independent of the heart's emotions.

Caleb frightened her because she couldn't control him as she could other men, which, unfortunately, was precisely the reason why she was so fascinated by him, and why her body responded to him when it had not responded to any other man.

Anastasia walked back to the railing and looked out at the sea below. There were times when she wished that she'd never started the game, that silly, dangerous game to protect herself from men who only desired her because she had wealth and power.

"You shouldn't stand so close to the railing."

For only a second, Anastasia flinched at the unexpected sound of the male voice. Then she did her best to keep the smile from her face. How ironic it was that Caleb, her bodyguard and protector, also represented the greatest threat to her! Granted, he didn't represent a threat to her life, but he made her feel things that she had never felt before, and he tugged at her mind as no other man had, so she could hardly think of him as anything *but* a threat . . . of the most erotically appealing, enticing variety!

"I can assure you, Mr. Carter, that I will *not* fall overboard. I've been on many ships and sailed to many countries in my life."

She did not turn around, though she could feel that Caleb was close behind her. Sometimes it was very eerie how he could move without making a sound.

"I'm sure you can keep yourself aboard, but I'd still

prefer it if you would step away from the railing. If you went overboard at this time of night, there wouldn't be a prayer of us finding you."

Anastasia turned slowly, and her blue eyes were bright and shimmering—like priceless pieces of polished sapphire—when she faced Caleb.

"And you'd search for me?" she asked, painfully aware that she was practically begging for a flirtatious response from the enigmatic American.

His eyes, dark and fathomless, bore into hers. There were several seconds of absolute silence before Caleb replied, "Yes. I would."

"Why? You don't like me. I've treated you badly," Anastasia said. For some reason, she felt more courageous aboard ship, embraced by the night, feeling the cool evening breeze playing over her, fluttering the skirt of her gown around her legs.

Caleb stepped closer, and for merely a breath, his gaze rove up and down the princess, his eyes registering no emotion.

"You have treated me badly . . . but sometimes it is as important to be patient as it is to be determined. You see, you want me, and that's why you hate me. I know something about you—something you never intended me to know." He stepped even closer, near enough for Anastasia to feel the passion he had bottled up inside him. "That's why you've been fighting me, because I know you're just a frightened little virgin, even though you've done everything you could to make people believe that you know what you're doing."

"I *do* know what I'm doing!" Anastasia snapped, unable to ignore the insult. Why couldn't Caleb simply compliment her, when that's what she clearly wanted more than anything else? Why did he always have to be so . . . complicated?

"Not in bed you don't," Caleb replied softly, with the absolute conviction of a man who didn't have a

283

doubt about what he spoke. "What happens in bed is a complete mystery to you, but you're too proud or scared or just plain too juvenile to accept the fact that you don't know everything there is to know, so you insult people and behave haughtily and pretend to yourself that your life is exactly the way you want it, when what you really want is to come to my room tonight. You want to experience with me what you've been dreaming about for days now."

Princess Anastasia Talakovich had never been spoken to in such a fashion, and it shocked her to hear Caleb's words. Worst of all, there was more than just a grain of truth in the words that he said. She *was* afraid, and she really *didn't* know what was supposed to be happening in the bedchamber, and it wasn't at all fair that the one man who could make her body cry out for more was also the one man who annoyed her most in the world, and the one she had the least power over.

"You're an insulting man," Anastasia said with not nearly the amount of vehemence in her words that she'd hoped for.

"I haven't insulted you. I've only told you the truth. Whether you dislike the truth and find it insulting is your own problem."

Caleb turned, about to walk away, and though Anastasia didn't want to, she reached out and grabbed the sleeve of his blue velvet jacket.

"Wait . . . can't we stop fighting?"

Caleb turned partially toward her, looking at her with dark, unreadable eyes. "I don't know," he said honestly. "I try to hold my tongue, but I just can't seem to."

Anastasia suppressed the smile that tugged at her lips, which glistened moistly in the moonlight. It appealed to her that she could keep Caleb from behaving the way he normally did. She wanted to be different to him, different from everyone he'd ever known, or ever would know.

"You don't have to hold your tongue," she said softly, her voice carried on the night sea breeze. "All you have to do is stop saying the things that I don't want to hear."

Caleb shook his head, his mouth pulling up grimly on one side in an expression that might or might not be a smile. "What you want me to do is say what you want to hear. I get paid to do a lot of things, but I'm not getting paid by you to lie. If you want lies to flatter yourself, hire someone to do it. The only reason you're angry with me is because I bring out the real Anastasia in you, the sensualist that you've always been aware of and always afraid of, probably ever since you were a little girl."

He turned and walked away, leaving Anastasia standing there, not sure whether she hated him more than any man who had ever entered her life, or whether she wished he'd stop being such a gentleman, take her into his arms, and carry her into his plush leeward cabin, where he could spend the rest of the evening teaching her all the things he'd hinted at the last time she was in his arms.

Twenty-one

Anastasia sat on the edge of her bed, feeling the gentle rocking of the boat. When she closed her eyes, she could once again hear every word that Caleb had spoken to her.

Damn him! Damn him to hell and back again! she thought angrily. He had no right to speak to me that way!

But in her heart, she knew that every word that he'd said was not only true, but irrefutably true.

How old was she when she first realized that her body responded to the touch of fine fabrics? How old was she when the touch of brick-warmed sheets against her body first drew a response?

Anastasia knew then that the need for a fabricated mystery man to protect her was there long before she'd ever come of age. She had needed to create the fantasy of the cruel man in Moscow to protect herself from the men in St. Petersburg who wanted her. She had not understood at the time how necessary it was, because none of the men she flirted with triggered the response within her, but that didn't matter.

Without being able to put words to it, she had known all along deep in her soul that she was the sensualist that Caleb accused her of being. It had just taken years for her to meet Caleb Carter to discover the single man she had to truly protect her virginity from.

286

She removed her clothes for bed, and an errant thought brought a smile to her lips. For once, without Marta to wake her in the morning, she wouldn't need to place a nightgown at the foot of the bed, near enough so that she could pull it on quickly when Marta came with breakfast on a tray.

All her life, Anastasia had resisted sleeping in a nightgown. She much preferred the feel of bed linen against her body rather than a nightgown, but to sleep naked was something that Marta considered a blasphemy of the highest order. So, since she was a teenager, Anastasia had slept with a nightgown at the foot of the bed, and when Marta knocked on the bedchamber door, bringing breakfast, Anastasia would hurriedly pull the nightgown on, and then allow her nanny to enter.

With a sigh, Anastasia slipped between the sheets and closed her eyes. She had put down extra money to make sure that she had good bed linen during her trip to France, and though the sheets weren't made of Chinese silk (as the ones she slept on at Castle Talakovich were), they were still smooth and soft against her skin.

Anastasia closed her eyes, and tried to close her mind as well . . . but the moment she did, Caleb's handsome face came into view in her mind's eye, his countenance as vivid as if he was standing right in front of her.

She opened her eyes and stared at the ceiling.

I'm not a sensualist! she told herself resolutely.

She closed her eyes and rolled onto her side . . . and she was able to feel every subtle sensation. She felt her naked leg sliding against the mattress, the contact smooth and gentle. She felt the faint friction of her thighs rubbing together as she got comfortable. She felt the gentle movement of her small, firm breasts as she rolled onto her side, and the way her nipples caressed the bed linen.

I am a sensualist! Anastasia thought with a strange

sense of dread, as though it were some terrible flaw in her character instead of a simple fact of life, like the color of her hair, or the shape of her body.

Very slowly, concentrating now on what she felt, Anastasia rolled onto her back, straightening her legs, and placing her hands lightly at her sides a little ways from her trim hips.

Feel . . . concentrate on what you feel, she thought.

She let herself think about Caleb, and when she did, even though he was not there, she felt the surface of her skin begin to tingle, as though she was being touched very lightly.

It isn't a bad thing to dream of him, she told herself.

She lay absolutely motionless in bed, her eyes closed, her mind whirling devilishly. In the depths of her brilliant mind, she conjured up once again all the sensations, all the sights, sounds, and tastes, that she had known when she was with Caleb.

His tongue . . . oh, his tongue! How strange it had first seemed when his tongue had slipped between her lips, entering her mouth. She had wanted to protest, but almost immediately the pleasure had erased whatever negative thoughts tried to spring to life. Oh, how erotic it had been to slide her tongue against his, the friction both wet and raspy!

She remembered how it had felt to have Caleb's mouth, so hot and wet, closing over the tip of her breast, his teeth and tongue alternating the sensations of sharpness and velvet-softness against her sensitive nipple.

With her eyes closed, Anastasia could feel her nipples, blunt and pink, become erect. She suppressed a smile, even though there was no one there to see the smile. There was no need to smile, she told herself, because she wasn't enjoying herself. Then, slowly and tentatively, she moved her shoulders just a little, just enough to turn her upper body sufficiently to cause her nipples to slide against the fine, light bed sheet.

"Oh-h-h!" she sighed as a tingle went through her, sizzling from the tips of her breasts throughout her body.

I'm terribly wicked, she thought, hearing the sound of her own sigh in the silence of her cabin.

She moved her shoulders once more, returning to her original position, and the sensation of the bed sheet sliding across the tips of her breasts was even more enticing than it had been the first time.

Caleb's to blame for this, Anastasia thought.

She caught her lower lip between her teeth and bit softly, telling herself this nonsense had to stop immediately. He was indeed to blame for making her aware of what she was capable of feeling, though criticizing him for his actions was incomprehensible now as she lay quietly in bed, more aware of her body than she ever had been before.

There were a thousand perfectly good reasons why she shouldn't be thinking about her own body, and about how it reacted whenever Caleb was near, Anastasia told herself. After all, she was headed to France, and from France she would get onto another boat and sail to England, where in London she would conclude business that would make it possible for Russia to defend itself. She could not sail directly to London because it was still illegal for the English and Russian governments to do business with each other.

Yes, there wasn't time for silliness and there certainly wasn't time for sensuality, and Anastasia knew that.

But her body didn't. Her body was alive to the possibilities of pleasure, at a heightened state of awareness . . . and all because of Caleb Carter, a mysterious American who, she was quite certain, she would have been better off if she'd never met.

With her eyes still closed, Anastasia was able to concentrate on the gentle motion of the boat. She felt then like she was floating, drifting in space, not laying upon

289

a bed on a ship. She was weightless, and nothing in the world mattered except being aware of her own body, nothing except her feelings . . . nothing except Caleb.

She was so deeply into the world of her mind, her inner world of awareness, that at first she did not hear the gentle knock at her door. Then, slowly, gently, a little sadly, she opened her eyes, blinked several times, and became aware of the physical world.

She heard the knock again, then Caleb asking softly, "Anastasia, are you in there? I must speak with you."

For a ragged moment she felt almost panicky. She had allowed her mind to wander into territory that was best left alone, and she felt almost unnaturally warm, heated to the core of her soul. She didn't *dare* let herself look at Caleb. He was much too handsome, and that dangerous quality of his, the one that whispered of intrigue and unspeakable pleasures, was much too intoxicating for her to risk being in the same room with him.

He knocked again, and this time when he spoke, Anastasia heard just a hint of worry in his tone. She could tell that he was keeping his voice muted so that he wouldn't draw the attention of any of the passengers or crew.

"Wait!" Anastasia replied finally. She kicked her feet over the edge of the bed, pausing a moment to compose herself. She felt jittery inside, and she made a promise to herself to never again let her mind wander like that. "I was sleeping."

"I have to talk to you."

"Why didn't you just barge in on me? That's what you've always done in the past."

She stood in the center of her quarters, her hair tussled, streaming over her slender shoulders, her emotions racing crazily in all directions, her mind suddenly quite incapable of logically deciding what her next move should be.

She was naked. Putting on a robe, or in the very least

her nightgown, *would* be the intelligent thing to do.

Keeping Caleb in a different country far away from herself would be the intelligent thing to do! she thought angrily, padding barefooted across the room.

"What is it, Caleb?" she asked, whispering, placing her hands against the door.

"I want to talk to you. I *must* to talk to you."

His voice was husky, passionate, thick with desire. It made Anastasia tremble. She closed her eyes, pressing her forehead against the smooth, hard, cool cedar door.

"Are words all you want?" she asked.

It took a moment for Anastasia to fully comprehend what she'd asked of Caleb. Then the reality of it — that her desire for him had forced her to voice a question that her better judgment knew she should not — filtered through the fog of her passion. She smiled sleepily when she heard the low, growling sound of Caleb's annoyance as he stood outside her cabin in the ship's hallway.

"No, it's not *all* I want," he said. "I want you. All of you. Every last bit of you."

"That sounds dangerous. But then, you're a dangerous man."

Anastasia's fingers toyed with the locking bolt on the door. All she had to do was raise the small handle, then slide the bolt through the locking hoops. She could unbolt the door without Caleb ever hearing it, then stand naked and defiant, separated only by an unlocked door, and taunt the passionate, virile man.

"Yes, I am a dangerous man, Anastasia. Especially for you."

She eased the bolt gently from its locked position. It was deliciously exciting to be talking to Caleb, teasing him mercilessly, while standing naked on the other side of the door, only inches apart. It was exactly the kind of thing that Caleb had taught her she craved, even though she'd never really understood that until she met him.

"I'm dangerous because I'm the man you can't run away from, and I'll teach you that you can't run away from yourself either," he whispered.

She leaned against the door, its smooth, cool surface a solid barrier against her breasts. She stifled the low moan of excitement, catching the sound in her throat, sure that Caleb would not control himself if he knew that all he had to do was push open the door and the bounty that had eluded him so long would be his.

"I'm supposed to be a very experienced woman," Anastasia said after a moment. "Maybe I could teach you something?"

"Your experience is all a myth, and we both know it." There was a growing, sharpening edge to Caleb's tone now. Anastasia sensed that she was playing a *very* dangerous game now . . . and she wasn't certain whether allowing Caleb to enter her cabin would make her the winner or the loser. "You're untouched."

"Not completely."

"No. Not completely."

She could almost feel his heat through the door, feel the hunger he had for her seep into the pores of her skin. She moved away from the door just enough so that her breasts no longer touched the smooth cedar. Her nipples throbbed with tension, hard little buds of pink flesh that responded to Caleb's voice, knowing the pleasure he could provide.

"Let me in, Anastasia."

"No. You'll have to kick it down. I won't let you in."

"Why would I kick the door in? I heard you throw the bolt."

Anastasia stepped away from the door, shocked. She hadn't even heard the bolt moving herself! Caleb had known all along that all he had to do was push open the door to enter her cabin!

She waited, certain that the door would burst open at any moment. Each second seemed to last an hour as

Anastasia stood, trembling from head to toe, staring at the door, her naked body tingling with anticipation for what was at last about to happen.

But she was greeted with nothing but silence.

"Caleb?" she whispered.

No response.

"Caleb, are you out there?"

Still no response.

"Caleb?"

Dead silence.

In the blink of an eye she pictured Caleb Carter, a lusty, virile man long accustomed to women satisfying his passion, deciding that she was no longer worth the wait. She saw in her mind's eye Caleb simply turning and walking away, no longer willing to play the cat-and-mouse game that had aroused her so completely.

She rushed to the door, heedless of her own nudity, and threw the door wide open.

"Caleb, don't you dare leave!" she shouted.

He was standing there, leaning nonchalantly against the door frame, a much-too-confident grin pulling at his lips, his dark eyes burning with passion.

"There's no need to shout," he said, as though he and Anastasia were once again in the library at Castle Talakovich, with Anton nearby, arguing about some method of procuring financing for their munitions purchases.

Anastasia teetered on her heels, very nearly in the hallway, breathing deeply with shock, reminded of her nudity only when she watched Caleb's eyes roam slowly over her in a perusing manner from head to foot.

"I thought you'd left me."

Caleb placed a hand on her shoulder, gently but insistently pushing her back into the cabin, and closed the door behind him.

"Princess . . . I don't think I could *ever* leave you."

She reached for him, trembling softly, terribly conscious of her nudity now, wishing to feel him touching her, needing to taste the sweetness of his lips against her own. As she slipped her arms around his neck, Caleb took her into his arms, lifting her scant weight easily, and carried her to bed.

Anastasia kissed him as though his lips alone kept her alive. She opened her mouth invitingly, and when she received his tongue, the purr from her throat was one of pure animal sensuality.

She accepted, then, all that Caleb had said about her being a sensualist. She *was* a sensualist . . . but only for Caleb. It was Caleb, and the nightmare possibility that he would leave her once again, that had made her willing to rush out into the hallway completely naked just to stop him.

The feel of his clothes against her naked body was suddenly intolerable. Even though Caleb wore fine clothes, their touch against her skin was almost painful. In the fevered state of her excitement, nothing less than Caleb, in all his naked, primitive, predatory animal magnificence, would suffice.

"Wait . . . easy," Caleb said as Anastasia pulled at his jacket.

She resented him a little for being so calm. When he rose to his knees on the bed to ease the removal of his jacket, she crossed an arm over her chest, and placed her other hand down low to hide her femininity. She was certain that a man of Caleb's sexual experience would prefer a woman of a more curvaceous physique, and she felt self-conscious when he looked down at her.

He stripped off his jacket and shirt quickly, then got off the bed to remove his trousers.

"Let me look at you," Caleb said quietly, yet commandingly. His breeches were opened, pushed very low, nearly exposing the manhood that was already swollen with passion for the princess.

Anastasia moved her hands away slowly, exposing

herself completely to Caleb in a way that was as emotionally opening as it was physically. He smiled then, a gently pleasing smile that touched Anastasia with its heat and wrapped her in perfumed folds of confidence.

"Now let me see you," she whispered, her mouth suddenly feeling very dry, though she was particularly moist down low, and the rest of her body felt heated.

Caleb pushed out of his breeches and underclothes, then returned to the bed, his flaring arousal standing out flagrantly, ready for Anastasia. He got onto the bed, and she rose up to meet him, sliding her arms around his chest to pull him close.

"Oh, yes-s-s!" Anastasia sighed, feeling the heat of Caleb's powerful chest against her sensitive breasts, the contact of him against her inflamed nipples one of such supreme satisfaction that she could not understand then why she had ever tried to keep Caleb away from her.

Caleb sensed her excitement, as well as her fear. Though he was inclined to allow this first moment of lovemaking to be a slow, leisurely expedition through the senses, Anastasia's volatile state and seesawing emotions made that impossible.

"Now . . . now . . . now," Anastasia whispered, shivering in Caleb's arms.

She felt his hand at her hip, the fingers trailing around to glide over the taut curve of her buttocks, then dipping lower to gently touch the moist petals of her femininity. She gasped when he touched her, feeling like she had been seared by the heat of his touch.

A thousand thoughts danced in Anastasia's mind, some of them delightfully pleasing, others annoying because they took away from the eroticism that was there for her to enjoy. She knew that she could not wait any longer for Caleb to become one with her. To wait one instant more would surely drive her mad.

"Now, Caleb! I can't wait any longer," she whispered, pulling him into her, opening her thighs to surround his lean hips.

She felt the hard, heated length of his arousal pressing against her belly, trapped between their bodies. It seemed to her then like an independent object, something separate from both her and Caleb.

When he raised his hips, Anastasia protested. She did not want him to break the delicious, full-length contact of their bodies. Then she felt the tip of his manhood against her, pushing firmly, insistently, and she realized why he'd raised his hips, and what was about to happen next.

For a moment, their faces very close together, they looked into each other's eyes.

"No matter what, you mustn't stop," Anastasia whispered, fear now mingling with the excitement that raced through her limbs. She had heard that it hurt terribly to lose one's virginity, and though she had no experience to compare Caleb with, he seemed a man of generous dimensions.

It took every ounce of will that Caleb possessed to control himself, but he did. He progressed slowly, with infinite patience, and when at last Anastasia opened to the entire length of his arousal, her short gasp of pain lasted no longer than a single breath.

To feel him inside her, gliding gently back and forth, was the unsolvable mystery that had eluded the frightened princess for so long. When Caleb held his weight up on his elbows, Anastasia pulled at him, her hands around him, her fingernails clawing at the smooth, muscle-rippled flesh of his back. She did not want anything separating them, either physically or emotionally, and when his chest was again pressing against her breasts, Anastasia sighed with sensual bliss.

She had thought that Caleb would be uncontrolled in his loving. Everything that she thought she knew about him indicated that he was extremely passionate, and such desire would surely burn too hot to allow for much self-control.

She couldn't have been more wrong. He seemed almost too civilized, and afterward, when he had gasped with ecstasy as his seed rushed from him into her, Anastasia felt a little guilty, as though her inexperience had somehow taken from Caleb's pleasure, inhibiting him, bridling him in when what he would really want to do was let his emotions run unchecked.

"I have to ask," Anastasia said, when she'd recovered her breath.

"Ask what?"

"You know."

"No, I don't know. What?"

"Whether I was . . . well, you know . . . whether it was any . . ."

Caleb smiled, at last deducing what it was that Anastasia had to ask while still lacking the courage to actually voice the question aloud.

"Ask what? You must tell me," he said, a grin now pulling at his mouth.

"Don't be coy with me. I'm not confident enough at this to be toyed with. Now give me an answer."

Caleb could see the sincerity in Anastasia's lovely eyes of sapphire blue.

"You were exquisite, my darling princess."

Anastasia smiled then, and even though she had been told a thousand times by a hundred different men that she was attractive, she never really believed it — not deep down in her heart — until that very moment.

Caleb reached out to cup the princess's face in his large hands. He thought it terribly strange that such a beautiful woman should be so insecure about her looks, that such a sexy woman should be so frightened of whether or not she was exciting to a man.

In truth, she had been rather tentative with him, but Caleb had expected as much, especially since it was her first time. That was why he had done all he could to make it enjoyable for her, and why he had been so careful to not let the passion, which he had kept bottled up for so long, become unharnessed.

Despite all the rumors, and her flamboyant and flirtatious manner of dress and behavior, Princess Anastasia Talakovich was in many ways a very young, frightened girl. She'd lived a life of bizarre isolation, separated by her wealth, her extraordinary intellect, and her vast beauty, from the rest of the world. Caleb was determined to keep her safe and protected, even from his most ardent animal desires.

Anastasia closed her eyes. She didn't want to cry, but she could feel tears brimming, though for the life of her she couldn't say why. She wasn't sad. Not in any way. Making love with Caleb had been everything she had imagined it would be. And though it had initially hurt to take him inside her, to be joined to him both physically and emotionally, the pain was short-lived, quickly supplanted by a pleasure far greater in both intensity and duration.

So why were there tears in her eyes?

"What's wrong?" Caleb asked, leaning close to Anastasia, looking intently into her face, searching for answers greater than those that would be spoken.

"Nothing," Anastasia said after a moment. Caleb's look bespoke of his disbelief. "I'm telling you the truth. Nothing is wrong. In fact, my life has never been so right."

She wiped away the tears, feeling a little embarrassed by them.

Why didn't men cry at times like this? she wondered. Perhaps they did, she decided, but they kept the tears to themselves. If they didn't cry, maybe they should.

"Tell me what you want," Caleb said.

She looked at him and smiled. So typically male to think that whatever she needed to make her happy would be something that could be bought. Mostly what she wanted was words, which she doubted would be fast in coming from a man like Caleb. More than anything else, she just wanted to know that she meant something to Caleb, and that she was more than just another sexual conquest. She wasn't asking for an eternity with him; she wasn't asking for a marriage proposal; all she wanted was a few tender words.

"Nothing, really," she said finally.

She had gotten Caleb to show a side of himself — a tender, caring side — and that was enough for her . . . for now. Later, perhaps, she would try for more from him, a deeper intimacy that had nothing to do with the ways of the flesh . . . but that was for later. For now, she would just be happy with what she had, which was him beside her, with his arms protectively around her.

"I've traveled to many countries, princess, but I've never traveled in this type of luxury," Caleb said. He was leaning back against the headboard of the bed, his long, lean body naked and relaxed and magnificent to look at.

"That's because you always travel alone, or with my brother," Anastasia replied, smiling, finding it difficult to keep from giggling as she plucked another cherry tomato from the bowl and popped it into Caleb's mouth. "Travel with me, my American lover, and you'll travel in luxury. I hate *anything* Spartan."

Anastasia was sitting with her legs folded beneath her, completely naked, and for the first time completely at ease with her nudity.

It was wonderful to see Caleb this way, relaxed and joyful, happily munching away on the delicious tomatoes, cucumbers in wine sauce, and cheese that she had ordered.

"I don't think I'll ever quite become accustomed to the Russian custom of eating so many tomatoes and cucumbers," Caleb said as a slice of cucumber was headed toward his mouth. Anastasia's hand stopped in midair, her gaze questioning. He caught her wrist and brought her hand close enough to bite the cucumber from her fingers. "I didn't say I didn't like it; I just said I won't get used to it."

"Will you get used to me?" Anastasia asked.

He looked at her, knowing that she wanted the compliment, and knowing that there was a timid little girl behind the flirtatious princess who *needed* the compliment. He watched as she tucked a lock of honey blonde hair behind her ear, in a sudden nervous gesture, shifting her position on the bed, clearly uneasy with his silence.

"Never," he said finally. He turned her hand to kiss the inside of her wrist. "I promise you that. I'll never get used to you, tired of you."

Anastasia closed her eyes for only a moment, savoring the sense of relief that she felt deep within. Everything about Caleb now utterly fascinated her, delighted her. She loved every line of his body, every hair on his chest, even the mysterious scars that looked like they'd been caused by a knife, though Caleb didn't want to talk about them.

"What do you think of the London deal?" Caleb asked then, never entirely comfortable with long silences in a conversation that had been tender and contemplative. He turned his attention back to the bowl of cheese on the bed near his hip.

Anastasia smiled, fully understanding why Caleb had so quickly changed the subject. She nibbled on a tomato and accepted the fact that Caleb would never be entirely at ease with heartfelt words.

"The London deal sounds fine. If he wants three percent interest, he's asking too much. And he's got to be the one to put his signature on the transit papers. I don't want a Talakovich signature on them."

"He'll agree to those terms. He knows that there's something not quite right about the loan," Caleb said. "That's why I'm certain we can buy him."

"He's crooked, but not so crooked that we can't do

business with him," Anastasia replied.

It was a statement, not a question, and it rather shocked Caleb. Sometimes he forgot how completely involved in the family business Anastasia had been over the years. Anton seldom mentioned Anastasia's contribution, or if he did, Caleb had not taken the statements as seriously as he should have.

"There's something about Parker Windom that just doesn't quite ring true," Caleb continued. "I sensed it right away — that he knew I was just a front man hiding someone else — and it didn't bother him at all."

Anastasia nodded her head, her lovely blue eyes now distant as she thought about a man she'd never met. "If he asks for any more than three percent interest on the money, I'll refuse the deal."

The steelish resolution in Anastasia's statement impressed Caleb. She might be insecure in the bedchamber, but she certainly wasn't when it came to business matters.

"Even if it comes to three and a quarter percent interest, with the loan we want that's . . . let's see, pounds sterling to rubles would be . . . a difference of nearly fifty thousand rubles," Anastasia commented. "For fifty thousand rubles, we can find someone else to do business with. Besides, as you well know, it's still illegal for Russian and British companies to do business together."

Caleb shook his head, thoroughly amazed that Anastasia had not only figured out what the difference would be for the interest rates on the loan, but also calculated the difference from English currency to Russian currency — and all in her head, without so much as the benefit of paper and pen!

"What will Anton say if you turn down the deal?" Caleb asked, his masculine sensibilities making it impossible to tell Anastasia how much she'd just impressed him.

Anastasia smiled, and her eyes became bright and

focused. "Anton trusts my judgment completely. He won't be angry with me at all."

She took the plate of cheese and moved it so that it was no longer between herself and Caleb, then stretched out on her stomach, her cheek against his chest.

"You and I are the only people in the world that my brother trusts. I wonder what he'd think about us being lovers?"

She liked the sound of that word. For so long, she had pretended to have a lover, a cruel and cold-hearted one who treated her badly. It was deliriously joyous now to finally have a lover who represented what the word was really supposed to mean.

"I've wondered about that myself," Caleb said, his fingers following the contours of Anastasia's shoulders, touching her lightly. "He'll probably want to kill me."

"That might be going a bit far," Anastasia chuckled. She turned her head just enough to kiss Caleb's chest. Her tongue flicked out briefly to graze across his nipple, and she received a soft moan of pleasure as her reward. "It seems to me that since we're already guilty, so to speak, we might just as well be magnificently guilty."

Anastasia rolled toward Caleb, letting her knee slide along his thigh. Her hand had been at his stomach, but now, with a courage she never really thought she possessed, she reached lower, blindly searching for the scepter of his desire for her.

He was not yet entirely ready for her, but when she took him into her hand, she felt him throb powerfully, coming alive. She squeezed him, and Caleb's moan was even louder than before, tinged with surprise and delight.

"That pleases you?" she asked, completely guileless, looking into Caleb's eyes as she stroked his burgeoning manhood.

He nodded. Anastasia tossed her knee over his lean hips, straddling him boldly the moment he had become fully aroused. He reached up to cup her breasts, and she tossed her head back on her shoulders, her moan of desire mingling now with his.

"Teach me to be a lover," she whispered, both hands moving along Caleb's turgid flesh, rubbing the crown of it against the triangular patch of honey blonde hair surrounding her womanhood.

"Teach you? My darling, you're a natural lover . . . a natural sensualist! My very own natural sensualist!"

As he spoke the last word, Anastasia raised her lean hips enough to get into position, then she descended upon him, taking his arousal fully within herself. To feel him spearing up into her, spreading her wide, filling her so completely, was such sublime joy . . . but Anastasia knew there was one thing missing, one vital facet of Caleb that she had yet to explore.

She looked down at him, and with challenge in her shimmering blue eyes, said, "Take me, Caleb. Don't hold back this time. I'm yours, all yours, take me there!"

She had wanted a response from Caleb, an unbridled response that spoke without words of the man inside . . . but she never dreamed it would be this commanding, or so satisfying.

Caleb's response was swift and sure. He raised himself up, and in one smooth, powerful move, had Anastasia supine beneath him a moment later, with her ankles up near his shoulders, and his dark eyes bore into her as his hips pistoned smoothly, powerfully, relentlessly.

"Yes-s-s! Oh, yes-s-s!" Anastasia sighed, feeling the extraordinary sensations of being both dominated and yet dominating, vulnerable and yet protected, powerful in the powerful response she'd evoked from Caleb.

Twenty-two

These were, without doubt, the best days that Ivan Pronushka had ever known in his entire life. He had money in his pocket to buy good food, fine liquor, and the most expensive women available.

The only problem, the only tiny factor that marred his existence, was the fact that he had not gotten as far as he had hoped. His journey to Paris was going to take longer than he had first thought. But even if he was a month late in arriving, he would *still* have money in his pocket, and the documents he'd stolen would still be just as valuable to Napoleon.

And there was also Rosto Rapp to think about. Ivan didn't trust his cousin completely. In fact, he trusted him hardly at all. He and his cousin were cut from the same cloth, and it was because of this that Ivan knew he could make a deal with Rosto. This was just the kind of deal that Rosto would find irresistible!

Ivan loaded his pipe with tobacco, then tilted it toward the candle. The tobacco was of excellent quality — the Balkan tobacco that Ivan had always enjoyed but seldom could afford — and the pipe was almost new, having been purchased during Ivan's last stop.

"Maybe I'll see you later," the prostitute said as she adjusted the bodice of her dress, then stepped out of the room, closing the door behind her, not even waiting for an answer from Ivan.

Ivan just smiled when the woman left. She hadn't been very energetic, though she was certainly pretty enough to please him enormously. Because she hadn't shown much enthusiasm for her work, he'd been rougher with her than he otherwise was with women he bought. She didn't like it, of course, but then Ivan wasn't really concerned with what she did or didn't like.

He rolled onto his side, continuing to puff away at his pipe, enjoying the tobacco. Too bad his hangover was as bad as it was. Ivan was determined that today he wouldn't drink at all, at least not until he found a carriage westward. He'd already spent more time in this village than he'd planned, and all because the liquor was cheap, the women attractive and available, and the inn clean.

At last Ivan kicked his feet over the edge of the bed and sat up. The pounding in his skull became even worse. He thought that maybe if he got something to eat, and had a drink or two just to calm his nerves, then his head wouldn't ache so horribly.

Time to get traveling again, Ivan thought with as much resolution as he was capable of mustering. He'd left behind several corpses in St. Petersburg, and a very angry family of royal blood with very close ties to the czar. That was reason enough to keep going.

He paid his bill with the innkeeper. Even after three days, the innkeeper still looked warily at Ivan, as though sensing that he was a murderer, even though Ivan hadn't done anything other than use prostitutes.

"What time is it?" Ivan asked, picking up his one piece of luggage.

"Nearly noon. My wife can fix you something to eat, if that's what you're asking." He didn't seem at all enthusiastic to have Ivan as a guest in his inn any longer than necessary, but since he offered a meal to all of his guests, he could hardly refuse Ivan.

Ivan thought about the offer for a moment, then declined. His stomach felt a little too queasy to handle food. Perhaps just a glass or two of some fine wine, and then he'd be right as rain and ready to travel hard for another couple of days.

He paused at the doorway, then pushed it open and stepped out into the sunlight that was so bright it was blinding, thrusting like daggers through his brain. He placed a hand over his eyes, standing motionless. The world reeled beneath his feet, and Ivan promised himself that he was going to take some time away from the women and liquor.

He still had a hand over his eyes when a sound registered in his brain. It was a strange sound, and not even the daggers that were thrusting and twisting in his brain could completely blot out the sound. But why did he care? It wasn't important enough to risk taking his hand away from his eyes.

Natasha!

It took several seconds, but then Ivan recognized the voice, and the recognition spurred him into spontaneous action despite the cruelty of his hangover.

She was far down the dusty street, approaching him slowly, bending over slightly as though that would somehow enable her to see more clearly. When Ivan looked directly at her, Natasha stopped walking. For a second or two, she just looked at him.

Ivan's first thought was that at last he was going to have the chance to force himself upon his niece, just the way he'd always wanted to, though Aggie never would let him. But then, further beyond Natasha, Ivan recognized another figure: a tall man with broad shoulders, blond hair, and an athletic stride.

Natasha hadn't come alone, and since the man with her was Prince Anton Talakovich, that could only mean that they'd been hunting for Ivan.

Ivan started to cross the street, hoping that perhaps Natasha didn't really recognize him. Then she called out again, drawing Anton's attention. And in the next instant Anton pulled a pistol from beneath his jacket, raised the long weapon with both hands, and squeezed the trigger.

Ivan felt the tug of his jacket as the heavy lead ball caught the collar of the new coat he'd purchased only a few days earlier. A couple inches to the right, and the ball would have gone through his throat.

In his fear he dropped his bag, heading back for the inn. Then reason—or perhaps it was greed—took over and stopped him in his tracks. He heard Anton shout. Ivan picked up the bag he'd dropped—the bag that carried the stolen papers, as well as his travel documents signed by the czar himself—and rushed back into the inn.

"Say a word where I've gone, and I'll put a knife in your back!" Ivan hissed to the innkeeper.

He rushed through the back exit and was outside again in just a matter of seconds. He knew that the innkeeper would tell Anton and Natasha where he'd gone, but maybe his threat would give him just a little more time nevertheless.

He ran down the alleyway, clutching onto the bag, his hangover completely forgotten now as perspiration began moistening the collar of his jacket—the collar that now had a tear in it from the bullet from Anton's pistol!

"He's here. He's here somewhere," Anton grumbled, breathing deeply, standing in the middle of the street, trying to catch his breath.

"He might already have gone on to another city.

307

We don't know," Natasha said, her words coming out haltingly with her ragged breathing. She didn't have the stamina that Anton did.

Further down the street, Natasha recognized the red and blue uniforms of the military men. Instantly, she felt a stab of fear go through her. As a commoner, she had a fear of the soldiers, though this fear was something that she was certain Anton would never understand.

She took Anton by the sleeve and pulled him a few steps back, so that he was partially hidden in shadows. Anger was making him incautious.

"We don't want the soldiers to see us," she said quietly.

"To hell with the soldiers," Anton replied. He looked down the street, away from where the soldiers were congregating, his attention still focused on trying to find Ivan. "I own my own soldiers."

"Yes, I know you do, but you don't own those soldiers . . . and right now, they're coming this way."

Anton was not so furious with himself for missing his pistol shot at Ivan that he missed the furtive quality in Natasha's voice. He allowed her to pull him around the corner of a small butcher shop, then he peered around the corner at the approaching uniformed men.

There were four soldiers, walking in a "Y" formation, just as they had been taught. Anton looked at the men and sized up his own options. He could confront the men and explain who he was, and why he had fired a pistol at another man. To do that would, of course, absolve him of all wrongdoing. A man of his social and political stature could do whatever he wanted to. But to say who he was would completely destroy his anonymity, and make it impossible for him to keep his search for Ivan Pronushka a secret. Once the secret was out, he was certain that it would only be a matter of time before some enterprising soul sold the information to Napoleon.

And, then of course, there was the possibility of enlisting the soldiers in his search for Ivan Pronushka.

"They're not *your* soldiers," Natasha said, standing behind Anton.

He looked over his shoulder at her and smiled. "I thought I was the one who could read thoughts?"

"I picked it up being near you," Natasha replied. It surprised her that she had accurately guessed exactly what had been going through Anton's mind, and she felt rather proud of her achievement.

"Still, they are soldiers, and soldiers follow orders."

"Only *your* soldiers follow your orders," Natasha repeated. The uniformed men, carrying long rifles with attached bayonets, were much closer now, stopping occasionally to talk to people. There was no doubt in Natasha's mind that they were looking for whoever it was had fired the pistol. "These men aren't going to be like those in Moscow or St. Petersburg. They're far away from any central authority here . . . and that means they're a law unto themselves."

Anton heard the fear in Natasha's voice now, and the sound of it surprised him. He'd never known a moment's fear from any soldier wearing the blue and red uniform. In fact, the sight of them had always been a comforting one, letting him know that he was well-protected against his enemies. He had heard the stories of atrocities and abuses of power by the soldiers when they were away from the watchful eyes of the commanders stationed in the large cities, but he'd never given the stories too much credence.

But he'd never really been on the run like this before, without all his wealth and power and authority behind him to protect him and give credibility to whatever he said.

309

"Damn," Anton hissed through teeth clenched in rage, realizing that he had to leave, or risk being caught by men who might or might not have any respect for the czar's laws.

He turned, took Natasha by the hand, and walked swiftly down one alleyway after another, staying to the corridors that were neither extremely crowded, nor completely barren, walking just fast enough to put distance between himself and the scene of the gunshot, and not so quickly that he drew undue attention to himself.

As the minutes ticked by, it became readily apparent that the soldiers were more than just a little bit interested in finding the man who had fired the gunshot. A hundred times Anton cursed himself for missing his one chance at stopping Ivan. He kept thinking that if Caleb had been with him, then the entire problem of the stolen documents would be over—because Caleb *never* missed his target when he squeezed the trigger of a gun.

"If we stay in this village long, eventually the soldiers will find us," Anton said quietly, standing near a small shack were cups of hot tea and bread were sold to the passing workers. "But I want to stay close. Ivan's here! All we've got to do is find him!

"No, we don't!" Natasha replied, her expression alight with excitement.

Anton's eyes narrowed suspiciously. "If you want to leave, I won't try to stop you. I'll catch him myself."

"That's not what I'm talking about. I'm saying we don't have to catch him here. He knows we're after him now."

"And that just means that he'll be traveling faster than ever."

"Not Ivan. That's not the way his mind works. Rather than trying to move faster than we do, he'll set up an ambush. That's what he did when he stole the strongbox. That's what he'll do now. He'll try to ambush us."

Anton's expression changed, transforming from one of suspicion that Natasha was going to leave him, to one of curiosity and interest.

"So what are you suggesting?" he asked.

"That we use my uncle's way of thinking to catch him," Natasha said, formulating the plan as she spoke, liking it more and more all the time. "We know where he's going—to his cousin in Paris. And now he's going to be traveling much slower. He'll have to set his trap for us, then wait there to catch us in it. Only we won't be following him. We'll be out in front of him, setting a trap for *him* when he reaches Paris."

"But the documents," Anton replied, his tone distracted. "I've got to get those documents before he can sell them."

"And he can't sell them until he gets to Paris," Natasha replied, confident that the logic of her plan was beyond reproach.

Slowly, as though he was trying to fight it all the way, Anton broke into a full smile, the one that made the dimple show in his cheek, and put a brightness in his cool gray eyes that Natasha so delighted in. It was the first time she could remember him smiling since their night of lovemaking at Castle Talakovich which seemed a lifetime ago.

"You're an intelligent lady, aren't you? I thought I was supposed to be the shrewd one."

"You are. You're just not alone," Natasha said. She felt as though the hand that had been around her heart, squeezing mercilessly since they'd left St. Petersburg, had finally decided to lessen its painful hold on her.

"Let's get out of here before we have to explain ourselves to the soldiers," Anton said, his hand lightly on the small of Natasha's back, touching her

311

in a way that he had not in a long time. "I'm sure we can find accommodations to Paris if we try."

The carriage came to a halt in Dresden, and when Anton stepped out into the cool night, he felt as though he'd been sitting forever. He turned to help Natasha out of the carriage. She groaned a little, though the sound was nearly inaudible. Anton knew that she was only trying to be brave. His body ached all over from the bumpy ride they'd taken for days now, and if his body ached, then he was certain that hers did, too.

"This place looks comfortable," Anton said, his hand at Natasha's elbow.

Natasha looked at the inn and sighed. She was out of the carriage finally, which meant that anything—including a stables with hay, if necessary—would look comfortable to her. All she wanted was a mattress, and she would be asleep in no time at all.

"Yes," she said at last, trying not to groan. The ride to Dresden had jolted her constantly, made even worse by the fact that the coachmen were behind schedule, so they'd refused to stop for anything other than calls to answer nature.

It had been days since they'd first spotted Ivan, and Natasha was certain now that they were far ahead of her evil uncle. During the trip, she had noticed that Anton's attitude toward her had warmed somewhat. He still wasn't granting the loving attention she had once known and had so appreciated, but at least now he wasn't scowling every time he looked at her, and he wasn't leaping away from her every time they accidentally touched.

It was especially nice whenever he touched her back, or when he let his hand rest for a second on her forearm, or when he opened a door for her. Those were the little things that a man did for a woman that he cared for—little things that he didn't really think about, but just did because they were the right to do, *natural* to do. And Natasha wanted Anton to feel natural and comfortable when he was with her.

"Just wait here," Anton said, once they'd stepped inside the inn. "I'll take care of everything."

Natasha nodded, remaining silent, feeling a little sad. What was it to be this time? Was she his prostitute? His sister? Each night there was a new story told to an innkeeper, and each time it was a lie that did not put her in a good light.

She was a little surprised when a cryptic smile danced on his lips when he returned. His eyes were still cool and gray, as unreadable as ever.

"Everything is taken care of. I think we'll be very comfortable."

She followed him up to their room, which was on the second floor of the inn. The room was rather large, and Natasha was pleased to see that the bed, too, was large. At least tonight she wouldn't have to hug the edge of the bed, trying not to fall out, trying desperately to keep from touching Anton because she knew he didn't want her to touch him.

"I'm exhausted," Natasha said, sitting on the edge of the bed.

Anton sat beside her, taking her shoulders in his hands and turning her so that her back was to him. He placed his hands on her neck and began kneading the tension-knotted muscles there. His touch felt heavenly.

"Feel good?" he asked.

"Exquisite," Natasha replied, thinking that his touch felt exquisite, but that wasn't as good as the simple fact that he was at last willing to touch her again, and not act as though to touch her was repellant to his senses.

"I'll wager you'd appreciate a bath, too."

313

Natasha smiled. "Yes, I would, but . . ."

"The innkeeper is heating the water right now. There's a tub in the back. You get it first, then me."

Natasha stifled the slight disappointment she felt. It would be asking for too much to have Anton share the bath with her, she told herself. It was good enough that he had wanted to please her by procuring a bath, and was even letting her use it while the water was hot and clean.

"You're being very kind," Natasha whispered. She rolled her head around her shoulders as Anton's strong, sure fingers slowly and inexorably loosened the muscles in her neck and shoulders.

"I've been very hard on you," Anton said quietly, feeling Natasha slowly relaxing beneath his fingertips. "We've been going since I can't remember. We both need a break. I'm sure we're way ahead of Ivan. Besides, if it wasn't for your plan, we wouldn't even be here."

"We don't know that the plan is going to work yet. It's still just a plan."

"Yes, but a good plan just the same. I've made a fortune being able to know a good idea when it's presented to me."

Natasha wanted to turn on the bed, take Anton's face in her hands, and kiss his mouth. It had been such sweet ecstasy to kiss him, to feel his lips against her own, taking her breath away. Even if he didn't want to make love to her, that would be fine with her—if only he would kiss her one more time.

But that thought was immediately followed with the realization that she desperately needed to bathe her body and wash her hair. Somehow, it didn't really bother her that Anton also needed to bathe, and he needed a shave. He looked good to her no matter what his condition; but she wanted to be fresh and clean for him.

"I suppose you're as sore as I am," Natasha said.

She was trying to not sound *too* forward. "As tall as you are, you were more cramped in the carriage than me."

"I'm fine," Anton replied.

I want to touch you, rub your neck and make you feel better, Natasha thought, but she couldn't force the words from her throat.

Before she could think of any other way she might be able to "innocently" touch and caress Anton, there was a soft knock at the door. Anton called out to enter, and a rosy-faced elderly woman of generous dimensions and a cheery demeanor stuck her head inside. She spoke quickly in German, and Natasha was surprised when Anton replied in German as well. Though Natasha did not speak the language, she heard the word "frau" spoken. Didn't that mean "wife" in German? She wanted to get clarification from Anton, but she didn't dare.

"Your bath is ready," Anton said when they were alone in the room again.

Natasha didn't want to leave Anton, because she didn't want him to stop massaging her neck and shoulders, but she also needed to bathe. As though he sensed her dilemma, Anton rose suddenly, stepping away from her.

"Take as much time as you like," he said, staring out the window of the room. "She promised me there would be as much hot water as we need. And she's making us something to eat. I'm starving."

"Me, too. And she looks like she can cook," Natasha said, recalling the old woman's rotund figure.

She wondered if she herself would look like that when she got old, and she decided that it wouldn't be so bad. The old German woman seemed genuinely happy with her life, and enjoyed helping make other people comfortable and well-fed.

She removed her spare dress from her bag. The dress was cheap but clean. It wouldn't be the impression that she wanted to give Anton when she returned, not the look of beauty and sensuality that a beautiful new gown might give her, but Natasha had no choice. It was either the plain, simple old gown that was clean, or the fashionable gown that was dirty because she'd had it on far too many days in a row already.

"The innkeeper is just outside the door. She'll take you where you have to go. Take your time. I'm in no hurry."

"If you want—" Natasha said, then cut herself off short. She had almost volunteered to share the bath with Anton.

"Want what?"

"It's nothing," Natasha replied, her courage failing. "I won't take long."

The tub was in a small shed behind the inn, where there was both privacy and a fireplace to heat the water without risking a fire in the inn itself. The innkeeper chatted away merrily to Natasha, and didn't seem to mind at all that her guest didn't understand a word of German. The water was steaming, the soap fragrant and nearly the size of a loaf of bread, and there were four towels on a small rack waiting to be used.

After the endless hours in the cramped confines of a carriage, it looked like heaven to Natasha.

The old woman looked askance at Natasha's soiled gown, and the moment she removed it, the gown was taken away, apparently to be cleaned, perhaps discarded altogether. Natasha couldn't be sure, and frankly, she didn't much care what happened to the sorry piece of fabric.

It was a large tub, allowing Natasha to stretch out her legs and still be in water almost to her chin, and as she luxuriated in the liquid warmth, she thought about the pleasure that Anton would feel when he was here. Then she thought about how much more she would enjoy the bath if Anton were in it with her—it was certainly large enough to accommodate both of them comfortably—and she realized with startling certainty that she was setting out to seduce Anton Talakovich because she loved him, and even if he didn't love her, there was the chance that someday she might regain his trust, and, in the process, earn his love.

Natasha sank beneath the water to wash her hair, but her hands moved of their own accord, doing what needed to be done while she thought about Anton, and her love for him.

Had she really fallen in love with him?

Yes, there could be no doubting it, no denying it. She loved him. If she didn't love him, if her feelings for him were something less than pure love, then she wouldn't be setting out to seduce him, as she was now.

And seduction—nothing less than that—was what she had in mind for this evening.

Twenty-three

A smile played on Natasha's full, sensual mouth. Yes, she would seduce Anton. He had kept his distance from her so far, but the distance was narrowing. There had been a light touch here and there to make Natasha believe that the fury of Anton's rage toward her was abating. He'd even gone so far as to massage her neck and shoulders. He wouldn't have done that if he hadn't forgiven her enough to care for her comfort. Natasha had enjoyed the neck massage, but Natasha knew Anton well enough to understand the pleasure he took in touching her.

It was going to be a long evening, Natasha told herself. Long, beautiful, and blissful!

She was finished with her bath before the innkeeper returned, but this didn't bother Natasha. Even though she didn't have any undergarments with her, she pulled her old dress over her head, buttoned it suitably, then padded barefooted up the rear stairway to the second floor to the room that she shared with Anton.

The first thing that hit her was the aroma. The scent of thick, juicy sausage, boiled potatoes, green beans, and wine made Natasha's mouth water.

"It's a feast!" Natasha exclaimed.

"Fit for a czar," Anton added, clearly pleased with

what he had accomplished, which was putting a smile on Natasha's face. "You were right about that woman. She's a magnificent cook. I couldn't resist nibbling."

Natasha noticed then that one of the sausages was missing its end, and that one of the glasses had some wine in it. If Anton decided to do a little nibbling on Natasha, she wouldn't mind at all, and she promised herself that later in the evening she would tell him as much.

Now that she knew exactly what she wanted — Anton's loving attention — the only question remaining was how precisely to go about getting what she wanted.

"I'd better take my bath now," Anton said.

"Eat first. The bath can be reheated; the food can't."

Anton chuckled. "You're right, of course. What did I ever do without you?"

Natasha didn't trust herself enough to answer aloud, because thoughts of all the women that had spent time in his bed came to mind, and she didn't want to bring up the past, especially when it wouldn't make either of them at all happy.

The food was spread on a small, circular table, and since there was only one chair, one of them had to sit on the edge of the bed as they ate. Natasha noticed, as the small table and chair were being moved into proper place, the way Anton looked at her. At first she was unhappy with it, but then she was pleased. The old dress she wore at first made Natasha think that Anton did not find it attractive. Then she realized that the dress was rather thin, and since she wore nothing beneath the dress, she was moving rather freely. Leaving a button or two unfastened might have drawn an even more favorable response from Anton other than a few looks that he tried not to be too obvious about.

They were both so hungry that they ate in almost total silence, with Anton sitting on the bed and Natasha in the chair. He poured her wine whenever she took more than a sip or two, never letting the glass get anywhere near empty.

"Your hair is so thick," Anton commented suddenly.

Natasha combed her hair a bit with her fingers. "It takes forever to dry," she replied, fluffing her auburn tresses as best she could over her shoulders.

"It's lovely. Even wet, it's lovely."

Tiny flutters raced through Natasha. That was the first compliment concerning her looks that she had gotten from Anton since Uncle Ivan's murderous behavior had turned her life upside-down. He had complimented her mind and her ideas several times, but he'd never said a word about how she looked, other than to ask whether she was tired now and then, and if she could continue to travel on.

He turned his attention back to his plate, and Natasha watched him surreptitiously over the rim of her wine glass.

It was entirely unfair, she decided, that Anton should look so appealing, even though he needed a shave and a bath. The beard stubble gave him a tough appearance, which he wore well. It made him look strong and defiant, and anything but the sophisticated Russian prince who had been educated at Eton, and was welcome in the halls of the most prestigious institutions in the world.

Natasha was absolutely sure that before she had bathed, she simply looked unwashed; Anton, on the other hand, appeared roguish, like a man who lived outside the conventions of society, and was capable at whatever he set his mind to doing.

In the back of her mind she wondered what it would be like to be with Anton now, to feel his body and beard stubble against her own body, which was

320

clean and pink and smelling of soap.

A shiver worked its way up Natasha's spine. She had to stop thinking of Anton, she told herself, or her little plan for seduction would backfire because she'd become too forceful. She wasn't entirely confident yet that Anton's desire for her would make him forget that she had betrayed him and his sister by telling Ivan Pronushka what she thought was useless information.

The knock on the door was familiar this time, and when the innkeeper stuck her head inside, Natasha gave her a pleasant smile. There was a brief conversation in German, then Anton said, "I'd better take my bath now. There's someone who wants to use it after me. Make yourself comfortable."

He left the room then, leaving Natasha behind to wonder just exactly what it was he meant by that last comment. Exactly how comfortable did he want her to get?

The innkeeper removed the trays and plates, and from what Natasha could guess, the old woman was pleased that there wasn't a morsel of food left uneaten.

Natasha patted her stomach to indicate that she had enjoyed the meal, and eaten quite a bit. The innkeeper initially mistook the gesture to mean that Natasha was pregnant, but the situation was soon straightened out. Then, when Natasha began worrying that soon Anton would return, she did her best to gently hurry the talkative old woman out the door.

What to do now? The waiting was intolerable to Natasha. She wished there was a looking glass in the room so that she might do something with her hair, which was only a little bit damp now. What had Anton said about her hair in the past? That he liked it best when she left it unbound, flowing free? If that was the case, it would only look its absolute best when it was completely dry.

She cursed herself for even worrying about such a little thing. After all, wasn't she wearing a very old dress? She didn't even have on stockings, or anything beneath the dress. She was anything but fashionable, and the gulf between her world and Anton's seemed larger than ever.

The smile that curled her lips spoke of sensuality and seduction. She might not have Anton's money, or have money like the wealthy debutantes who had seduced Anton so often in the past, but she had intelligence, and she knew what Anton liked, and she was going to use every trick she'd been taught about seduction by the master of seduction himself, Prince Anton Talakovich.

Natasha slipped off the bed, and after just a moment of doubt, she pulled the dress over her head, neatly folded it, then went back to bed. She slipped between the covers, pulling the blankets up to her underarms, being careful to conceal her breasts, yet show enough cleavage so that when Anton looked at her, there would be no doubt in his mind that she was naked, and waiting just for him.

She smiled serenely, imagining the pleasures that would soon be hers, the pleasures she could share only with Anton.

He had stayed away from her long enough, kept his anger at a fever pitch long enough. Now it was time to put past mistakes behind them, and get on with their life . . . and renew the passion Natasha was absolutely convinced was shared by both of them!

It was a minor point, but one that Anton took pride in. Despite the lust burning in his veins for Natasha, he had managed to stay on his side of the small table all through the truly delicious dinner of sausage and potatoes the innkeeper had made. It hadn't been easy to keep from rushing around the table to take Natasha into his arms. Memories of the loving times he'd shared with her were much stronger than the negative thoughts about her betrayal.

A smile tickled his lips. He was certain she would be receptive to making love. The iciness that had existed between them had thawed; the chasm narrowed. All he had to do now was reach across the small space that still separated them, take her hand in his, and tell her that she meant the world to him.

There was still the matter of Ivan Pronushka to be dealt with, but once Anton's rage had cooled, he was able to look back upon what had happened with detached objectivity. It was clear to him that Natasha had been in an untenable position, and that when she had given her uncle the information about the coach arriving without armed escort, she had neither understood the value of what was in the carriage, nor the potential for violence that Ivan Pronushka was capable of.

She hadn't really meant to cause the harm she had. Natasha Stantikoff's gentle heart simply was incapable of fully understanding the evil that Ivan was, nor did she understand the extraordinary responsibility that Anton and Anastasia carried when they went about the daily routines of operating the various Talakovich business interests.

Anton worked a thick lather into his hair once again, then dipped below the surface of the water to rinse. It felt magnificent to be clean once again. Thank goodness he had fine, clean clothes to return to the room in. He wanted to look his best when he returned to Natasha. It had been disconcerting to be sitting there in the room with her smelling so clean and sweet, while he felt so sweaty and foul.

If it hadn't been for the vast difference in their cleanliness, Anton might very well have rushed around the table, taken Natasha into his arms, thrown her onto the bed, and done his best to have his way with her.

Closing his eyes, he thought about her, and how she'd looked with her hair wet, her spirits buoyed, her smile at last unguarded after so long. There could be no denying that beneath the thin, old dress she wore, she wore nothing but skin.

It was ridiculous, Anton told himself, to let his blood get so heated just because he could see the way her breasts swayed and moved beneath the dress. He *had,* after all, seen her breasts before—seen them, and much more than that. So why was it so tempting to his senses to watch them move gently beneath the old dress?

Anton could not explain it. There wasn't a logical explanation as to why Natasha excited him as much as she did. Yes, she was beautiful, but then Prince Anton had surrounded himself with the most attractive women in Russia and Europe for many years now. Having beautiful women near him was hardly a unique experience.

There was no explanation for it, Anton finally decided. Everything he thought he knew about himself, and about women, was subject to question now that Natasha had entered his life. And enter it she had. Whether he was happy about it or not mattered little. The fact was, her life had collided with his, and not even Czar Alexander himself, with all his power, could prevent the collision from taking place.

It was thinking about the czar that convinced Anton he had to return to his room. It wouldn't do to think too much about the czar because sooner or later, Alexander would surely catch wind of what had happened with the documents, and he'd ask Anton about it. When that happened, Czar Alexander would probe for facts until Natasha's name came up. Then Alexander would demand to know why Natasha had—

Stop it! thought Anton angrily as he stepped out of the tub and reached for a towel.

He was imagining the worst possible scenario, and doing that, at least now, accomplished absolutely nothing. Once the documents were recovered from Ivan, then Anton could worry about keeping the entire incident a secret from Czar Alexander. Until that time, worrying about the czar would only keep him from concentrating on the problems—and the delights!—that were more pressing at the moment.

He shaved quickly, using the small looking glass he kept in his kit, then dressed with care, using the brush he'd brought with him to smooth his wet hair back. The jacket was aqua green, and though it wasn't the best one he owned, it was the best one he was traveling with.

When the innkeeper spied Anton returning to his room, she just smiled and turned her eyes down.

"Been married a month," Anton said in German as he passed the blushing old woman. "The meal was wonderful."

Anton bounded the stairs up to his room, taking them two at a time. Despite the exhaustion that had been pulling at him, he felt edgy, invigorated. Tonight, if only for tonight, past transgressions and wrongs would be forgiven, if not completely forgotten. He knocked softly, waited for a response, got none, then entered.

She looked angelic with her head on the pillow, her satiny auburn hair spilling out everywhere, dark against the white linen, soft lashes curling against her cheeks. Anton stood for a moment, transfixed by what he saw. He watched the gentle, even rise and fall of her breasts beneath the sheet, and he knew that she was naked beneath the blanket.

He closed the door quietly, careful not to disturb Natasha's sleep. He knew that Natasha had undressed for him, and had intended on being awake

325

for him once he got back from his bath. Only fatigue prevented her from being awake for him now, nothing more.

A sweet smile of understanding crossed Anton's face, and if he could have seen it, it would have surprised him, because he'd never thought himself a sentimental person. The pursuit of passion and fulfillment had always been paramount in his life, but he would be satisfied tonight to just hold the sleeping Natasha Stantikoff in his arms. To do that, on this night, was enough to make Anton a very happy man, and this was a stunning revelation, since he'd always thought he could only really find happiness with a woman by having sex with her.

He eased himself into the bed after undressing, and very gently took Natasha into his arms. She murmured softly, sleepily, then placed her head upon his shoulder, her eyes never opening. Anton put his arm around her naked shoulders, feeling the warmth of her plush breasts against his chest.

Let her sleep, he told himself. She's exhausted, and so are you. Just let her sleep.

Prince Anton Talakovich did let Natasha sleep. From that evening forward, he would consider it his greatest act of self-control.

Natasha awoke slowly, gently, and was aware of nothing more disturbing than the simple fact that she wanted to sleep just a few more minutes before getting up. It was so nice and warm in bed, and Anton's shoulder provided the perfect pillow for her head.

She sighed, yawned, and snuggled in a little closer to Anton. With her ear against him, she could hear his smooth heartbeat. In the sleep-foggy recesses of her mind, she listened for Anton's breathing, and when she recognized that its even, regular tempo meant he was asleep, she was happy. He'd been so dominating lately, always keeping them moving westward to France. From the moment he awoke to the time they collapsed into bed, he was pushing, pushing. So it was nice now to lay next to Anton, feeling his arm around her . . .

Anton . . . arm around her . . . naked!

Natasha's eyes opened wide, but she never moved a muscle. She was naked, in bed with Anton, and he was just as naked as she.

For a few delirious seconds, Natasha tried to reconstruct the events of the previous evening. Had they made love? Natasha searched her brain, trying to remember the last things she'd done, the last thoughts she'd had before going to sleep.

She remembered taking off her dress and crawling between the cool sheets, thinking that Anton could hardly fail to get the hint that she wanted to make love when he discovered that she wasn't wearing a stitch of clothing. She remembered wondering how long it would take for Anton to bathe, and that her eyes felt heavy.

And that was the last thing she remembered.

She'd fallen asleep waiting for Anton to return, and she hadn't awakened, even when he got into bed beside her and took her into his arms.

But Natasha was fully awake now, and she rolled away from Anton carefully. His arm fell away from her shoulders, and she lay on her stomach, looking at him, wondering what he must have thought last night.

Why hadn't he awakened her? she wondered. He couldn't have failed to notice that she was naked, and there could only be one reason why she was. And he was naked, too. There could only be one reason for that!

She eased the sheet down Anton's body just enough to look at his stomach. His chest, shoulders, and stomach all spoke of controlled, masculine power, and the sight of him touched Natasha deep inside, making her feel warm.

When Anton's eyes opened, he blinked them twice, and was fully awake.

"How late is it?" he asked, spinning away from Natasha, kicking his feet over the edge. He rubbed his face in his hands. "Do you know what time it is? Did we oversleep?"

"The carriage isn't scheduled to leave until nine," Natasha said, just a little irked that the first thing Anton could think about was getting on the road to Paris once again. She propped her head up in her hand, laying on her side as Anton ran fingers through his dusty blond hair. "There's no need for haste. At least not to get to the carriage."

"Of course there is."

In a more stern voice, Natasha declared, "Anton, there's no need to hurry out of bed."

He turned to look at her. Natasha's dark eyes were fixed upon him, the smile on her lips faint, confident. Her breasts were bared to him.

"Anton, I am not leaving this bed until you make love to me," Natasha said quietly, with conviction and authority that would make an empress proud. "I know you're in a hurry, and that we're still days from Paris. I'm also aware that we have spent many nights together, but we haven't made love in far too long. Now the longer you sit there looking at my breasts, the less time you have to touch them. And if you really must sit there motionless, please turn more toward me, so that I can see as much of you as you can of me." She reached out and ran her fingertip along Anton's thigh. "I get excited looking at you just the same way you do looking at me."

Anton turned toward her, but that wasn't as far as he went. He took Natasha into his arms, stretching his long, lean body out beside her, pulling her in tight so the full length of their bodies touched with legs entwined.

"I'm not accustomed to taking orders," Anton said, grinning as he kissed Natasha on the neck.

"Learn," she replied, shocking even herself at her forcefulness.

When their lips met, Natasha felt the kiss from the top of her head to the tips of her toes. She felt fused with Anton, more than just a woman beside him. She felt a part of him.

She twisted her leg a little more tightly around his, pressing her womanhood against the solid mass of muscle that was his thigh. When he cupped her buttocks and pulled her against him even more tightly, her low purr of pleasure was simultaneously kittenish and vixenish.

"It feels so good to hold you in my arms again," Natasha whispered when the kiss finally ended. She rolled just a little onto her back, pulling Anton with her. It always pleased her to feel his weight pressing down upon her. "I was afraid—"

"Sh-h-h!" Anton said, placing his fingertip against her lips to silence her words. "No more talk like that. I don't want you ever to be afraid again."

Natasha kissed his fingertip, then let her tongue curl out around it. She sipped at his fingertip, her dark eyes alight with mischief and passionate hunger.

"Holding you in my arms last night without touching you the way I longed to . . . it was the hardest thing I've ever had to do."

"But you *were* touching me."

"Not the way I wanted to."

Natasha took Anton's right hand by the wrist. "Not like this?" she asked, placing his hand upon her breast.

Anton's strong fingers pressed into her breast, and she arched her back, pushing herself against him as warm tingles passed through her. When Anton caught her nipple between his forefinger and thumb and pinched firmly, Natasha issued a short, sharp cry of ecstasy.

"You excite me so much," she whispered, shivering a little in her lover's arms. She felt his manhood coming to life between them, stretching out, pressing against her, heated and insistent. "Kiss me!"

He kissed her mouth, and Natasha opened her lips invitingly. When she tasted his tongue against her own, it was as though there had never been any moment in time when she had not loved Anton completely, with all her heart and soul.

Perhaps he did not trust her completely, but she loved and trusted him with every fiber of her being, every nerve in her body, and all she could hope for was that someday, when the danger had passed, he could love and trust her in return.

"Kiss me!" Natasha repeated moments later, only this time she demandingly pushed Anton's head downward, directing his hot, searching mouth to the tingling crest of her breast.

She pushed her fingers through Anton's thick, blond hair, holding him securely as his lips and tongue worked their special magic upon her senses. When she felt Anton's hand sliding around her hip, she turned away from him, opening her legs willingly, freely availing herself of the majesty of his caresses.

"My darling! Oh, my darling, we must never fight!" Natasha whispered as the fire within her belly burned hotter and hotter. "We must never be apart! You can see that, can't you? Tell me you can, and I'll be yours forever!"

Anton pulled away from Natasha just enough to look down into her face, into the beautiful brown eyes that he had always been able to read so easily. What surprised him most about what Natasha had just said was that he couldn't argue with any of it.

330

Every word that Natasha had just said made perfect sense to Anton.

So did that mean he was in love with her?

It was a frightening possibility for a man like Anton to seriously ponder. He loved *making* love, but that didn't necessarily mean he was comfortable with the idea of being *in love* with any one woman.

"Anton, what have I said? If I've said anything to make you angry, I take it back! I take it all back!"

Anton moved up on the bed to kiss Natasha's mouth again, stopping her words, kissing her slowly and sensually from one corner of her mouth to the other, then slanting his lips over hers in a single searing kiss that left her breathless and trembling.

"Never take back what you've said," Anton replied, his gray eyes vividly intense, boring into Natasha's. "I want to hear your voice the first thing every morning. That's what I want out of life, Natasha. That's all I want!"

I should tell her I love her, Anton thought, but he could not force the words—those three words he'd never told any woman—from his tongue.

He was not given the chance to think about what words he should say, because Natasha's desire was burning more feverishly. She reached between their bodies to curl her fingers around the throbbing shaft of his manhood, her actions bold and sure. Anton's words, combined with the nights of loving she'd already experienced in his arms, had given her confidence in such matters.

"I'll always be with you," Natasha whispered, kissing Anton's neck, wriggling against him, moving lower on the bed beneath Anton while her hand worked upon his aroused flesh until it was fully, gloriously distended.

Natasha wasn't exactly sure what she wanted to accomplish, except to show the man that she loved that though she might have less experience than the other

331

women that he'd shared his body with, she lacked nothing when it came to energy, enthusiasm, and creativity.

"Tell me you want me," Natasha said, her tone making it a command, a royal decree of such authority that Anton dared not refuse.

After she spoke the sentence, she bared her teeth and bit Anton's stomach hard enough to draw a gasp from him, letting the prince know that she was not to be denied when she was in this mood.

"Ouch! I want you! I want you! Don't bite me again!" He moved higher on the bed, placing his hands against the wall, not entirely certain what Natasha had in mind, but certain that whatever it was would be an adventure that he would not soon forget.

After some fumbling about, with neither Anton nor Natasha quite certain of what she was trying to accomplish, she eventually had Anton above her, straddling her with the length of his phallus trapped firmly between her breasts, which she held together.

"Don't move," Natasha whispered, looking up into Anton's eyes. "I don't want you to move a single muscle."

Anton's lips moved, but no words were formed. To feel the length of his arousal trapped between Natasha's warm, soft breasts was something he'd never imagined, even in his most erotic dreams and fantasies.

"Tell me . . . what you want . . . me to do," Anton said.

He licked his lips. His mouth was bone dry. At that moment, though he had always resisted anyone being in control of a situation but himself, he was willing to relinquish complete control to Natasha. Whatever she wanted he would provide. He was captive, in complete thrall, to her charms, her beauty, her erotic imagination, to the strong and yet entirely feminine essence of her.

Natasha's eyes were locked with Anton's when she raised her face just enough to flick her tongue against the tip of his phallus. The contact, sensual both on a physical and a visual level, jolted Anton powerfully, making him pull away from her.

Perhaps earlier in their relationship, Natasha might have taken Anton's reaction to mean that he did not like what she had just done. But now she knew better. Hardly had Anton pulled away, when he thrust his hips forward, driving his manhood once again through the tight valley of Natasha's breasts.

"You've slept with many women, haven't you?" Natasha asked tauntingly.

She laced her fingers together over her breasts, holding them together, trapping Anton's arousal, which throbbed lustily, between them.

"I've stayed awake with many woman. You're the only woman I've slept with."

"A minor distinction." Natasha flicked her tongue against Anton again, and she watched as his eyes widened in shock. She felt powerful because of the desire she could elicit from Anton, secure in the hold she had over his emotions. "Do you think of them often?"

"Not often."

"I don't like you thinking of them at all."

Anton moistened his lips again. His heart was pounding, and remaining motionless was the most difficult thing he had ever done.

He still wasn't quite sure what it was that Natasha was trying to accomplish, but whatever it was, it had made him more agonizingly aroused than he could ever remember being. He wanted to spread himself over Natasha and thrust himself deeply into her, but he also wanted to wait and follow her orders, because every time he had, he was rewarded for his obedience in the most erotic of ways.

"Move your hips," Natasha said.

Anton began pumping his hips.

"Slower!" she commanded.

He followed her command. It felt like his flesh was on fire.

"I don't know what it's like for you, but for me when you move so fast, though it all feels good, I can't feel *everything,* all the tiny, delicious sensations that I can feel when you move slowly."

For a few seconds, Natasha closed her eyes and concentrated on what she felt. The heat of Anton's manhood seemed to burn the soft, inner flesh of her breasts. She could feel his heartbeat through his phallus. When she opened her eyes and looked up into Anton's face, she saw the wonder in his expression, and she knew that she was exciting him in a way that he had not expected, in a way he would never forget.

"Do you want me?" Natasha asked, a sultry smile curling her lips. She felt completely in control.

"You know I do," Anton replied without ever once slowing the undulations of his hips.

"But do you *really"* — she drawled the word out slowly, giving it great meaning — "want me? Want me as you've never wanted any woman in your life?"

"Now you're teasing me," Anton said.

Natasha watched as his expression changed just slightly, just enough to show the side of him that was always in control, commanding and authoritative under any conditions.

"Yes, I'm teasing you," Natasha said. And then, to emphasize her statement, she once again danced her tongue over the sensitive tip of Anton's manhood when he thrust near. "What are you going to do about it?"

Without missing a beat, Anton reached behind him, sliding his hand between Natasha's tapering thighs. He cupped her moist mound firmly, rubbing the sensitive bud of her desire with the heel of his palm.

Natasha gasped with pleasure as heated desire surged through her. In an instant, she had gone from being completely in control of the situation to questioning whether she could give Anton enough pleasure to make him lose control, or whether he would be the one to drive her over the edge of ecstasy with the manipulations of his skilled fingers.

"Yes, I want you, Natasha," Anton said, inserting a fingertip between Natasha's moist petals. "But no more than you want me. And don't try to tell me otherwise. I can feel that you want me."

Natasha released her breasts, reaching up to Anton. "Enough of this!" she cried out. "I need you inside me!"

Whether he needed her more than she needed him was a matter of debate. Anton thrust himself into Natasha's honied core, burying himself deeply as their mouths fused together in a fevered kiss.

Their loving was volcanic in its intensity, made more frantic and feverish by the ever-present danger, by the days of abstinence, and by the sense that they had surmounted an enormous chasm that had separated them, and at last they were again together in body, mind, and soul.

Twenty-four

Rosto Rapp leaned back in his chair and let the sun shine directly upon his face. It was unseasonably cool in Paris, and he was not at all looking forward to winter. He hated the cold, and one of his fantasies was that some day he would make enough money to move to Sicily. He'd heard the weather was beautiful there, always warm and sunny, and the temperature gave the women of the island warm and sunny temperaments.

It seemed like an ideal situation to Rosto. All he had to do was make enough money to set himself up comfortably in Sicily, because he certainly had no intention of going there and living like a pauper. Not when life in Paris was becoming lucrative for him, and his connections to Napoleon Bonaparte's inner circle continued to trust him more and more all the time.

Beside Rosto at the small, round table in the outdoor cafe was Pierre de Gruzin, prefect of police for Paris. Pierre, like Rosto, was a man of considerable ambition. But whereas Rosto was more interested in money and living a leisurely life, Pierre coveted power, and the pleasures that could be gleaned from being in complete control over one's own life, as well as over the lives of as many other people as possible.

"I hate it when it's cold," Rosto said, never bothering to open his eyes.

"Then move to Sicily. You're always talking about it." Pierre wasn't in the mood to listen to Rosto's complaints. "You've got enough money for it."

"I'd have enough if I had the ability to live a meager existence, but I don't, my dear friend. I need fine and beautiful things surrounding me, just as you need . . ." He was suddenly at a loss for words, having no real idea of what Pierre needed. Nothing seemed to give the prefect any happiness.

"Like I need young and beautiful women?" Pierre volunteered.

He resented the fact that Rosto, who really had no employment, should make so much money because he had ingratiated himself to certain people in circles of power, yet he, Pierre de Gruzin, prefect of Paris, should be forced to extort money from business owners just to live in reasonable comfort.

"Whatever . . . I still don't have enough money to live the rest of my life on, and that's the key to it all, don't you see?"

Pierre was silent. He sipped his tea, then cast an angry, sidelong glance at the cafe owner's niece. The young girl scurried over to place a new teacup before him, and filled it quickly.

For a moment, Pierre thought of pulling the girl onto his lap, but he controlled the impulse. The owner had paid his protection fee in full and on time, which meant that Pierre was rather duty-bound to avoid causing him or his niece any trouble.

Pierre de Gruzin was a thief, rapist, and extortionist, but he never went back on his word. The way he saw it, as long as his promises were good, then he was a good man.

"Have you heard any interesting stories lately?" Rosto asked. He was sitting up again in his chair, watching the people walking by along the boulevard.

Pierre shrugged his shoulders. Rosto was always fishing for dirty facts on people, bits of information that he could use to elevate his power and influence.

"Nothing interesting. Well, there is Michel Tott. I'm sure you remember him. You introduced me to him a year ago, or so. I believe the two of you were in some enterprise . . . weren't you?"

Rosto's expression didn't change at all, but his tone was guarded when he replied, "Not quite an enterprise. I hardly knew him."

"Well, you did introduce him to me. As I recall, you thought it was important that the two of us meet. Well, Tott is in my prison now. I'd be very much surprised if he survived the month."

Rosto looked away, the faint shrug of his shoulders suggesting that whatever happened to his former partner failed to affect him. But inside, he felt his guts tighten.

People who crossed paths with Pierre without showing him the proper respect often ended up arrested, usually in the middle of the night. They were in prison long before they could defend themselves properly in court, and not long afterward they would conveniently hang themselves, or miraculously stab themselves in the back, or they'd fall down the stone stairs and have their skulls smashed in, or their necks broken.

No one really believed all these deaths were accidents or suicides, but Pierre's power extended far into the prisons. If he wanted to make an inmate's life easy, that was well within his power; if he wanted to make an inmate's life end abruptly, that, too, was easily and swiftly accomplished.

"I never did trust that man Tott," Rosto said absently, hoping that he hadn't done anything to earn the prefect's wrath. "Tott was most untrustworthy. He spoke from both sides of his mouth."

Pierre hid his smile. He had interrogated enough strong men to detect fear in a man's voice, no matter how well-concealed.

"He was disrespectful," Pierre said. "A man should never forget to show respect."

"True, true," Rosto replied.

He wondered if the sabre and scabbard that he'd just obtained — both objects showing craftsmanship and engraving that made them exceptional works of art — would be fully appreciated by Pierre.

Two men passed by on the boulevard, speaking Norwegian, and Rosto scowled.

"Foreigners, all the time foreigners," he said, shaking his head. "Pretty soon we'll have more foreigners than Parisians!"

The prefect remained silent. He didn't actually mind foreigners coming to Paris. They tended to be hard-working, for the most part honest, and when he said they needed to pay him money if they wanted to live in his city, they paid without causing too much trouble.

A coach came down the boulevard, rattling to a stop at the tavern across the boulevard. The door opened and a tall blond man leaped out, then assisted a beautiful young auburn-haired woman to the cobblestones.

"Now there's a fellow who has his cake," Rosto said softly.

He was instantly envious of the man's looks, his exquisite clothes, and the stunning, curvaceous woman at his arm, who smiled when she looked at him. Rosto had always wanted that kind of love from women, and he'd always resented the fairer sex for never giving him such adoration.

Pierre paid the man only passing interest. It was the woman who held the prefect's gaze. There was a sweet smile upon her face, and the way she looked up and down the boulevard with almost childlike curiosity and enthusiasm suggested to him that she was new to the city.

A myriad of scenarios began formulating in his head, ones that led invariably to the point where he and the auburn-haired woman would be alone together in a room, and in one way or another, she needed his help with some vital matter.

"Do you recognize that man?" Rosto asked.

The intrusion of Rosto's voice annoyed Pierre. He wanted to let his mind fantasize all the erotic possibilities to be found with a woman like her. He certainly didn't want to talk to Rosto, and most definitely not about the young woman's escort. What was the man to her? wondered Pierre. Brother? Husband?

Had to be a husband, Pierre decided. No sister ever looked at her brother with so much love in her eyes.

It was a pleasing revelation for Pierre. A woman in love would do almost anything to protect the man she loved, especially if that man should get arrested and be thrown into prison, where only the prefect of police had the influence necessary to free him, and then only if he was given enough incentive by a beautiful woman!

"I know I've seen that man somewhere before," Rosto continued. "Do you suppose he's a politician?"

"Here? He's a nobody if he is. Besides, I don't care about politicians. They don't bother me, and I don't bother them."

"I *know* I've seen that man in Paris before, and I know he's a foreigner."

Pierre waited until the man and woman had disappeared down the boulevard before he finally turned his attention to Rosto.

"If he is a politician, he's a rich one. What would a politician be doing here?" He waggled a finger in Rosto's direction. "Whatever you've got planned, you make sure that I don't have to get involved. I don't want any trouble here in Paris."

Rosto hardly heard Pierre's words. He was trying to go backward in time in his mind as he attempted to place where he'd seen the tall, handsome, well-dressed blond man before.

It didn't surprise Rosto at all when Pierre de Gruzin stood, and without a word of farewell, walked away, leaving the unpaid bill for the meal and drinks for Rosto to worry about.

"This city is just too exciting for words!" Natasha exclaimed.

Anton chuckled, patting her hand which was on his forearm as they walked down the Paris boulevard, on the west bank. "For being too exciting for words, you're using quite a number of them."

He delighted in Natasha's expression of wonder. She was so happy, it was almost as though they really weren't in Paris to set a trap for her uncle.

"If I couldn't live in St. Petersburg, then I'd live in Paris," Anton explained. He kept his voice a little lower than normal, not wanting everyone to hear his Russian. "Without comparison, they are the most exciting cities in the world."

Natasha felt a number of deeply buried emotions when she considered that Anton had travelled widely, yet chose to spend precious time with her. She wondered if there would ever come a time when she would completely shed the insecurities and hidden scars on her soul caused by living with Ivan and Aggie.

"And I'm here," Natasha said, now keeping her voice down as well. "I never thought I'd travel."

Anton couldn't tell Natasha that they were far from the sophisticated section of Paris, that part of the city that he was most accustomed to, and most yearned to show her. Here on the west bank, they were in the heart of the underground community. Anton had several spies in Paris, and they all lived in the west bank. On the edge of impoverished areas, yet near enough to the heart of Paris where the hangers-on could feel a part of the action, Anton decided this was the logical place to begin their search for Rosto Rapp.

"First, we'll get a room, then I'll begin asking questions," Anton said. "You can stay back and rest a while."

"Rest? I'm so excited right now I don't think I'll ever need to rest again."

Anton looked down at Natasha, smiling gently. "Actually, my darling, I don't want you with me. You see, I'm going to be traveling in some . . . *unsavory* sections of this city, and it wouldn't be safe for you."

"If it wouldn't be safe for me, then it wouldn't be safe for you. You'll be better off with me beside you."

"Not this time. You see, your French isn't what it needs to be."

Natasha wondered if Anton was telling the truth, or if he was just saying that to protect her. Either way, the fact that her French wasn't what it should be reminded her of the happiness of her youth, when her parents were alive, and the squalor she knew later, when she went to live with Uncle Ivan and Aunt Aggie.

She was certain that if her parents had lived, she'd have gotten the tutoring necessary to speak French in such a manner that she wouldn't prove embarrassing to Anton.

Anton bought Natasha a rose from a street vendor, and tried to put his mind at ease. After days of bruisingly hard travel, they had time to settle in and become comfortable, he told himself. Ivan had to be days behind, even if he had the stamina and will to push himself as hard as Anton and Natasha had.

As they walked past the small shops and vendors, inhaling the delicious smells of fresh baked bread and exotic pastries that Natasha had never heard of, Anton became more and more convinced that he would find Rosto Rapp here in the west bank of Paris.

He could almost smell the greed mingling with the aroma of the bread, the smell of fear and power of living on the edge of a slum on one side, flanked by the edge of the most glittering city in the world on the other. The struggle to move one way and not the other was what made the west bank the ideal place to live for people who danced just outside the law, but wanted nothing more than the appearance of respectability and decorum.

Parker Windom closed the window to his office. It was an unseasonably cool, windy day in London, and he wasn't in a mood to put his jacket back on, preferring to work in his shirt sleeves.

He sat back down at his desk, and picked up the red leather-bound ledger that had been consuming his thoughts for the better part of the past three weeks. The ledger was in his own handwriting, and in it was the sole record of the money that he had embezzled from his bank's accounts.

The problem was all with the widow, Mrs. Erickson. Now that her husband's will had been properly processed through the courts, she had decided her money would be better placed in a bank nearer her home in London. If she would just be content to leave the money where it was, then the fact that Parker Windom had depleted the account by nearly ten thousand pounds would never become known.

Parker had been able to stall the old woman, saying that before she made such an enormous decision, she would do well to give the matter a week's thought. Two weeks would even be better, Parker insisted, but the old woman would hear none of it. She was determined to move her money, and stubbornness was her most dominant characteristic.

The only way Parker could put the missing ten thousand pounds back into Mrs. Erickson's account was if he robbed Peter to pay Paul, and take money from other accounts.

He sighed and rubbed his eyes, which burned from staring at the same columns of figures for too many hours. In his heart, Parker Windom knew that sooner or later his superiors at the bank would discover what he had been doing. They weren't exactly stupid men, though Parker had never really considered the six old white-bearded men who oversaw all bank operations as his intellectual equals.

Who would he take the money from? One account? Perhaps one thousand pounds from ten different accounts?

It wasn't time to make the big break, Parker told himself. Not just yet. When he was ready to leave the bank, then he'd spend a week or two embezzling every sixpence possible, transferring the money from one account to the next, to the next, and then finally into his own pocket.

And at last, when he figured he'd taken as much as he needed—for at least as much as he possibly could—then he'd go before the leaders of the bank and tearfully explain that his mother was gravely ill, and needed him to be at her side immediately. He'd tell the old men that though he did not want to tender his immediate resignation, he simply had to. Family responsibilities were too grave to allow personal ambition to supersede them, he would tell the sentimental old men, and maybe if he told his story with enough pathos, he might even get a final bonus from them, just to tide him over with his mother's overdue bills.

Parker stood and went to open the window. The cool, fresh air might revive his brain, he decided.

He had to stop thinking about what it would be like once he decided to put an end to the embezzling, and concentrate on the problems that the widow Mrs. Erickson now represented. She could cause an investigation, if Parker wasn't careful, and he simply did not have enough money set aside to live comfortably in some other country now.

There was a knock at his office door. Parker returned to his desk and closed the red leather ledger, returning it to the lower left desk drawer and locking it before he allowed his personal secretary to enter.

"There's someone here to see you, Mr. Windom," the efficient young man said.

Parker looked at his secretary, wondering what made the young man, who was quite intelligent and a perfect employee, satisfied with his salary. Parker just couldn't imagine living such a meager existence when there was so much money everywhere for the taking.

"Who?"

"A Mr. Carter, and a woman."

"Mr. Carter?" The name meant nothing to Parker.

"A Caleb Carter. I believe he's an American, sir."

Parker took his waistcoat from the coattree and

began putting it on. "Give me three minutes, then send them in. You did say he had someone with him, didn't you?"

"Yes, sir."

Parker's mind was spinning, and he said a quick prayer of thanks that a new victim had been found.

He remembered Caleb Carter clearly. He was a lean, dangerous-looking man. After their initial meeting, Parker had hired men to check into Caleb's background. Almost by accident, Parker met a man who had known Caleb back during their days together at college. From there, it was fairly easy for Parker Windom to deduce that Caleb Carter was acting on behalf of his old college friend, Prince Anton Talakovich.

As long as there were sanctions in place preventing Russians from doing business with Britons, then any transactions would be outlawed, and if Parker Windom understood anything, it was that an outlaw cannot cry foul and run to the local constable for help if his own hands are buried deep in the till.

Parker forced himself to become calm. It wouldn't do to let them smell his fear.

What had his plans been? Those plans he'd concocted so long ago, when he first discovered there was a connection between Caleb Carter and the Talakovich dynasty and fortune?

A slow, creeping smile curled Parker's lips as he recalled those plans he'd made. He hadn't really thought there was any chance in the world that they even had a chance of coming true, but now they could prove something more than a tentative fantasy.

He had people to contact. As much as Parker loathed to talk to the dockside characters who were so prone to violence, he had to see them again and purchase their services. They were dangerous and untrustworthy men, but he had no alternative.

As he took his seat behind his large, formidable cherry wood desk, the door to his office opened, and Caleb Carter and Princess Anastasia Talakovich entered.

Parker's first thought was: my God, she's beautiful! His second thought was: she has the most beautiful breasts in the world, and she's not afraid to show them!

His thoughts, however, did not register in his well-schooled expression. He rose partially from his chair to extend his hand casually to Caleb. When he took Anastasia's hand in greeting, he bowed and kissed the back of her hand.

"I am so glad that you've come to me," Parker Windom said after introductions were made. He found it very difficult to keep his eyes from the princess's enticing decolletage. "I trust you've had a safe journey?"

He was much more curious as to whether Anastasia and Caleb were lovers. He figured they had to be. Any woman who wore a gown like that had to be completely indiscriminate in the men she brought to bed with her.

"Very long and tiring, I'm afraid," Anastasia replied, seating herself in one of the chairs that faced the banker's desk. "Nevertheless, I must say that I am happy to be here."

Parker smiled warmly, quite pleased that Anastasia's English was excellent. At least that wouldn't be a barrier they'd have to challenge.

They chatted briefly, with Parker asking a few questions but not really caring about the answers. Mostly what he wanted was the time to collect his senses, rearrange his thoughts, and figure out what the next logical step was. There was the widow Mrs. Erickson to contend with, a missing ten thousand pounds sterling, and an astonishingly beautiful princess from Russia, who just happened to have enough money to make the amount missing from the widow's account look like purse change.

Twenty-five

"Please, try to understand that I'd like to help you, and I *am* willing to help you, but there are certain considerations that must be taken into account if we're to reach an agreement that benefits all of us," Parker Windom said more than an hour later.

Anastasia was getting frustrated, though she was still bubbling inside at finally being a player in the action. For once she was something much more than just Anton's sister, a spectator who was only allowed to watch from the sidelines.

She had come to London prepared to make a deal for the financing, and now all Parker Windom seemed willing to do was talk about the "unfortunate" political situation, and proclaim the dire consequences should anyone discover that a British bank did business with a Russian princess. The scandal, he moaned, would rock the foundations of the Empire.

"I'm aware of the legalities of the situation," Anastasia continued, trying hard to keep annoyance from darkening her tone. "That's what Caleb can do for us. He can be the American businessman on paper, so that your British bank *won't* be doing business directly with myself *or* my country."

Parker nodded, his eyes focused on something on

his desk.

Anastasia wasn't sure if he had heard a word of what she'd just said. It seemed perfectly clear to her that, on a purely moral level, the banker had no problems making the loan to a nation that his own country was currently feuding with. Equally true was that the more Anastasia explained how using Caleb to sign all the documents would completely free both Parker and his bank from any legal wrongdoing, the more Parker seemed to draw away from her.

She watched as he wiped his brow with a handkerchief. He hadn't been perspiring, so the move drew attention. *Was he nervous about something more than just the loan?* Anastasia mused.

From what Caleb had learned of Parker Windom, he'd had some minor problems in the past with gambling debts. If he was a card player, then he should be able to hide his feelings better than he was, she thought. And as a gambler, he obviously wasn't that concerned with the mandates of convention concerning right and wrong.

"I think we should continue this discussion at another location," Parker said suddenly, rising to his feet and forcing a smile to his mouth. "Sometimes, it is easier to discuss matters more freely outside the office."

"Particularly if what must be discussed is illegal," Caleb commented drily, looking unwaveringly at Parker.

"Exactly, Mr. Carter, exactly," Parker replied.

"I don't see why we had to change hotels," Caleb said quietly, his booted foot up on the window ledge, looking down at the bustling London street below.

He didn't like the new hotel that Parker had insisted they move to. Rather than being in a fine section of London—a section of town that Anastasia felt comfortable in, and Caleb felt was safe—they were now near the pier, and all a man had to do was look at the people walking the cobblestone streets below to know the difference in what the citizenry was like.

"He said it was important," Anastasia replied, walking up behind Caleb. She slipped her arms around him from behind, sliding her hands inside his jacket. She loved the feel of his muscles through the fabric of his shirt. "You don't have to worry about *everything*, you know."

As she squeezed Caleb tighter, twisting her arms further around him, she felt the leather sheaths that carried the daggers beneath his right and left arms. The touch of the weapons disturbed her, reminding her that Caleb believed there was danger lurking about in every shadow.

"This isn't a safe place for you," Caleb continued, hardly paying any attention to the beautiful woman who held him close. "I don't trust Parker. He's a different man now than when I first met him. He's . . ."

His words trailed away. He couldn't put words to the feelings in his gut. The banker *was* a different man, but exactly *how,* Caleb couldn't say. There was a desperation to him now, he thought, though Parker Windom hadn't done anything overt to indicate he was in any way desperate. But that's the way Parker made Caleb feel, and Caleb had long ago learned to trust the whispered warnings of his instincts.

"How is he different?" Anastasia asked.

She placed her cheek against Caleb's back, and when he spoke, she could hear his voice rumbling through him. She wished that Caleb weren't so worried about the change in hotels, because she was suddenly feeling the need to have his body, gloriously naked and moving with all that supple grace that she had come to know and adore during the passage from St. Petersburg to London, moving against her own.

"He's just different," Caleb replied after a long pause.

The knock at the door was expected, though it still startled Anastasia. When Caleb opened the door, Parker Windom was there in the hallway, only now he had another man with him.

"I thought it would be best if we discussed these delicate matters while moving, that way, well, I'm sure you understand," Parker said, twisting his walking stick slowly between his gloved hands.

"Actually, I don't understand," Caleb said, slipping past Anastasia, about to step into the hallway.

He was stopped by Parker, who placed a hand lightly upon his chest. "I'm sorry, Mr. Carter, but what is to be discussed is private, between Princess Talakovich and myself. No one else. You understand, I'm sure."

Anastasia thought for an instant that Caleb was going to strike Parker. When he didn't, when he merely pushed the banker's hand away, she breathed a sigh of relief.

"Not only don't I understand it, I won't agree to it. Anastasia's not leaving my sight."

Parker turned to Anastasia, his eyes almost pleading for understanding. "Whether you want to discuss with Mr. Carter the arrangements and agreements we come to is entirely up to you, but I have always worked on the basis of strict confidentiality, don't you see? *You* can divulge whatever you want with him, but only after *I* am no longer directly involved. I'm sure, if you think about it, you will see that my desire to observe strict confidentiality is in everyone's best interests."

Caleb said quietly, vehemently, "I don't like it one little bit, and I won't tolerate it."

Anastasia replied, "I understand completely, Mr. Windom."

She turned to face Caleb, looking up into his dark, angry eyes. She was too close now to at last securing the loan that her country needed, and she was finally being asked to make the big decisions that had always been left up to her brother. *Nothing* was going to stand in Anastasia's way now, certainly not an over-protective lover who, she still suspected, believed in the deepest part of his heart that a woman just isn't strong enough to go toe-to-toe against a man in a business setting.

"I'm sure this shouldn't take more than an hour," Parker continued, pressing his advantage when it became clear that he had convinced Anastasia. "Caleb will be comfortable here until we return. I've a trusted coachman hired, but he won't hear a word we say."

Anastasia noticed that Parker was now referring to Caleb by his first name, and that there could be no doubting that he had been dismissed as merely an employee. She wanted to comment on this, to defend Caleb, but she kept her tongue, not wanting to offend the banker.

"Don't worry," Anastasia said to Caleb, hoping he wouldn't make more of a scene than he already had. "I will be fine. I'll see you in an hour or so, and then we'll go somewhere to celebrate. How does that sound?"

"Watch yourself," Caleb said quietly, wondering if he was doing the wrong thing by allowing her to leave alone with a man who couldn't be trusted.

The carriage drew attention because it was so beautiful, completely enclosed and whispered of wealth, in stark contrast to the dray wagons and poorly dressed dockworkers who milled about.

353

Anastasia stepped into the carriage, expecting Parker to follow her in immediately. Instead, he stepped away from the carriage and spoke to four men wearing fine clothes. The men nodded, then stepped away, and Parker returned quickly to the carriage.

"Who were those men?" Anastasia asked once the carriage was under way. "I thought the purpose here was anonymity."

"Those men are occasional associates of mine. There are times when their services are most valuable to me."

"They looked like—" Anastasia said, then pretended to not know the right word in English to use. She had seen their type before, hard-edged men who knew how to fight with guns or knives or fists or swords, yet wore fancy clothes and tried to look like gentlemen of leisure and good breeding.

"What do they do for you?" she asked.

"Very shortly, they'll go into the hotel and tell your friend—he is your friend, isn't he? lover?—Caleb that unless a sizable portion of the Talakovich fortune is immediately transferred to my account, then you'll be killed."

The change in Parker's tone first caught Anastasia's attention, then the reality—the cold, brutal reality—of his words struck her.

"Are you going to kidnap me?" she asked, her blue eyes wide with shock. She was so stunned she wasn't even afraid . . . yet.

"Princess, I already have," Parker replied casually. From between the carriage seat cushion he withdrew a small pistol, and very deliberately thumbed back the hammer. Guns made him uncomfortable, and he was not good with them, but he used them whenever necessary. "I've already loaded this, so please don't tempt me. I know that right now you want to rush out the door, but I will shoot you in the back

354

should you try. You see, there was never any reason for you to come to London. I *could* have done business with your American friend, if I'd so chosen. But the thought of either you or your brother, with all that money you've got between the two of you . . . well, it was a fantasy that has come true."

"You bastard," Anastasia whispered, rage battling for supremacy over fear in her heart.

Parker chuckled softly, holding the pistol trained on Anastasia. "Perhaps. It doesn't really matter what I am. What you are, however, is important. You see, you are kidnapped, and unless Caleb can provide the ransom, I'll have to kill you." Parker spoke calmly, as though he was discussing just another business deal instead of Anastasia's life. "By the way, might I say that I find your Russian gowns not only very revealing, but really quite feminine and delightful. When you entered my office this afternoon, I could hardly take my eyes off you."

Anastasia sank back in the seat, crossing her arms over her breasts to cover herself, even though the dress she now wore was modest, even by London standards. She wasn't at all fooled by the casual, almost friendly tone that Parker Windom spoke in — she knew that behind that gentle facade was a killer . . . or worse!

Caleb heard their boots against the wooden stairway before the knock on the door. Even before he opened the door, he was immediately certain of two critical things: that Anastasia was in desperate danger; and that the longer he waited to take action, the less likely his chances were of rescuing her.

He opened the door to find four men standing shoulder to shoulder. The more professional of them had hard looks in their eyes, and in the set of their jaws; the less professional ones had smirks of derision on their lips.

"Where is she?" Caleb asked, not even bothering to pretend that pleasantries or introductions were in order.

"Somewhere safe," the apparent leader of the four said. He walked into the room, pushing Caleb aside, secure in the belief that as long as he had three of his friends with him, then Caleb wouldn't attack. "We're here to let you know what you've got to do now if you ever want to see her alive again."

A muscle twitching in Caleb's jaw was the only emotion he displayed. He watched as one of the men went to the bag that Anastasia had left behind and began rummaging through it, fondling the fine silk undergarments, and showing them to his friends. Another of the men patted Caleb's body, and quickly removed the two daggers he wore.

"He wants gold," the leader said, rocking slowly back on his heels, eyeing Caleb cautiously. "At least fifty purses full of it."

Caleb rolled his eyes. "If he thinks that I can get my hands on that much gold in a short time, then he's—"

"He thinks you can," the leader cut in, and now he, too, wore a derisive smirk as he looked at Caleb. "And don't take too much time in getting it. We'll be entertaining the lady, and if you don't hurry, she'll be entertaining *us*, if you catch my drift." He chuckled malevolently. "She's got a funny accent. Where's she from, anyway?"

"Kiev," Caleb lied.

"Kiev? That near Ireland?"

"Very near," Caleb replied.

It was clear that these four men were not close partners with Parker Windom. They were hired thugs, men who were bought cheaply.

The sight of them disgusted Caleb, and perhaps

356

what bothered him most was that when he looked at the four men, he wondered how much difference there was between them and himself. Wasn't he, too, a hired thug? A mercenary whose services were essentially the same as those provided by these men, with the exception being the skill that Caleb possessed, and the pay he received for his services?

No, Caleb told himself, he wasn't at all like these men. True, the things that he did were often outside the exact boundaries of the law, but he didn't kidnap innocent people, or hurt innocent people, for money. He worked for one man, and one man only, and every assignment he'd ever undertaken for Prince Anton Talakovich, he knew exactly what he was doing, and why.

"What's the next step?" Caleb asked, beginning to size up his opponents.

"You get the gold, and be back here in one week. Just wait here and don't go anywhere. Once we get the gold, we'll let you know where you can find your lady." He chuckled, the sneer in his eyes letting Caleb know that he didn't think much of him. "Just be smart and do what the banker boy says, and you'll see your lady. 'Course, she might be a little different than what she was when you last saw her, but that's to be expected, once a woman's been with me. They see life differently after that."

All four men chuckled then. The shortest of the bunch was holding a pair of Anastasia's pantalets, rubbing his cheek with them.

Caleb looked at the men and began making decisions of what needed to be done. Within the inner ear of his mind, he could hear his old, Oriental instructor whispering, telling him that he must be calm, and never allow emotion, such as rage, dictate his actions, especially not when he went on the attack.

"So then, what you're telling me, is that when you leave here, you'll see Parker Windom, then help yourself to the lady. Correct?"

The leader chuckled again, enjoying this more and more. "That's about it. 'Course we may stop and have an ale first, just so's we get in the right frame of mind when we see your lady. But don't you think of following us. This ain't your city. It's mine, and nobody follows me through the streets unless I let them. Clear?"

Caleb turned away from the leader. He moved closer to the small man who was continuing to fondle Anastasia's silk undergarments. The largest of the four men, an enormously broad-shouldered fellow with a sizable belly from too many pints of rich ale, stepped over, blocking Caleb's path, just as the American mercenary had hoped he would.

"Where you goin'?" the fat man asked.

Caleb looked at the fat man, and within the confines of his mind he could hear his old Oriental mentor whispering that when outnumbered, and a fight was inevitable, it is always best to strike first, strike hardest, and attack the strongest element of the opposition.

"Listen, mate, I asked you where you were going," the fat man repeated.

Caleb came to a stop very close to the man. He had to look up to see into his eyes because he was several inches shorter than the burly Englishman. The short man who had been fondling Anastasia's undergarments moved closer, sensing a fight was at hand and wanting to witness it, certain that Caleb did not stand a chance against his giant of a friend.

"You'll be returning to Parker Windom to inform him that I've been told of the ransom demands," Caleb said.

The big man's expression twisted quizzically.

"Didn't we jus' say that?"

The men moved in closer, surrounding Caleb, curious as to why he seemed to have such a difficult time understanding what was glaringly obvious, others smelling a fight in the air and wanting to partake of it.

"Do you know what I think?" Caleb asked.

"I don't care what you think," the giant replied.

"I think only one of you will return to Parker Windom."

"I think you're wrong," the giant replied, the last word exiting his lips a moment before the breath gushed from his lungs as agonizing pain shot upward from his shattered knee.

Caleb was moving away from the giant immediately after kicking him hard on the inside of the left knee, forcing the joint to bend it in a way nature insisted it could not, causing ligaments and cartilage to yield to brutal strength.

Spinning, crouching, Caleb struck at the leader of the foursome, pouncing upon him like a puma. The man was struggling for the knife that was inside his jacket, but he never removed it from the sheath. Caleb's powerful hands found the man's soft, vulnerable throat, and the man whose life had been spent brutalizing innocent people was himself brutalized, and died before his body struck the floor.

The third man to receive Caleb's attention was the silent one, the man who hadn't spoken, who had stood back and watched, ever cautious. He was attacking now, rushing toward Caleb, but caution had caused him to delay his charge just a fraction of a second too long, so that by the time he reached Caleb, the leader was already dead, and his charge could be met and concentrated upon.

The silent man never did understand how Caleb could take the dagger from him so quickly and easily, and as the dagger was used against him, he thought it terribly unfair that he should die by his own weapon.

The small man who had been fondling Anastasia's clothing was, as Caleb had surmised, a coward. He was still standing with pantalets clutched in his hand, his eyes wide with horror at the sight of two of his comrades already on the floor, their bodies unmoving. Caleb looked at the little man and dismissed him from his immediate attention. The little coward was dangerous only so long as there wasn't the slightest chance that he could be hurt.

But the giant with the shattered knee was not cut from the same bolt of cloth. He had withdrawn his dagger, and with a wide swing of his long arm tried to cut Caleb's throat. Caleb was able to bend backward just quickly enough to avoid the blade's deadly razor-sharp edge.

The giant was big and strong, but he was not terribly quick, and that was his fatal flaw against a man like Caleb. A fraction of a second after the blade barely missed his throat, Caleb leaped forward and went for the giant's throat, only all he needed was the edge of his palm. The giant fell backward, his throat crushed, his astonished eyes frozen open in death.

"Oh-h-h! Oh, God!" the little man whimpered, unable to quite fully comprehend the fact that his three friends were now dead, killed by an unarmed man.

"Be quiet," Caleb said, advancing slowly.

The little man was apparently trying to beg for his life, though his entire body was shaking so hard that his words were almost undecipherable.

"I'm not going to kill you, but only as long as you do everything I tell you," Caleb said, his voice perfectly calm, his mind racing far ahead, thinking of all the things that had to be done if he was to get Princess Anastasia Talakovich back into his arms, which, he realized with pristine clarity, was where she belonged.

The little man fell to his knees, promising to do whatever Caleb asked. The sight sickened Caleb.

"You'll return to Parker Windom, and you'll tell him what I've done here. And you'll tell him that I agree to his terms, and that I'll have the gold for him. But you'll also tell him that if Anastasia is hurt in any way, there won't be a rock large enough for him to hide beneath. I'll find him, and I'll kill him. Do you understand me?"

"Yes, yes, yes!" the coward whimpered. "I hear you!"

"Tell him everything I've just said. Don't forget a single word. If you fail to do this, you'll join your friends in hell," Caleb said, waving his hand at the three corpses on the floor.

The coward stood, about to rush for the door.

"And one more thing," Caleb said. "This is for touching her clothes."

He brought the heel of his boot down hard on the little man's instep, breaking bones with a sharp snapping sound. The little man cried out in pain, but Caleb quickly hauled him to his feet and shoved him out of the room.

"Hurry now," Caleb hissed, his dark eyes deadly with intent. "Straightaway to Parker Windom, and don't forget a word of what I've said!"

The little man hobbled down the hallway, quite certain that he was the luckiest man in the world to walk away from an angry Caleb Carter with nothing worse than small broken bones in his foot to show for his efforts.

Twenty-six

Parker Windom looked at Anastasia, thinking that whatever unfortunate things should now happen to her were entirely justified. It was not at all fair, he decided, that she should be a titled woman, a woman of striking beauty, and a woman of considerable intellect. She had no right to be *all* those things, so whatever happened to her now, Parker decided, was just a matter of evening the score.

"You changed dresses," he said, walking slowly around her in the warehouse. She was sitting in a chair. Parker had tried to sit, but he was much too anxious for his men to return from the hotel to remain seated for very long. "Why?"

"You know why," Anastasia replied, fighting to reveal more anger and less fear in her tone.

"Yes. Such an indecent dress."

It was a gown, not a dress, Anastasia thought contemptuously. And it wasn't indecent! Just because the English have cold blood, it doesn't mean the Russians do as well!

"Are you and the American lovers?"

Anastasia was shocked at the question, though she realized that she shouldn't be. After all, if this man was unseemly enough to kidnap her,

362

then he lacked the graces to realize there were some questions a gentleman just didn't ask a woman.

As she looked at him, she realized that there was much about the world beyond the glittering salons of St. Petersburg that she knew nothing about. She had thought she would know what to do once she got to London because she had for a long time dealt with the facts of what it was her brother did. What she was only now beginning to realize was that she had always concerned herself with the facts of her family business while insulating herself from the people. The facts are constant; it is only the people who can be treacherous.

"I asked you a question. Aren't you going to answer me?"

Anastasia looked at Parker and tried to smile confidently, failing only slightly. She leaned back in the chair and crossed her legs at the knee.

"That is none of your concern."

"Ah, but it is. If you're lovers, then maybe he'll be more interested in producing the ransom money." Parker smiled, calm and in control, secure at last in his belief that he had thought of everything that was necessary, and that finally he would have the money to live the life that was due him. "Personally, it matters not at all to me if you're spreading your legs for him. I've had an affair or two in my life myself."

"With women who needed a loan from your bank, no doubt."

Parker grinned crookedly, his opinion of Anastasia going up slightly at the accuracy of her assessment. "Actually, it was their husbands who needed the loans. Bad business moves, a few changes in a man's fortunes, and the next thing you know, they're sending their wives to me to get the money they need to keep them afloat. Men can be very reasonable about such matters."

"What do the wives think of it?"

"Wives don't think," Parker replied with blithe unconcern. "They do what they're told."

Anastasia shook her head slowly, realizing finally that there were men in the world who were beyond the evil that she had thought existed. Caleb was something of a chauvinist, but it was within his ability to change his views and reform; Anton, certainly, saw her very much as an equal while accepting simultaneously the fact that few businessmen would consider a woman an equal. But Parker Windom was beyond belief, beneath contempt.

"Change that expression right now," Parker said slowly, his countenance hardening with savage speed. "Change it now, or I'll really give you something to scowl about."

Anastasia did as she was told, immediately and without reservation. Parker Windom dressed like a prominent banker, but his heart was as black and void of compassion as the worst cutthroat killer. Unless she did everything he demanded, she was certain he would think nothing of killing her.

"I apologize, she murmured softly, dropping her eyes down to the floor. "I didn't mean to offend you."

When she looked up at Parker again, she saw that he was smiling, standing with his hands clasped behind his back, rocking slowly on his heels. He was again at peace with himself and his world. He liked it when she looked demure, when she appeared frightened of his power over her.

"That's better," Parker said in that faintly condescending tone bankers so often use. "You see, I'm really not a difficult man to get along with."

Anastasia tried to smile then at Parker, but as

364

she did so, she thought, *Caleb, please hurry!*
This is a madman we're dealing with!

Caleb had no difficulty in following the little
man through the crowded streets of London. The
broken bone in the coward's foot kept him moving slowly, and the general expression of fear,
pain, and unspent violent rage prevented the occasional hansom cabs that appeared on the street
from stopping for him.

In the pit of his stomach, Caleb felt the slow,
burning rage for Parker Windom, and a fear for
Anastasia's safety. He should never have allowed
her to leave St. Petersburg, where she was safe,
he told himself. But even as he thought this, he
knew that she would never have stayed at Castle
Talakovich, and he never would have been able to
keep her there.

It was her feistiness that appealed to him, that
made her different in his eyes and gave her a
place in his heart that no other woman had ever
occupied, even as it was her feistiness that made
her the most frustrating woman he'd ever known.

And now that feisty woman that had stolen his
heart was being held captive by a treacherous
banker who would not hesitate to kill her if that
meant destroying all evidence of his crime.

The little man was thirty yards ahead. He tried
to hail a cab, but the coachman merely cocked
his arm, threatening to whip him if he didn't
move away.

How much pain was he in? Caleb wondered.
How swollen now was the broken foot inside his
boot?

He pushed the thoughts aside, forcing them
from his mind. They would lead to sympathy,
eventually, and that was not an emotion that Ca-

leb could afford—certainly not for a sick little man with savage tendencies who enjoyed fondling women's undergarments.

They had covered nearly a mile, moving along the water's edge, when the little man finally stopped and looked behind him to see if he was being followed. Caleb ducked into the entryway of a fishing net maker's office.

"Can I 'elp you with something?" an attractive woman in her early thirties inquired.

Caleb looked at her and smiled. "No, thank you."

"More's the pity," she replied, amber eyes twinkling. She enjoyed the cut of Caleb's clothes, the look of his face, the line of his body. Among the unwashed dockworkers the pickings of men—gentlemen, that is—was meager.

The little man was on the move again, and Caleb moved out of the entryway, weaving his way through the crowds of people, following at such a distance that it was extremely unlikely he would lose his prey, yet not so close that he would likely be spotted.

There wasn't any need to panic yet, Parker repeatedly told himself, though it didn't do anything to bolster his courage.

The simple fact of the matter was that the men should have returned at least an hour ago, and they hadn't.

Parker told himself that the men were unskilled, unschooled, lowlife pier scum that could be bought cheaply, and who would do anything for a shilling. Quite likely, they had stopped off at a tavern somewhere on their way back from seeing Caleb Carter, and they were probably now drinking ale and bragging of their own courage.

Parker walked over to the window that looked down at the pier. He wrinkled his nose at the smell of fish that hung heavy in the air.

His back was to Anastasia, but he wasn't afraid that she would try to run. He had the key to the only door to this second floor warehouse, and even if she did manage to get out of the huge room, she probably wouldn't make it down the stairs and out of the streetside door, which was also locked. Besides, he'd let her know with hints and innuendo that as long as she cooperated with him, she wouldn't be hurt, but if she didn't do as she was told, she'd be given to the lusty, lowlife thugs that would soon be returning to the warehouse.

Parker had seen Anastasia shiver when he made the threat, and he wondered if she wasn't a virgin. It seemed very odd to him that being gang-raped would be frightening to a woman who wasn't a virgin.

He turned away from the window and looked at Anastasia. She was much easier on the eyes than the sailors, prostitutes, stevedores, and foreigners of every stripe and color who populated this section of the city.

Almost idly, he wondered if he should rip her clothes off and force himself upon her before the cretins had their turn with her, but he decided against it. He was too nervous for sex, and he highly doubted that he could achieve and maintain the necessary state long enough to properly accomplish the act.

His reoccurring impotence had been a source of frustration for him, and one that had caused him to punish three different women who thought it humorous that he couldn't rise to the occasion, even when he had gone to considerable lengths to use extortion to force the women into his bed.

"My family has a great fortune," Anastasia said, feeling chilled to the marrow of her bones whenever Parker looked at her. "You'll be a very wealthy man when this is over, as long as I'm alive and unharmed."

She had always prided herself on her ability to read a person's thoughts, but with Parker, she drew a complete blank. He was too different, his thought processes too convoluted and twisted, for her to even attempt to comprehend his thoughts. She could tell that with each passing minute he was becoming more agitated, but beyond that, she wasn't certain of anything at all.

"I'll be a very wealthy man one way or another," Parker corrected. "Whether you stay alive or not depends upon your doing exactly what I tell you to, and whether that American you're so fond of can follow orders." Parker's lips twisted derisively. "I've always loathed men from the colonies. Have you noticed they've an air about them, an attitude as though they're better than everyone else? Disgusting, all of them."

Anastasia thought, *Hurry Caleb! For God's sake, please hurry! He's completely insane!*

Caleb was only a little surprised when the little man hobbled to a dingy abandoned warehouse. He went to a waterside door and struggled with it, trying to open it and failing. Then the little man went to the north side of the building, and climbed up a rope ladder to a broken second floor window and crawled through it.

A thousand questions exploded in Caleb's brain, and he felt the surging rush of adrenaline pump through his veins. He knew he was close to Anastasia now, and to Parker Windom as well. Within the next few minutes, or perhaps the next few hours, he would need all the skills he had learned during his years of living on the brutal edge of society if he was to rescue Princess Anastasia Talakovich alive and unharmed.

He moved out of the shadows, walking down the cobblestone alley. The first thing he had to do was make a circle of the warehouse, and familiarize himself with it and its surroundings as much as possible. Once that was accomplished, he would determine exactly how many men were inside, and how close Anastasia was to them. It wouldn't accomplish anything for him to rush blindly into the melee. Such rashness would only be suicidal, and would not help Anastasia at all.

The sun would be down soon. Darkness might help his assault on Parker's position, Caleb told himself. But darkness might also impede him. Whoever was inside the warehouse would surely know the building better than Caleb, and would be less hindered by the darkness.

When he'd completed his trip around the warehouse, Caleb had learned a great deal. It was clear that the warehouse had not been in use for several years. There were four entrances to the large building—one on each side—and all four large doors were chained and locked. But there were several windows on each side, and almost all of them had at least one or more of the glass panes broken. Two windows were completely void of glass, so Caleb was certain he could gain entrance to the building without cutting himself, though whether he could get inside without being seen or heard by the guards was a question that could not be answered in advance.

He crossed the alleyway, melting into the shadows to watch the building and let his mind consider all the possible moves he could make next. He saw the little man peer from a second-floor window. The face was in the window for only a second or two before disappearing, but in that time, Caleb was able to conclude several things: that the little man was afraid he'd been followed; and that there might not be as many men inside the warehouse as Caleb had first suspected. Surely, the little man's foot must be causing him unbearable agony by now, but he was still acting as a sentry.

Caleb knew that he had done the smart thing by killing the other three messengers in the hotel when he'd had the chance. It sent a message to Parker Windom that left absolutely no room for misunderstanding, and judging by the way the little man continued to peek his head out the window every minute or two, it put more than just a little fear into their hearts.

He wished that he had weapons—a sabre, several throwing knives, a rifle or pistol. Anything would be more than what he had: his hands and a single dagger.

Caleb shrugged away his doubts. He had to fight this battle on another man's ground, but that didn't mean he had to fight it on his enemy's terms. He could skew the odds more in his favor.

The sun was casting long shadows through the high buildings now. Inside, it would be quite dark, though not completely dark. Heart pumping, nerves finely tuned for action and yet perfectly calm, Caleb crossed to the north side of the warehouse, and wasn't at all surprised that he was able to slip through the window there to crouch in the shadows inside completely unnoticed by his enemies.

The conflagration had begun. Caleb knew in his heart that he could not negotiate for Anastasia's release—not with a man like Parker Windom. To negotiate with him would be to have faith in Parker's honesty, and only a fool would make that mistake. No, one way or another, Parker had to be dealt with swiftly and surely, and when it was over and the bloodletting had ended, either Caleb would have freed Anastasia, or he would have died in the attempt.

He drew comfort from believing completely that what he was doing was the only thing to be done, giving Caleb a deep, abiding sense of confidence. He headed deeper into the warehouse, thinking that the only thing that could make him feel more confident was if Anton were by his side.

Parker Windom was murderously angry. "I ought to shoot you in the other foot!" Parker hissed, aiming his pistol at the little man's ankle.

"Don't! I tell you, I never seen a man move that fast ever! He was on us in a blink of a cod's eye, an' killin' 'fore I 'ad the time to gut him with my knife!" Fear was making his cockney accent even thicker than normal.

Anastasia was still sitting in the chair, and it was taking all the self-control she possessed to keep from smiling. The little man had related his story to Parker Windom, complete with all the gory details of how Caleb had fared against three armed, dangerous men, killing them in less than fifteen seconds with just his bare hands. Parker Windom was frightened by what he heard, but not impressed.

"And he said he'd have the gold, right?" Parker asked. It was at least the tenth time he had asked the question.

"That's what 'e said. The three—they was just 'is way of proving that if you didn't release the lady 'ere when you got the gold that 'e'd track you down and—"

"Shut up!" Parker snapped. He did not need to be told one more time that Caleb intended to kill him if Anastasia was harmed or assaulted in any way. "I know what that bloody fool said!"

He walked close to Anastasia and pointed the pistol at her face. The muzzle looked as large as a tunnel, and black as hell itself, but Anastasia refused to tremble with fear. Caleb had something planned. She was certain of it. However much she had always abhorred those strange, deadly skills that he possessed and that her brother had always found so useful to employ, it was now obvious that without Caleb and his deadly abilities she did not stand a prayer of being alive in the morning.

"Maybe you're more trouble than you're worth," Parker said quietly.

"He'll come with the gold. If you kill me, you'll ruin the only chance you have of getting rich. I know Caleb. He won't give the gold away until he's certain that I'm safe."

"She's a liar!" the little man whined. "Don't trust 'er! Let's get out of 'ere, Mr. Windom. Let's just kill 'er and leave and pretend this whole bloody business never got started at all."

Parker turned slowly, and raised the pistol to aim it at the little man. "Back to the window," he said, his voice was hoarse with tension. "I want to know when they get here."

They? wondered Anastasia, her confidence that she would be rescued by Caleb diminishing rapidly.

The little man looked out the window again, then let out a little shout of approval. "They're here! The carriage is nice and big, too!"

Parker said, "Get down there and unlock the

door." He fished a long key from his jacket pocket and tossed it to the little man. "And be quick about it."

The little man started to say once again that his foot had been broken, but he thought better of it, and hobbled out of the room as quickly as he could.

"What's going to happen to me?" Anastasia asked softly, the tremble in her voice apparent despite her efforts to hide it.

Parker grinned broadly. He hooked his thumbs into the waistband of his breeches, and looked down at Anastasia in a beaming way that bespoke soaring confidence. "When I told the American long ago that he wouldn't get the loan unless he brought whoever he was fronting for to London to sign the papers, I never really thought he'd do it," Parker explained. "Then when you showed up at my office, I had to make plans quickly. I've been saving this warehouse for just such an occasion for a while now, but this isn't safe enough. Not for you. Not when it'll take your American friend a while to come up with the gold that I'm demanding. So we're going to put you into a little box, and carry you away to some place . . . safe."

Anastasia felt as though all the air had suddenly been sucked out of the room. How much was he demanding for her safe return? Could Caleb gain any access to the considerable Talakovich funds that were in numerous banks all through Europe?

The sudden possibility of weeks or even months of captivity brought tears of horror to Anastasia's blue eyes.

"No, please," she whispered, rising from her chair. "I can't do that! You can't just keep me locked up! I haven't done anything to you!"

Parker had enjoyed Anastasia's fear in the past, and he positively relished it now. He was laughing heartily when the large door opened at the north end of the room, and three well-dressed men walked in, two of them carrying a large chest.

"This going to be big enough for what you want, Mr. Windom?" the one not carrying the trunk asked.

Parker nodded his head in Anastasia's direction. "Harry, all you have to do is fit her in the trunk. I think you can accomplish that, don't you?"

Harry looked at Anastasia, clearly impressed with what he saw, making no effort to hide the wickedness in his leer. "Yes, sir, Mr. Windom, I'm real sure I can get her in the trunk. She's just a little thing. A pretty little thing, but a little thing just the same."

Anastasia looked at the trunk, and the scream that was ripped from her throat echoed off the walls of the huge warehouse.

Twenty-seven

If there had ever been any doubt in Caleb's mind as to whether his love for Anastasia was real, it vanished the moment his heart was pierced by her scream. At that point, nothing mattered to him but rescuing her; not his sense of caution, not trying to reclaim his sense of calm essential to a warrior, not even his own life mattered.

He bolted up the crumbling wooden stairway, knowing that he was rushing unarmed into a room which only moments earlier he'd watched three villainous-looking scoundrels enter, carrying a large trunk. His boots pounded against the wooden floor landing, and though he knew that he was making too much noise to facilitate a surprise attack, speed was more essential to Caleb now than stealth.

He burst into the room, and in one sweeping glance took in the entire situation. Anastasia was sitting in a simple wooden chair in the center of the room. From what Caleb could see, she was not tied to the chair. Standing near her was Parker Windom, holding a flintlock in his hand, the pistol appearing reasonably new, in well-oiled, working condition.

Immediately to Caleb's right were the two men

who had been carrying the large trunk. The little coward with the busted foot stood by them. And just to Caleb's left was Harry, who was still grinning wickedly, even though he'd heard the sound of Caleb's hurried approach.

Caleb's dagger was in his hand, and he used it on the closest man, one who held an end of the trunk. Blade met flesh and not even a sound was emitted from the dead man as he slumped to the floor.

"You bastard!" Harry screamed, wheeling away from Caleb, removing a large-bladed knife from beneath his jacket. Though a savage killer, Harry was loyal to his men, and he always took it as a personal offense whenever one of them was injured by anyone other than himself. Once he had the weapon in his large hand, he started toward Caleb, intent on revenge.

"That's 'im! That's the bloke!" the little coward screamed, his eyes wide with shock, his brain unable to fully comprehend the fact that he would be witness to Caleb's lethal wrath twice in so short a time. "Kill 'im!"

Parker Windom raised his pistol, trying to aim it at Caleb. He held his finger from the trigger, knowing that he had only one shot to kill his enemy. The problem was that Caleb moved swiftly, and never in a straight line, moving in this direction, then that one, his attack precise, acute, and deadly.

One man had already fallen, and a second was holding onto his stomach, trying to staunch the flow of blood that oozed quickly through his fingers. His knees were bending slowly, and soon he, too, would be just another corpse.

"You fool!" Parker hissed, suddenly turning upon the little man he'd hired earlier that day. "He followed you here!"

Parker aimed his pistol at the little man, but again he held his finger from the trigger. There would be time enough for revenge after the American had been dispensed with.

Caleb sized up Harry, feigning a lunge to test the man's reflexes. Harry moved quickly out of the way of the dagger, lithe on his feet for a big man, and Caleb knew he had a dangerous foe to deal with. He also knew that the moment he stopped moving, the second that he and Harry settled into a serious knife fight, was the moment that Parker Windom would at last be able to train his pistol upon its target.

"Drop the knife, or I'll kill the whore!" Parker shouted, suddenly turning his attention from Caleb to Anastasia. He aimed the pistol at her chest, a cruel smile of victory twisting his lips.

Anastasia shouted, "Get out of here, Caleb! He's going to kill me anyway! Save yourself!"

Harry was a skilled, experienced knife fighter. When Parker first shouted, he began maneuvering himself so that he had Caleb trapped between himself and Parker. The moment Caleb would turn to look at either Parker or Anastasia, he'd thrust his huge knife into the American's back, and that would be the end of the fight. He could almost taste the cool ale he'd be drinking and hear the eloquent, bawdy toasts he'd give for his fallen comrades.

Never for even a split second did Caleb consider leaving Anastasia, or consider dropping his own dagger. The princess had assessed the situation accurately when she said that Parker was going to kill her anyway, no matter what course of action Caleb took.

Caleb had been taught to use more than just his eyes to see his world. He could see, with that sixth sense of danger that had protected him for

377

so many years, Parker turning the gun away from Anastasia and toward him. Caleb tried to move so that he was not directly between Parker and Harry, but the burly knife-fighter only shifted to keep him trapped.

A macabre grin danced on Harry's face. He kept his distance, a patient fighter willing to bide his time until just the right moment presented itself.

Becoming more desperate by the moment, Parker Windom sensed the end of his dream at hand. Too many people had already become involved in the kidnapping of the Princess Anastasia Talakovich for word of his involvement to remain a secret for long. He knew this with the certainty of a man who knew that his luck could not last forever, just as he knew that the reason his luck had come to such an abrupt and untimely end was that Caleb Carter had not been the passive victim that Parker had counted on.

Contempt for men from the colonies had always burned hot in Parker's veins, but never so hot as at that moment.

He aimed at Caleb's broad back and squeezed the trigger.

Anastasia saw the blood on Caleb's back, and she began to scream, her eyes squeezed tightly closed, the horror of what she had just witnessed too hideous for her to ever again want to open her eyes.

It had not been the first time that Caleb's powerful body had been violated by the ball of an enemy's flintlock, though it was certainly the most painful.

At the instant that Parker squeezed the trigger, Caleb's instincts had warned him. He leaped to the left, twisting as he did so. The pistol's heavy lead ball ripped a jagged hole through his coat, striking flesh, leaving a long and bloody tear in Caleb's back before moving on.

It was the look on Harry's face, one of surprise, resentment, and lack of pain, that told Caleb that Harry would soon be dead. He had taken the lead into his stomach, and the force of the ball hitting him staggered him back several steps.

"Damn it, Mr. Windom, I think you killed me," Harry said quietly, more confused than angered by the unexpected turn of events.

The heavy-bladed knife fell from his fingers, suddenly much too heavy for him to hold. He fell to his knee, his eyes still fixed upon Caleb, then fell face down on the hard wooden floor.

Caleb turned away from Harry just in time to see Parker Windom rushing from the room. Caleb took two steps after the man, then stopped. He would not leave Anastasia alone with the little coward.

"Oh . . . don't . . . not me . . . not again," the little coward babbled, whispering, trembling.

It was only then that Anastasia opened her eyes, and when she did, she let out another shout, only this time it was of joy. Caleb was bleeding badly, she could see, but he was still on his feet, and if she knew anything about the man it was that he was strong. If he could take the ball from Parker's pistol and not be knocked off his feet, then he would live to fight — and love — again.

She leaped from the chair and rushed to him, completely ignoring the little man.

"You're bleeding," she whispered, wanting to take him into her arms.

He moved away from her, his dark eyes hard and cold upon the little man still in the room.

"You sit," Caleb said to the little man, pointing

379

at the chair. To Anastasia he asked, "Did they hurt you?"

"No. They would have, but you came in time." Anastasia was not interested in discussing the ordeal that she'd just been through. It meant nothing to her now. What concerned her was Caleb, and the amount of blood he was losing.

Using two large swatches of her petticoat, Anastasia bandaged Caleb's wound as best she could. The bullet had broken a rib, and left a long rip in the flesh of his back, but from what she could see it had not damaged any of his internal organs. The wound was painful, but as long as she could stop the bleeding and keep the wound free of infection, Caleb would recover with nothing more than another scar to show for it.

"Let's go," Anastasia said, sliding under Caleb's arm to help him, keeping her hands far from his painful wound. "It's time for us to return to St. Petersburg. We never should have come to London at all."

They were almost out of the warehouse when Caleb eased himself out of Anastasia's embrace. He looked down into her eyes, his fingertips light against her cheek.

"Wait here. I'll be right back."

"Caleb, you're not going to . . ."

"Don't worry, I'm not an evil man."

Caleb returned to the warehouse room where Anastasia had been held captive. He found the little man going through the pockets of the men who'd been killed, taking whatever valuables he could find. The sight of it disgusted Caleb, and if he'd had any doubts as to what course of action should be taken if justice was to be served, they vanished in an instant.

"You were going to hurt her, weren't you?" Caleb said softly, his voice almost thoroughly void of emotion.

The little man, kneeling by Harry's corpse, picked up the big knife that had fallen from his dead fingers.

"You would have raped her if you'd had the chance," Caleb continued. He didn't bother taking his own dagger from its sheath. "You must be punished for what you did to Anastasia. You must be held accountable for that. And if I let you live, you'll rape someone else sooner or later, won't you?"

"Who I rape is none o' your business!" the little man whispered, feeling really quite confident because he held a very large knife in his hand, and Caleb's entire left side was red with blood. "A man's got to take care of his needs."

The little coward shouldn't have felt so confident.

Parker Windom had stood in the dark, shivering with fear, waiting for eight o'clock until the bank opened. He'd been walking the streets of London for hours, not daring to return to his home for fear that Caleb would find him there. But the American surely wouldn't dare show his face at the bank. Parker might not have killed him with the shot, but he'd wounded him badly.

"He's probably lying somewhere, bleeding to death in his lady's arms," Parker said aloud, needing to hear the sound of his own voice to bolster his waning confidence.

He heard the chiming of a distant clock. At exactly that moment, old Sean McWilliams unlocked the huge oak front doors of the bank, exactly as he had done every working day for the past twenty-seven years. The bank was nothing if not punctual.

Parker crossed the street, smoothing his hair as best he could with his hands. He had left his hat behind at the warehouse, and his clothes were a little damp from the fog, but he still appeared somewhat presentable. Though this had not been how he'd always planned he'd make his exit from the bank, there was a certain peace of mind in knowing that at last he would stop living the lie. On this day, he would transfer as many funds as he possibly could, and with any luck by noon or perhaps even sooner he would have embezzled enough funds to live comfortably, at least for a couple years, under an assumed name.

He smiled at the thought. It would be fun to pick a new name and identity for himself.

"Good morning, sir," Sean McWilliams said as Parker stepped into the bank.

Parker ignored the greeting, just as he had ignored it every day that he'd worked as an executive at the bank. He'd never before found it necessary for a man of his stature to respond to greetings from such low-level employees as the security guards and the bookkeepers, so he wouldn't change his position now. He *did* notice that McWilliams had given him a funny look, obviously aware that Parker wasn't immaculately groomed. Parker had no intention of explaining anything—certainly not to a guard.

He passed other people, ignoring their greetings as well. When he passed his secretary's desk, he was surprised that the slender young man wasn't there, as he normally was. Parker could feel eyes upon him, but he dismissed this as the bank employees merely noticing that he looked as though he'd slept in his clothes.

He was two steps into his office when he stopped dead in his tracks.

The six old men were crowded around his desk,

all of them trying to read at the same time Parker's personal red leather-bound ledger, the one that listed the accounts that he'd embezzled money from, and the amounts that were missing. Parker's secretary was in the room, too, and when he looked at Parker, undisguised contempt filled the honest young man's eyes.

"Mr. Windom, under other circumstances, I'd say that you have some explaining to do," the white-bearded chairman said gravely. "However, this ledger seems to tell me everything I need to know."

Parker turned on his heel, intent on making a furious escape, but two constables had already moved into position behind him, blocking his exit, and beyond them, he saw two more waiting. He turned back to the six old men.

"It's not what you think," Parker said, blood draining from his face.

"Mr. Windom, if I have any say about it, you will never set foot outside a prison again in your life," the chairman said with quiet hatred. "And believe me, I'll have a lot to say about your sentencing. Lord Baldridge and I have belonged to the same club for more than two score years, and when he's called a man who upholds the law, it means he believes criminals should be imprisoned for years and years."

Outside the bank, as a light drizzling rain began to fall, Anastasia and Caleb watched as Parker was led away, surrounded by a half dozen constables.

"That's the end of it," Anastasia said. "I don't know what they got him for, but by the looks of it, it must be something pretty horrible."

Caleb was holding the bandage tight against his ribs. The throbbing ache set his teeth on edge, and he felt weak from the loss of blood, but at least he knew that Anastasia was safe.

"We didn't get what we set out to," Caleb murmured. He had been successful every time he set out on an assignment from Anton, and it bothered him to think that this time he had failed.

Anastasia turned toward him, her eyes bright blue and shining with the brilliance inspired by a new idea. "Wait right here. I've an idea," she said, and was crossing the street toward the white-bearded old men before Caleb had the chance to stop her.

Twenty-eight

"You're sure he'll be here?" Natasha asked.

Anton looked around the small tavern that was filled with smoke, crowded with men and a few women. Some of the patrons were poorly dressed; others immaculately attired. It was, as Anton had suspected it would be, a crossroads tavern, one where a man with enough money might buy a prostitute, or a politician.

"It's been a long time since I've been absolutely sure of anything," Anton finally replied. He sipped the wine and grimaced. It was positively foul.

It had taken three days to get word to Rosto Rapp that a meeting would be profitable for him. Though Anton's French was excellent, it was not without accent, and suspicion of foreigners in Paris was running high. Everyone knew that Napoleon was making plans for *something,* but exactly what that something was, nobody but the emperor himself could say. To be within the inner circle of Napoleon's advisors, to possess such information and be willing to sell it, was the French government's worst fear, and a political opportunist's fantasy.

As he looked at the men who were, in turn, looking at them seated in a corner table in the back, Anton sensed once again that he should not have allowed Natasha to follow him into the tav-

385

ern. He could not tell whether the men were looking at Natasha because she was an outsider and had drawn suspicion to herself somehow, or if the men were simply looking at her because she was beautiful, and they lusted after her. Either way, Anton didn't like it.

"That man over there is looking at us," Natasha whispered, leaning closer to Anton, her hand resting lightly on his knee beneath the table. "I think that's Rosto Rapp."

Anton glanced at the man she referred to. He was in his early forties, with hair salted with gray and combed back into a queue. His clothes were of fine quality, though a bit too flamboyant for a man who occasionally walked within the political circles of Paris.

"I don't think so," Anton replied. "And I don't think he's looking at both of us. You're an extraordinarily attractive woman, my darling. You must start remembering that."

At that moment the man under Natasha's scrutiny rose from his chair and crossed the crowded tavern. He smiled down at Anton and Natasha, nodding slightly, and said in the most courtly manner imaginable, "Monsieur and madame, allow me to introduce myself. I am Rosto Rapp, and I understand that I can be of service to you. May I be allowed to sit?"

Natasha and Anton exchanged a glance, and Natasha raised her auburn eyebrows for only an instant to silently say: I told you so!

Introductions were quickly made. Natasha noticed that Anton provided only their first names, and—surprisingly—Rosto accepted this without comment. Natasha felt an eerie sensation in the cold pit of her stomach that many things were happening in this tavern that she did not know about, and that if she did know, she would not be pleased. But however much it disturbed her that strange and dangerous things were happening, there was an adventurous side of her that was gloriously happy to be in the heart of this particular storm.

"My time is valuable, and I'm sure yours is, too, so I'll not waste it," Anton said to Rosto. "Soon there will be a man coming to Paris. When he does, he will be looking for you. When he contacts you, I want you to contact me."

"And why should I do that? Why should this man want to contact me? I am just a simple servant of the people, doing my best to put bread on my table."

"You're a political whore who'd sell out his own country in a second if he thought he could turn a profit by it," Anton replied.

Natasha watched Rosto's expression change infinitesimally. She saw the glint in his eyes harden, and she could not understand why Anton would go to such lengths to antagonize the man whose good graces they needed if they were to set this trap for Ivan.

Then, after a lengthy, silent pause, Rosto smiled a little. "You are correct, of course, and though I appreciate your honesty, I cannot abide your bluntness. I don't consider myself a political whore, merely a politician." Rosto's grin spread completely across his face. "But then, both apples are red, are they not?"

The men smiled then, and even laughed a little, but Natasha knew Anton well enough to see that in his heart he did not find anything funny about what had been said, and that he did not like or trust Rosto Rapp at all, no matter how cordially Anton appeared.

"Tell me now, who is this man who will seek me out, and why will he do this?"

"The man is your cousin from St. Petersburg,

Ivan Pronushka."

"And you want me to betray my own cousin?" Rosto placed his hand over his heart, as though the suggestion itself horrified him.

"You'll be paid for it."

"Very well paid," Rosto replied.

Natasha listened to the conversation, astonished at how quickly and easily loyalties changed. Could it really be possible that she had blood ties to men like Rosto Rapp and Ivan Pronushka? Nothing about them seemed to her worthy of respect, and in some ways they seemed inhuman, incapable of holding any semblance of goodness and decency within their breast.

"He's in possession of some letters that would be embarrassing to Czar Alexander should they get into the wrong hands."

"Letters? Of what nature?"

"Do you need to know?"

"If I am to help you, we need to trust each other, at least a little. I like to know exactly what it is I'm going to betray my own beloved cousin for."

Anton nodded. "The letters are personal correspondence between a nephew of the czar, and another young man. Just letters, that's all."

Rosto grinned and tugged at his lower lip. "Letters which suggest something more than merely a friendship between the young men?"

"If a person was suspicious by nature, then perhaps the letters might indicate their affection for each other was more than brotherly," Anton replied. "Since the czar of Russia and the emperor of France are such good friends, I've been sent to see that the letters are destroyed so that the enemies of our countries cannot use these silly, boyish letters to embarrass either country. Surely, you can understand that Napoleon would not want his name associated, however remotely, with such a matter."

The lie was an outrageous one, and Natasha felt as though she had been given yet another lesson in what the world of politics was really like. Anton was lying through and through; but Rosto believed that the only part of the story that was a lie was the part about not wanting a hint of scandal to touch Napoleon.

Natasha couldn't imagine what difference it would make to the two governments if the czar's nephew was a homosexual, but obviously it was something that could be used to embarrass or blackmail Czar Alexander.

"Yes, yes, yes," Rosto said after another long pause. "I can see how it would be most embarrassing to have such letters circulated through Paris."

"Then it is agreed that you will contact me when Ivan contacts you?"

"How did my cousin obtain these letters? I would think that the czar's nephew would have gone to considerable lengths to keep them discreet."

Anton just looked at Rosto. Such a question was beyond answering, his silent look said. Natasha knew that the real reason Anton said nothing was because he would only be adding yet another lie to the mixture, and he'd already put forward quite a few.

A tall, slender man with sinewy features and eyes that Natasha thought looked like those of a snake, approached the table. He had an authoritarian bearing to him, a way of standing and moving that Natasha thought was militaristic.

"Good evening," the man said, forcing himself into the conversation.

"Good evening," Rosto replied. He made a vague gesture toward the one chair still open at the small, round table. "Please, have a seat. Madame and monsieur, I'd like you to meet the prefect of police for Paris, Monsieur Pierre de Gruzin. Pierre, meet

389

Anton and Natasha. They are visiting our fair city in hopes of finding something they've lost."

"Something has been stolen from you while you have been here in Paris?" Pierre asked, his brows beetling. If there was going to be any stealing done in Paris, Pierre was going to be the one doing it.

"Not in Paris," Anton explained.

Natasha did not know what to think. When she first learned that the new stranger was the prefect of police, she thought that at last they could somehow use the normal legal channels to regain possession of the damning documents. But then, watching Anton, she realized that he was as doubting of Pierre's integrity as he was of Rosto Rapp's.

"So many thieves in the world," Pierre said with a weary sigh, as though his days and nights were completely consumed by the pursuit of justice.

A waitress hurried over and placed a drink in front of Pierre on the table. Everyone at the table noticed that the woman did not wait to receive payment for the drink.

Pierre turned his attention from Anton to Natasha, and he smiled. She thought it looked more like a wolf's snarl just before it attacked than a man's smile.

"Surely, such an attractive young woman as this cannot be a party to theft, unless it is the theft of a man's heart," Pierre said.

Not knowing what the appropriate response was, Natasha smiled and cast her eyes down. Then she felt Pierre's hand on her knee beneath the table. Her body flinched for only an instant, then she froze.

Pierre was the prefect of police, and if he wanted to, he could cause problems for her and Anton. That was the reason why Anton had been more than cordial and less than honest with the prefect. That was also why Rosto Rapp had invited Pierre to join them at the table, even though his intrusion into their conversation made discussing the imminent arrival of Ivan Pronushka impossible.

The men resumed their conversation, but there was such a ringing in Natasha's ears that she could hardly hear what they were saying. She knew that Anton did not realize Pierre had his hand on her knee, and for this, she was thankful. He would, she was certain, react strongly if he knew, perhaps even challenging Pierre to a duel.

And what if that's what Pierre wanted all along? What if he was intentionally trying to provoke Anton into reacting violently.

Natasha told herself that Pierre wasn't really touching *her,* he was touching her dress. It didn't bother her at all, she tried to tell herself . . . but she felt soiled just the same, especially when he squeezed her thigh.

He's an evil man, Natasha thought. *My instincts from the very beginning were right about him. Pierre de Gruzin is a dangerous, evil man!*

Then, just as abruptly as he had arrived on the scene, Pierre rose from his chair. "I trust our guests in Paris will enjoy themselves immensely, and will recover what you have lost," he said, smiling easily. "If there is anything that I can do for you while you are in the city, please call upon me."

He took Natasha's hand and kissed the back of it, and when his eyes met hers, she shivered and looked away. Having him look at her and touch her—even though it was on her knee through her dress—made her feel as though she'd been spit upon.

With Pierre gone, Rosto sighed heavily, just a bit theatrically. "You can both do yourself a favor by staying as far away from that man as you possibly can. Here in Paris, his power is absolute. If he accuses you of a crime, then you are guilty of that crime, and you will be punished for that crime."

"But what about your courts? France is not an uncivilized country," Natasha interjected, still not quite believing that the abuse of power could be as openly known and yet unchecked as it seemed.

Natasha had read of how in France every citizen was allowed the right to have their opinion heard in court, and given a fair and impartial hearing, no matter what their station in society. France was not like her Russia, where the landed gentry ruled with total power, and punished with complete impunity.

Rosto smiled at her naivete. "No, madame, France is not an uncivilized country. But whether we want him or not, France has Napoleon Bonaparte, just Paris has Pierre de Gruzin, and wishing it were different would be to wish the moon and the stars were different. Destiny cannot be changed."

"What are you thinking?" Anton asked as they rode in the carriage on their way back to their hotel.

"I'm thinking that it is unfortunate that politics has to be this way," Natasha answered. "I just never dreamed that there was so much dishonesty and greed everywhere."

"It is the world I live in, I'm afraid," Anton replied. "It is the world I've always lived in. I was raised for it."

"You never had any choice in the matter?"

"Not really. Not much of a choice, anyway."

Anton turned away from Natasha to look out the carriage window. He would have liked to show her the city at night, but that was out of the question. Plans had to be made, and somehow he had to set up a post so that he could spy upon Rosto Rapp.

Though he had paid Rosto a partial payment in advance for informing him when Ivan arrived in Paris, Anton had no doubt at all that Rosto would betray him, just as he would betray his own cousin, when the time came for that. Rosto would get as much money for himself as he could, then try to distance himself from the carnage and conflict that would ensue.

They arrived back at their inn, and Natasha sensed that something had made Anton unhappy, though she wasn't sure what. Twice she tried to draw him out, to get him to talk of his feelings, but he dismissed her questions, once with a joke and once with a mumbling comment about nothing being wrong at all.

"Do you know what I think?" Natasha said, when they were locked away in their room, undressing for bed.

"What?"

"I think that what you need is some gentle loving," Natasha replied. She stepped out of her dress and tossed it aside, then crossed the room to stand before Anton, wearing only her chemise and pantalets. She slipped her arms around his neck, pressing her breasts against his chest. "Some gentle loving like only I can give you."

Anton eased his hands around her waist, loving the feel of her against him. "I think you're right. I've got so many things on my mind, so many things to think about . . . tonight. For a little while, all I want is to think about you, make love with you, and show you how much I love you."

For an instant, Natasha pulled a bit away from Anton. Had she really heard him correctly?

Then Anton realized what he'd said, and a smile graced his features, and a happy light sparkled in his gray eyes—a light that had not been there in some time.

"I love you." Anton said the three words as though tasting them. Then his smile became even broader. "I *do* love you. I don't know if I ever really, completely realized it until this moment, but I love you, my precious darling, with all my heart!"

"I love you, too," Natasha replied.

It was not quite the declaration of love that she had hoped for. Anton had almost fallen into it, saying the words first and then only later realizing that the words were the truth. But at least the declaration had been made, and all she had to do was look into his eyes to know that he was telling the truth, and that his love for her was genuine and unforced, as indeed she had known for some time.

Anton looked at her, battling with himself against old prejudices, against ways of behaving and thinking that he now found repellant. She was a commoner, yet she was the least common woman he'd ever known.

Prior to meeting her, he'd never really thought of the woman he'd marry. He knew that it was necessary for him to produce an heir, a masculine child to carry on the Talakovich name. But the woman who did that had always been a faceless entity in his mind, just a dynastic cog in the gears of Anton's plans.

Then Natasha entered his life, with her spirit and her wisdom, her love for the people, and by loving her, Anton was able to see the error of his ways in thinking that only a woman from the aristocracy was fit to bring his child into this world.

"I want you to be my wife," Anton said. He pushed Natasha just far enough away from him so that he could get down on bended knee. "Will you honor me with your hand in marriage? Say you will marry me and I will be the happiest man in the world."

Natasha blushed. Anton was being swept away

by the moment, she told herself. Maybe he didn't really know exactly what he was saying. She felt a little silly standing in a sheer chemise and pantalets while Anton was still fully dressed.

"Say you will marry me," Anton said, more than just a hint of a command in his voice now.

Natasha felt tears pool in her eyes. It shocked her that Anton was clearly fearful that she might not agree to become his bride. That was why he had become almost stern, she realized.

"What woman wouldn't rejoice in marrying you?" she asked.

"I don't want to know what other women would do; I'm only concerned with what *you're* going to do, now and for the rest of your life." Still on one knee, he squeezed Natasha's hand tightly in his own, looking up at her anxiously, a man entirely unaccustomed to having to ask for anything twice, much less getting down on one knee to pose the question.

"Yes, my prince, I will marry you."

Even before Anton could leap to his feet to take her into his arms, the door to their hotel room splintered into dozens of pieces, and nearly a dozen heavily armed soldiers rushed in, throwing Anton face down on the floor, and knocking Natasha aside.

"He's being brought to the post," the leader of the soldiers told Natasha in response to her shocked demands to know what was happening, as Anton was hauled bodily away, kicking and fighting for all he was worth. "You can see him in the morning."

"I want to go with him now!"

The soldier placed his hand upon Natasha's breast, pushing her back against the wall. He looked into her eyes, a faintly cruel, lascivious smile twitching at the corners of his mouth. His fingers pressed deeply into her breast, touching her through her chemise.

"You can't be with him, but you can be with me if you cause any trouble."

There was no doubting that what the soldier said was true. If she caused any trouble, she, too, would be taken away by the soldiers.

Natasha felt as if her entire life had been ripped from her heart when she met Anton's eyes one last time as he silently communicated his love for her before being dragged away. Only moments earlier she had proposed that she and Anton make love, and then he proposed that they become husband and wife . . . and now she was alone, and what was happening to the man she loved was quite likely a living nightmare that turned the blood to ice in her veins.

Twenty-nine

Ivan slung the cloth sack over his shoulder and smiled. Paris. He was finally in Paris. After all his journeys, he had at last reached his destination, and for a man who had completed very few of his long-range plans throughout his life, he felt as though he had accomplished something truly spectacular, even heroic, in scope.

He still possessed the documents he'd stolen so long ago, though most of the coin that had come with the theft had been spent during his flight from St. Petersburg. He still had some money left, but not much. He had enough to see him through until he could meet with his cousin, Rosto Rapp, and they could split the bounty received from the stolen documents.

Ivan had been thinking about Rosto quite a bit, more and more the nearer he got to Paris. If there was anything that he had learned about himself during his trek from Russia, it was that once a man has killed, killing a second time is easier, and by the time he kills for the fifth or sixth time, he doesn't even hesitate at taking a life.

On four occasions he had been challenged by men as he traveled to Paris. The first time, Ivan had backed away from the fight. He then cursed himself for days for not having shown the courage to kill the man. When he passed through Germany, Ivan killed a man who had shown an uninvited interest in what valuables Ivan might have with him.

After that, Ivan felt much better about himself. Eventually, he killed two more men who looked at him in either a curious or a threatening manner, or appeared as though they were sizing him up for a robbery.

And lastly, only days earlier as he first entered France, he killed a prostitute with his knife, taking her life while her back was turned to him as she counted the money he'd given her in return for sexual favors.

He killed her simply because he'd never killed a woman before, and the simple truth of it was, he wanted to know what it would feel like.

He had liked the way he felt afterward. Women had been a constant source of frustration to him his entire life, but that would change soon. Once he had sold the documents, he'd set himself up somewhere nice, and then he'd buy two or maybe even three women to tend to his every need. And if they talked back to him at all, or gave him those cross looks like Aggie always had, he'd take a leather belt to their backsides. One way or another, they'd learn to pay him the respect he deserved.

But that was all for later. His first task was to find his cousin, and then together they could decide what the next step would be.

As Ivan headed deeper into Paris, he conjured up images of what Rosto must look like now. The only thing he was certain of was that he wouldn't hesitate to kill his cousin if he tried to take a larger cut of the profits than was his due.

A slow, creeping smile spread across Ivan's face as he walked on, his clothes in tatters, the cloth sack slung over his shoulder carrying documents that could drive two powerful nations to war.

There really wasn't any reason at all that Rosto deserved any of the profits, Ivan told himself. All Rosto needed to do was make an introduction or two, and then Ivan would take it from there. Hadn't he proven his own resourcefulness by travelling completely across Europe? And if Rosto didn't like being cut out of the profits, he could get his throat slit just as easily as the prostitute had a week earlier.

Ivan Pronushka felt as if all his plans, all his glorious dreams of happiness, were at last within his reach.

"He can see you now," the sergeant said.

Natasha rose from her chair, promising herself that she would keep her temper in check. She stepped into the office, and all she had to do was take one look into Pierre de Gruzin's eyes, and she knew he was responsible for Anton's arrest the previous evening.

"How lovely to see you again, Natasha," Pierre said after the young sergeant had left the office, closing the door behind him. Pierre moved quickly around his desk and ushered Natasha to a small sofa situated along one wall. "Please, be seated, and we will discuss this terrible mistake."

"Yes, mistake is the right word for it," Natasha said, then bit her lip, remembering what she had just promised herself.

She sat, and Pierre sat beside her, close enough so that their knees touched. He put his left arm around her, but rested it against the back of the sofa so that he didn't actually touch her.

"All I want to do is get Anton free," she added, a bit more softly.

"Yes, yes, that's what everyone wants," Pierre replied. He was looking at Natasha's face, admiring the line of her nose, the beauty mark near the corner of her mouth, the long curl of her lashes. "If we work together, I'm certain everyone can get what they want."

Natasha stiffened at the comment. Did that mean what she suspected it did? She didn't entirely trust her grasp of the French language, so there was the possibility that Pierre's words were completely harmless . . . but there was no language barrier separating them when his arm dropped from the back of the sofa to her shoulder.

"You've got to set him free immediately," Natasha continued, her heart fluttering wildly in her chest. She was staring straight ahead, not wanting to look at Pierre, hating the fact that she could feel his hand upon her shoulder. "I know Anton. He'll die in prison. He has to be free. You'll kill his spirit unless you get him out immediately."

"*I* will kill his spirit? My dear, you misjudge me. I did not arrest Anton, nor do I have the authority to simply free him from our prison. There are rules that must be heeded."

He inched closer to Natasha, so that they were now touching from hip to knee. His arm around her shoulder tightened just enough so that the tips of his fingers now hovered very close to her breast.

"I will not be falsely modest by telling you that I have no power at all in Paris," Pierre continued. "I have, after all, reached a position of some stature, and there are those men — men such as our emperor, Napoleon Bonaparte — who understand the value in having Pierre de Gruzin as a personal friend. But I am not the emperor, and I cannot simply create laws by decree, nor can I free a man imprisoned simply because I believe him to be innocent. His innocence must be proved, don't you see?"

"Yes, I see very clearly," Natasha replied softly.

How far would she go to get Anton out of prison?

Pierre wanted to make love to her, Natasha knew. As soon as this thought entered her head, she realized that it was wrong, completely wrong. What Pierre de Gruzin wanted to do to her had nothing to do with love. In fact, it was just the opposite of love. He wanted her body, and he wanted his own lusts fulfilled.

"I am a very influential man, Natasha," Pierre said in a softer tone, admiring the curve of her ear. He used his right hand to smooth a curl of auburn hair behind her ear, and though she flinched at the touch, she did not try to escape. Pierre smiled, his confidence mounting that he had her within his power, and that everything would turn out exactly as he had planned. "And you are a very attractive woman. But my work . . . my work keeps me very busy . . . too busy, I'm afraid, to allow for much socializing . . . the kind of socializing that a Frenchman, strong and virile as myself, needs. You can understand that, can't you?"

He waited for Natasha to speak. When she did not, he felt heat begin in his stomach, the slow burn of anger. It was always so much better, so much more fulfilling, when the women showed him sympathy, when they told him how they understood that he was very busy, and that was why he was not married, with three or four mistresses on the side.

Pierre was not a rapist—at least he did not see himself as one. Rather, he was a man who knew how to make the most of a situation, and how to position himself so that he could profit most by his foresight.

"You can understand that I'm a handsome man, who really is shackled by the responsibilities that the good people of Paris have thrust upon me. You can see that, can't you?"

"Yes, I can see that," Natasha murmured, still staring ahead of her at the floor.

What did he want her to say? Natasha tried to

think as Pierre would think, but she had no possible frame of reference to have any comprehension of how his mind worked. He wanted to have sex with her. Natasha realized this. He had power over her. Natasha accepted this, even if it appalled her. But what did he want with this babble of his?

"That's very, very good," Pierre said, turning just a little more toward Natasha, his leg still against hers. He placed his right hand on her knee, and the tips of his left hand brushed lightly, briefly, over Natasha's breast. "I knew that you would see things my way. I knew that you were an intelligent woman from the very beginning."

Memories of the sweet pleasure that she had known when Anton touched her breast came to mind, but Natasha knew she mustn't dwell on the thought. Surely, Pierre would know if she was thinking of another man, and he would be furiously offended by it. Natasha tried to understand what pleasure Pierre could possibly feel in knowing that his touch was a defiling one and that the women he coerced into his bed had not come willingly. She could never be in the least bit satisfied by the touch of any man who she did not love, so how could Pierre possibly find any pleasure in it?

Natasha decided there were a thousand things about men that she did not understand, and never would.

Pierre was continuing to talk, explaining to Natasha how he did not need to use his power as prefect of police to lure women to his bed. They would go willingly, he assured Natasha, if only he wasn't so busy all the time. Then his hand closed over Natasha's breast, and she was jolted out of her thoughts by the ugly harshness of Pierre's touch.

"I understand everything you're saying," Natasha replied, speaking slowly and as clearly as she could in the foreign tongue. "And I also understand that a man as virile as you has needs, strong needs that must be satisfied if you are to be happy."

For an instant she closed her eyes, summoning all the courage she possessed, struggling mightily to ignore the feel of his fingers encircling her breast. She knew that she would do anything to see to it that Anton was freed from prison and once again safe in her own arms, even if what had to be done would turn Anton against her.

She opened her eyes, took a deep breath, and said, "But there is something that *you* must understand as well."

Pierre asked, "And what is that?" though he hardly paid any attention at all to what Natasha was saying. He was looking at her face in profile, thinking that she was easily the most beautiful woman he had ever enticed into his bed, and that her breast, so large and firm as it filled his hand, would taste sweeter than anything he'd ever known.

"It is that I am willing to satisfy you as no woman has ever satisfied you."

She turned on the sofa to look straight into Pierre's eyes, and when she did, she managed to get his hand from her breast. The sight of him appalled her, but Natasha knew that she had to do whatever was necessary if she was going to free Anton.

"But not here," she said with quiet, intractable resolve. "At your house. I'll satisfy you in ways you've never even thought possible."

"Splendid, my dear."

"But you've got to have Anton there. I'll please you . . . but not until I'm certain that he's free, safe, unharmed."

She stood abruptly, pulling out of Pierre's embrace, not really certain that she was doing the right thing, but too far into her hastily concocted plan to back out of it now.

"Shall we say nine o'clock? A nice meal and a

good wine would be appreciated before we . . . consummate our agreement."

Pierre told Natasha where he lived, then smiled. He hadn't expected her to be so bold, but it was her boldness that heightened his appreciation of her charms. When he had her gown in tatters, her hair in his hands, and her body trembling and vulnerable beneath him, then she wouldn't be so quick with the tongue, then she wouldn't tell him what she would and would not do.

"Nine o'clock it is," he said.

"If Anton's not there, I'll be very disappointed," Natasha said quietly, hating the words coming from her lips. "You'll be disappointed, too, because without Anton's freedom, you'll never know the pleasure that I can give you."

Then she walked out of the office, feeling as though she'd just been cursing like a sailor, and needed to wash her mouth out.

Would she really sleep with Pierre to free Anton? And if she did, and Anton found out about it, what would Anton think of her? Would he still love her, and want to be her husband if he knew what she'd done?

She stepped out into the street, feeling disoriented. Corruption was everywhere, she now realized. She'd always assumed that it was just a Russian malady, but now there could be no denying that the French who held power had just as much of a problem with honesty as her own country's power wielders.

What was her next move? She had hours before her meeting with Pierre de Gruzin at his home. That was exactly how much time she had to think of a way of setting free Anton so that she wouldn't have to sleep with Pierre.

Rosto Rapp?

Natasha loathed Rosto, but he understood how the French government worked, and he might be able to help. Natasha had already teased and flirted with one man to achieve her ends; perhaps she could do the same one more time, no matter how personally loathsome she found the act.

She hurried down the boulevard, her destination now determined, her stride long and quick. Rosto was a hideous scoundrel, and that just might be exactly the kind of man she needed if she was to again see the man she loved.

It was surprisingly easy to find Rosto. Natasha went to the west bank, and it took only four inquiries before she found his apartment. He was basking in the sun on his balcony, his eyes closed. Natasha was surprised to see that he had a servant to tend to his needs, as well as a cook. He was, she realized, a man with a considerable need for comfort.

"Madame Natasha, it is so good to see you again," Rosto replied, taking her hand and kissing it formally. "Please, do have a seat and enjoy this sunshine. Then tell me everything, absolutely everything! I can see in your eyes that your heart is troubled, and a woman as lovely as you should never have a troubled heart."

"It is Mademoiselle, not Madame," Natasha said as she took her chair, angling it so that, like Rosto's, it faced the sun directly. "Anton and I aren't yet married."

Rosto smiled, liking the turn of the conversation already. "And why do you tell me this?" he asked, looking at Natasha out of the corner of his eyes.

"Because last night Anton was arrested. Pierre de Gruzin had him arrested so that he'd have power over me. He wants me in his bed." Natasha spoke the words calmly, as though this was nothing different

405

than a business negotiation that had taken a nasty turn.

"And I take it that you're not particularly interested in joining him there."

"You are a perceptive man, Rosto. That's why I'm here. I'm in need of an intelligent, perceptive man. I want to get Anton out of prison, and I believe you're just the man to do it."

Rosto was openly smiling now. "Pierre's up to his old tricks. He's done this before. Many times before, in fact. I suppose I should have warned him that Anton was on a very important mission . . . but then, I suppose, Pierre would only use that information against your friend, wouldn't he?"

"I suppose. What is it going to cost me to get your help?"

Natasha's heart was slowly and steadily accelerating. She was getting better at this strange life, she realized. She was learning the rules and how to get what she wanted. She just wasn't entirely certain it was a skill to be proud of.

Rosto again glanced at Natasha, looking at her through eyes just barely open. She was beautiful, but he was a man much more interested in acquiring wealth instead of women.

"That is something I'll have to think about," he said slowly, wondering how much leverage he had over Natasha. The truth of it was that if Anton was already locked away, then there really wasn't anything he or anyone else could do to get him free. Only Pierre de Gruzin possessed that kind of authority, and he wouldn't use his personal power until he'd gotten what he wanted, which was Natasha. "I've always found that thinking and eating go well together. Perhaps you might be interested in dining with me?"

Natasha only then realized that she was famished. She hadn't eaten a morsel since long before Anton's abduction and arrest, and at the mention of food her stomach tightened into an empty knot.

"I would enjoy that very much," she replied.

It was Natasha's guess that Rosto wanted to show her off, to be seen in public with her like she was some kind of trophy. She didn't care, as long as it would enable her to free Anton. If Rosto wanted to publicly humiliate her, she'd accept that, too. Her own pride, her own safety, were secondary concerns to her now.

Rosto took her to a small tavern which he claimed served the finest food in all of Paris, and at a price that was surprisingly modest. The greatest surprise to Natasha was that the place existed at all, considering the number of people she could see nearby who appeared to have no food or money at all.

Rosto and Natasha were escorted to a table near the front windows, where everyone passing outside could see them. The little old man who escorted them to the table spoke in French that was much too quick for Natasha to understand completely. What was clear to her was that Rosto was a frequent patron of the establishment.

The wine arrived quickly, and though Natasha tried to keep Rosto on the topic of Anton, and what could be done to free him, Rosto's attention was continually being taken up by the people who came to the table.

Before an hour went by, Natasha figured out that Rosto was a man who did all his business in the tavern and eating establishments in Paris's west bank. People came to him with information to sell, which Rosto would then sell to someone close to the political circles for more money than he'd bought the information for. Other men came to Rosto needing a favor for this or that, and in return for the favor, they would owe Rosto, and promised to do anything he requested at a later date, if only he would help them out of this or that little problem.

"Rosto, what can you do to help *me?*" Natasha asked, the annoyance she felt showing clearly in her tone. She was willing to be a prop to bolster Rosto's ego and be seen with him, if that's what he wanted, but only so long as what she was doing was working toward Anton's freedom.

"Actually, there are a number of things that I can do," Rosto replied, his tone just a little haughty.

He had received even more people than he'd expected, and everyone who had come to him had looked at Natasha with envy. His prestige in the community of thieves and spies had gone up considerably on this afternoon, and he sensed that it would only be a matter of time before he would be sitting at Napoleon's right elbow, whispering cogent advice into the emperor's ear.

"Such as?" Natasha prompted.

"You're being impatient," Rosto replied. The day had been going splendidly, and he did not want Natasha destroying the illusion he'd created. It wouldn't do his reputation any good at all if she should create a scene, openly being disrespectful to him in public.

It was at that moment, just when Rosto was about to tell Natasha a new lie about how he could bribe a minor official to get Anton out of prison, but he'd need money from her, that he noticed a man standing hardly three feet away, just on the other side of the window.

"Isn't this simply too perfect," Rosto said, his beaming grin spreading from ear to ear.

Natasha followed the direction of Rosto's gaze, and when she did, she nearly fainted. Standing so close that she could have touched him if the glass hadn't been there was her uncle, Ivan Pronushka.

For a moment Natasha and Ivan simply looked into each other's eyes, neither quite believing what they saw. Then Ivan turned on his heel and walked away at a quick pace that would put distance between himself and Natasha without drawing undue attention.

"That's him! Rosto, that's him! We've got to stop him!" Natasha shouted, rising from her chair, nearly stumbling in her haste.

Rosto had his own reason for wanting to speak with Ivan, and it wasn't so that Anton could be freed, or that embarrassing letters could be destroyed. With Anton in prison, it was clear that it would be intelligent to befriend his cousin, who possessed embarrassing letters that would be worth a fortune once they were sold to the right person in Paris.

As Natasha rushed out of the tavern, Rosto followed hot at her heels, reaching forward to grab her by the shoulder.

"Wait! Don't draw attention to yourself," Rosto hissed angrily, suddenly wishing that his servant hadn't allowed Natasha into his apartment at all that day. "There are soldiers everywhere."

Natasha pulled out of Rosto's grasp, frantic to catch her uncle. She had travelled too far and for too long to allow the opportunity to catch him slip through her fingers.

Rosto noticed Ivan again looking back over his shoulder as he pushed his way through the people in the street. Ivan had aged badly, Rosto could tell. His face was lined deeply from the ravages of intemperance, and despite the distance that separated them Rosto could see the hatred burn in Ivan's eyes.

"Wait! I need to speak with you!" Rosto shouted, wanting to stop his cousin without actually having to break into an undignified, attention-getting run to do so.

Rosto grabbed Natasha by the wrist, and when she started to pull away from him, he whispered, "Don't fight me now. I'm only trying to help you. Isn't that what you want?"

Natasha didn't trust Rosto. He'd already proven himself to be a corrupt, immoral hedonist, but she had no choice except to follow his instructions. She had travelled across Europe in hopes of stopping her uncle from selling stolen documents—documents that never would have been stolen if she hadn't told her uncle about a mysterious carriage that would be arriving at Castle Talakovich on that ill-fated day a lifetime ago.

Ivan continued walking, but his pace had slowed somewhat, and Rosto could tell that he was deliberating what he should do next. Several soldiers were watching intently, Rosto could tell, but he was not sure whether it was because he had just raised his voice, or because Natasha was with him, and men always watched her.

"You'd better speak in Russian, if you can," Natasha said, hurrying now to keep up with Rosto, deciding that she had to trust him. "He speaks French worse than I do."

Rosto had learned Russian at the same time he learned French. In the language of his father, he called out, "Ivan, my cousin, haven't you journeyed far enough already? Slow down, and let us speak as family."

A curse was trapped in Rosto's throat while he watched as several uniformed soldiers, bayonets fixed to their rifles, began moving closer, curious as to why one man would be calling out in a foreign language to another man who didn't seem willing to slow his pace.

My cousin is an idiot, Rosto thought angrily, wondering what lie he could tell the soldiers so that they wouldn't bring him to their headquarters for further questioning.

And then suddenly Ivan turned toward Rosto and Natasha. He smiled and raised his hand in greeting, though he did not say anything. He gave the appearance of a man who had not realized he had been followed, and Rosto gave a sigh of relief. The soldiers continued to watch carefully, but they were no longer moving closer.

"He's a murderer," Natasha whispered.

She wished she had a knife with her, though she couldn't really picture herself using the weapon against her own uncle, no matter how well-deserved it would be. But she wanted something so that she could defend herself against him, if it came down to that.

"He's many things, and none of them good," Rosto replied under his breath so that Ivan couldn't hear as he approached. "Now just keep quiet and leave everything to me. All your troubles are about to end."

Natasha's hands felt clammy. She tried to dry them against the skirt of her dress, but they still felt wet with perspiration.

Ivan . . . after so long . . . and yet the sight of him was even more repellant to her senses, more of a violation to her perceptions of truth and goodness, than ever.

"You've come so far to see me," Rosto said in Russian when only a few feet separated him from Ivan. "It seems a shame that you would run from me now." He looked over at Natasha, whose wrist he still held tightly in his hand, then back to Ivan. "You needn't worry about her. Her lover's been arrested. He'll probably be dead by morning. And I've already been told that you are in possession of some personal letters that will be most valuable, should they make their way into the right hands."

Ivan grinned then, nodding. "I thought I'd left her and that damned prince long behind me." He looked at Natasha, and the lust and sense of triumph he felt over her was like a slap on the cheek. "This wench has caused me much trouble, my cousin. Why is she

411

with you?"

"She was hoping I would help her, but I'm willing to believe that she's more valuable to you than she is to me."

"How right you are." Ivan opened his waistcoat just enough to show the dagger tucked inside the waistband of his breeches. There was a spot of dried blood on the wooden handle. "I've got something here for her, and I'm willing to pay you, dear cousin, for the privilege."

It never really occurred to Rosto that Natasha might not just meekly go along with whatever he and Ivan had planned for her. When she rounded on him, her fingers hooked into claws to rake across his eyes, then shouted for help, he released his hold on her wrist, spinning away from her to put his hands over his injured eyes.

"Help! Help!" Natasha screamed.

Ivan went immediately to his knife, pulling it from his waistband, jabbing at Natasha. She leaped out of the way of the blade, but stumbled on the cobblestone street and fell hard to her knees. Before she could get back to her feet, a soldier stepped between her and Ivan.

The soldier had believed that his uniform would protect him, since everyone in Paris knew that to injure one of Napoleon's soldiers was a death sentence that no one would escape from. But the soldier erred in his assumption that his uniform would earn him fear and respect from Ivan Pronushka. Ivan stepped past the soldier's long rifle and thrust his dagger into the young man's stomach.

Ivan ripped the rifle from the soldier's hand, turning at the same time. He had intended to use the bayonet on Natasha, but the onrushing soldiers presented a much more pressing problem. He aimed at the nearest soldier and pulled the trigger, and though he wasn't a good shot, he struck the soldier solidly enough to knock him off his feet.

In the confusion that followed, Ivan escaped, with Rosto following closely behind him. Rosto was furious at the sudden turn of events, murderously angry at Ivan for his willingness to kill French soldiers, and at Natasha for causing the bloody melee in the first place.

Rosto didn't know yet how he was going to do it, but somehow he was going to get the damning letters from his cousin, and once he did that, then he was going to somehow make sure that Ivan—and Ivan alone—took blame for the murders of the soldiers. Rosto was certain that Pierre de Gruzin had been waiting for just something like this to happen so that he would have an excuse to have him arrested. Once arrested, Rosto knew that he'd never live through the night.

Thirty

Natasha played the role of the injured, innocent woman magnificently, and the soldiers believed every word of it. She told them of how she was new to Paris, and how she had been befriended by the men, and how they had suddenly turned into monsters, assaulting her, and trying to do much worse.

The soldiers, with one of their ranks already dead, and another badly injured, with a gunshot wound to the shoulder, saw absolutely no reason to disbelieve Natasha's words.

When she told them that what she really needed was just a few moments of privacy to regain her composure before she went with them to their post to talk to their commanding officer about the incident, they didn't have a suspicion in the world . . . until she disappeared into the crowd that had gathered.

Natasha walked the streets of Paris, her mind spinning as she pondered what her next move would be. An almost overpowering sense of rage washed over her when she thought about how close she had been to at last catching and stopping her uncle, and how Rosto had turned against her when he had been telling her all along that he was on her side. She had been foolhardy to put even scant trust in the scoundrel.

No matter how she looked at it, she could see no alternative: she had to go to Pierre de Gruzin and throw herself at his mercy.

He would violate her. She was certain of that. But at least when it was over and he'd had his fill of her, then she would have freed Anton.

Anton might not love her after that. Natasha realized this, and accepted it as a price she might have to pay if she was to save the life of the man she loved. If he would later hate her for what she had done, she would accept that, at least knowing in her own heart that she had done all she could, sacrificed all she could, to save the life of the man who meant more to her than life itself.

Her decision made, a strange calm descended over her. She would go to Pierre immediately, and do whatever he asked of her — but not until she had proof that Anton had been freed, and would remain that way.

"You are a madman, my cousin," Rosto said, shaking his head slowly in disgust. "There was no need to kill those soldiers. Killing the woman — if that was necessary, then you could have done it later. Killing those soldiers without even trying to talk your way out of it first . . . it was murderous, savage!"

"What's done is done," Ivan replied quietly, cradling the wineskin in his large hands like it was a precious child. "My knife does all the talking I need to do."

They were sitting in a small stable not far from where the killing had occurred. The owner of the stables owed Rosto a favor, and it was being collected on now, because when the soldiers showed up asking questions, the stable owner said that he hadn't seen two men rushing by.

"Tell your knife to stay silent," Rosto said to his cousin. "When it talks, trouble follows."

Ivan was undeterred. The cloth sack, which held the stolen documents and what was left of his money, lay on the floor between his boots. He hadn't removed the knife from the soldier's corpse, so he no longer had that, but he wasn't terribly concerned about being without a weapon. He had his cousin with him now, and that's all he really needed if his dreams were to be realized.

"Let me see these letters," Rosto said. "I want to see what has caused all this trouble."

Ivan didn't trust his cousin, but he had no choice other than to hand over the documents. He needed to find out just exactly how valuable they truly were. He watched, silent, as Rosto began looking over the papers. As he read, his mouth at first dropped open in shock, then pulled into a wide grin.

"That lousy liar," Rosto said quietly. "I was told that what you had were personal letters concerning a sexual matter. These have nothing to do with that at all."

"Then they are valuable?"

"In the right hands, very valuable," Rosto said, still reading over the columns of figures, and the names attached to them.

"Who will you sell them to?"

Rosto shrugged his shoulders, continuing to read, speaking absently. "First thing, I'll talk with the prefect of police for Paris, a man named Pierre de Gruzin. He's a beast, but he's a man who understands the value of money, and I can reason with him."

"And he will pay good money for those papers?"

"But of course he will."

Rosto flipped from one page to another, amazed at what he was reading. It shocked him to discover that the Russians didn't trust France, and were preparing for a French invasion. He'd always thought the Russians were a bit dull-witted, and he never dreamed that they were clever enough to see that an invasion was forthcoming, or that they needed to disguise their own military fortification if they were to maintain a temporary peace with Bonaparte's government and military.

Ivan watched Rosto reading, and judging from the

expression on his face, the documents were even more valuable than he had dreamed.

He slowly got to his feet, stretching his muscles, pretending to be stiff from his long journey. Slowly, he walked in a small circle, and from the corner of his eye checked to see if Rosto was paying him any attention. Rosto's complete concentration was consumed by the papers he held in his hands.

"This Pierre de Gruzin . . . he's a man you've done business with before?" Ivan asked, moving behind Rosto.

"Many times. He's got his fingers in everything, and he always turns a profit."

"And I suppose you'll take a percentage of what de Gruzin pays?"

"That's only fair," Rosto replied quietly, his eyes focused on the papers.

Ivan picked up a pitchfork, gripping the handle tightly in his hands. He had proven to himself that he could come up with an idea, then see the idea through to its conclusion without needing help from anyone else. There was no reason he should share the profit to be made by selling the documents, especially not now, when it was clear that they were worth even more than he had first hoped.

"What's fair is fair," Ivan said softly.

He rushed forward, holding the pitchfork tightly in his strong hands, watching as the long, sharp tines met with his cousin's exposed back.

Natasha was tired, but she knew that wouldn't last long. The moment she was alone with Pierre de Gruzin, she would be wide awake and frightened beyond words.

The house was unimpressive, though in a pleasant section of Paris. It looked like exactly what it was—the modest home of a bureaucrat, living well, but not lavishly, on an income determined by the emperor.

Before knocking on the door to announce herself, Natasha patted her hair, thinking that it would be better if she had a brush, and some combs to hold her auburn tresses in place. Then she realized that there was no need for her to make herself appear more attractive—not for a man the likes of Pierre de Gruzin. He wanted her sexually, but there was hate in his heart along with the want, and it was an ugly combination of emotions that disgusted Natasha.

She approached the front door of the small cottage home slowly, and when she was very near, she saw the slight movement of one of the curtains. She had been watched from inside. Before she knocked on the door, it opened, and a woman in her early twenties attempted what Natasha suspected was a smile. It looked more like an expression of sadness and sympathy, though this didn't seem at all in accord with an ally of Pierre de Gruzin.

"You're a bit early, but he's expecting you," the woman said.

Natasha entered the house, and the door was closed and locked behind her. Then, for a second or two, Natasha and the servant simply looked into each other's eyes, neither one quite knowing what the next move should be.

"I'm supposed to take your wrap, but you haven't got one. I'm terribly sorry, mademoiselle," the woman said softly. This seemed to bother her greatly, and her anxiety confused Natasha.

"It's not your fault I don't have a wrap."

"Lots of things aren't my fault, but that doesn't mean I don't get blamed for them." She looked away, literally biting her lower lip to keep more words from spilling out. "I'm very sorry, mademoiselle. I didn't mean to say that. I'm truly happy here."

"Why are you here? It's obvious enough that the prefect of police scares the soul out of you."

418

Again, the two women exchanged a long, questioning look. Natasha's strength of will was greater, causing the woman to tremble with fear, and tears of frustration to glisten in her eyes.

"He's got my husband locked away," she said softly, her voice trembling with emotion. "A couple hours ago his soldiers just came and took my beloved away. Then de Gruzin says that if I don't do what he says, I'll be a widow by morning." She placed her hand lightly over her stomach. "I have one baby already, and I think another on the way. I can't manage alone. I need my husband, don't you see?"

"I see quite clearly," Natasha replied with a smile. She patted the woman's arm. "What's he asked of you?"

"Make food for you and him, clean his home nice and spotless, and see to it that everything is just right for the two of you."

"Listen to me carefully. What is going to happen to me isn't any of your fault, so don't blame yourself for it," Natasha said. "I, too, have a man I love who is in Pierre's prison, and the only reason why I'm here is because I want him freed."

"You've a big, handsome man, I believe. Wears nice clothes, has light hair, and a little line on his chin, here?" she asked, touching the tip of her chin.

"A cleft chin? Yes, a little," Natasha said, her throat suddenly tight. "Have you seen him? Where is he?"

"I don't know exactly, mademoiselle. I saw the man brought through the back way. His wrists were tied with a rope. Soldiers brought him in, then they left quickly."

The sound of footsteps came from their left, and the woman gasped softly, turning toward Pierre de Gruzin, who stood at the end of the hall, looking regal and menacing in full uniform, his eyes black with anger.

"Good evening," Natasha said, forcing a smile to her lips. "I've just been discussing the menu with your servant," she said, lying in hopes of preventing the young woman from suffering needlessly. "The meal sounds wonderful. I couldn't have selected better myself."

Slowly, Pierre's fierce scowl changed into a soft smile. "I'm glad you approve. Everyone in this sector has heard about the magic Nadine performs with food, and what she can do with sauces. She's really quite magnificent.

"I don't doubt that at all."

Nadine disappeared discreetly.

Looking at Pierre, Natasha could tell that he had gone to considerable lengths to look handsome and commanding, though there was absolutely nothing he could possibly do that would make her think that he was anything but repulsive. She did not, however, allow this emotion to show in her eyes.

"Shall we retire to the dining room?" he asked as he moved closer.

As Natasha started toward the dining room, Pierre moved with her, slipping his arm around her back. She impressed herself by not even flinching, even though she knew she would remember as long as she lived the incredible frustration and helplessness she felt at the moment.

The dining room looked like it also doubled as a sun room, and might also be where Pierre did any work that he took home with him. Natasha could see ink stains in two different places on the table.

Pierre was trying hard to make himself appear wealthier than he was. She knew then, as she looked around the sparsely furnished little room, that in Pierre's mind, this wasn't an evening of extortion for sex, or even rape. To him, this was seduction, and because he thought of it as such, Natasha realized that he was even more dangerous than she'd previously imagined.

"I have given the servants — all but Nadine — the

night off so that we might enjoy our privacy," Pierre said. He went to the far side of the table, where there was a bottle of wine waiting. "I'll serve, if that's acceptable to you?"

"Yes, of course," Natasha replied, but she wasn't fooled at all.

She knew the prefect of police didn't have any full-time servants to dismiss. A man with as many secrets as he possessed, a man who committed as many foul crimes as he apparently did, couldn't risk the possibility that his servants would find out what he was doing. He couldn't take the chance that wagging tongues would put the word out on the streets of Paris of what kind of hideous monster he really was, so he'd live alone, shielded from the contemptuous looks that would surely come his way if anyone knew the full extent of his villainy.

He helped Natasha to her chair and poured her wine, then bent down low to kiss her lightly on the cheek. He touched her chin, trying to turn her face toward him so that he might kiss her mouth, but Natasha resisted, even though she knew this would make Pierre angry.

"Please . . . not until I know that Anton is safe," she said quietly.

Natasha saw the anger burn brightly in Pierre's eyes, flaming instantly to life.

"I could make you get down on your knees right here," he threatened in a soft tone of pure malice.

Natasha smiled at him, and let her lashes dance against her cheeks coyly for a moment.

"Yes, of course you could. But that wouldn't really be much fun for you, or for me. And what's more, it would all be so unnecessary. Why take that route when we've a wonderful meal on the way, and we haven't even touched our wine? Everything you want will be yours . . . in time."

"Yes, of course," Pierre replied after several seconds

of deliberation.

"All I'm asking is that I see him. Nothing more than that."

Pierre was standing very close, looking down at Natasha, and though he was inherently intimidating towering over her like that, she was not at all fearful of him.

I've got you! she thought angrily, feeling Pierre's eyes raking over her body, touching her with their invisible yet defiling caresses that could never possibly elicit any pleasure at all.

She had power over Pierre, whether he realized it or not. He could rape her, and she couldn't stop him; but his sense of self-worth would only be heightened if he could pretend that Natasha really wanted him, and that he had succeeded in seducing her.

Natasha at last was able to understand how Pierre's mind worked, and even though the knowledge horrified her, it also made her feel strong, because she finally realized she was not entirely powerless.

"The longer you stand there just looking at me, the less time we'll have when we're finished with our meal," Natasha said in a sultry purr.

Pierre stepped aside enough to help her out of her chair. He was smiling, and when she hooked her arm around his, it gave all the outward appearance of a man and woman walking into a ballroom to hear a piano recital.

"Now, my dear, you must understand that you are not allowed to speak. And, in fact, you may consider not seeing him at all. We've developed such a romantic atmosphere this evening that I'd hate to see anything spoil it."

This is a vile, insane man, Natasha thought. She said, "I'm not that fickle. My mood doesn't change so quickly."

He escorted her to the upstairs floor, where there were three doors leading to the three bedrooms. In a horrifying instant, Natasha realized that one of the rooms was Pierre's bedroom, where she would likely soon be while Anton was being held in another room.

Would Anton be able to hear the activities that were required if she was to secure his freedom?

"Is something wrong? I knew we shouldn't have come here," Pierre said. He was oblivious to the immorality of his actions.

"It's nothing," Natasha said quickly, shocked that her feelings had shown in her expression. "Really, it's nothing to concern yourself with."

"Very well, then."

He stepped up to the door nearest the stairway, and opened it just an inch. Natasha was allowed only a second or two to look inside, and what she saw took her breath away.

Anton was seated in a coarse chair, his hands bound behind his back, his ankles tied to the legs of the chair. There was a gag tied around his mouth.

In that fleeting moment she was allowed to see him, she noticed that there was redness and puffiness around his right eye, but that he was struggling against his binds. That was a good sign. He'd been beaten, probably struck with fists by the soldiers while they struggled to arrest him the previous night. But other than that, he looked healthy, and as long as he was angry, Natasha knew that he would eventually be fine . . . as long she could secure his freedom.

Pierre closed the door before Anton had the chance to look in their direction.

"Now, let's progress with our evening," Pierre said, speaking as though he and Natasha had at last concluded some troubling business matter, and could now behave in a more romantic manner.

As they returned to the dining table, Pierre chatted away happily, oblivious to Natasha's mental agitation. She kept looking over at Pierre, wondering what she would think of herself after she had performed whatever hideous acts the Parisian demanded of her.

She had no doubt that she could go to bed with him. The only question remaining was whether she could pretend that Pierre's touch didn't offend her as badly as it did, and whether she could keep the look of utter revulsion from showing in her expression as he violated her.

Once she had gained Anton's freedom, and she herself was free from Pierre, then she could concern herself with Anton's emotions, and how he would react to the horrible truth of what she'd been forced to do to gain his freedom.

They returned to the dining room, and this time when Pierre bent low to kiss Natasha, she did not resist, though she kept her lips tightly clamped together for fear that he would attempt to taint her mouth with his tongue.

"Our meal should be ready soon," Pierre said, refilling Natasha's wine glass to the brim. "You arrived early. I'm afraid you've caught me a little unprepared."

There was a soft knock on the dining room door, then Nadine stuck her head inside.

"Is the lamb ready?" Pierre asked. There was a twinkle in his eye and a lightness in his voice. All was as it should be within the confines of his fantasy world.

"Not yet, Monsieur de Gruzin. There's a man here to see you," Nadine said quietly.

"I told you I'm not to be disturbed this evening," Pierre replied sharply. "How many times do you need to be told what is expected of you?"

"This man is different, very different," Nadine answered, the tremulous quality of her voice testimony to how afraid she really was of the police prefect.

"That will be all," Pierre said to Nadine. When she had closed the door, and he was again alone with Natasha, he offered her an indulgent smile. "Remember how I told you my work keeps me continually occupied? I'm afraid you're witness to it now. There's been a disturbance this evening, and one of my men has been killed, and another is likely to die soon. I'm sure that's what this is about."

"The people of Paris are indebted to you," Natasha replied, hiding her hands beneath the table for fear that Pierre would see them tremble.

What if soldiers had come to the house, and one of them recognized her as the woman who'd been at the scene of the murder? The thought sent a shiver through Natasha.

"Quite so. Please excuse me. This won't take long." Pierre rose from his chair, and when he attempted to kiss Natasha before leaving, she offered her cheek, unable to bear the thought of tasting another of his kisses.

The instant Pierre was out of the room, Natasha rushed to the door. She could hear voices risen, one in anger. It took a couple seconds for Natasha to realize what it was that made the intruder so "different" in Nadine's eyes—he didn't speak French. He spoke Russian instead, and he wasn't at all happy that neither Nadine nor Pierre spoke his language.

Natasha rushed back to the table, grabbing the short, sharp knife used for cutting meat. Then she dashed out of the room, moving as swiftly and as quietly as possible because there could be no mistaking Ivan Pronushka's guttural voice.

Though Natasha was able to exit the side door of the dining room, she still had to cross the hallway to reach the stairway leading to the bedroom upstairs. While she was in the hallway, she'd be visible to the men standing at the front doors.

She pressed herself against the wall and cautiously peered around the corner. Uncle Ivan was standing with his hands on his hips, the cloth sack containing his precious documents clutched in his left fist, telling Pierre in Russian that he had travelled completely across Europe to make Pierre a wealthy and famous man. Pierre, meanwhile, was beginning to understand some of what Ivan was saying, though he was more interested in seeing what was inside the sack than in continuing the stilted conversation any further.

Knowing that the moment the two men reached some kind of agreement her time would be up, Natasha steeled her courage and stepped into the hallway, crossing it as silent as a prowling cat until she was up the stairs.

Please, dear God, don't let the door be locked, Natasha prayed as she reached the bedroom where Anton was being held captive.

The handle turned easily in her hand. Why lock the door to a room where the man inside is bound hand and foot?

She rushed to Anton, pulled the gag from his mouth, took his face in her hands, and kissed him hard on the lips.

He wrenched his face free instantly, "Sweet Natasha! Cut me free!"

Natasha dropped to her knees to saw away at the ropes around Anton's ankles. She had left the door open, and from downstairs she heard that the tone of the discussion had changed. And, her senses keenly aroused with the awareness that a mistake now meant certain death, she heard Ivan say her name, and then Pierre asked, "Natasha? What does she have to do with this?"

The language barrier was crumbling quickly, leaving Natasha vulnerable.

"Hurry!" Anton whispered.

Natasha sawed furiously at the coarse rope. She had freed one of Anton's ankles, and was working to free the other. Twice she had accidentally touched him with the blade, and a trickle of blood ran down his foot.

"Where are your boots?" Natasha asked, a strange, disembodied panic now beginning to grip her. There were much more pressing problems to think about than her lover's missing boots.

"The soldiers stole them. Don't worry about that now! Cut the damn ropes!"

She could hear the pounding of boots along the hallway floor below her. Pierre and Ivan would first go to the dining room, then, seeing that she wasn't there, come immediately to Anton's room. And nothing she could do would make the knife cut the rope any quicker.

The heavy boots were pounding on the stairs now, and she was only halfway through the thick hemp.

She'd come so far, gone through so much, sacrificed so much—only to have it all end here. To fail in her quest now seemed an act of unmanageably cruel divine vengeance for an offense—that of disloyalty to the Talakoviches—that she'd been forced by circumstances to commit.

Anton, too, heard the boots on the stairway. Balling his hands into fists, he strained against the ropes with all his might. The muscles in his arms, chest, and shoulders bulged with the effort, the tendons and veins in his neck stuck out. His face turned crimson with the struggle.

And the ropes came free!

Thirty-one

With Ivan and Pierre just seconds from entering the room, with Natasha's life in dire jeopardy, Anton's will to live was stronger than any rope.

Anton pulled the knife from Natasha's hands and pushed her behind him, shielding her body from the onrushing attackers with his own in case they were armed with pistols. When Ivan and Pierre entered the bedroom, each with a dagger in hand, Anton knew he was in trouble, but at least he had a fighting chance of success.

He lunged forward, stabbing straight ahead with the short knife Natasha had taken from the dining table. The move, though hardly threatening, caused both Ivan and Pierre to leap backward and reconsider how badly they wanted to attack the prince from St. Petersburg.

"I knew you'd make it here eventually," Anton said in Russian to Ivan. "Your kind are like rats. You seem to survive everything . . . until now."

Anton circled slowly to his right, motioning with his left hand for Natasha to stay behind him. He was stalling for time, needing to postpone the actual fight for at least a minute. The tight ropes around his wrists and ankles had cut off his circulation, and though he had the appearance of a knife fighter ready and willing to bring blade to flesh, the truth was that he could hardly feel his fingers curl around the handle of the knife. His toes were tingling as blood was only now flowing to them. If it was necessary for him to be nimble-footed to either attack Ivan and Pierre, or leap from their attack, he was certain he'd fall to the floor.

"You've caused me nothing but trouble, you stinking dog," Ivan shot back, fury now welling up in him at the sight of the prince whose life seemed to have been charmed.

Natasha could not hold her tongue, even though she knew that what Anton wanted her to do was just stay quiet, and remain behind him.

"All the bad things that have happened to you have been your own fault!" she shouted, looking over Anton's shoulder at her uncle. "You've blamed Anton and his family for all your misfortunes, but the truth is that you're just a lazy drunkard, and that's why you've never had anything! You've never worked a day in your life! You blamed me and you've blamed Anton, and you even tried to blame Aislyn, but we've given you everything and still you haven't been happy!"

"I ought to whip you," Ivan shot back.

Anton appreciated the talk because it accomplished two very valuable things. The first was that he now was in full control of his hands and feet, the blood pumping strong and true through his veins. The second was that the conversation, in Russian, was confusing Pierre de Gruzin. In Russia, a person could not be considered truly educated who did not speak French; however, the reverse was not true for the French, where the educated elite considered their own language so superior to all others that learning a language such as Russian was a guttural task not worth undertaking.

"Those days are over," Anton said softly, balancing nimbly on the balls of his feet, waiting for the attack, his eyes dancing left and right to measure each move his two enemies made.

A trickle of sweat rolled from Pierre's hairline down

his cheek. This was not the kind of fighting that he was accustomed to. He had been a leader of men for years, and if ever there was the need for violence, he simply assigned the task to several of his men. It had been years since he'd actually jeopardized himself with a direct fight with a competent opponent . . . but he wasn't at all afraid to find out how much was left of the once-ferocious fighter that he had been in his youth. In Anton, he saw a powerful young man in the prime of his physical and mental capabilities. To have such a man's woman at his mercy after killing such a man would be justice in its purest, most primitive form.

Ivan moved so that he was no longer directly beside Pierre, positioning himself so that it would be more difficult for Anton to keep an eye on both his opponents simultaneously, and impossible for him to keep Natasha completely shielded from them with his body.

"Tell me, nobleman, whether you think your soul will go back to Russia when your blood is spilled in Paris?" Ivan laughed, enjoying the odds of the fight, and the way Natasha trembled as she stood behind Anton.

"I'll tell you this," Anton said, then made his move.

He faked a lunge toward Ivan, then shifted his weight and cut through the air with his knife, trying to stab Pierre, who had only begun to move in. But Anton's knife was made for dining, not for fighting, and it wasn't particularly sharp. When he hit the thick, heavily laced cuff of Pierre's uniform jacket, he cut through the cloth, but did not even draw a single drop of blood.

Pierre leaped back. A chill went through him — one that warned he'd escaped a serious injury by the smallest of measures — and he welcomed the sensation. It had been many years since he'd felt this alive, this much in touch with his true, barbaric nature.

He started to laugh softly, and even though he did not speak the same language as Ivan, he understood what was expected of him, and he moved to the side, positioning himself to prevent either Anton or Natasha from making a break for the only door that represented an escape.

Out of the side of his mouth, under his breath so that only Natasha could hear him, Anton whispered, "Get ready. You'll only have one chance."

Natasha did not want to leave Anton, but she could see what Pierre and Ivan were doing just as well as Anton could. As long as she stayed with Anton, she would be a hindrance to him, and if there was to be any chance of success, any real chance of escape for the two of them, then she had to be the first to leave, which would allow Anton to fight unhindered by her presence.

When Anton made his second lunge, imitating his first attack by beginning his move toward Ivan, then changing direction to actually go after Pierre, Natasha knew what was expected of her. As Pierre and Ivan leaped away from Anton's knife, she bolted between them, heading straight for the door.

"Run!" Anton shouted, leaping into the fray, stabbing at Ivan's face to force him backward.

The moment that Natasha was out of the bedroom, Anton spun, blocking the doorway to give her as much time as possible to escape. He couldn't hold his position more than a couple seconds before Pierre and Ivan coordinated their attack in such a way that made continuing to block the doorway an act of suicide.

Ivan's moves were slow, brutish, and Anton had no difficulty in either anticipating them, or avoiding them. Pierre de Gruzin had not spent years in dissolute squalor, and his reflexes were not dulled. In his eyes burned a blood lust that Anton had seen only a few times before, and always in desperately evil people.

When Ivan stabbed at Anton, he forced him backward, and Pierre acted immediately, cutting sideways with his dagger. Anton felt the bite of the knife as it cut through flesh and muscle high on his left shoulder. Pierre had tried for a lethal cut to the throat, and though he failed, he had succeeded in leaving a short, deep gash in Anton's shoulder.

Blood ran from the wound, but Anton dared not give the injury any of his attention, or surely he'd feel the blade again, and the next time it would prove fatal.

Ivan rushed from the room, scrambling madly after Natasha, who had at least a fifteen second lead on him.

"Run, Natasha! Run!" Anton shouted, furious with himself for not having been able to protect her better than he had.

When he looked at Pierre, there was something maniacal in the Frenchman's eyes that had not been there earlier. It was the gleam of a man no longer young, believing that he was still all the powerful, deadly things that he had been in his youth.

Anton backed away, sizing up Pierre, trying to see into his soul to gauge what he would do next.

The two men circled each other slowly. With each step he took, Anton could feel the pounding in his ribs from the fists of the soldiers who had arrested him, and he remembered how casually Pierre had ordered his minions to beat him.

Lunge and parry, attack and retreat, Pierre and Anton tested each other out, attempting to get an accurate assessment of the other's strengths, weaknesses, and reflexes.

Anton felt the flow of blood from his shoulder soaking into his shirt. It was a painful wound, but he knew that in and of itself, it was not a fatal one. Not unless he lost so much blood that it weakened him, or slowed him down, at which point Pierre would surely be able to capitalize upon the weakness.

"I do not know what this is all about," Pierre said, a faint smile curling the corners of his mouth, "but I assure you, when you are dead and Natasha is once again under my control, she will tell me everything." He laughed then, a hollow, breathy cackle of triumph. "There's never been a person in my dungeon who has not broken down and told me everything I wanted to know. Mademoiselle Natasha will tell me everything . . . and I will take the greatest pleasure in extracting each morsel of truth, and every cry of agony, from her."

Anton's teeth clenched in rage, and he almost went on the attack again. He would have stabbed at Pierre had not the inner voice in his mind, the one that he always listened to and had learned long ago to trust, warned him that what Pierre was trying to do was goad him into attacking rashly.

No man lives long by fighting as his enemy wants him to, and Anton accepted this as an irrefutable law of nature and war.

"It never fails that your type likes to hurt women," Anton replied, forcing a smile to his lips. He waited several seconds, knowing that Pierre, despite himself, was curious as to how the statement would end. "When a man hasn't the ability to give a woman sexual pleasure, he always resorts to hurting them." Anton laughed then, and he saw a vein pulsing hotly with anger in the Frenchman's throat. "I've long heard that you Frenchmen were all talk, talk, talk, and when the moment of truth comes with a woman, all you can do is still talk, talk, talk about it!"

Anton laughed louder, though it wasn't a real laugh. Just the same, it had its desired effect.

"Swine!" Pierre hissed through clenched teeth.

Anton had guessed that Pierre would attack from the left, trying to take advantage of his wounded shoulder, and he'd guessed correctly. When Pierre moved forward, Anton met his charge, bending his knees low so that the dagger cut through the air six inches above his head. Anton stepped in close and stabbed with all his might, driving the knife to the hilt through the Parisian prefect of police's uniform tunic, and deep into his chest.

"You pig," Pierre said in a bubbling whisper, his face just inches from Anton's. "You swine. I'll kill you for this."

His knees buckled, and he fell to the floor, hating Anton to the very end, believing that he really would see the time when he could order the execution of Anton and Natasha.

Downstairs, Natasha reached the ground floor and raced to the dining room, where she knew there would be at least one more knife on the table that she might use as a weapon. Love for Anton and fear for his life put speed in her step, and she moved down the stairs and hallway with astonishing speed.

Nadine was standing in the dining room, her face pale and drawn. A delicious meal was on the table, and she was clearly concerned that with all the commotion going on in the house that somehow she would be blamed for people not sitting down to dine.

"Get out of here now!" Natasha told Nadine.

The frightened young woman could only stare back silently, her gaze blank and uncomprehending. Only then did Natasha realize she had spoken in Russian. She repeated herself in French while grabbing the sharp knife that had been placed beside Pierre's plate.

At that instant, Ivan's boots thudded loudly against the wooden stairway. Nadine began to shiver, then she knelt on the floor, wrapping her arms over her head protectively.

"Nobody will hurt you if you get out of here," Natasha said, furious that anyone should frighten an innocent woman so completely.

Before Ivan entered the dining room, Natasha knocked the candle out of the heavy brass holder, then grabbed the candlestick with her left hand. When Ivan saw her, he stopped, furious and excited with the chase, yet still not wanting to rush into a fight with a

434

woman armed with a knife and bludgeon.

"You really think you can best me?" Ivan asked. He was smiling. His small, dark eyes glittered menacingly. "You can't show your uncle any love, eh, niece of mine?"

"You're sick," Natasha whispered. "You murdered those people in St. Petersburg for no good reason at all. You could have stolen without killing."

"I could have, but why risk the chance that someone would talk? There's a finality to murder that is most reassuring." Ivan chuckled again. He moved to his right, and Natasha also moved, keeping the long table between them. "I thought you wanted this fight? Don't run from me now, Natasha. Pretty Natasha, always so proper, pretending to be a lady of class. Remember how you always looked down your nose at your old uncle? Remember how you never showed me any love at all, even though I took you in when your parents died?"

"I remember how you were always looking at me, always sticking your nose into my bedroom, that's what I remember most about you," Natasha replied, moving a little to keep the table between herself and Ivan. "And when you're dead, that's the memory of you I'll keep with me. You're exactly the kind of man I loathe most in the world. You're lazy, and you always blame everyone else for your problems." Natasha squared her shoulders, and consciously looked at her uncle in a manner that was ostentatiously condescending. "You're nothing but a peasant," she whispered, knowing how it would infuriate her uncle, who'd always carried pretentious notions in his heart that he was something more than that.

Natasha had been feeling more confident as she talked with her uncle that everything would work out for the best. From upstairs, she could hear Anton shouting, first triumphantly because he had dispatched Pierre de Gruzin, then frantically because he was frightened for Natasha's safety.

With the table between herself and Ivan, Natasha was well-protected, and it was only a matter of time before Anton arrived.

Ivan, too, sensed that within seconds he would be outnumbered. But within the pocket of his jacket was the cloth sack which held his stolen documents, and as long as he possessed them, he would be a wealthy man. All he needed was a hostage to assure him safe passage from the house, and the world would be his for the taking.

He went for Nadine, raising his hand high, the knife gleaming and deadly in his fist.

"No!" Natasha shouted, sure that her savage uncle was going to kill the cowering woman. She leaped onto the table, trying to shorten the distance between herself and Ivan, cutting him off before he could reach the woman.

Ivan turned on her, his attack almost identical to the one Anton had used earlier. In mid-attack, he turned from Nadine to Natasha, stabbing straight ahead with his dagger.

"Wench!" he hissed as his dagger found its target at precisely the same instant that Natasha brought the heavy brass candlestick down upon his skull.

She felt the burning of the blade enter her, and heard the scream of rage as Anton burst into the room.

She felt him take her into his strong arms, cradling her head to his chest. "My darling, you mustn't die!" he whispered. "I can't bear to live without you."

"I'm sorry," Natasha whispered, her eyelids feeling heavy, her entire body so terribly weary after all she'd been through. "I tried. I really tried. I will always love you."

Thirty-two

Natasha gazed out of the window of the carriage as the countryside rolled by. Under her breast, slipping gently across the silk of her gown, Anton's fingers gently traced the path of the scar that Ivan had inflicted five long years ago. From the moment she had recovered consciousness in his arms, through marriage, childbirth, and the strain of dealing with St. Petersburg society, she had never once doubted this man's love. A soft, contented smile curled her lips. Tonight had been more than successful, it had been triumphant. At least five different women at the wedding dance of Anton's cousin Rachel were wearing a gown she'd designed. The past—her personal history that had been changed so drastically on that day so long ago, when she'd been called to Castle Talakovich to interview for the position of Princess Anastasia's personal seamstress—seemed to have been several lifetimes ago. To think that there was a time when she had been afraid that she would never be a part of the elite society of St. Petersburg that Anton had been born into! Now, here she was, five years later, the toast of the city!

"That's a smug smile if ever I've seen one," Anton whispered in her ear.

Natasha's grin broadened as she turned her face more toward the window so her husband wouldn't see. "It is not," she replied in a whisper.

On the opposite seat of the carriage, Caleb and Anastasia snuggled close together. "Smug is a word that fits as well as your gowns," Anastasia said.

"You weren't supposed to be listening!"

"I can't help it. I was born curious."

Natasha gave the princess a theatrically furious look, not all angry. "You're just like your brother," she said, though it didn't sound at all like an insult.

"Is that why you married him?"

Natasha made a harrumphing sound, which brought soft laughter from the occupants of the lavish carriage.

She reached out for Anton's hand, and they shared a smile. It had been a glorious evening for Natasha. Although, as Prince Anton's wife, her power was unquestioned in St. Petersburg, she had always doubted whether she was accepted by the aristocracy, who had been part of Anton's life.

The wedding, and the dance that followed, had set all of Natasha's fears to rest, once and for all. In addition to seeing her gowns worn and admired at the gala event, several husbands had approached her, insisting upon an original creation for their wives.

Natasha promised that she would have her staff begin the new orders just after the crack of dawn, though she knew that wasn't at all possible, since nobody worked on Sunday morning in St. Petersburg. Natasha was not so far removed from her days as a common worker that she had forgotten what it was like to take orders instead of give them. She never asked anything from her workers that she wouldn't ask of herself.

The large, six-horse carriage reached Castle Talakovich, and Caleb and Anastasia headed down toward the east wing of the castle, while Anton and Natasha headed toward the west wing.

"I'll check in on Josef," Anton said.

"I'm not tired," Natasha replied.

Actually, she was quite tired, but she wanted to look in on her child anyway. She knew what it was like to not have parents, to sleep fitfully, to never be sure if she would be sleeping in the same bed the following night. She had made a solemn vow that her son would never know those things. Never, not even for the most fleeting moment, would Josef wonder whether his parents truly loved him.

They opened the door to the bedroom slowly, Natasha leading the way with Anton looking over her shoulder. Little Josef, not quite three, was sleeping, as he so often did, with his small, sturdy body sprawled at an angle on the mattress, the blanket pulled up to his nose, one foot kicked over the edge, peeking out from beneath the blankets.

Anton nudged the satin trim of the blanket down just enough so he could see all of his son's face. The boy's face blended features from both his mother and father; he had Natasha's dark hair, and Anton's gray eyes. The prince made a mental note to have yet another portrait painted of his son, even though the last one he'd commissioned was not yet six months old.

"Look at him," Anton whispered. "He looks so innocent, so at peace."

"Let's hope he always looks that way," Natasha said.

There was a moment of silence as the parents looked at their sleeping child. They both realized that Josef would not always sleep so peacefully. As a Talakovich, he was born into luxury and wealth, but along with that came great responsibility that had to be shouldered personally, and could not be relegated to underlings. But those days of weighty responsibility were many years—and countless hours of lessons at his father's side—in the future.

Natasha eased Josef's foot back onto the mattress

and pulled the blanket over it. But, even before Natasha and Anton had left the bedroom, Josef kicked his foot out from beneath the blankets, and pulled the blanket up so the satin trim again touched his nose.

"He's incorrigible," Anton murmured with a smile. In his eyes, his son could do no wrong.

"Just like his father," Natasha replied.

They left their child's bedroom, closing the door carefully behind them. Anton slipped his arm around Natasha's waist as they made their way down the hall to their own bedroom.

"Did they really like my gowns?" Natasha asked, entering the enormous confines of their bedroom.

"You know they did."

"Then tell me."

Anton grinned as he walked to his own closet, pulling loose his tie and unbuttoning his waistcoat as he walked. "Natasha, how many times do I have to tell you, everyone adores your gowns, and they adore you. Did you see the way Alexander kept looking at you?"

"The czar has a roving eye," Natasha said with mild censure.

Natasha knew she was being silly, that she was letting old fears crop up where they didn't belong and were no longer relevant. Just the same, it reassured her to hear Anton say she was accepted by St. Petersburg's elite.

How many times had she stared at the ceiling at night, wondering if Anton would end up paying some terrible price for falling in love with a woman of common birth, and then doing the unthinkable by actually marrying her? And how many times had Anton held her tightly in his arms, kissed her tenderly, and reassured her that the only person's opinion that meant anything to him was hers?

"It *was* icing on the cake tonight to see so many

women wearing my gowns," Natasha said, standing at the doorway to her own closet.

Behind her, she heard the soft *clink!* of Anton's onyx button studs being removed from his shirt and dropped into the small gold plate near his side of the bed. She'd given him the gold plate for the studs so that he wouldn't have to spend every morning searching for them.

Natasha turned to watch her husband undressing. Though she had watched him doing exactly the same thing nearly every night for the past five years, she never failed to feel a small thrill, a little catch deep within her, when he took his shirt off. As he moved his arms, she was able to watch the muscles move beneath the surface of the skin, the deep, barely contained power of a stalking lion.

She turned, openly staring at Anton now, her full, lower lip caught slightly between her teeth as she welcomed the familiar, hot stirring in her lower body. When Anton was completely naked, she released her breath in a slow, audible sigh.

Anton looked at her, and their eyes met, the communication between them silent and profound.

"And what are you looking at?" Anton asked, mildly teasing, still looking over his shoulder at his wife.

Natasha shrugged her shoulders, her eyebrows dancing. "Nothing."

"Nothing?" Anton asked, as though he had been terribly slighted.

"Well, not as much as I'd *like* to look at," Natasha replied.

Anton turned so that he faced her, and once again, Natasha's breath caught in her throat. It wasn't fair, she thought, that she should be so susceptible to his animal magnetism, to the potency of his presence. Time had diminished none of the excitement that Natasha felt for her husband, none of the sense of wonder she felt when in the sensuous throes of his rapturous caresses.

Anton stepped toward Natasha, but she shook her head slowly, stopping him. "Go to bed," she said, and the sudden strain upon her senses showed in her tone of voice.

A crooked smile pulled at Anton's lips. "I've never been very good at taking orders, not even from my wife."

Natasha thumbed open a single pearl button of her bodice, smiled wickedly, then flicked open a second.

"Trust me," she said softly, her voice a throaty purr of pure sensuality as smooth and refined as the best Chinese silk.

Years earlier, the sound of her voice, filled with such passion, shocked her; now she accepted it as just the way she was, as completely natural when she had romantic designs on her husband, when her body, heart, and soul sought that special connection with him.

Anton moved to the bed, a faint smile floating on his lips. He raised a pillow to the solid headboard, fluffed it, then got onto the bed, leaning back negligently, one knee raised, looking at his devilish wife with eyes that glittered mischievously.

"You were worried about not being accepted?" Anton asked rhetorically. "I'm at a loss to imagine any situation in which you could not take complete control."

Natasha eased out of her gown slowly, loving both the words that her husband had just spoken, and the way that he looked at her. She knew that he enjoyed watching her disrobe, knew that it touched a responsive nerve within him to watch her revealing herself to him slowly until, at last, she came to him, naked and unashamed.

"Did you enjoy yourself tonight?" Natasha asked

with calculated nonchalance, as though she didn't realize the strain she was putting on Anton's inclina-
tion for action, immediate, decisive, conclusive.
"There seemed to be an awful number of men who
needed your attention, and there were as many
women who were tugging at your sleeve, trying to get
you to look at them. Or were they wanting more
than just a conversation with you?"

Natasha eased out of her gown and disappeared
into the closet to hang it up. When she re-emerged,
she wore only her pantalets, chemise, and stockings.
She began rolling the stockings slowly down her legs,
turned precisely so Anton could see her in profile.

She had, in fact, noticed the looks that Anton received from the women at the wedding, but after five
years of marriage, she had finally accepted the fact
that she had married a man who would always draw
the attention of women. All Natasha could do was
accept that fact, and make sure that when the passionate gleam was in his eye, he was looking for her.

"Women? What other women?" Anton asked. "I
was unaware there was any woman at the dance but
you."

Dressed now in only her chemise and pantalets,
Natasha grinned at her husband. "You're a liar. A
charming liar, but a liar just the same."

She unknotted the chemise and let it slide down
her shoulders and off her arms to the floor, then
pulled the drawstring of her pantalets free, and with
a wiggle of her hips, sent the garment slithering
down to her ankles. She stepped out of her pantalets, and told herself once again that it was silly that
the heat of her husband's eyes should still excite her
the way it did.

"Will you do me one favor?" she asked.

"Name it."

"Always be my personal liar," Natasha said, walking slowly toward the bed. "I know that there are

women who will look at you, and I know there will be times when you just can't help but look back, but—"

Anton moved swiftly off the bed, his body a symphony of grace and strength as he took Natasha into his arms, crushing her naked body to his.

"Don't! Don't you know that you'll always be the most beautiful woman in the world to me? Don't you know that I would never do anything to jeopardize the life we've made for ourselves?"

"I'm just trying to be a realist," Natasha said, just a little alarmed and overwhelmingly reassured by the intensity of her husband's words.

"You're my wife, mistress of Castle Talakovich," Anton explained in a softer tone, bending low to kiss her forehead, then cheek. "You don't have to be a realist." The tip of his tongue traced the circumference of her ear.

"But—"

"No buts."

"But . . ."

Natasha was going to say more, but she could not because Anton was kissing her words away. And though the bed was only a few steps away, he picked her up, lifting her easily in his arms, and placed her gently upon the bed.

She pulled Anton so that his weight was upon her. There was something special about knowing that his heart was so close to her own, to feel his weight pressing her deeper into the thick feather mattress that Anton had specially built when Natasha had agreed to become his wife. Her legs wound around his, and she wiggled just a little beneath Anton until their bodies found that perfect fit. She felt his burgeoning manhood throbbing heatedly against her abdomen, growing quickly despite being trapped between their bodies.

"It is a beautiful life we share, isn't it?" Natasha

said, kissing Anton's cheek, dragging her tongue upward to his earlobe, which she caught briefly between her teeth, biting just hard enough to bring the rumble of pleasure from her husband's chest.

"Yes. Unbelievably so." Anton arched his back, pressing his chest a bit more firmly against Natasha's breasts. He felt himself growing longer, thicker, felt the heat of Natasha's desire, and he wondered if tonight they would create another child.

"I don't know what I'd do without you," Natasha said quietly, moving very subtly beneath Anton. She ran her fingernails over his naked flesh, from buttocks to shoulders. She felt him responding to her touch, and she became even more moist and heated with the awareness of the pleasure that soon would be hers.

"That's a question you'll never have to answer," Anton replied softly. He pushed a hand between their bodies to cup one lush breast, catching the erect nipple between forefinger and thumb to pinch with just the right amount of pressure for Natasha's pleasure. "You'll never be without me. I'll never leave you, and I'll never let you leave me."

"You're so possessive," Natasha purred, moving her hips beneath Anton, her fingers kneading the taut muscles of his buttocks.

"Possessive? Tell me you want me to possess you, Natasha," Anton whispered, raising his hips sufficiently to be poised above her. He felt her hands, small and trembling with need, touching his arousal, running back and forth over its pulsating length.

"Anton, please . . ."

"Tell me," he said, feeling her heat, the wetness of her desire.

"I want you now." It was a soft, pleading sound.

"To what?"

"You *know* what," Natasha said, pulling at him, trying to make their connection complete.

"Tell me," Anton insisted, still refusing the sensual pleasure he knew was his for the taking, just as he knew it was hers to command.

"Possess me," Natasha said at last.

He did. With one long, breathtaking plunge, he possessed Natasha, taking her as his own as she, in her own way, possessed him, their bodies becoming one, joining spiritually, physically, in a love that would last beyond the far reaches of forever.